Ann Lingard was formerly a lecturer and researcher in zoology and parasitology. Her other published works of fiction include two novels and various short stories, and she has written and broadcasted about 'the science of the countryside'. She lives on a small-holding at the edge of the Lake District and rears Herdwick sheep. For further information see www.annlingard.com

Also by Ann Lingard

FIGURE IN A LANDSCAPE
(1996, Headline Review. ISBN 0-7472-5296-3)

THE FIDDLER'S LEG
(1996, Headline Review. ISBN 0-7472-5297-1)

(To order, contact Littoralis Press or www.amazon.co.uk)

SEASIDE PLEASURES

Ann Lingard

Copyright © 2003 Ann Lingard

The right of Ann Lingard to be identified as the Author of this work has been asserted by her in accordance with the Copyright, Designs and Patents Act 1988

First published in 2003
by Littoralis Press

Printed in Great Britain by Fir Press
5a Buddle Road, Clay Flatts, Workington, Cumbria CA14 3YD

ISBN 0-9544572-0-X

LITTORALIS PRESS
Plumbland House, Plumbland, Aspatria, Cumbria CA7 2HD
www.littoralispress.co.uk
tel: 016973 22815

Further copies can be ordered from Littoralis Press,
or from Beagle Direct Ltd.,
Colletts House, Crane Close, Denington Road, Wellingborough NN8 2QH
tel: 01933 443862; fax: 01933 443849; email: info@beagledirect.co.uk

CHAPTER 1: ELIZABETH

The door beside the south gable of the Shell House hides a path that leads into a steep garden, inserted between the cottage and the carved-out hillside. The garden is moist and sheltered and its walls and grassy terraces are awash with a profusion of creepers and green foliage. It is exuberant, like Barbara herself; lush and extrovert. With some surprises. Interspersed among the shrubs are stones and salt-bleached wood that she has collected, amused by their miniaturised resemblance to the sculptures of another Cornish artist with the same first name as her own.

'My Hepworths,' she calls them, but she points out (in case the subtlety is overlooked by the observer) that she has not sought their internal tensions, but has positioned them, instead, with reference to the sun. The tallest, a curved cylinder of wood, which she has stained brown to show the grain, casts its gnomonic shadow against an arc of smooth white pebbles set in the grass of the upper terrace.

That is where she is sitting when I arrive. She is lying in the wicker garden-chair, and has kicked off her navy espadrilles with their down-trodden heels, and pulled up her skirt so that the sun's warmth is on her legs. Her eyes are closed and I think she is asleep, so I walk quietly up the stone steps and sit near her until she should wake. I notice that the scarlet varnish on her toenails is chipped, and her grey hair is escaping in long wisps from the loosely-pinned coils.

I sit and wait, and by now I know she is not asleep. I wait. The harsh calls of gulls, so familiar as to be almost unheard, occasionally jar the peace. A robin sings loudly from the rock wall somewhere behind us, and its bright, fluid notes are a reminder of winter.

'Wait until the shadow reaches Bob,' Barbara says, and she opens her eyes and smiles at me.

'Who's Bob?' I ask, wondering if she is rambling, half-asleep.

'Bob Hepworth. The first white stone on the right, the one nearest the house. Go and pick him up and look underneath. Go on, it's all right, I'm not going daft in the head.'

I do as I am told, grunting a little as I get up from the grass; on the base of the stone, partly obscured by dried earth, is the name 'Bob', written in black, waterproof felt pen.

'Why Bob?'

'I don't know, lovey. Matt named him. When he was little he thought of the Hepworths as a family, and gave them names, Bob and — oh, I don't know, Tom and Cindy, I can't remember the rest. Bob's the only one who has a written name — I expect Matt still thinks that his scribbles are a secret!' She laughs gently, but then her face becomes sad. 'Put him back — is the shadow there yet?'

'Why are we waiting?' I ask, as I go across to her and kiss her.

She just shakes her head, and I suddenly feel apprehensive, waiting for the earth to turn, for time to pass.

'I wish I could stop the sun,' Barbara must have been reading my thoughts, and she reaches out and takes my hand. 'Then time would stop, too. It's nearly there. Wait.'

The dark finger of shadow strokes the edge of the designated marker, and Barbara's grip on my hand tightens.

'Lizzie, I need to say this quickly. I went for a check-up on Tuesday — I didn't want to tell you I was going, because — oh, never mind. I've been ignoring the signs, Lizzie — and I don't just mean the backache, the physical signs. The consultant used the word "metastasis", you'll know what that means, and told me that I'd have to have more tests and various sorts of therapy. But I told him I wouldn't bother. It was pointless. And I've checked and it was predicted, it's just that I've kept ignoring the signs ... And the other thing I have to tell you is that I've asked Hazel to come.'

The Tourist Information leaflet lists the Shell House as one of Polkenna's attractions: it 'has been decorated since late Victorian times with intricate patterns of local shells.' A cautionary note is added, that 'the hill up to the Shell House, at the top of East Polkenna, is very steep and the road (which is impassable for cars) may be slippery in winter and wet weather.' Despite this, a few middle-aged or retired people make the climb and are relieved to be able to sit on the wall for a rest, and to admire the façade and the view. But when I first visited I was fortunate in that Barbara Lewisham had let me into a secret, that I could drive there by a narrow road that came to a dead-end behind the cottage.

I had parked the car, and walked down steep rocky steps. The Shell House appeared to have been embedded in the cliff; the north side was separated by only a few feet from the hacked-out rock-face that rose darkly and damply, its crevices supporting pennywort and green encrustations of moss and liverwort, to the height of the chimney. The cottage itself was unexceptional; an engraved stone above the door was dated 1860, but an ugly glazed porch had been added and modern dormer windows projected from the slate roof. Interest focussed on the face the cottage presented to the world: the pale-pink visage was decorated with beauty spots and patches — squares and fans, spirals and curlicues, constructed of the cockles, cowries, limpets, topshells and twenty or more other species that give the Shell House its name.

Barbara had seen me standing at the front, and came through the garden door to greet me (the porch door was apparently permanently swollen by the damp sea air) and we had examined the shell patterns together. At first sight they had seemed large and crude, but when I had begun to look more closely, I had discovered the smaller, more intricate patterns around the windows and dotted about the façade, scattered almost teasingly as though challenging the viewer to find and identify their gems: the most unusual shells, sometimes one, sometimes several with the same or different markings, were framed within interlocking rectangles, superimposed triangles and looped circles of small shells.

'This is extraordinary, Barbara! Whoever did this really knew his marine shells. And he had a sense of humour, too — come and look at this one.'

I had glanced around at Barbara, who was sitting on the wall. She had bent forward to re-tie the scarf that kept her long grey hair back in a ponytail, and her still-full bosom had fallen against the low neck of the peasant blouse that she used to favour in those days. She had straightened up and unselfconsciously had adjusted her clothes, her dark eyes crinkling with amusement.

'How do you know it was a man? Maybe this amateur shell collector was a clever woman with a sense of humour. Like you. Though to be fair, Elizabeth, I suppose I don't know you well enough yet to know about your humour, but you certainly seem to know a thing or two about shells. Come on then, tell me about this shell-collector's joke.'

I think I had looked at her rather uncertainly, not sure how to interpret the remark, but I had seen that she was laughing at me, teasing me, and so I had shown her the object that had been placed as the stem of a stylised flower.

'Oh, the bullet. That's what I call it, anyway. What's so funny about it, then?'

She had made me feel like a child, so I had replied pompously in my awkwardness.

'It's a belemnite, which is a fossil and not a shell at all — in the sense that all the others are external coverings. It's actually a rod that was the internal skeleton of an animal a bit like a squid or cuttlefish, that lived 150 million years ago, and so if you know it's a fossil you know it's out of place here. But the joke, of course, is that the animal that surrounded the rod was a mollusc, just as all these winkles and cockles are molluscs. It's subtle — a clever joke that only a few cognoscenti would recognise and enjoy!'

'Well, there you are, Elizabeth — it was a joke waiting for your arrival, a hundred or so years later! The chosen few — it was obviously your destiny to find it.'

But I had wanted to know more about the pattern-maker.

'Do you have the deeds? It's possible they may contain some sort of clue about the shell-collector. Or we might be able to find something in the local archives, or the library.'

Barbara had shaken her head. 'It was in the past, Elizabeth. It's enough that you're here now, enjoying the joke in the present. And looking towards the future.'

That theme, I came to learn, was integral to Barbara's thinking.

Metastasis, the changing from a stable state; an instability, a movement of no-longer-static cells. Cells that have multiplied, released from internal control, and have lost contact with each other, migrated, been swept by blood or lymph to distant sites, there to settle down and multiply. Again and again. It's biological, nothing to do with the stars. Astrological mumbo-jumbo, probabilities and coincidences. Mars enters Libra and Jupiter goes into retrograde motion, so the wandering mutant cells set up home in the bone marrow, and Barbara says that it's all been predicted and preordained. Time arrows forward, the biological process is irreversible and Barbara's lifetime will soon end ...

So I sit on the front wall and try to finish the drawing. Sitting like a child, Barbara calls it: a childlike pose. I perch on the low wall in front of the Shell House, feet on the back rung of a chair, knees bent to support the large sketchbook. The tin box with pencils and old but treasured Rotring pens is on the wall beside me. (In the garden, I had sat with my head in her lap, silently grieving as she stroked my hair. I could not bear to think about the future, to think that she would leave me again. This time would be for ever.)

The drawing is almost finished; I have outlined the front elevation and drawn in the intricate patterns of the shells. Around the margins I have added enlarged portraits of individual shells to show their characteristic details, and I intend to touch in a few colours here and there with water-colour; to add a few muted shades, faded like the crumbling shells on the wall yet hinting at the original colours.

I can see Barbara inside, in the dimness of the dining room. She is standing quite motionless and staring out at me. I point at the right edge of the façade and smile, and then I take out my medium-fine pen and label a shell-portrait in the margin: *Tiphobia horei*. She gives a little wave and smiles back, because she has guessed that I'm pointing at the new pattern that we had constructed.

There had been a patch of rotten and rust-stained rendering near the drain pipe, so Barbara had designed the pattern and I had supplied the shells, and we had mixed new mortar according to early recipes; but in our first attempt we had included too much lime so that the mortar had set before we had finished the pattern. So we had to chip it off and start again, and we had learnt through trial and error (and considerable hilarity) to cover only a small area at one time. Our new pattern is of concentric circles formed from *Turritella* spires; within the inner ring are several orange-banded dogwhelks, *Nucella lapillus*, and in the outer ring there is a single red-flecked queen, the beautiful scallop *Chlamys*. But the single *Tiphobia* lies at the very centre and is my own contribution to the Victorian shell-collector's joke.

CHAPTER 2: MATTHEW

Funny how when I get to the Tamar Bridge I always start to yawn. It's not the bridge's fault, though it has a weird effect on you — as though the grey struts are falling and rising, falling and rising outside the train window. You look down and see the moored yachts and, if you're lucky, a destroyer or some other hulking grey symbol of Britain's ruling the waves, and then you know you're crossing into Cornwall. I guess I was about fourteen when I first did the journey on my own, worrying whether I'd get out at the right station or if the door wouldn't open and I'd be stuck inside, Granny B out on the platform ... Sitting there with my can of coke and sandwich papers, too scared to get up for a pee in case someone took my seat!

Okay, so why am I yawning now? Twenty years old and I'm nervous as a kid just because Hazel will be there, and I said I'd spend the summer at Polkenna, and now I'm wondering why the hell I said that. But where else could I go? Gail getting all fat and broody and Dad gloating over his daughter-to-be. They had a scan, they know it's a girl, a little step-sister for dear Matt. God, she gave me a shock, she did it on purpose, telling me like that, knowing I'd be quickly counting back — and then I'd see that it couldn't have been me, I was safely tucked away at college. I'm relieved, but I'm jealous, too, jealous of my own father for getting his 'partner' pregnant. So now, at last, he decides he'd better ask Hazel for a divorce, so he and his partner can get married. And Gail will be my step-mother, and strictly off-limits; fucking your dad's younger partner is different from fucking your dad's younger wife. God, I revolt myself. But I'll miss you, gorgeous Gail. 'There were times, I do declare, when I took some comfort there. Li-li-*li*, li-li-*li*-li, li-li-*li*, li-li-*li*...'

And Hazel will want to know about Dad and will talk about the divorce. He told me once that she'd wanted to come back to him, but by then it was too late, he'd got together with Gail ... If she had come back, after sleazy Edward — would I still call her Mum?

It's going to be strange at the Shell House without Granny Barbara, I hope I can hack it.

Of course, when the train gets to the station, Hazel isn't there. Fucking bloody typical! I have a hell of a job getting the bags out of the door, the rucksack strap gets caught, and I practically fall out onto the platform. So I just hang about getting more and more pissed off, and when she finally appears at the top of the ramp she comes hurrying down, full of incredibly boring *rustic* excuses about getting stuck behind tractors or cows or something. And I just kind of peck her on the cheek and say, 'Hi, Hazel,' and that probably makes her feel worse, and she tries to carry the sports bag and it keeps thwacking her across the calves.

She still looks good, despite her age — what is she, about forty-one or -two? Nice short-sleeved denim shirt, oatmeal-ish trousers, and her hair is still brown. I like the bob, it makes her look quite young. But I still can't tell what she's thinking — it's those eyes, they always seem to be partly-hidden by the heavy lids, and her face is always so calm, almost immobile sometimes, so that I can't read her at all. Not like Granny Barbara. Her eyes were brown and deep-set but they were always sparkling with laughter and nearly hidden in creased flesh. Everything was up-front with Granny B, I always seemed to know what she was thinking and where she was coming from. It's going to be awful without her, just me and Hazel, no mediator, no jokes …

I'd forgotten how narrow the lanes were, you can't see a thing over the bloody great banks. Perhaps she really was stuck behind a tractor. There's a lane that takes you to the top of Polkenna, a dead-end that stops practically above the Shell House. It's only ever used by the people that live at the top of the hill, and the view is fantastic. After she's parked, I get out and stand there, and look down at the harbour and out to sea, with that incredible smell of the coast blowing in, seaweed and cliff-top smells, and a bit of fish thrown in from the market down on the quay. And there's always the sound of gulls, sort of echoing between the houses, you even hear it in the towns inland. If I hear it somewhere else it makes me kind of homesick for Polkenna.

Hazel insists on taking the bag again, though the steps are really difficult, the way they're all uneven and cut into the rock. You can't see the Shell House from the top, but then you suddenly find that you're walking down past the chimney and the end wall. When I was a kid I used to hunt around for cigarette butts and stones and things, and drop them down into the gap between the cottage and the rock.

There's an old couple sitting on the wall. We must have given them a hell of a fright, suddenly appearing at the bottom of the steps next to them, and they get all flustered. Hazel doesn't say anything, I can't believe it, she just bumps past them with the bag, doesn't even acknowledge them, and pushes open the side-gate. The old chap is quite taken aback, he's quite breathless when he stands up, and he clutches his handkerchief, full of apologies.

'I'm so sorry. We were just admiring the shells. Catching our breath from the climb. I do hope you don't mind.'

They're a nice-looking couple, probably in their seventies, smartly-dressed, sensible shoes, and the like. And a warm day in spite of the wind.

'No, no,' I say, 'you just carry on sitting there. It's a tough climb, isn't it? You need some time to have a good look at the shells.'

Hazel has gone through the door and out of sight. I look at the front of the house to remind myself of the details. God, how often I used to look at it, playing games, trying to find matching pairs, or yellow ones, or whatever.

'The best ones are in these more complicated patterns round the window. You can come closer, if you want, we really don't mind. Please, just come on over and look.'

The old chap gets out his glasses, and the woman stands up and takes his arm. They are a bit anxious, but they are smiling, and I show them the cowries and things.

'Oh yes, darling, look,' she says. 'I hadn't noticed those ones before, look at the little ones in the middle.'

'Yeah. They're kind of framed, aren't they? Oh, sorry about that.' The rucksack swung forward as I bent down and knocked against the old man. 'Sorry. But you should look at this one, apparently it was put there as a joke because it's not a proper shell, it's a fossil. It's part of a squid or something, that hung out in the seas around here millions of years ago. I can't quite remember why it's a joke, actually —,' (damn, that *really* spoilt the effect!) 'but the amazing thing is that it ended up here. You have to think about that —.'

(I could so easily see Granny B telling me: she had been stroking the smooth grey stone of the fossil as she told me about it.

'Wouldn't it have been astonished to know its destiny — that it would end up here? You have to think what this little rod has been through, Mattie — the poor old squid had to die in just the right place and in just the right way. If it had been swallowed by a shark — were there sharks around then? I don't know, you can put me right, you're doing your O levels or whatever they're called these days — that little rod might have been crushed or at least stayed inside the shark. So for the rod to get here, the squid had to die of old age or disease, or something like that, and drop down into the mud — and then its body got covered up by more mud and rotted away and all that was left of it was the little rod. Which became a fossil, as the mud was squashed together to make rock. What happened then? Let's think.' She had stopped and frowned, and then given a triumphant grunt. 'Ah yes! A friend told me all this, you see! Yes, so then the sea receded and the layers of rock were pushed up, and buckled and eroded away again, and perhaps the sea came back again — I don't know. Squeezed and probably pushed all over the place.' She had kneaded her hands together to show me, and had laughed. 'It doesn't bear thinking about, darling, does it? Millions of years of being pushed about. And perhaps the squid's rock was covered with earth and trees, and then someone decided to build a road or a house and dug the rock out. Or the ice or floods exposed the rock with the fossil in it. And then — and this is the way *I* like to think about it! — along came an amateur geologist with a hammer and chipped our little stone bullet out of its resting place. And he gave it to a friend, or he sold it to a fossil-shop like the ones in Lyme Regis. Or — who knows, lovey? — perhaps our jokey shell-collector found it herself!'

'*Her*self? Why do you think it was a woman?'

'Why not?' That was all she would say, and she had put her arm around me and squeezed me; she was very warm and — soft. I remember being a bit embarrassed, and she must have noticed because she laughed again.

'Good gracious, boy! You're already taller than I am. I'd better stop giving you cuddles, hadn't I?'

I remember that she laughed — she was always teasing me — and pushed me away.)

'You have to think what has happened to it between the time it died and the time that it was stuck on here.'

I know I sounded a bit vague, but I could still feel Granny Barbara's arm, and almost smell her patchouli or sandalwood or whatever it was and her warm hair. Now, though, I was old enough to wonder how she came to know all that stuff. I can just see Hazel, inside in the dining room. She's peeping out at me, and I wave, to show that I can see her, spying.

'Extraordinary, indeed,' the old chap says. 'Very good of you to show us. Somebody told us that the decorations were Victorian. Is that true?'

Victorian? God, I haven't a clue!

'Well, all I know is that they must have been here when my grandmother bought the place — and that would have been 25, 30 years ago? I could go and ask Haze — my mother. She might know.'

The woman laughs and shakes her head.

'No, no, please don't bother. You must go in and put your bag down. We'll just have a quick look and then we'll be off, won't we, darling?'

They look such a kind, well-established sort of couple, really comfortable with each other, that suddenly I don't want them to go. I can't believe the way Hazel ignored them, and I don't want to be left alone, with Hazel, in Barbara's house.

'Hey, I've got a good idea! Why don't you come inside? Come in and have a cup of tea, you'll need something after that steep climb and I'm sure we can tell you more about the house.'

'Goodness, no. It's really very kind of you, my dear, but really we must be going. We shall be quite all right.'

And with quite a little a flurry of protestations and thanks, and anxiously-crumpled handkerchiefs, they step back onto the road. So I have no option but to go inside.

I dump my rucksack at the bottom of the spiral staircase and look round to see what Hazel has changed. It smells different — Granny B's smell was very distinctive — and it feels warm and damp from being shut up while Hazel was out collecting me, but it's brighter and emptier than it had been before, less clutter, more white paint. And Hazel's sanded and varnished the floor. It looks okay. She's put the table against the window at the dining room end, and her word-processor and fax and all that stuff are there. Different. She's in the kitchen, that extends back from the dining room into the garden.

'Do you want a cup of tea? Did you get any lunch? I can make a sandwich.'

She's always so bloody calm, it's infuriating.

'I'd rather have a beer. I asked that old couple in for tea. But I rather panicked them.'

'Why? I mean why did you ask them in?' She stares at me.

'They were old and tired and hot. And Barbara would have. She was always asking people in, folk who came up to see the shells. It was great, you ought to keep up the tradition. It would liven things up. We might meet some interesting people.'

I don't mean to sound so spiky, but she really irritates me. Anyway, she doesn't answer but just goes to the fridge and gets out a can of beer.

'I don't think many people come up here these days, because I asked the Tourist Office to omit the house from this year's leaflet.' She is drawing patterns in the condensation on the can with her fingertip. 'Anyway, I've put your bag upstairs. You're in the old studio. You can move things round a bit if you want.'

So I take the can and the rucksack upstairs, cursing because, as usual, the straps and things get caught and bang against the metal handrail. That spiral stair is really incongruous, stuck in the middle of the downstairs, like a sort of barrier between the sitting and eating ends. Whoever thought to put that in? Bad design! But then the whole house is crazy, with these attics opened up to make two bedrooms and the bathroom tacked on at the back of the kitchen downstairs. Bloody inconvenient when you've been out to the pub and had a few. Barbara said she used a potty when she was desperate, though I never saw it.

The studio looks so different! I used to sleep in here when I was a kid, but then it was a matter of fitting in amongst the painting clutter. The bed used to be pushed against the wall, and I had to dodge around a couple of tables, the easel — oh yeah, a stool, and all the stacked canvases and boards and picture frames, and stuff. Jars with brushes. And the smell — a different smell in here, linseed oil and dust, and hot slates in the summer. There wasn't a carpet before, just the varnished chipboard all spattered with paint, but this is pretty cool, I like the blue and white rug on dark blue varnish. Not bad. Nice plain mirror — reflecting the sky. Shit, you look a mess, boy! Watch your head on the bloody sloping ceiling. I'm a lot taller now, Granny B. Oh God, I wish you were still here. You'd have asked them in for tea. Look at them, poor old people, walking slowly down the hill, down to the teashop on the front for a nice cream tea. Pot of tea for two, and scones and jam and cream. You'd have given them black tea in mugs, because you always forgot to buy the milk, and ginger biscuits. Wouldn't you?

You gave me hugs and cuddled me! And when I got too tall, Gail gave me hugs, instead, lovely big soft cuddly Gail. A bit more than hugs — but we only did it twice, the first time because we'd drunk too much. And the second time was your fault, Granny B, because I had seen you dying. How about that? A year ago, when you lay across the hall, where Hazel sleeps now. And I came to see you, didn't I? Not knowing that I would see a … a shrivelled skeleton in the bed, that you would be hurting and peevish and not wanting to talk, except to mutter on about your fucking horoscope. And how we should all stop fussing because you were glad. *Glad?* You didn't know what the hell you were saying, did you? The real you had gone away, and I hadn't had a chance to say goodbye. And you made me get some stupid dolls off the dressing table, a chain of painted paper dolls, all dusty and faded. Badly made, too, something odd about them, only one plait. And you muttered on about bows and arrows or something. I thought you had gone mad — and I wished I hadn't come. And I would have liked my *mum* to have given me a cuddle, but Hazel was too tired and distracted being your daughter, and dealing with nurses or whatever. She did try to talk to me and explain, but it wasn't any good, and I went home. All alone on the train, Barbara. No cuddles, no jokes to send me on my way.

But Gail was there, swallowed me up and looked after me, none of that garbage about 'big boys don't cry'. A bit naughty, eh? But that's what it's all about, being a bit naughty, getting a bit of a thrill. And sex has lots of bonuses — it's exciting, good exercise, it's comforting and it helps you sleep. Sooo fulfilling!

What the hell am I going to do all summer? Perhaps I'll borrow the car and head to the north coast and the surf, hang out and try to pull a few babes. 'Pull a few babes', huh? Get real, Matthew lad. Get a job in the beach café or something. Make a start and get this stuff unpacked.

I throw everything into one of the cupboards and lie on the bed for a while, staring at the ceiling. There's this kind of frenetic buzzing in my mind, all these thoughts, and I need to slow it down, make it all quiet again inside. Hazel has done a good job, tidying everything. It must have been pretty bad for her. Barbara was her mum, for Christ's sake, even though I don't think they were that close any more. (Is Hazel close to anyone any more? She's so remote. Though maybe she doesn't know where she's going to, I don't know. Yet she said she wanted me to come.) I used to want to sit in those cupboards when I was a kid, I liked the way they covered the whole end wall, like a secret room — I quite fancy sitting in one now. The other one's full of garbage, though, rolls of cartridge paper and boxes, stuff that she hasn't wanted to throw out, I suppose. Maybe some of it is Hazel's own stuff.

Lying on the bed doesn't help. I'm going to have to look in Hazel's bedroom, too — she's downstairs and there's no point trying to sneak in (and anyway, why should I?), so I just clump across the landing and lift the metal latch and go in. The room looks okay, she's moved the furniture round a bit, and must have brought some of her own things from the flat. I guess she doesn't have much, really, and she's probably not very well off. Copy-editing, or whatever it is she does these days, doesn't sound like it makes you rich.

There is a photo on the chest of drawers, in a plain wooden frame — Hazel's graduation photo, Hazel with long brown hair and short black skirt, wearing a gown and clutching a rolled certificate. She looks really embarrassed — and a bit resentful — but she is smiling. And there is Granny Barbara, dressed to kill in flaming poppy flowers, down to the middle of her calves, and with a wide straw hat! Standing on a lawn in front of a building covered in incredible carved stonework, a college or chapel, I guess. If you had seen them apart, you wouldn't have thought they were related, but seen together, they have — they had — the same broad cheekbones, the same smile.

Next to the photograph is a shell lady. She's kept it all these years. I cannot believe that. Had it really seemed so important? I pick it up, I have to ask Hazel.

'Hey! I remember making this!'

I clatter down the stairs, looking for Hazel. She is sitting on the sofa with her feet tucked under her, just staring at the wall, but she gets up at once.

'What? What have you found?'

'A shell lady! It was in your bedroom — sorry, I just looked in. I saw your graduation photo — awful hair, by the way, it's much better the way you have it now.'

She takes the shell lady from me and we look at it. The skirts are made from two creamy-yellow limpet shells, conical and ridged like gathered material. The woman's upper body is a faded brown-black winkle shell (which gives her a corsetted, boobs-tightly-controlled look) onto which I'd glued two spiral white shells — are they dog-whelks? I can't remember — for arms. Then there is a rounded yellow shell for the head, and a small flat white shell, with a speckled brown pattern, for a hat. Very jaunty! And a dried branched frond of pinkish seaweed is stuck to one 'hand' like a parasol, or perhaps it was meant to be a fan.

'I remember making loads of these. It was raining — wasn't it always? — and I was probably driving Barbara mad. She hauled me off to the beach in the rain and we had to gather shells. I was really pissed off with her, it was so baby-ish.'

'You were thirteen.'

'Yeah. Was I?' I think back, and grin. 'Yeah, thirteen-year-olds think they're a bit grown-up for that sort of garbage. And she made me wash and dry all the shells, and then she sat me down with newspaper on the table and a tube of glue, and showed me what to do. Not bad, is it? Quite artistic, a promise of things to come! I do remember that I made loads. I didn't know she'd kept any.'

'I'm not sure she did. I don't remember finding any when I cleared up,' Hazel puts the shell lady carefully on the mantelpiece. 'That one's mine, actually. Don't you remember that you sent it to me?'

'*Did* I?'

I'm really surprised: I wouldn't have done so, because she must have been with Edward. Or maybe she had just left him. But even as I ask the question, I realise that Granny B must have sent it, from me, probably with a note like 'I promised him I'd package it and take it to the Post Office', or something.

'Of course, I remember now,' I nod quickly.

But she must have realised, too, because she gives a wry kind of smile and a little shrug.

'I treasured it all these years. Well.'

'Hmm. That's good, then, isn't it? I'm glad. Thanks.' How awful! I change the subject. 'I guess you had a lot of sorting out to do. It looks good upstairs, you've made it look — good.'

'Yes, well, you know what it was like. Clothes and things. Lots of bits of driftwood and pebbles.'

'You didn't chuck out the Hepworths, though, surely?' I'm horrified.

'Of course not! Come out and see them, they're still there, Bill and Bob and —'

'*Bob!* Yeah!' I punch the air.

We step out of the French windows onto the slates of the lower terrace, and climb up the granite steps. The 'sundial' is still in place and I pick up Bob and turn him over.

But he's changed sex. His name has been altered with black felt pen to 'Babs'.

I hold the stone out to show Hazel.

She looks at it and begins to laugh, softly. 'I think the joke's on you, now, don't you?'

'I didn't realise that she knew.' I want to laugh, but I suddenly have this awful feeling that I might cry instead. '*Babs*!'

Hazel is staring at the stone, tilting it, and then she puts it back very carefully and sort of frowns and put her hands in her pockets.

'I threw out all her magazines,' she says, 'all the horoscopes, even the ones cut out of newspapers. I didn't take them to the recycling skip, either. I put them in the bin.' She sounds really angry for a moment. 'I couldn't bear to think of that rubbish being recycled.'

'I think she died when she did just to fit in with the bloody astrological predictions. She didn't *have* to give in, why didn't she fight it? She was so strong!'

I can't help it, it just comes out. I don't mean to make Hazel cry, but it's as though the tears jump into her eyes.

'Matt! Of course that isn't true. She was really ill.'

I feel awful. But then I realise what Hazel has just said.

'Wait a minute — did you just say it was rubbish? I thought you believed in all that stuff, too.'

'Me? Of course I don't believe in it. How could the positions of planets and stars possibly affect one's life? Starlight's old news, in any case. We might as well be robots, given instructions from outside. But *Mummy* believed in it, Mattie. And it gave her comfort, she had to believe in predestination, that whatever happened to her had already "been decided". That knowledge helped her accept what was happening — and there was no way of stopping the progress of the disease. It was a comfort, don't you see? She felt that "something" — heaven knows what! — was watching over her.'

Hazel has surprised me. She'd understood and been prepared to put up with Granny B's daft beliefs, and all I had done was sneer. I really respect her for that. But the whole idea was just so weird — and pointless.

'But for what purpose?' I can't help asking. 'Is there some sort of astrological afterlife? Did Granny Barbara just hope she'd become a star?'

CHAPTER 3: ANNE: JULY 1855

'Emily? Emily, come and see!'

I hear him, over and over again in my mind. I saw her cheeks flush pink. She must have been conscious of our covert glances. Although she smiled and hastened over, she perhaps thought it was a little improper that he should so summon her. In the middle of a class!

'Would you allow Mrs Gosse to have a look?' he asked more courteously, more correctly, and so we all moved aside in the small and crowded room to allow his wife to pass and reach the table on which his microscope was standing. He had been showing us the barnacles, in the easy manner of his teaching, that is part-conversation, part-lecture.

'Now, without disturbing the busy fishing of this colony of barnacles, I ask you all to take your seats in front of this aquarium,' he had summoned us, his students. 'And with a lens before your eye observe the creatures which are closest to the side. From one and another, every instant, you will observe that a delicate hand is thrust forward and then withdrawn.'

We had gathered around, taking turns to peer through our lenses, each exclaiming at the feathery limbs.

'What is the purpose of this elaborate appendage?' Mr Worthington had asked, although he must surely have known that Mr Gosse would explain.

'Ah, it is the net, Mr Worthington, with which the little fisher takes his food — see how his fingers form a sieve, so that the minute animalcules that form his food are sifted out of the water around him ... Now, here in this jar you see the large individual which we collected yesterday. It has been throwing off dense clouds which, if we examine them with a lens, are seen to be composed of thousands of minute dancing creatures, resembling the water fleas that we examined the other day. Now ... if I can catch some of these little dancers with the aid of this glass tube ... and eject them into the glass cell ... which we place upon our microscope stage ...'

He had bent to the microscope, turned the focussing knobs, shifted the glass cell until it was correctly placed.

'There! Come and look at one which I have captured here. Look at its tiny swimming legs, the intensely black eye ...'

One by one, we had sat down to look. I had looked at him, too, covertly, at his own dark eyes; he was not looking at me — his wife, sitting at the back of the room, was the object of his own intense regard.

As we each took our turn, he had continued speaking.

'From the researches of Mr Darwin we know that this tiny active waterflea will be transformed, in ways which the Wisdom of God has ordained, into a stony acorn barnacle that must sit for ever in one place ... Imagine, imagine if such changes as these took place in the history of the *horse*, for instance. If it was born in the form of a fish, passed through several changes of this form, imitating the shape of a perch, then the pike, then the eel, by successive castings of its skin —'

He was in full stride, standing with his back against the blackboard, enjoying himself; but always glancing at his wife.

'Then by another shift it appears as a bird — then, glueing its forehead to a stone with its feet in the air, throws off its covering once more and becomes a foal — which gradually grows into a horse!'

By now he was the focus of our attention, and many were smiling their appreciation.

'Should we not think that wonderful? Yet it would not be a whit more wonderful than the changes which the great God has caused to occur in the barnacle!'

He could restrain himself no further: there occurred a momentary hiatus in the queue for the microscope and he suggested, 'Perhaps Mrs Gosse might like to look? .... Mrs Gosse? Emily! Come and see!'

'Emily! Emily!' Over and over again in my mind. 'Anne! *Anne!*' I imagine myself hastening to his side at his urgent command.

'Anne! Wake up.' Sarah giggles, staring at me in the mirror. There are dark patches on its uneven surface that spoil our unfreckled complexions. Mrs Gosse — *Emily!* — has freckles, her skin is very fair. 'You have been standing quite still with the brush in your hand for the past minute.'

'Are you sure it was quite a minute? Did you count every second?' I resume brushing her wavy hair. 'You are becoming very precise, Miss Nisbet, in your observations. Our esteemed tutor would be very pleased with you.'

'Well, I am not entirely the pretty and brainless young creature that I choose sometimes to portray. *Ouch!* Be careful!'

'Oh, but who will marry you if you become too clever? "Your locks are as fine as a mermaid's hair, tresses of seaweed, tangled and fair." Tell me quickly, what species of seaweed?'

She wrinkles her nose. 'I don't think there is a fair one, is there? I shall have to settle for that brown slimy one, the sort with the long thin strands. And now *you* are being precise. Anyway, who were you dreaming about? I am sure it was Mr Worthington, he was being so attentive this afternoon. Oh do please stop, my poor scalp feels quite *raked*! I heard Mr Worthington telling Mrs Pettifer that the common sea mouse —'

'*Himanthalia.*' I put the hairbrush down on the tiny dressing table that is so cluttered with our assortment of potions and ointments, and sit down on the bed next to Sarah. '*Himanthalia* has the long brown strands. Mr Worthington wanted to carry my basket, being convinced that the jar of seawater was "far too weighty and cumbersome" for me to manage. I suppose he thinks that the basket should be filled instead with freshly-cut roses or *herbs*, something more befitting a young lady. Sarah, I could not *dream* about Mr Worthington — it would rather be a nightmare.

And besides, he has a wart beneath his ear.'

Sarah shrieks. 'No! That is too disgusting! I must contrive to examine it with my magnifying glass!'

We both burst out laughing.

Knock! Knock! Knock!

It is Miss Shipton's stick against the wall.

I hide my face in the pillow, still gasping with laughter, as Sarah whispers, 'Oh dear no! *Sssh*! She will come in, and you know how frightening she looks in that ugly cap!'

'And she will be sad and sorrowing. "The lilies of the field ..." No, that's not apposite. "Wherefore do ye not ...?" etcetera.'

'There will be wailing and gnashing of teeth.'

'Beating of breasts.'

And we are off again, imitating the bewailing hordes, hooting with unladylike mirth until our eyes run with tears.

So naturally our good chaperone comes to remonstrate, replete with righteous indignation.

'Miss Church, I had really hoped that, as my elder charge, you would set a good example.' (I am twenty-two, as opposed to Sarah's twenty, years of age.) 'Your voices, dear young ladies, must surely be heard throughout the house.'

'Miss Shipton, we are so sorry that we disturbed your sleep. I think perhaps we have been a little over-stimulated by our most interesting and informative day.'

But Sarah is not in a mood to be mollified. 'The walls are so thin, Miss Shipton. We can hear that dreadful Mrs Parker coughing from two doors away. I wish we had procured an apartment in one of those handsome houses by the sea. Then we would not have so far to walk and you would be able to watch our shore classes from your window.'

'It is true, Miss Nisbet, that these rooms are not all that we might have wished for. But if this is what the good Lord intended for us, then we must abide by His decision and look to find His meaning.'

Miss Shipton sighs and leans heavily on her stick. I am certain she exaggerates the discomfort in her limbs. She stands upon the threshold, with her wrap pulled tightly across her nightgown; her cap is laced so severely under her chin that I think her face must surely turn purple, but her skin is as sallow and sere as ever. I hope I *never* grow to look like that at forty, she is so *old* and seems always to be unwell. Sarah and I have admitted to each other that we have each held fantasies about running away from her along the promenade ... but of course we have to behave decorously, like the marriageable young ladies that we are. (I wish I were married to Mr Gosse. Then I would not need a dreary chaperone. I would run to him along the shore when he called 'Anne, Anne, come and see!' My bonnet would fly away and I would pick up my petticoats and *run*, uncaring who might see.)

But Miss Shipton is not to be escaped; she sits down — very slowly — in the single armchair.

'It cannot be denied that it is a long and tiring walk to the shore. But if it is the Lord's Will, so be it that we should love Him a little more through our own suffering — He has given us extra time to reflect upon His goodness before we immerse ourselves in the business of the day.'

'Is it also the Lord's Will that the Gosse family should have an apartment overlooking the promenade?' I cannot help myself, even though I know what will follow. 'That surely must indicate that Mr and Mrs Gosse are more favoured in His eyes.'

'The Lord Jesus could not fail to do otherwise in His Wisdom, Miss Church. Dear Mrs Gosse in particular lives only to proclaim His Name. She was explaining to me the other day how they came to find their apartment. As you know, they —'

'Oh, do tell us what their apartment is like inside, Miss Shipton.' Sarah wriggles up to the head of the bed and tucks her nightgown around her knees. 'I imagine it to be full of microscopes. Are there jars everywhere full of sea creatures? *Oh!*'

She catches my eye in horror and coughs, trying to disguise her exclamation, as we both remember our own glass jar. I rub my hand over my forehead to hide my glance towards the window, but our little secret is invisible behind the curtains. Fortunately Miss Shipton seems unaware of our conspiracy and merely continues with her remonstrances as she rearranges her cap.

'Miss Nisbet, it would be most improper of me to gossip about Mrs Gosse's apartment, especially to the pupils of her dear husband.'

'Of course, Miss Shipton. You are quite right.' But Sarah and I well know that the information that we desire will soon be forthcoming. Indeed, Miss Shipton barely pauses to pat her cheeks (to remove what, I wonder? — they are so parched that a desert would seem wet in comparison) with her handkerchief before she continues.

'It is, of course, a well-proportioned apartment, and at present is much given over to books. Mrs Gosse informed me that they conveyed here nearly two trunkloads of books, as well as the three boxes of Mr Gosse's collecting equipment. But yes, I do recall that there were several large vessels of sea water containing creatures which doubtless you young ladies would now be able to name.'

'I do wish we could see them. Could you not contrive that Mrs Gosse might invite us to accompany you there?' How I wanted to see where Mr Gosse lived!

'Miss Church, you know that is quite out of the question. It is indeed a very well-positioned apartment from which Mr Gosse can pursue his work with ease. Dear Mrs Gosse pointed out to me a few of its disadvantages, but she acknowledges herself that the few imperfections are quite unimportant, because —'

'The Lord Jesus showed them the Way!'

'That is so. My dear friend recounted how she and Mr Gosse had placed the matter before the Lord, and He had — as always — answered. They are such excellent examples to us all.' Such is Miss Shipton's enthusiasm for her new friend that her face appears almost healthy in the lamplight. 'Mrs Gosse told me, "Miss Shipton, if

I have want of a pin and cannot find one, I place it before the Lord. I tell Jesus and He always finds me one. And so it is with our apartment." To tell Jesus! That is what we must all resolve to do.'

'How wonderful! To have Jesus arrange every aspect of our lives.' Sarah is irrepressible. 'Everything one dreams of finding. Just think of it, Anne, you must lay the matter of Mr Worthington before the Lord. And we must encourage Mr Worthington to do the same in respect of you.'

This time she has been too outspoken, verging on blasphemy, and our chaperone cannot let this pass. (I am almost prepared to do so — far better that Sarah should imagine that I yearn secretly, despite my protestations to the contrary, for the attentions of Mr Worthington. She must never guess the true object of my secret love.) Miss Shipton taps her stick on the floor in her agitation and, breathing rather fast, struggles out of the chair. I hurry forward to take her arm, and frown warningly at Sarah.

'You have been overtaxing your mind, Miss Nisbet, and it is time that you calmed yourself and retired to bed, so that you may be alert and responsive in the morning. Then perhaps you will consider your words with more care. Mrs Nisbet would find it hard to forgive me if I return you to her in such a feverish state. Good night, Miss Church.'

'Sarah,' I say, after Miss Shipton has left us with a final admonitory quotation, 'you must not tease her so. She is annoying and unamusing, but perhaps that arises from her always being unwell. And we would not have been able to come to Ilfracombe without her. I have to keep reminding myself of that. It is kind of her to accompany us.'

'She is being paid well,' Sarah replies brusquely. 'And she has little to do, when you and I are occupied with our classes, other than to occupy herself in whatever way she chooses. With Mrs Gosse, poor woman.'

I can think of no suitable reply so walk across to the window and pull the curtain aside to reveal our secret.

'Surely it is dark enough now?' (It is indeed well past ten o'clock and almost dark. For Sarah the early dusk is a continual source of surprise and dismay: 'In Helensburgh it remains light until almost midnight at this time of year,' she tells any fellow student that expresses an interest, and she then must explain — with much finger-pointing and tracing of maps in the air or on the table, guaranteed to acquire an attentive audience — that Helensburgh is 'on the westerly coast of Scotland, just to the North of Glasgow.')

'Is anything happening?'

We peer into the jar; it is a glass preserving jar which we have persuaded the landlady to lend us, telling her that we had need of it in order to help the 'famous Mr Gosse' with an experiment. She was unimpressed however, and grudgingly agreed only after we had promised to return it thoroughly washed and cleaned. At present it appears to contain only sea water.

'How disappointing, it is quite dark.'

'We must tap it or stir it, do you not remember?' I remind Sarah. 'We can use the handle of my comb.'

I want so much to be the first to make the experiment — but Sarah has already flicked the jar with her fingertip. At once the water glows and glitters with minute but brilliant sparks.

We are both entranced, but remember to whisper our amazement.

'It is just as Mr Gosse told us.' I grip Sarah's arm as I lean forwards.

'They're fading. It is your turn, Anne — try stirring it.'

I plunge the handle of my comb into the water and stir it gently: a sudden luminosity swirls and spirals in the jar.

'Can you imagine seeing the sea like that? He said he was on the paddle steamer, did he not?'

'Yes. Yes, he did. Here, you try it now.' Handing her the comb, I turn away quickly to hide my expression, and busy myself searching for my notebook.

The luminous sea: he had described it in the class. We had finished with the acorn barnacles and Mr Gosse had taken a sample of seawater from another jar and placed it in a glass cell; he had written the name, Noctiluca maritima, on the blackboard. As we each took our turn to examine them — the little objects resembled minute blobs of jelly — he had spoken to us about his experience with *Noctiluca* when he had travelled by the Bristol steamer. He had finished with a quotation from Sir Walter Scott: ' "Awak'd before the rushing prow, The mimic fires of ocean glow, Those lightnings of the wave; Wild sparkles crest the broken tides—" '

How wonderfully he had spoken the poetic lines! I shall read Sir Walter Scott's poem and memorise it in full, so that I shall *never forget* that moment.

But while I sat there with my pencils and notebook, pretending to concentrate on the task in hand, I had seen him catch his wife's eye — and *such* a glance had passed between them that I had had to look away. He had approached his wife, and I had busied myself with searching for another pencil in my bag.

'Henry, I must leave now and collect Willy from the Pollards'.' Mrs Gosse had spoken quietly and touched his sleeve. He had replied softly, too, almost whispering, so that I had to strain to hear.

'Do you remember, Emily, that night at Tenby? We watched the steamer from our window — she was at the pier, turning her paddle —'

'And the water blazed!'

'The Quay Steps were covered with sparks like diamond dust ...'

'You seized a bottle and a stick, and we left Willy asleep and hurried down to the quay so that you might take a sample of the water to see which animalcules produced the light —'

'And when I dashed a large stone into the water — every drop of the spray was luminous, a star with many rays of light!'

'Yes! I remember how a great circular wave of brilliant light spread out across the water. So that passers-by stopped to see what we were doing, and threw in their stones too. *That* was a time, Henry!'

I had watched Mr Gosse and his wife, and had seen his severe features soften and his brown eyes grown tender; the most gentle (and loving, oh, how he loved her!) smile had lit his face ...

I catch my breath, remembering how I had spied on their moment of intimacy — and Sarah looks at me quickly.

'What's wrong, Anne? You look so agitated.'

'Nothing is wrong at all. I was merely thinking how strange it is that the *Noctiluca* appear so unexciting in the daytime and yet now — they are *magical*. Is it not like magic? You wave your wand and set the water on fire!'

'Conjuring something from nothing — they are invisible to the eyes of ordinary mortals. Thus — *abracadabra*!'

'Ohhh.'

We sigh our disappointment in unison and this causes us to giggle again.

'*Sssh*!'

'They have stopped, we have exhausted them.'

'What fun we should have if we were really able to weave spells,' Sarah muses, and for a moment her face looks so wistful that I am taken in.

'Why, what would you wish? Do you have an unfulfilled dream?'

She tiptoes rapidly to the bed and scrambles beneath the covers, laughing softly. 'Well, of course, dear Anne, I would bind you and Mr Wart together with a spell.'

I am so cross with her that I slap my notebook hard down on the bed. '*Stop it*! Forget about Mr Worthington.'

'Ouch! You hurt me. You have no sense of humour.' She flounces her body and tugs the sheet so that the quilt slips to one side.

'And *you* are so childish. Nor have you said your prayers.'

'Well, you had better "tell Jesus" then!'

It has been a long day and we are both tired and overwrought. I lie stiffly awake beside her, my mind unable to rest: the mattress is lumpy, the room is stuffy, and my nightdress confines my hot limbs. I want to drag it over my head and throw it in the corner. To lie naked and cool ...

But the sheets are rough and would chafe my skin. I try to imagine how it would be, to run down to the sea and cast myself into the waters, to glide in the water like a fish. But there are waves and the sea is cold. (Mr Gosse does not mind the cold. His natural element is the sea. I have heard that once, when he was collecting at Capstone Rock and thought himself unobserved, he was seen to strip off his clothes and plunge into a deep pool — and to emerge clutching a specimen which he then most carefully placed in his jar before he attempted to re-clothe himself). Yet ... to swim in a *luminous* sea, to be cloaked in spangled light ... both of us, side by side ... playing like ... porpoises. Rolling and cavorting ... My own body ... buoyant ...

no, no, NO. The idea is too horrible, it is disgusting. I must stop, think pure thoughts, tell Jesus. Dear Jesus, help me, please!

I can see the jar of *Noctiluca*. Are they shining? No, all is dark. I must lie still, Sarah grumbles and mutters in her sleep. I wish we did not have to share a bed, I wish we had more comfortable lodgings. Like the Gosses. No, no, think instead of Mr Wart. Even he has found somewhere more suitable. How I dislike him! I swear that even thinking his name is sufficient to give me nightmares. But he is merely unattractive, poor man, and ineffectual. I do him an injustice, I should try to be more charitable. I have him to thank for my meeting with Sarah and Mrs Nisbet, and if that had not taken place I should not be here. When was that? It was last winter, in late November, or perhaps it was in December? There was untrodden snow on the ground in Regent's Park. I described it, as is my habit, in my journal. I could look, and check the details — and, since Sarah sleeps, perhaps write something of my observations of today's events. But if I light the lamp, she will wake ...

'I could almost read the small print of a book'. That was what he told us. (Darling Mr Gosse!) Will the *Noctiluca* be persuaded to light up again for me?

I slip out of bed and carefully open the drawer of the dressing table to find my journal. By touch alone, I am able to unclasp it and open it somewhere towards the beginning (my uncle gave me the book as a present in October of last year). I pray the rustling of my nightclothes will not wake Sarah as I step softly across to the window. My comb is still there, I see it by the dim light that comes in from the street, and I take it up and stir the contents briskly (carelessly striking the side, but the cracked-bell ringing of the glass does not cause Sarah to stir). An ethereal glow of pale-green light springs into life and hastily, oh so hastily, I turn the pages looking for the date ... there is nothing in December, nothing at the end of November ... the light is waning ... and there it is, November 23rd . 'Today Papa took us to the Zoological Gardens at Regent's Park.' I hold the journal closer and closer to the dying light. 'A gentleman interrupted Papa's monologue to inform us that the word 'aquarium' owed nothing to the Revd Mr Kingsley but had been coined by the well-known naturalist, Mr P.H. Gosse. He showed us ...' But now the animalcules can no longer help me, they will not be aroused again.

He showed us a book, *The Aquarium*. The eavesdropping gentleman on November 23rd 1854 was Mr Worthington and since that time he has persisted (with Papa's vague approval but without the least encouragement from me) in his attentions.

Just one day in my life, yet an entry into so many new directions! Thence to marine natural history, to Sarah, to Mr Gosse and North Devon. How can *one day* make such a difference?

All thought of returning to bed has left me, although I know I should try to sleep for the sake of my complexion (just as I know that brushing my hair one hundred times each night will make it shine, and eating the crusts on my bread will make it wavy!). Instead, I curl up in the armchair, sniffing at the comforting smell of my leather-bound journal, and try to recollect the details of that momentous day.

It had been Mama's idea to go up to London; I can remember that so well. She had longed for the chance to shop for new fabrics and trimmings, and to see the exhibition of Sir Joshua Reynolds' portraits that had been so much talked-about. And my brothers and sister and I had also longed to go, for a variety of reasons — to visit the shops, to travel on a train, to walk in St James' Park and see Buckingham Palace! Papa had strongly resisted such a protracted visit on the grounds of expense (and perhaps also because he preferred to go to Town and to his club unencumbered by his family). But clever Mama had thought up a ruse: for some time Papa had talked admiringly of the Reverend Charles Kingsley's ideas (he had made his acquaintance at a dinner some months previously and had subsequently travelled to Eversley to talk with him further) — so my clever Mama had reminded him of the dear Reverend's connection with the new marine vivaria at the Zoological Gardens and persuaded him how useful it would be, and how instructive for his children, if we were all to make a visit. So, after spending a day or two in giving serious thought to the matter, and convincing himself that his patients could survive without him, Papa had agreed and had managed even to persuade himself that the expedition was entirely his idea. How Mama and I had giggled together in the privacy of her sewing room, and how I had hugged her! She herself was like a girl again in her excitement. And we were thrown into such confusion and despondency in the planning of what we should wear!

Mama does not at all care for Mr Worthington. I wish she were here now, instead of that awful Miss Shipton who preaches at us day and night ... Suddenly I feel quite *homesick* and long for the comfort of our own house, and my own bed, and a hug from Mama — and the *safety* of it all.

However, I am 22 years of age and should be looking for a husband, not crying for my Mama. Mr Worthington — despite his wart and pale eyelashes, and disconcerting habit of talking only to Papa when we are all together, as though I were a mere female without a brain in my head, and therefore worthy only of wife-hood — is judged to have 'good prospects'. He is hardly a Christian Socialist, which is what Papa — in admiration of the Reverend Kingsley's principles — now claims to be.

The Zoological Gardens! Papa was informing us quite loudly (possibly so that others might hear!) how Mr Charles Kingsley had contributed a great number of the specimens in the marine vivaria. We — Papa, my younger brothers and sister, and I — were wandering from tank to tank, amazed by their size and the large collection of sea-plants and animals contained therein. I recall there was a sea-star, its rows of suckered feet waving palely as it moved laboriously across the glass. And a fish (I did not know what species — I think now that it was probably a wrasse. How ignorant I was then!), distorted by the glass into a grotesque gulping monster, which caused little Tom to shriek with delight and fear and hide himself behind my skirts.

What an attraction the vivaria had become! At times we were hard-pressed to get close enough for a view. A lady standing nearby told us that she came there frequently as the collection was always changing. It seems the Zoological Society had been quite overwhelmed by the public enthusiasm for Mr Gosse's idea and had been persuaded to increase the number of the tanks to seven.

'To keep the tanks well-stocked is an onerous task,' Papa replied with great authority. 'When I last saw him, the Reverend Kingsley told me he had been much engaged in dredging off the Devon coast, in all kinds of inclement weather — with the express purpose of sending hampers of specimens up to London for Mr Gosse's perusal.'

Papa waved his hand vaguely in our direction. 'It seems that even Kingsley's children help him in the quest for ever-more unusual exhibits. He told me he was very proud of a strange creature — what did he call it? "a creature with no stomach", a sort of sea spider I believe — that his little boy had found. "If it has no stomach, how does it eat?" I asked him,' Papa laughed loudly, 'but of course Kingsley could not give me an answer.'

'Can we go to the seaside, Papa? I want to find a big crab,' Tom interrupted, pulling at Papa's coat (something which annoys Papa intensely — Tom is sometimes slow to learn.)

'Elizabeth and her sisters went to Bournemouth with their Mama,' my younger sister chimed in, with her usual lack of relevance. 'She went in a bathing machine — she said it was horrible. I should not like to do that, would you, Anne?'

But I was somewhat distracted by a gentleman standing nearby, because it seemed that he had become rather too interested in our wayward conversation. He was staring at Papa in an intense fashion, perhaps made more profound by his peculiarly pale eyebrows and lashes. I glanced at Papa to see if he had a mark on his face or was incorrectly dressed, but could find no cause for alarm or embarrassment.

Suddenly, the gentleman lunged forward and spoke out, blurted, even: 'The "creature without a stomach" to which you referred, sir, is no doubt the pycnogonid, a most unusual creature that appears to be composed entirely of legs, so small are its thorax and abdomen.'

I think we all recoiled a little, so *unexpected* was the gentleman's assault. Indeed, several people turned their heads, and I happened to catch the eye of a fashionably-dressed young lady, of about my age. Her eyes — and mouth — were wide open, and her expression was of such quiet hilarity that I could not help but smile back.

This gentleman, having succeeded in silencing Papa, now proceeded to lecture him (and indeed anyone else who would listen) about the origins and maintenance of the 'aquarium'; he held in his hand a book by Mr Gosse that described the process and the *scientific* reasoning behind it. That was the book I mentioned in my journal, *The Aquarium*, a book with which I have become so familiar.

'Ah, we have an expert in our midst,' the amused young lady whispered to me, then turned to her elegant chaperone. 'Mama, do you not think we should buy this Mr Gosse's book so that we too may become experts?'

'I have heard that smaller versions of these "aquaria" have become the latest object with which to ornament the drawing room,' her Mama replied, with a rather superior smile. 'Collecting sea creatures is becoming fashionable in the extreme.'

'Do walk around with us while your poor father is held captive. My name is Sarah Nisbet, and this is my Mama.'

Thus did I meet the Nisbets. Thereafter Sarah and I spent as much time as was permitted in each other's company while we were both in London. After she had departed on the railway train to Scotland, and I had returned to Winchester, we were happy to keep up a regular (and often irreverent) correspondence. As for Mr Worthington, he had inveigled himself into Papa's good books through his wide (but superficial) knowledge of the sciences, and took many opportunities to journey to Winchester to acquaint himself further with our family.

One day a letter arrived from Sarah asking if I would accompany her to North Devon in the summer, to attend the marine natural history classes arranged by Mr Philip Henry Gosse. 'My aunt has arranged a chaperone,' she wrote, 'a very Christian lady who will attend to our morals. Do say you can come, dear Anne. We shall have such an exciting time — free from the confines of our families! My Mama will write to yours if you think there is any hope!'

Considerable discussion ensued between my parents as to the suitability and cost of such a course. How unfortunate that, after agreement had been reached, Papa should let slip to Mr Worthington that I was to go to Ilfracombe. Mr Worthington declared that he himself had known of these classes for several months but had been uncertain whether he should himself attend — but now, by *great* good fortune ... etcetera, etcetera.

Mr Worthington found a pycnogonid yesterday and was able to occupy a great deal of Mr Gosse's attention. But I was able to busy myself with attempting to identify worms of the polychaete class, and so avoided having to admire his catch.

'Anne — *Anne!*'

Sarah's sleepy voice makes me start and I realise that I am quite chilled and stiff.

'Why are you sitting there? I'm sorry I was unkind — please come back to bed!'

CHAPTER 4: HAZEL

'How did they get the coffin down the stairs?'

I was dozing, lulled by the scent of thyme and rabbit-cropped turf, and the sound of the sea, but now I turned and squinted at Matt, who was sitting upright, elbows on bent knees. I wondered if he was trying to shock me, but I could see that he really did want to know.

So I told him, and it made him laugh.

I had been waiting for a fax to come through, with answers to some queries about a manuscript, but when it hadn't arrived by mid-morning, I had decided to go out instead. Matt had been pottering around, up and down the stairs, between the kitchen and his bedroom. On impulse, I had asked him if he wanted to come for a walk along the cliff path: on impulse, he had agreed.

We walked down the hill, legs stiff against the steepness, and took the passenger ferry across the estuary. In a couple of weeks the ferry steps would be crowded with rucksacked walkers, and children waving gaudy shrimping nets and squalling at their parents, who would be laden with baskets bulging with towels and enough food for a prolonged siege — but right now the boat was able to accommodate the whole queue; apart from us, there were two retired couples and three local women, one of whom I recognised, all carrying bulging supermarket carrier bags.

On the far side of the estuary Matt and I climbed again, on worn granite paving stones that were smeared with dried dog shit and gobs of phlegm; up a narrow street between a pub and the Methodist chapel; past cats, curled, eyes closed, on window sills, and cottage doors that opened onto the pavement; and so up to the cliff-top path.

I was glad Matt had agreed to come. Walking is a good way of talking; it's not necessary to make eye contact and you can interrupt awkward topics to climb stiles or catch your breath. Pauses assume much less significance. Matt had spent several hours job-hunting yesterday, and was explaining about the part-time bar work that he had managed to pick up in 'The Anchor' on the main quay. He'd been lucky because the vacancy had only just arisen, and he would mostly be required to work evenings, which would leave the daytime free for the beach.

'I'll give you something towards my keep, if you want,' he said.

I was touched. I should have replied, 'You don't need to, you're my son not a paying guest', but I didn't. I looked over my shoulder and smiled at him, and just said, 'Thanks.'

Springy turf was dotted with sea-pinks, and then the path plunged us into a tunnel that had been worn between banks of stunted, sloping trees and tight-knit gorse that, earlier in the summer, had been heavy with scent. The trapped air was hot and moist, and there was a smell of warm earth. Out again, onto the level headland, the breeze cooling our sweat, and then a knee-cracking descent to a deep hollow where a footbridge took us over a stream that carried hints of bovine life upstream.

Matt was striding ahead of me up the wood-fronted steps, his arms swinging and thigh muscles and buttocks straining against baggy checked shorts, but as he neared the top I could see him slowing and he bent forward and rested his hands on his thighs. By the time I reached him (breathing deeply myself but smiling, trying to show that although I was old enough to be his mother, a steep climb wasn't going to defeat *me*!), he was sprawled on the grass, his head resting on his balled-up tee-shirt and his chest slick with sweat.

'Christ! Why did I say I'd come out with you? I should've stayed in bed.'

'You've got a good tan. I didn't realise Art and Design was such an outdoor subject.'

When I sat down beside him I could smell his hot skin and damp hair. A manly smell, but one which suddenly also brought back the smell of the boy, the sweetish, musky, child-smell that bonds mother and offspring. I sniffed, and breathed in deeply, trying to recapture that elusive memory.

'What's wrong? Do I smell bad?' He was trying to sound belligerent, but I just grinned at him. 'Anyway, we get loads of free time so we climb out onto the roof and sunbathe. Or hang out in South Park. Whatever.'

'Watching the girls.'

His grunt was non-committal and he closed his eyes again; the rhythmic rising and falling of his chest slowed, and it was obvious that he wasn't intending to move for a while. I untied the cotton pullover from round my waist and arranged it as a pillow, then I lay back, too, enjoying the warmth of the sun on my face and arms.

'I'm glad you don't wear a medallion. Or nipple rings.'

'Why? Why are you glad?'

'Oh — I don't know, really. They're sort of indicators, aren't they? — signalling a certain viewpoint, or a certain self-vision. I suppose if you had a medallion nestling in your chest hair that would indicate to me that I really knew nothing about you, after all. Which would be my fault. Of course.'

I didn't really mean to sound so ironic. The sun pressed on my eyelids and made me sigh with pleasure.

I added, 'But anyway, you're an adult. And so you're entitled to do whatever you want, I suppose, nipple-rings, tattoos or whatever.'

'Is that what being an adult is about, then? Doing what you want, whenever? That really explains things, doesn't it?'

I waited for him to bring up the subjects of Edward, and David, and divorce, but instead he surprised me with that question.

'How did they get the coffin down the stairs?'

I opened my eyes and turned to stare him, but he was sitting up and his eyes were closed, and he wasn't smiling. The question was clearly of some importance to him.

I could have said, 'Oh, it was a struggle but they managed'; but I didn't want to lie.

'They didn't. They couldn't. It was impossible.'

The funeral director and his assistant had been quite unsettled. I had waited in the kitchen and had heard them going up and down the stairs, and their whispered conversations. The director had blown his nose, he had cleared his throat, and had called out (softly, of course), 'Mrs Myers? Would it be possible to have a word ...?'

They had explained the problem, with subdued and balletic pointing and miming.

'Well, you'll just have to leave the coffin down here and carry her down.' It had seemed so obvious. 'It's quite all right, I won't be offended — and nor, come to that, will she. I'll go out into the garden while you transfer her.'

'They were really rather embarrassed,' I told Matt. 'It just was not etiquette. But what else were they to do? And, anyway, Mummy — Granny — didn't seem like my mother any more. She had gone. Do you see? I don't know how they did it, I didn't look.'

Matt stared at the sea: gulls were stationary white specks on the water, rising and falling with the swell. He was silent for a while and I thought he was angry, but then he nodded and looked down at me.

'It was okay. It would have made her laugh if she'd known. Were the undertakers — "funeral directors" — good-looking? She'd have made a joke about that, being carried by a bloke and so on.' He grinned, a little tightly.

'Well, no, not really. The helper was plump and balding, from what I remember. He was very self-effacing. And the man in charge was — I hate to say it — cadaverous!'

Matt burst out laughing, then pulled at his lower lip.

'A bit grim for you, though, on your own.'

'Well, yes. It would have been nice if ... But Jamie came back for the funeral. And I think you were sensible not to come, there would have been no point. I *did* understand, really.'

After all, there had been no point; Matt's Granny Barbara had gone. But the memory of Matt's absence could still hurt, if I let it. Thank heaven that my brother, at least, had been there.

'Yeah. Well, you know, I didn't think I could cope, and ... well, we did discuss it at the time, didn't we, and ... Sorry. But it was good that Uncle Jamie could come. Do you mind about Dad? Finally asking you for a divorce, I mean?'

This particular question wasn't unexpected, in fact it was one I had asked myself several times and had answered to my own satisfaction; yet I wasn't too sure what our son wanted to hear from me, it was not a matter that he and I had ever discussed. I rolled over and sat up, too, resting my arms and chin on my knees.

'No, Matthew, I don't mind. I'm pleased for him — after all, he and Gail have been together for six years or so. I would have minded very much if he'd asked for a divorce then, just when I'd left Edward.'

' "Sleazy Edward".'

'He wasn't sleazy, I don't know why you always say that. He was smart, and senior management and — oh, anyway. I suppose I kept on hoping that I could just come back to you both and forget what had happened, that you'd forgive me and I could pick up where we'd left off. Perhaps your father should have insisted on a divorce right then, but he was happy living with Gail — you *both* seemed to be happy.' I looked at Matt quickly for confirmation but his expression was distantly-focussed and uninformative. 'So we drifted along on our own separate ways, growing further and further apart. After a while I stopped even thinking about us getting together again. The three of you seemed like a family unit ... It makes sense for him to want a divorce now. I can see why he and Gail want to get married, now that there's a baby due. Nice for them to have a child. But how do you feel about it, Matt? Do you mind? It's your home, you've lived with them all this time. Do you feel a bit jealous?'

Was the threat of exclusion why he had decided to come and stay with me?

'*Jealous!*' Matt's voice was loud as he stared at me. Astonishingly, his neck and throat began to blush. 'Why do you think I'd feel jealous?'

I think I understood, then, but I didn't want to know. It would not have been surprising, because Gail was midway between Matt's and David's ages; she was comforting, and comfortable — everything that I was not. I stood up and picked up my pullover and shook off the adhering strands of dry grass.

'As long as your father doesn't find out,' I murmured,

'Find out what?' Matt asked, a little aggressively. He wiped the back of his hand over his face.

But I didn't repeat myself, or explain, merely shrugged and wandered back towards the path. A blue launch, half-full of sight-seers, was idling at the bottom of the cliff, riding the smooth swell. A man's amplified voice was explaining about kittiwakes and, obligingly, nesting birds called to their circling mates. Cormorants stood motionless on a white-splattered rock and hung out their wings to dry.

Nothing surprised me: people live and interact in an infinite variety of ways. Some drift, some are decisive, many are victims of circumstances and their gonads. I hoped Matthew would not be like me, wouldn't drift ... I tried not to wonder about his absence from the funeral. I glanced at him and saw that he had put his shirt back on, but had taken off one of his trainers and was picking at a toenail; a displacement activity.

'What are you going to do with your life?' I called across to him. 'Do you have a Plan?'

He stopped his pedicure and glanced back the way we had come. Two women in their late twenties, coastpath walkers with rucksacks and boots, were climbing up the steps.

'Yeah. Do you want to hear it? I'm going to put my trainer back on.'

The woman at the front, who wore a square plastic map-case suspended from her neck, spluttered with laughter, and they both looked at us appraisingly as they passed. The one at the back wore a denim bikini top with her shorts, and she had a large purple birthmark across one shoulder-blade. Even as I laughed at Matt, I wondered why she wanted to display it.

'Come on, then, put your Plan into action and let's get to the headland so we can see round into the next bay, and then we'll go back and have a pint.'

I linked my arm through Matt's when he joined me, but the path narrowed after a few yards and he was able to disengage himself.

On the headland the gorse and scrub had been cut down, and the cleared land was now fenced off and cultivated. The wind blew in rhythmic waves across the barley so that the whiskery seed-heads soft-focussed the field. ('Metachronal waves': I suddenly remembered the term from student days.) Now we were able to look down into the next bay, where a strip of grey sand and yellowed grass separated the sea from the steep-sided, wooded valley. Headland after headland faded into blue haze and distance towards the West, black rocky outcrops splitting and churning the waves so that dark land and blue, glittering sea were separated by an uneven milky line.

My eyes began to water from the glare and I blinked. Then my nose prickled and an unpleasantly hot tightness seized my face. The sneeze exploded out of me, flexing my body backwards then forwards.

'Oh no!' I just had time to gasp before the next sneeze roared from my mouth and nose. They were unstoppable, one after another, full volume, and my panicky hands searched pockets for a handkerchief while my nose and eyes streamed liquid. One small crumpled tissue — but it would have to do!

'Shit! Can't you do that quietly?' Matt looked round appalled. 'You've even scared the gulls away. No, you *can't* use my tee-shirt as a nose-rag!'

'It's not my time of year for hayfever,' I moaned. 'What started this? Perhaps it was that barley.' I dabbed ineffectually, feeling weak and feverish, and as though my face would burst. 'Are those women still in sight? Perhaps one of them can give me some tissues.'

'God, no. They're running away as fast as their boots'll take 'em. Come on, we'll just go back — you'll be okay when you get away from whatever started it off, won't you?'

Unfortunately, the cure was never that simple and I knew that the symptoms would persist for an hour or more. Staggering up and down those steps with bloated face and impaired vision did not appeal, yet there seemed to be no alternative. I walked on a short way, hoping to see a miraculous speedboat or a bus labelled 'Polkenna', conveniently waiting around the corner.

'There's a house down there, look. I'll see if they can give me some Disprin and some tissues. You wait here — then you won't have to be embarrassed.'

'Don't be daft. You'll probably fall over and break your leg, the state you're in. I'll go, Hazel — you wait.'

'They won't even answer the door to you! We'll both go.'

I stumbled and oozed along the path, with an occasional sneeze. Matt grumbled and swore softly, but he kept close to me and occasionally grabbed my arm. Fortunately, the path was well-trodden and firm, the last part dropping down through the edge of a cool dark wood that held the sharp, clean smell of wild garlic, and we came out through a kissing-gate at the head of the bay. A narrow tarmacked path, raised above the beach on a stone embankment, led to the house. The house *nestled*, there was no other word for its appearance. It seemed to have gathered the natural features of its surroundings onto itself. Its roof and upper storey were hung with brown-flecked grey slates; Virginia creeper clambered over the drain pipes and the stone porch, holding on wherever it could to form a dense green cover; even the rough stone wall around the garden was overgrown with ivy, and the trees in the garden merged with the enclosing woodland. Swallows and house martins swooped over the garden and the shore, and there was an impression of completeness and warm, moist air; smells of sea and slatey sand, dried wrack — and something sharper, unnatural, like a solvent.

'There's a car in the garage, so there must be someone there. Go on, then. Go and ask,' Matt urged, as I stood and looked.

'Hi there! Can I help? You guys look lost.'

The voice was startlingly close. A young man stood below us, looking up from the shore. He wore only faded shorts and red rubber flip-flops, his body was tanned and well-muscled, his dark-brown hair was pulled back into a ponytail, and his smile showed perfect teeth. A wooden boat was upturned on fish crates beside him and an open pot of varnish explained the solvent-smell.

'Hey, I didn't mean to startle you.'

He really *is* American I thought, erratically, as I stared at him. Give him a board and he'd be at home in the North Coast surf. A real Beach Boy. I could feel how Matt, with scarcely perceptible movements, began to disassociate himself from me. My water-logged, hot face flushed even more.

'Oh, that's quite all right. We don't want to disturb your work. I was actually just about to call at the house. Do you live there, by any chance?'

'Sure, for the moment, at any rate.' The American was peering at me with a slight frown. 'Hey, you don't look too great. Are you allergic?'

'I have hay fever — something triggered it off back on the coast path. I don't suppose you have any Disprin in the house, do you? I wonder if you could let me have a couple? They're usually the most effective cure.'

'Disprin? I don't know what that is, but we'll go see. Wait there.'

He propped his paint-brush across the top of the pot of varnish and walked across the shingle to a concrete slipway. Until then I hadn't noticed the short stone jetty that followed the contours of the rocks at the edge of the bay. The sea wall on which we stood curved round to join it, and the beach in the crook of the elbow, where the American had been working, was banked up with grey sand, shale and wind-blown plastic jetsam. The corner would only be flooded in a storm or at very high Spring Tides and now, on a warm summer afternoon, it formed a hot, dry workshop. I thought the new varnish might blister and wondered how much the young man knew about boats.

He held out his hand to introduce himself.

'Hi, I'm Jim Steinberg.'

'Hallo. I'm Hazel, and this is —'

'Matt,' Matt interjected quickly, before I could say 'my son'.

'Hi, Matt. Why don't you guys come along to the house and we'll see what we can. find. I'm sure Elizabeth will have something stashed away.'

The tarmac path led through the garden gate to the front door and then around the house. As Jim led us round to the right I noticed that gales had caused their usual damage to south-facing paintwork and window-frames. A broken slate lay where it had fallen, and a window-ledge was thick with sparrows' droppings beneath the creeper. But although the path was cracked and blistered by erupting weeds, the rest of the garden was immaculate. Jim Steinberg's bare back was smooth and confident and his ponytail flopped against his neck as he walked ahead and pushed open a side door into the house.

'Come right on in and I'll go tell Roger you're here.'

He waited while we walked down a short concrete ramp that led straight into the kitchen, then he picked up a mug from a rack beside the sink and ran cold water, testing it with his finger.

'I guess tap water's okay to drink? Help yourself — you too, Matt. I'll be right back.'

I filled the mug from the tap and took a drink, and realised that my symptoms were already easing; a few moments of apprehension, an outside interest that briefly supplanted self-appraisal and self-pity — sometimes that was all it took to dispel an allergic response. The triumph of 'mind over matter'! I raised an eyebrow at Matt, and he shrugged and continued looking round at the plain, cream-painted cupboards, the pine table and the stone-flagged floor that was partially covered by woven rush mats. A greying teatowel, stiff and dusty, hung from the wooden rails of a clothes-drying rack that was hoisted up against the ceiling.

We could hear Jim ('There's a woman, she's sick…') and, presumably, 'Roger' talking in the distance. Feet pounded up stairs and, soon, pounded down again. Jim reappeared, a tee-shirt draped around his neck and not at all out of breath, and held out a bottle.

'Soluble aspirin, right? How're you doing?'

'Improving.' I smiled at him. 'That's good of you.'

I dropped a couple of tablets in some water in the mug and watched them froth and shrink.

'So are you guys from round here, or are you on vacation?' Jim's voice was muffled because his head was inside his tee-shirt.

Matt's shoulders were slightly hunched and I could see that his hands were bunched in his pockets. I wondered how he would reply.

'Hazel —,' he jerked his head towards me, even though Jim could not see. 'Hazel lives here, over at Polkenna. And I'm visiting. Sort of on holiday, though I'm going

35

to be working in The Anchor.'

Jim's emerging face was laughing. As he pulled down the shirt I saw that it said *'Evolution is ...'* beneath an obscure design. 'Sounds like me — I'm sort of on holiday, but sort of working, too. It's a pretty place but kinda quiet.'

'Where are you from?' Matt asked.

'Oregon. If you know where that is — most people don't. Top left- hand corner of the States, just below Washington State. Corvallis, which isn't exactly New York. How're you doing, Hazel?' he asked again. 'Is that aspirin kicking in yet?'

'Much better. I'm really grateful — but we better be going and let you get back to your varnishing.' I had been looking round, hoping to see a box of tissues or some kitchen towel, but none was visible. 'Would you mind if I just used your bathroom before we go? If I could just swill some cold water over my face and wash off the pollen or whatever it was that started it.'

'Sure — there's a bathroom along the corridor. And you needn't rush off on my account. Come and meet Roger — he's getting bored with his own company.'

I ignored Matt's pointed glare and followed Jim into the narrow corridor that seemed to lead along the centre of the house. The back of his tee-shirt said '... *chaos with feedback'*; I was no wiser. Like the kitchen, the corridor was stone-flagged and partly covered by a woven sisal runner. The bathroom nearly lived up to its name, and was not just the American euphemism for loo: there was a toilet, a glassed-in shower cubicle and a wide ceramic handbasin with thick, old-fashioned taps. It was a spacious room with cream-glossed walls, but there was little evidence of luxury apart from a two-bar electric fire fixed to the wall above the door, and the only hint of non-functional decoration was the shell of a pearly nautilus, sliced through to show its whorl of glistening empty chambers. Poor thing.

I washed my face and dried it with toilet paper, then folded another wad of paper and put it in my pocket for a handkerchief. The low toilet was fenced in at each side with a chrome handrail, and now I saw that there were other rails inside the shower. At once the relevance of the kitchen ramp and the incongruously tarmacked path was apparent — 'Roger' must be disabled, and perhaps Jim was temporarily looking after him. Perhaps while 'Elizabeth', whoever she was, was absent. It seemed that Matt and I were to provide Roger with his entertainment for the day. I pulled my jumper over my cotton vest top, raked my fingers through my hair, and wished I were wearing a skirt instead of shorts; but my eyes were not as puffy and bloodshot as they felt and my nose was not, after all, a swollen red balloon.

I followed the sound of the three men's voices, amused to hear that Matt, in my absence, was sounding animated, and crossed a front hall, shadowy with hanging coats, towards a door that led into a drawing room. Matt and Jim were standing together at the far end of the room, where Roger (presumably) was seated on a swivel chair in front of a computer screen. The room had a low ceiling and was surprisingly long, with three recessed windows that contained deep, cushioned window-seats where one would be able to sit and look out over the bay and the headland. I had an impression of blowsy old roses on dark blue linen — an attempt had been made to unite and harmonise the odd collection of chairs and stools and sofa, but the loose covers were old and faded about the arms, and the chairs still managed to look individual and undistinguished. Books and papers were piled on every surface, including the floor, and it was noticeable that the removal of dust and sand was not a high priority.

'Hello!' I called. 'Can I come in?'

'Hazel, hi. We're just discussing screen savers — computers geeks, right? Come and meet Roger — Roger this is Hazel, who's allergic.'

Roger swivelled his chair to look at me and I caught a glimpse of the brightly-coloured moving patterns on the screen behind him. He stood up and walked towards me. He was not at all disabled, not even the slightest limp, and when we shook hands, his grip was positive and firm.

' 'Morning,' he said, and he was English, too. 'I gather you've been suffering — bad luck. But I hope the Disprins are working? I'm Roger Trenton, by the way.'

He could have been in his mid-forties, although his glasses, and the brown beard and moustache that were streaked with white, made it difficult to tell.

Multicoloured, patterned fish were swimming, circling and shoaling, between weeds and rocks on the screen behind him; the moving pictures drew my attention, and Roger turned to watch, too, smiling.

'Jim just installed a new screen saver, and unfortunately it's proving a real distraction from writing. We keep looking for patterns of behaviour and hypothesising about predator-prey relationships. There are one or two carnivorous species,' he explained.

''Hazel uses hers to remind her who she is,' Matt said.

I grimaced. 'I'm afraid I have one of those where your name goes spinning around the screen. I never seem to get around to changing it.'

Roger's computer was set up on a broad and ancient desk, and I could now see that pages of a printed manuscript were piled all around it. Two mounted photographs lay beside the keyboard but their subjects were indistinguishable because each was covered with a tracing paper overlay on which letters and arrows had been drawn in black pen. A ruler lay on top of a numerical Table in a reprint from a scientific journal.

'You must be some sort of a biologist.'

'How can you tell? Are biologists so stereotypical?' Roger looked down at his plain blue shirt with the rolled-up sleeves and his denim jeans. 'No sandals — though I acknowledge I've got the beard.'

I laughed, and he joined in.

'No, just the words you use — and the fact that you have a reprint open at a table of DNA sequences.'

'Heck, who have you let into the house, Jim? Are you a spy from the opposition? Or are you a biologist, too?' He looked doubtful.

Matt and Jim had been watching the screen and discussing the piscatorial happenings, but now they both looked up and listened.

'I *was* a biologist, a long time ago — I read Natural Sciences at Cambridge.' That sounded too grand and I didn't want to appear cleverer than I was. I added hastily, 'But I only got a Lower Second and I went into publishing and editing.'

'Ah.' Roger seemed relieved: perhaps, for a moment, he had felt threatened by a superior intellect. 'I'm a biochemist, though I like to call myself a molecular biologist these days. And Jim here is a mathematician, slumming it with the biologists in the interests of epidemiology.'

Jim grinned at me. 'Yeah, they're not too good with numbers.'

'Why are you both *here*?' Matt asked. 'It's a bit out of the way, isn't it? I mean, you haven't got a lab tucked away somewhere in a shed, have you?'

'No, we're visiting Dr Wilson. She lives here — she's a retired biologist, a malacologist, actually.' Roger Trenton looked at me to see if I understood the word, and I nodded. 'I've been doing some work on speciation with her, and I've come down for a few weeks to work on the manuscript of a book we're writing together.'

'And I'm here for the summer because Elizabeth and I are trying to hack some stuff on population biology and parasite transmission. Hey, if you like this screen-saver, come and see mine. My desk's in the next room.'

But I was more interested in the owner of the house, and let Matt be taken off by Jim. The name 'Elizabeth Wilson' had rung a bell.

'The owner of the house is Elizabeth Wilson, is that right?' I asked Roger. 'In her sixties, rather wiry, with short dark hair going a bit grey?'

'That sounds like her, yes. Do you know her?'

'Not really. But she knew my mother, I don't know how well, but they certainly knew each other.'

Now that I had made the association, I could remember my first meeting.

'I met her outside the Art Gallery in Polkenna — my mother was the artist, Barbara Lewisham.'

But Roger shook his head. 'I'm sorry, I don't know her work.'

'She always exhibited some of her paintings in the summer exhibition, and I remember going down to the Gallery with her to change a frame that she wasn't happy with, and we met Elizabeth Wilson and her husband outside. She — Elizabeth — was exhibiting some drawings, I think. But her husband was in a wheelchair and they were having a bit of a struggle trying to get it into the Gallery.'

'That would have been Allan — Allan Galbraith. Elizabeth kept her maiden name. He had some sort of strange wasting disease, I don't know quite what, but it was thought that he picked it up in Africa. He's dead now, you know. He died, oh, three years ago. All rather grim and tragic, I believe.'

'The ramp in the kitchen and the handgrips in the bathroom — they make sense now. He seemed rather a nice man — though I only met him briefly. He had a beard, too, didn't he?'

A silvery, neatly-trimmed beard and moustache and a tanned face that looked both kind and tired. My mother and I had helped Elizabeth Wilson half-carry, half-bounce the wheelchair down two steps. I had been at the front, lifting the foot rest, and I had seen how his legs were thin and wasted inside his trouser-legs, and that his hands were emaciated, with knotted veins. I had recognised Elizabeth at my mother's funeral, too, but she had not come to the wake and I supposed Jamie must have spoken to her at the door of the chapel, because I couldn't remember talking to her. But then one doesn't remember much from such occasions.

'Poor man. And poor Elizabeth, too.'

'Yes, but she keeps very busy. She's an astonishing woman. She may have retired from active research but her mind never switches off. People in the field — parasitologists, malacologists — constantly cite her work and lots of people still come to visit her. She's on her way back from Bristol today, that's why she's not here now, otherwise I'm sure she would have been glad to see you.'

'So what does she work on? Snails and parasites, so that must be — sheep liver fluke?' I made a guess. 'Goodness, that's scraping around in my memory a bit.'

'Not bad! But it's actually human urinary bilharzia — *Schistosoma haematobium* in African *Bulinus* snails. Were it only that clear-cut! The dividing lines between the species are always shifting.'

'I remember now that my mother introduced her as a biologist, and I thought that it was unusual that a scientist should be an artist, too. Drawing rather than painting, wasn't it? Though perhaps she did watercolours, too?'

'I know scientists who are artists, poets or good musicians,' Roger said, rather primly, I thought. 'Those are Elizabeth's drawings on that wall.'

But why hadn't I noticed the painting before? The furniture and the people had occupied my attention, I had ignored the walls. The painting was on the long wall opposite the windows, and the bold colours were unmistakable; bold colours for a minute detail, a fragment of a stone quay, an orange rope trailing from a bollard, green weed on wet steps, deep blue shadows, and at the bottom on the strip of muddy sand, the empty red shell of a large edible crab.

'My mother painted that.' I went up to it and found her initials in the bottom right corner. 'There. "B.L." ' I touched them and stroked the frame.

I could see why the composition might have appealed to the biologist in Dr Wilson. It appealed to me, and I could suddenly see my mother painting it, see how she saw it. The unexpectedness of the discovery, of my mother's work, threatened to make my eyes water again, and I had to blink quickly.

'Did she? What an extraordinary coincidence. It's very dramatic, isn't it? And these are some of Elizabeth's.'

Roger took me over to look at several portraits of seated figures and nudes, fluidly drawn in pen and ink or red crayon. I commented on their spare outlines and accuracy.

'Yes. There are lots of her snail drawings next door in the room that Jim uses.

Accuracy is very important there, as you can imagine.'

I smiled at him. He had taken off his glasses and they had left accurately-placed red marks on each side of his nose. He cleaned his glasses on his sleeve and after he had put them back on he stared out of the window for a few moments, as though to re-set his vision, then looked back at me. I felt that he was looking properly at me for the first time.

'You said you lived in Polkenna. That's rather an attractive little fishing village, isn't it? But I suppose it's rather quiet in the winter — how do you find living there all year round?'

I told him the usual sorts of things that tend to confirm an outsider's prejudices, and we discussed the wonders of the electronic age that allowed me to work from home and send information along telephone wires. It must be clear that I'm not entirely stupid (after all, I have a degree in a science from a highly prestigious university!) and I found it amusing and also a little irritating that Roger didn't know whether to treat me as a colleague, as a poor woman recovering from hay-fever or as an attractive young woman. (I was probably only a year or two younger than he, and not that much shorter, but he did rather exaggerate the manner in which he bent forward to hear what I was saying. But he was courteous, and his laugh was genuine.)

Eventually, I said, 'I think I had better go and find Matt, it's time we were going. Thank you for the Disprin — and for being so welcoming.'

'You look much better already. I'm glad we could help. Drop in again next time you're walking this way, I'm sure Elizabeth would be very pleased to renew acquaintance with you.'

As we wove our way through the books and small tables (how had Allan managed to negotiate a passage?) towards the door, I asked where he normally worked.

'London, King's. I live out at Croydon, so it's a hell of a commute — but it's pleasanter for my wife and the boys out there. Elizabeth was lucky, she and Allan had a little flat in South Ken, but it all got too difficult when Allan became less mobile. So she chucked it in and moved down here.'

'Chucked what in?' I had obviously missed something.

Roger looked blank for a minute, then realised. 'Oh, she used to work at the Museum — the Natural History Museum on Cromwell Road. Sorry, I thought you knew.'

Matt was in the kitchen, eating a slice of bread and jam. He and Jim already seemed to be good friends and were making plans to meet up again.

When we left, I saw that the garden gate had a name cut into the wood and although the letters were cracked and ingrained with green slime, I could still see that it said 'Nancarrow House'. The name rang a faint bell and I realised that my mother had probably mentioned the place to me.

'There was a painting by Granny Barbara in the drawing room,' I said.

Matt stopped. 'Why didn't you tell me? I would have liked to see it.'

'Because it nearly made me cry. And I didn't know how to tell you without giving you a shock.'

CHAPTER 5: ELIZABETH

One afternoon, after Barbara had taken a shower, I went upstairs to ask if I should make some of the ginger tea that she liked, and I found her sitting on the end of her bed. The top of her dressing gown was open and she was staring at her reflection in the mirror.

'I've grown used to the effect of gravity,' she said. 'I can put up with the sagging flesh and wrinkles and the flab, you expect that at our age. But I still can't get used to the idea of being *asymmetric*, Elizabeth. Everything we look at is symmetric, animals and flowers, almost everything living. Even this bed, the dressing table, the window! We expect things to be symmetric, we appreciate the symmetry. When I'm painting I look for the symmetries — if only to avoid them! But look at me —,' she straightened her back and tried to laugh, although I could see that she was on the verge of tears, 'I'm like a broken statue — Venus with half a nose, David with only one ball. I'm not sure that I can ever feel comfortable with myself again.'

I looked at her back, staying silent, not wanting to look at her face because I didn't know what to say: because what she had said was true, symmetry was perceived as the normal state and, for whatever reason, our brains were programmed to search for it and respond to it. Our perceptions, however artefactual, are biased towards the search for visual perfection — whether it be an intricately-decorated Gothic arch, Blake's 'tyger', or a starfish. For even a starfish, rotated, has symmetry, and the halves of other animals are usually mirror-images of each other. As Barbara's halves were not.

A broken statue; a broken symmetry. There was a key there. Broken symmetries were functional, they had purpose.

'An Amazon!' I was inspired. 'That's your new function, you're to be an Amazon. You must go out and fight!'

For a moment, it seemed so simple.

She stared at me in the mirror, laughing and shaking her head.

'An *Amazon*? I'm struggling, Lizzie, to find the relevance of your metaphor. I assume it is a metaphor? Who am I to fight? My own personal bogey-men?'

She flung out her arms in an exaggerated operatic pose, and sang out,

' "Bring me my bow of burni-ing gold, bring me my a-rrows of de-*sire*",' but then quickly dragged her dressing gown tightly closed and looked away from the mirror.

'What desire could there possibly be? At this age and in this state?'

I had been no help. I did not know what to say, and I sat down next to her and held her head against my own, rocking her gently. I tried not to look in the mirror, not wanting to see those two ageing women; not wanting the viewpoint of the detached observer who sees the image only and nothing of the reasons and hidden emotions. But the pinpoint of an idea expanded and developed, and the fantastical nature of it began to delight me.

'Wait a minute. I want to show you something.'

I let go of Barbara, slipping off my shoes and climbing onto the bed, shuffling round to kneel behind her. I put my hands on her shoulders.

'You and the woman who is your mirror-image are symmetrical. Lift your right hand — go on, just wave it around. And do you see how your double is waving her *left* hand?'

I pulled open her dressing gown and slipped it off her shoulders, reaching down to place my own right hand over the thin white scar (sad, dry, crumpled skin). Then the warm reality of her made me catch my breath, and for a moment I closed my eyes, and bent my head into her neck, feeling her heat, smelling her smell, almost overcome with love. I made myself look again at our images, saw her eyes, too, half-closed.

'With which hand has your double's companion touched which side of your double's chest?' I asked. 'Let's forget that we are looking at ourselves, and pretend that those are different women in front of us.'

'This is a sort of voyeurism, isn't it?' Barbara gave a brief, deep chuckle, but she was puzzled, and intrigued, and she eventually shrugged slightly, and she pressed my hand more firmly against her skin, shifting against it. 'Well, all right, lovey. It's their *left* sides that we're talking about, I can see that, but ...' She shrugged again, and smiled at my reflection and leant back against me, wriggling her shoulders and murmuring, 'So what? Lizzie darling, are you going to lecture me?'

'You have to concentrate!' I was trying hard. 'Look — there *is* a symmetry. Those two women are symmetrical with both of us and, more important, *you're* symmetrical with your reflection. If you and your mirror-double joined hands and stood side by side — like two of a chain of paper dolls — the pair of you would have symmetry. And that's how you see yourself, isn't it? You and your image make a pair. And who's to say which is real, because it's your *joint* perception that counts. The two of you observe each other!'

And now she stared into the mirror, and held out her left hand as though to grasp the right hand of her other half.

'There are times when one feels detached from oneself, as though one is an observer, watching one's own behaviour ... It's a common feeling, isn't it?' She spoke slowly, looking at the two not-quite-touching hands. 'I believe lots of people experience it. I don't know what that says about those people's characters — too self-regarding, perhaps? Or too unsure? But yes, you're right — I and my other half there make a whole. And with you too, my love, the four of us make quite a party, don't we?'

Barbara leant her cheek against my hand that was on her shoulder, and then she drew that hand down so that she was encircled in my embrace.

CHAPTER 6: ANNE: 1863

'Anne — my darling! Are you in pain? Has it begun?' Duncan has just entered my bedroom, some papers in his hand, and he rushes across to the bed and kneels beside me.

I shake my head, momentarily unable to speak. He grasps my hand and lays his head gently on the mound that is my stomach.

'He knows that I have returned! He is moving in response, I can feel him. Dearest love, what has upset you so?'

My eyes are wet but I smile at him and stroke his already-greying hair.

'We cannot be certain that it is a boy. I keep telling you so. Why have you come back so soon?'

'Why have I returned? I came to collect these papers that I had forgotten.'

I see that he is not entirely telling me the truth: after breakfast he had been so loth to leave.

'Perhaps you felt the urge to be with your wife again. Perhaps I should have allowed you to stay.'

'You have been reading Miss Shipton's book.' He takes *'Tell Jesus!'* from my hand and places it on the floor. 'And it has upset you, as I knew it surely must. Now let me stay, to comfort you.'

'You may only stay if you will first sit on the chair beside me and read certain passages.' I dry my tears as best I can, using the gathered cuff of my gown, and gently push his head away. 'Please, Duncan.'

'Let us be done with the book quickly, then. Where do I start?' He hands me the book and settles himself on the chair.

'She has mentioned Sarah and me, although not by name. Read from here.'

' "A lady, almost a stranger, called" —'

'That was Sara's aunt. She is a Presbyterian and very strict.'

'—"and requested, as a personal favour, that I would accompany a young relative to the coast, partly with a view to change of air, but more particularly to give her and a friend the opportunity of meeting with Mr Gosse, for the purpose of studying the world of wonders beneath the waters" — I rather like that alliteration, I must make sure to use it myself.' He reaches across to stroke my cheek and I take his hand, gripping it for comfort. ' "I consented to accompany her young friends to Ilfracombe …" '

'If you turn a few pages you will find us mentioned once more.' I attempt to reach across and turn the pages for him, since I have captured his free hand, but my body is too unwieldy and I release him.

'Ah yes. "While Mr Gosse and my young friends were exploring, with the ardour of naturalists, the treasures of the deep with the dragnet, or rambling over the rocks…" Surely you cannot be upset that she refers to you as "my young friends?" Forgive me, darling, I should not be so frivolous.' He turns the page, reading silently, stopping now and then to read more carefully. 'Especially when I can see that there is much here to cause you distress.'

There is much indeed, and the greater part of it, at present, is too heavy a burden to contemplate. I do not wish to delve too deeply and instead I find myself resorting to petulance at the extent of Miss Shipton's self-delusion, her misinterpretation, indeed her re-interpretation of events.

'I should like you to read aloud a certain passage — and then I shall recount to you the tale behind this story, or *parable* if you will. It is early in the work, at page six. It is two pages long, so you must be patient and keep reading.'

Duncan turns to the page, and bends to kiss me; he has resolved to humour me.

' So. "I was sitting, in a time of weakness and loneliness, on the sea-shore — a stranger in a strange place. It soothed me to watch the tide, as it ebbed, sweep away or deposit some stray shell or weed upon the strand; and I mused on the mission of some of the treasures that, in its mighty tidework, the sea brought or left behind. It was an evening in autumn, and not a loiterer was left on the shore, excepting a nurse and two young children — the elder a fine boy of about four years old. The child looked wistfully at me. I smiled at him, and he smiled in return. In a few minutes I felt a light touch on my arm, and his blooming cheek was laid on my knee, as he earnestly gazed in my face with an expression of loving sympathy. Perhaps he had some sick one at home, and knew the power of his sweet smiles. No matter: God sent him. We talked together like old friends, and my heart lost its loneliness beneath the loving ministration.

"At length he started off beyond my reach. I watched him eagerly seeking among the weeds for shells. One after another he held them to the light, casting aside each one that was broken, as unsuitable for his purpose. At last his busy fingers held up one which gave him satisfaction, and after examining it carefully, he polished it with his coat, and then, with a triumphant smile, advanced and laid it on my knee. Stepping back a few paces, evidently pleased at my unfeigned delight, he lisped out, "For *you*, only for you — all for you," as if I might doubt my right to the gift.

"The shell lay in my hand; my soul had risen like a lark above the clouds; and, with a glad "Hallelujah," I praised the God of the whole earth. I do not own many treasures; if I have any, I count that fragile shell among the choicest of them — a token from my heavenly Father's hand … a tiny transparent shell, that not a wave could break without His will." There, my darling, I have done! Now you must tell me what concerns you so, and then we shall think of other matters.'

Duncan put the book down on the floor, and clasped his hands and waited.

'The description must surely refer to an incident at Ilfracombe, which involved Master Gosse and a shell. Miss Shipton has altered the circumstances — of course there was no nurse, and there was only one boy, young Willy … and he was certainly seven years old not four …' I faltered; perhaps Miss Shipton had after all recorded another, separate, incident? But I was unwilling to believe this, for had not *Willy* presented her with a shell?

'Tell me your interpretation, my darling, and I shall act as adjudicator.'

'How can you, when you have no means of distinguishing the truth? Help me up, for I must look for my notebook from the shore class — there is a drawing that you should see.'

'Remain where you are, dearest, and be calm. Tell me where to look and I shall fetch it for you.'

How I detest this bed! It seems that I am to be imprisoned in my bedroom as my time for confinement nears. I scarcely dare move: I cannot lose this child, too. Our baby moves vigorously inside me as though to emphasise its agreement.

Duncan returns with the notebook, *'Ilfracombe 1855'*. I used it for nothing else, its contents were too precious to share with observations from other times and places. I hold it to my face and sniff it, hoping to catch the tang of seaweed, the sharp smell of shellfish, but after eight years it smells a little musty — like the room where our 'indoor classes' were held. Here is my drawing of the cuttle bone, and notes which are direct transcriptions from parts of Mr Gosse's lecture (I hear his voice as I read them: my heart aches again and *again*, now doubly so); drawings of seaweed, of tiny crustaceans and polychaetes, of actiniae and medusae, the skeletons of cup corals and —

'Yes, here it is. Do you see? This is the shell that Willy Gosse found.'

'I can tell it is a tellin.' Duncan smiles broadly, his face crumpling on the verge of laughter, and then sings tunelessly, ' "You can always tell a tellin." And what is that written beside it? "This shell was found by Master E. Wm. Gosse".'

'He asked me to write that. You are correct, the shell is very like one of our tellins. But I was also *certain* that he had taken it from a box of shells that Mr Gosse had brought for us to examine — and all those shells had been collected on the Jamaican coast. However, let me tell you what happened. After I had drawn the shell — Willy sat next to me, instructing me what to show, he could be quite imperious on occasion — he then insisted that we should take the shell and the drawing to show his Mama. She was there, in the classroom, with Miss Shipton — I no longer recall the reason why, but perhaps they had come to collect Master Gosse.'

I could still remember Emily Gosse's lively features and her windswept auburn hair, and how Anna Shipton had sat and watched her — with a curious sort of fascination or, even then, perhaps devotion.

'And was this "fragile shell" rejected by the dear Mama, that it ended its long journey in Anna Shipton's hand?'

'No.' I shook my head slowly, trying to recall exactly what had occurred. 'Mrs Gosse praised the drawing, agreed that the pink colour of the shell was very beautiful. Miss Shipton praised it, too, and would perhaps have liked to touch it — I think she earnestly wished to be Master Gosse's friend. Then Mrs Gosse asked him, quite quietly, did he really find it himself? He said he did, but I am certain she did not believe him, for she took him aside and spoke to him. I observed how his expression became quite sulky and he took — indeed, he *snatched* — the shell from his Mama's hand. Then, he looked at Miss Shipton ... he put on a sweet smile and he took the tellin to her. "This is for you." He may even have said, "All for you." '

'Had this minor altercation between Master and Mrs Gosse escaped Miss Shipton's notice, then? So that the gift seemed genuine, if we are to believe her parable?'

'I believe so, yes. She was a little hard of hearing, and in any event I remember that we had been distracted briefly by some remark of Mr Causley's — about the use of cowries as barter for wives, as I recall. Devonshire cowries are very small, so Mr Causley speculated that the wives thus bought would necessarily be dwarves.'

The memory of his quiet, dry humour cheers me for a moment.

'Poor woman.'

I regard my husband with surprise. 'Poor deluded woman,' I correct him.

'Perhaps so. But I receive a strong impression of a lonely woman who is suddenly almost overcome by the apparent sympathy and generosity of a child — and translates that feeling into an even greater reverence for the Lord. "Thy Will be done".'

'But that belief, the 'tell Jesus' creed, is an abdication of responsibility! It makes it an impossibility for us to have any control over our own destiny. So that the Lord must even decide whether an empty shell should or should not be broken by a wave!'

'Why did you consent to draw Master Gosse's shell in your notebook? No doubt, my darling, you had your own reasons ... We each have the choice between right and wrong. That is most important. But as for *love*, and ... the ebbing and flowing of the tide ...'

Duncan's mouth tightens into a sad line and he shrugs almost imperceptibly: we avoid each other's eyes. He retrieves his papers from the chest and pulls out his pocket-watch.

'They are waiting for me at the office.' He stoops to kiss the top of my head, and then he is gone.

CHAPTER 7: MATTHEW

I sometimes think Hazel's quite weird, she's so quiet, and while everything is going on around her there are different things going on inside her head. Or that's the way it seems. As though she's moving along inside a kind of opaque, soundproof bubble. And just when you think she's on another planet, she comes out with something that shows she really has been watching and analysing, all along. Like that business with Barbara's horoscopes — Hazel not even wanting to recycle them in case they contaminated someone else.

And she can be so stubborn, too. I couldn't believe that she was going to go and ask at that house for aspirin. But on we had to go, never mind her blotchy face and Jim watching us from down by the boat. No, she ignores the chance to make an excuse and run away, and we all have to march off in a line to the house.

But it worked out okay, it wasn't quite such a disaster after all. Jim seems like a good bloke, we got on like a house on fire towards the end. When I saw him there with his fancy shorts and the worked-out body and heard he was from the States, I had this feeling that he might be gay, especially when he started going on about 'Roger'. If he'd said he was from San Fran, I'd have been dead certain. But then it turns out that this Nancarrow House belongs to an Elizabeth Wilson, and Roger's married and got kids, and so on. Roger seemed okay, too, but I have a feeling he got up Hazel's nose a bit, though that may be because she was pissed off that he wasn't ecstatic about Barbara's painting.

Apparently Hazel had quite a shock when he stood up because she thought he might have lost a leg or something, because of the ramp in the kitchen and handrails in the bathroom, apparently. She was quite funny about it later, said she felt a bit like Jesus Christ and the lame man at Bethesda (not that I knew who *he* was, of course, so she had to explain that bit — 'rise, take up thy bed and walk' — which rather spoilt the impact of her joke. But it was funny, though).

While Hazel and Roger were busy trying to impress each other, Jim took me through to his workroom to look at his screensaver programme. It's a weird house, quite a weird set-up, the three of them — with this Elizabeth, who owns the place — all working away on a project to do with snails and the worms that they carry, which can infect humans. Jim said the worms, blood flukes they're called, live in the blood vessels around the bladder.

'When the infected person urinates, the worm's eggs are flushed out in the urine.'

'Hang on! Worm *eggs*? And how do eggs get from blood to pee? Or don't I want to know?'

'Okay. Eggs because the worms mate, right? They've got to reproduce, everything living has to reproduce. And the eggs have hooks, and get squeezed through into the urine when the bladder muscles contract. The point is —'

'— Sharp. Ouch.'

'Yeah, you're pretty sharp too, Matt! The point is, the eggs have to get into water because the next stage of the lifecycle needs a freshwater snail. The larvae that hatch out of the eggs have to get into a snail to develop.'

'Why? Why snails? That's crazy!'

'That's evolution for you. Parasite evolution's crazy, enough to turn people into Creationists. Just accept it, man. And you have to remember where this is all happening, these aren't people using the bathroom. These are people using rivers for washing and irrigating their crops. Kids fooling around in the water, women washing clothes. Okay? Snails, water, then humans — the larvae burst out of the snails into the water —'

'Sounds like "X-files". You know — aliens growing inside then bursting out through the bloke's throat.'

'Other way round. The larvae swim around and find a nice bit of bare human skin, and burrow *in*. Then off to the bladder wall — eventually. Incredible.'

'Grim. That is really gross. I didn't know things like that existed.'

'Oh, there are other types of schisto in the blood vessels around the gut, and their eggs come out in the shit. Hey, this'll disgust you even more — researchers looking at the incidence of infection have to sift through shit samples and count eggs. We're doing some work on those schisto species, too.'

I glanced around quickly.

'It's okay, we don't get our hands dirty like that. I work with nice clean computers.' He showed me.

'The sort of calculations I'm doing need a whole load of extra memory, so I just brought my own PC with me. It was a hell of a hassle getting a transit permit, they're paranoid about letting this stuff out. But it means I can do a lot of what I want here, and Elizabeth has fixed up with the Oxford people that I can go up there if I really need to.'

'So what are you doing? Why have you come here? It's not exactly a humming metropolis.'

I looked around the room. The dining table had been covered by an old khaki blanket, I suppose so it wouldn't get scratched. There were only a couple of chairs left at the table, and the others were stacked in the corner of the room. (Seeing the legs sticking up like that brought back a funny memory, it must have been at primary school, coming into the classroom when it had been cleaned. We did daft things like tying string round the legs before the teacher came in, making sort of cradles for our toys — I can't remember why.) And there were books everywhere, on the sideboard, on a wheeled wooden trolley, on the bookcases … Jim saw me looking round and laughed.

'Crazy, I guess. She just buys books like, well, like I'd like to buy beers! She sure doesn't seem to buy much else.' He shrugged. 'So, what am I doing? Well, I majored in math, but it's kind of rarified out there, and I wanted to stay in the real world. I like working on models and trying to see what the world's going to do — so I shifted into epidemiological modelling, trying to predict outcomes for disease spread. That's what I did my doctorate in.'

'Guesstimates.' I grinned at him.

'What? Hey, no. This is based on hard data, man.' But he grinned, too, and leant back against the sideboard, crossing his arms. 'You build the equations and you talk to the biologists about the variables, and then you say, "Hey, you guys, we need some numbers. Get your asses into gear and get the data." Then I punch in the numbers and see how they affect the outcomes.'

'Of what?' I didn't like to admit that I hadn't the faintest idea what he was banging on about.

'Whether the infection will become endemic or die out, what proportion of hosts need to be infected for the disease to — hell, there are a whole bunch of factors, snail genetics, human immunity or susceptibility, water temperature, worm genetics. Whether they're one species or not, that's where Roger inputs ... Yeah, yeah, I can see you really want to know, your eyes are going kind of glassy! Okay. Come and look at this program, anyway.'

He switched on the computer, waited while it clicked and whirred, then clicked the mouse button and waited again.

'It'll boot up after a minute. So what do you do, Matt — when you're not "sort of on holiday" or working in a pub?'

'I'm doing a BA in Art and Design — just finished my first year.'

'Oh okay, you'll like this screen saver then. You enjoying your studying?'

'Yup, it's really good.'

It's funny how, if someone asks you what you're studying, you suddenly feel about eight years old, explaining to an auntie or uncle what you did at school today. 'It's really good.' God! Puerile, or what! I should have explained to him the buzz and the challenge, and how you really envy someone who comes up with a great design. But I was saved from further embarrassment by the monitor, which at last clicked into a wild display, swirling patterns of deep blues and purples, shot-silk shimmering like oil on water, and twisting off into related patterns in dark green and red. The whole screen seemed to be slowly pulsing. It was certainly attention-grabbing. If I'd had that on-screen I'd never do any work, I'd be sitting and watching it all day. I stared at it, trying to figure it out, and soon the underlying pattern got through to me and I remembered what it reminds me of.

'It's Mandelbrot, isn't it? Just a little piece of it. Incredible.'

'You got it, Matt! Mr Marzipan himself. Never mind the math, as graphic design it's way up there.'

Marzipan? What the hell was he talking about now? But fractals I knew about. Ferns and snowflakes, coastlines and rocky shores, pebbles and grains of sand — there were pictures and photos kicking about all over the place, in books and posters. But wasn't it all a bit *eighties*? I'd a feeling the craze had been and gone. But then again, perhaps having a moving Mandelbrot, a little bit of it, turning through different axes, and with changing magnifications ... Mandelbrot moving, with a practical purpose. Ironic, really.

Jim bent over the table, staring at the screen.

'There! That's the one I was waiting for. Elizabeth really likes that one, she thinks it's like a section of a spiral shell and then she says it turns into a seahorse's tail.' He looked up at me. 'You can see whatever you want, can't you? It's kind of addictive after a while.'

'Saves spending on alcohol or prohibited chemical substances,' I agreed. Mr Supercool, that's me. Huh. 'But what's Elizabeth like, then? Do you all get on okay together? I mean, do you sit around and talk about snails all day?'

'Well, she's pretty relaxed about it all, I guess. We kind of drift in and out of each other's rooms — I guess we talk shop at mealtimes quite a lot. But, you know, it varies from day to day. We each do our own thing. If I want to work on the boat, I do that thing. Roger goes back to see his wife and kids when he wants — but he's only here about a month, I think. But we're not prisoners, we don't have to put in "x" number of hours a day. And Rog and I help with the cooking.'

'And housework and stuff like that?'

'Well, yeah, that too. Though as you can see, Elizabeth is pretty relaxed about that as well. She can get real focussed on her work — even though in theory she's retired. She's quite an artist, too. Those are some of her snail drawings, but there are some sketches of people in that other room that we were in.'

The framed drawings were propped against the wall, on top of a wooden cabinet of some sort. They were (I assumed) accurate and detailed reproductions of snails, in ink, and the fancy name of each one had been written beneath it in neat black letters. They were biologist's drawings for, I guessed, identification purposes: graphic — but not art.

I touched the smooth polished surface of the cabinet.

'What's this — with all these strange little drawers?'

Slotted brass plates on the front of each drawer contained cards with names.

'It's part of her snail collection.' Jim pulled at the flat brass rings on a shallow drawer that was labelled '*Bulinus*', and the rings turned into handles and he slid it open. It was filled with a collection of small white cardboard boxes, all different shapes and fitted tightly together like a jigsaw, so that I wondered how long it took to arrange them that way. They didn't have lids and each contained loads of tiny glass tubes with cork or rubber stoppers.

'Can I look?'

'As long as you put them back in the right place.'

I took a couple of tubes out of a box. At the bottom of each one were small empty snail shells, and the rest of the tube was filled with a plug of cotton wool. I looked at the hand-written label on one tube but I was none the wiser: '<u>Bulinus forskåli</u>, L.Tana'. I lifted up tubes at random from other boxes; some had shorter, more rounded shells mixed in with the cotton wool, in others there were whole pickled snails in some sort of pale yellowish fluid. Most of the snails looked much the same to me, about a centimetre long, brown with a tinge of green, thin almost transparent shells. Boring.

'Why collect so many of the same?'

'You'll have to ask her that — but they're all *Bulinus*. If you read the labels you'll probably find they're all one species, but slightly different variants or from different localities. That's the problem, you see — they may not be the same species, or they may be different genetic stock with different susceptibility to the parasite. And that makes a big difference when you're looking at transmission rates. That's the rate of flow of parasites through their hosts — potential levels of infection, if you like.'

'Yeah. Right.'

He closed the drawer, then opened and closed several others lower down. There was one that didn't contain boxes, but was lined with a layer of cotton wool, like a nest, for the empty shells that lie on it.

'These look more interesting.' Jim squatted down and peered at the label. His ponytail was held back by a green rubber band. Not so perfect. 'Thiaridae. Lake Tanganyika.'

The shells were much bigger and much thicker than the *Bulinus*, and their shapes were very varied. There was one which was particularly striking, several centimetres long and spiky, a bit like the new one on the front of the house, the one that I'd noticed when I was showing that old couple the shells. I squatted down too, which was difficult because there wasn't much room. We pulled the drawer out further and it came whizzing out and would have fallen on the floor if we hadn't both grabbed the back of it.

'Shit, that was close!'

We were both kind of twitching with shock and laughter and we had a job to keep the drawer steady and slot it back in. I guess the shock kind of broke the ice, and it was kind of easier to talk after that.

'Imagine if they'd broken! They're probably irreplaceable.'

'You could have come and chipped some off the front of our house — it's completely covered with shells.'

'It is? Why so?'

'It's a tourist attraction. Or at least it was until Hazel objected. It's called the Shell House — in Polkenna, at the top of the east hill.'

'It's Hazel's house, right? You're staying with Hazel?' He seemed a bit puzzled.

I nodded; I was puzzled, now. 'The house was her mother's. She died — and left it to Hazel.'

'Oh. Right.'

Then I saw what his problem was and I didn't know whether to laugh — or be disgusted. Though the idea of being some woman's toy boy — some *rich* woman's toy boy — might have had some attractions. For a while.

'Hazel is —' I began to grin, even though I was a bit unpractised with the words. 'Hazel's my mother. Supposedly. It's a long story.'

'Hah!' Jim began to smile, too, and suddenly we were roaring. When I stopped I realised I was hungry and my stomach was groaning. I looked at my watch.

'Christ, it's nearly one o'clock, no wonder I'm starving. Typical bloody Hazel not to think about lunch, she'll probably only need a Ryvita and a lettuce leaf in any case!'

'There's bread and cheese in the kitchen. Come and grab something while your *mother —*' he grinned again and shakes his head, 'talks to Roger.'

So we ambled into the kitchen and I snooped around a bit, poked at things and picked them up and put them down — the way one does — while Jim found the soft marg and some cheese and pickle; but the cheese was Stilton so I just had some strawberry jam, or 'jelly' as Jim called it. He was an okay guy; we talked about this and that, and he said he was doing up the boat, which is some sort of local class of sailing dinghy — it belongs to Elizabeth and her dead husband — so that he could use it, and that I should come and help. We agreed that would be good, we could potter about and I suggested we could invite girls for picnics at otherwise-inaccessible beaches, and the like. Dream on. I suggested he came over to the Anchor in the evenings, though apparently he'd have to borrow Roger's car or Elizabeth's old Volvo, unless he wanted to walk. Anyway. Whatever.

Hazel looks a bit hungry so I give her some of my third jam sandwich after we leave. She looks better, in fact she looks quite good. I know she looks younger than she is, but I don't tell her what Jim had thought about our relationship. It made me a bit embarrassed, really. We stop and look at the dinghy. I bet the brush has gone hard, being left uncovered like that. I tell her that I'm going to help Jim get the boat seaworthy.

'I don't know what needs doing, though. I suppose the mast and things are in that garage.'

'It's a Redwing, I think, because it's clinker-built. They're fairly heavy to sail, they generally need two big lads to keep them balanced. There are Redwing races off Polkenna on Wednesday and Sunday afternoons, if you want to go and watch. You might pick up a few tips.'

'How do you know all that?'

'Oh,' she smiles and makes a funny sort of pout with her mouth. 'You'd be surprised what I know. Actually, I know someone in Polkenna who owns one, he's a dentist. I crewed for him once but we capsized, and I was too light to get the boat back upright again.'

'I didn't even know you knew how to sail.' I think about the dentist. 'Is he nice?'

She's finished the piece of sandwich and is wiping her fingers on some toilet paper that she's taken from her pocket.

'He's pleasant. Why? Do you think I'm having an affair with him?'

I waggle my shoulders crossly, and humph.

'Does it matter?' she persists. 'Matthew?'

'Oh, I don't know. I don't want to talk about it, anyway.' And I really don't know. We're walking up through the wood by now and it's steep, so there's an excuse not to talk; but Hazel stops at one point and says,

'To put your mind at rest, I barely know the man. He came to a party your grandmother organised, several years ago. He wanted a crew, that was all. And he's not my type, Matt — for goodness' sake, he stares into people's mouths all day. And his eyelashes are too pale. But you mustn't forget that we're all grown-ups here — that means you *and* me.'

'Yeah, yeah.'

We walk on in silence for a bit and then she tells me about Granny B's painting, and we both get a bit emotional and have to look where we're putting our feet.

When we reach the wider path on the cliff top I'm surprised to see those two women walkers again. They're just climbing up from somewhere below the path so I suppose they have been having lunch or sunbathing or something. I thought they'd gone on miles ahead. The one with the purple parrot-mark on her shoulder has put on a pullover. She smiles and says 'hello', and I think about taking off my trainer and making them laugh again; but then I decide against it. The one with the stupid map-case must be cold because her nipples are sticking out against her top. It's hard not to look at them, those little rigid points. I quite like the idea about being a grown-up. Hadn't Hazel said earlier that it meant that one could do what one wanted?

It seems a long way back to Polkenna. I scrounge a couple of quid off Hazel when we get to the first pub, and promise to pay her back as soon as I get my first wages. I need a pint and a pasty, but she doesn't want to stop, says she has to get back. She's gone all inscrutable again. So I sit on my own at the bar and fantasise for a bit about breasts and boats and night-time barbecues, that sort of thing — and finally wander down to the quay singing 'Red sails in the sunset' over and over (where the hell did that come from, Blue Peter? — and it's the only line I know), just in case anyone thinks that makes me look kind of fun. Sad git!

CHAPTER 8: HAZEL

'*Fucking* tomatoes!'

Matt had been chasing a tomato round his plate, trying to spear it with his fork; predictably it had shot onto the floor, like a bullet. He had balanced his tray on his knees and was having to perch on the front edge of the armchair because there wasn't room for his elbows. His hair was wilder than ever.

I decided to ignore the expletive.

'You'll have to get a table, this is stupid. We can't keep eating on our knees.'

To point out that the dining room table was now my desk would have been inappropriate; his criticism of our dining arrangements was justified. He picked up the tomato and bit into it, which is what I would have done in the first place.

' And another thing —' he wiped the tomato juice from his chin, 'I don't understand why we've only got two of Barbara's pictures. Where are they all? We can't live in her house without her paintings — you haven't given them away, too, have you?'

I'd noticed earlier that he had decided to drop the 'Granny' epithet, and wondered whether he was attempting to distance her or wanted to imply familiarity. We'd had an odd few days and I felt unusually disorientated, both in space and time: there had been the walk, and the business at Nancarrow House but also, perhaps mostly, there was the strain of trying to come to terms with my volatile son — the steps forward, the slips backward, sometimes gaining ground then losing my foothold again. I didn't even know how to feed him: the microwaved jacket potatoes and the cold chicken and salad looked dull and insubstantial. My mother's painting at Nancarrow had almost made me cry and now Matthew was demanding more. But there were no others; and the Shell House wasn't her house, it was mine. I put down my knife and fork and tried to speak calmly.

'She painted for other people, Matt — and to make a living. She exhibited her work and she sold it. There wasn't any unfinished work in the studio — I think she made a big effort to finish everything when she knew time was running out. There really wasn't anything left apart from the two paintings in this room.'

'But that's terrible.'

'Yes.'

'Perhaps we can find out who's got them and we can buy them back. What about the one you saw this morning, at Jim's place?'

'I don't think we can do that, I don't know Dr Wilson well enough. Also I'm not sure I could afford to buy them back, even if anyone wanted to sell.'

'I spent ages hunting through that cupboard in my room this morning, before we went out. I thought perhaps you'd stashed some away in there — but there's nothing but a few studies, and a weird pattern, and stuff like that.'

'Mmm.'

'What's in the leather suitcase that's locked?'

I frowned, trying to visualise the case in question.

'Oh, it's not locked, I think the lock's just stiff. As far as I remember there's nothing very much in it, but I only had a quick look — some old natural history books, or something like that. Why don't you go and fetch it and we can have a look? There certainly aren't any paintings, I'm afraid.'

'Damn. I hoped it would be full of used tenners. Oh, these tomatoes are crap, why couldn't you cut them up before you put them on the plate?'

I didn't say anything, merely resumed eating, and he glanced across and said 'Sorry.'

It is, I suppose, the nature of the dance: Matt and I will adapt to each other with time. I've little authority over him because I've failed him as a parent, and I'm too old to be his friend, so perhaps it will take as long as the eight or ten weeks that he plans to be here. But the situation will resolve itself — as situations always do.

'Go on, go and fetch the case,' I prompted again, as I took the trays into the kitchen.

'I bet it's really boring.' But he padded upstairs with bare feet and I heard his heavy footsteps overhead.

The leather was scratched and dry, flaking at the corners, but although the salty air had corroded the lock we were able to free it with some drops of cooking oil and a kitchen knife. Matt wiped his rust-smeared fingers on the tea-towel and then scratched his head, and took the case through to the sitting area and sat cross-legged on the rug. I sat on the sofa and watched. The body of the case was half-filled with books, and there were flat pockets in the lid for paper and envelopes and soft suede loops for pens and pencils..

'See — it's just old books. What's this? It's a sort of diary — no, a nature notebook, "A.B. Church" written inside. Who's A.B. Church? Here's another. And another.'

He handed several black cloth-bound books to me; the yellowing, brittle pages were covered with hand-written notes and sketches, and I put them aside for now.

' *Seaside Pleasures* by P.H. Gosse. That sounds interesting, must be about bonking bathing belles. Nope, looks like nature rambles. Hey, perhaps that's what those two girls on the cliffpath were doing.'

'Oh, no doubt.'

'*The Aquarium*, P.H. Gosse. What *is* all this? I didn't think Barbara was into marine biology, weird. *Actino* - something, *Actinologia Britannica*'

He snorted incredulous amusement as he piled the books on the floor next to him and then peered into the pockets and slid his fingers around inside.

'Aha! Jackpot. A folded sheet of paper, with the map showing where the treasure is.'

He peeped inside secretively, then sighed exaggeratedly and handed the paper to me.

'That's all. You can have it. You can solve the mystery and find "X". I can't be bothered.'

'In that case, any treasure's all mine,' I warned, and I pulled the books across the floor towards me.

Matt yawned and stretched. He shuffled his bottom backwards until he was leaning back against the chair, and then he flicked through the television channels with the remote control, grumbling that there was nothing worth watching, but eventually settling on a sports quiz that seemed to be nothing more than a pretext for *doubles entendres*.

I started with the folded paper and, in a way, it was a map; a map of a family's genealogy — my family's, although the final twig was my mother's, and Jamie and I had not yet been born. It was hand-drawn, not very carefully, in pencil, and some of the names were hard to decipher, so I worked backwards through the ones I knew.

'Barbara Meyerscough, b.1933; m.1954 John Lewisham.' My mother and father, both now dead.

Back a step to maternal grandfather, 'Harold Meyerscough, b. 1889; m. 1932 Catherine Corbett.' I had seen photographs of my grandfather; he was portly and balding, with a large moustache, and he looked jovial. Catherine had been his second wife. The son from his first marriage had emigrated to South Africa, as far as I could remember.

It occurred to me that grandfather Harold could well have drawn up this family tree. He and his siblings, Marion and George, dangled from the same branch, and the three of them had all sprouted from Samuel Meyerscough, who had married, 1881, Caroline Robertson.

At the top of the page, a crooked arrow led from 'Anne Church' to Caroline. Anne Church, whose name was on the notebooks, had lived to a good old age, from 1833 to 1911, and in the interim she had married one Duncan Robertson. But these two people were not directly linked to my mother's roots, because their names were placed in the top left-hand corner, not the centre, and alongside the crooked arrow were written the words, 'D.R. gave books to his niece'.

I worked backwards through the tree again: Caroline and Samuel were my mother's grandparents, Duncan Robertson had been Caroline's uncle, so he and Anne Church had been my mother's great-great-uncle and great-great-aunt. Or something like that.

'This Anne Church is some sort of relation,' I told Matt, who was sniggering quietly.

'Mmm? What? Right.'

I opened one of Anne Church's notebooks and saw that it was indeed a 'nature notebook', as Matt had said; but of a sophisticated kind. On the first page she had written 'Ilfracombe, July 1855', and nearly two-thirds of the book was filled with careful sketches of marine shore life, both animal and vegetal. Many of the sketches were partially or fully hand-coloured, and all were accompanied by notes and descriptions in ink or indelible pencil. I supposed that this littoral content might explain why the Gosse books were also in the leather case.

The final third of the book was left blank and it seemed to me that this extravagance could indicate the importance of the Ilfracombe period in her life. It wasn't to be mixed with any subsequent endeavours or investigations. (Alternatively, she could have completely lost interest in marine biology and natural history. Or even become a botanist, God forbid!)

The green, cloth-covered boards of *The Aquarium* had come unstuck and had at one time been carefully mended with a strip of glued paper, but the first few gold-edged pages still remained loose and fell out in my lap. 'A.B. Church, 14 Portarlington Road, Winchester' was written on the yellowing fly-leaf. There was a beautifully-coloured frontispiece of 'The Ancient Wrasse', lurking amongst artistically weed-covered rocks; I liked the 'ancient'. The orange reticulated pattern of his upper body was rich and strong, and his gaze was upward, perhaps waiting for his captor to scatter food on the surface of the water.

What next? Matt's bonking bathing belles, *Seaside Pleasures*. Tan leather binding, marbled edges to the pages — and the title page signed by 'P.H. Gosse' himself, in July 1855, a surprisingly untidy pencilled holograph. Presumably this was why the book had been passed on as a family heirloom. Fun to speculate that Anne Church had bumped into him at Ilfracombe; perhaps she had waylaid him on the shore and demanded his signature, and his hands were cold with all that guddling around in rockpools or aquaria! The book seemed to be a series of descriptions of parts of the Devonshire coast and the animals he had found, with quite a few anecdotes and stories. It was illustrated with some attractive engravings, although I didn't much care for the gloomy Valley of Rocks. How strange! Here was another signature, by another Gosse: I struggled to make it out, for the writing was all over the place. Emily. Emily Gosse, signed above the chapter heading. Suddenly the book began to look more interesting.

'This book could be quite valuable, Matt.'

He showed a bit more interest then. 'Will you sell it and buy me a car? Christ, this programme's so crap, I can't believe I used to think it was funny.'

'Good to know you're maturing with time.'

'Huh.' He flipped channels until he found something that was presumably less faecal.

Meanwhile, I opened the thick book with the grand title of *Actinologia Britannica: A guide to the sea-anemones and corals of the British Isles*. This time I turned at once to the title page and there was a beautifully neat handwritten dedication: 'To Mr and Mrs Duncan Robertson, this book is given with my heartfelt thanks. Ph. H. Gosse. 1860.' So now Anne and Duncan were married and had both done something that had caused the author to be grateful.

It was a beautiful book; the engravings appeared to have been coloured by hand

and the colours were still rich and warm, the sea-anemones in life-like poses, adherent to rocks, often several species in each illustration. As I turned the pages I came across a torn fragment of newspaper but I couldn't make any sense of it until I realised it must have been part of a bookmark. The plumose anemone, *Actinoloba*, was described on the pages, a lengthy and detailed description which was followed by a paragraph that listed the contributors who had either sent specimens to Gosse or had noted localities where *Actinoloba* could be found. And there was 'Miss Anne Church, Clyde, near Glasgow (at low ebb).'

'*Aha!* Now what about Duncan Robertson?'

'What are you muttering about?'

'Yes, here he is. "D. Robertson on Cumbrae".' I turned back a page to see what he had found. ' "*Sagartia bellis*, the Daisy Anemone".'

Cumbrae was an island in the Clyde, not far from Glasgow. Love among the actiniae! Drawn together on a Scottish shore by a passion for sea-anemones? Well, perhaps.

I was on the point of telling Matt about this fascinating piece of family history when the telephone rang, and he jumped up and went to answer it. I looked round, expecting the call to be for me, but judging from what he was saying, and his now-animated expression and gestures, it must have been for him. The loud telephone conversation and the inane laughter from the television were unbearable.

'*Matthew*!'

I sighed and got up to turn off the television. Matt, who was wandering round near the kitchen, clutching the portable phone in one hand and plucking hairs from his eyebrow with the other, shrugged and wandered over to the French windows and out into the garden, where he could talk with fewer inhibitions.

The sofa was now a mess of books and paper and I collected it together. When I picked up *The Aquarium*, the fly-leaf and adherent pages fell out again, and as I reinserted them and tucked in other loose pages, I noticed that the last page of the book was smaller and rough-cut; it was a Sale List from a Marine Aquarium supplier, Mr Alfred Lloyd, of Portland Road, Regent's Park, who 'ordinarily keeps a stock of 15000 specimens, comprising 200 genera.' But it was the full-size page opposite the advertisement that really caught my eye.

<u>MARINE NATURAL HISTORY CLASS</u>

In the summer of 1855, I met at Ilfracombe, on the coast of North Devon, a small party of ladies and gentlemen, who formed themselves into a class for the study of Marine Natural History. There was much to be done in the way of collecting, much to be learned in the way of study. Not a few species of interest, and some rarities, fell under our notice, scattered as we were over the rocks, and peeping into the pools, almost every day for a month. Then the prizes were brought home, and kept in little Aquariums for the study of their habits, their beauties to be investigated by the pocket-lens, and the minuter kinds to be examined under the microscope. An hour or two was spent on the shore every day on which the tide and the weather were suitable; and, when otherwise, the occupation was varied by an indoors' lesson, on identifying and comparing the characters of the animals obtained, the specimens themselves affording illustrations. Thus the two great desiderata of young naturalists were attained simultaneously; they learned at the same time how to collect, and how to determine the names and zoological relations of the specimens when found.

A little also was effected in the way of dredging the sea-bottom, and in surface-fishing for Medusae, &c.; but our chief attention was directed to shore-collecting. Altogether the experiment was found agreeable.

'Those interested' were invited to apply to P.H. Gosse at 58 Huntingdon Street, Islington, for further details. So that was why Anne Church had been at Ilfracombe, and that was how she had met Mr Gosse. So simple, no mystery there at all.

I gathered up the books and returned them to the suitcase, then carried them over to my table — and jumped when I saw Matt in the garden. I had forgotten that he was there.

'Are you *still* on the phone? You've been talking for ages.'

'What? Oh. Nearly finished. So you did. Okay. Speak to you soon. Cheers, then.'

He telescoped the aerial with a '*clack!*' and came back inside.

'Is everything all right?'

'Uh-huh. That was Steve, he's a mate of mine at college.'

'Is he coming to stay?'

'No. So, was there anything interesting in all that junk?' Matt jerked his head at the leather case.

'An interesting bit of family history. I hadn't realised that one of our relations, Anne Church, was on close terms with Gosse. He was a famous Victorian naturalist.'

'Really?'

Matt didn't sound very enthusiastic, but he opened the case again, rummaging around until he found the folded diagram of the family tree. He had obviously been keeping half an eye on what I'd been doing earlier. He opened the paper and stared at it, wiggling a lock of his hair round his forefinger.

'I wish I'd known my grandfather John. Barbara never talked about him — nor do you.'

'Well, I told you lots of times — Dad died when I was three, and he and Mummy had only been married five or six years. Jamie was four and I was three.'

'How did he die? It was something to do with a train crash, wasn't it? I was never too sure.'

'Train, yes, but crash, no. He became a statistic. He was one of those people who were killed by train doors coming open before the train has slowed at the platform. You know — passengers open the doors too early and the doors swing out. It was at Marylebone. He was waiting to get on the train to come home, and a door flew open and hit him. Awful. It must have been terrible for my mother. But neither Jamie nor

I remember much about it apart from everybody being very upset. And then we went to live with my grandparents — that's Harold and Catherine — for a while, and I think it was Catherine's parents helped my mother financially, Catherine's side of the family were fairly well-off. But the three of us eventually moved out and went to Gloucestershire.'

'I'm surprised Barbara didn't get married again. You'd have thought men would've been falling over themselves to get her. In a manner of speaking.'

Matt grinned, and caught my eye so that I couldn't help snorting with laughter.

It was strange to imagine my mother as an object of desire. But then, most of the time she had not seemed like a mother, possibly because she had so often had only her two children for company and so she had treated us as equals, as though our opinions counted. She had also ignored us whenever it suited her, and so Jamie and I had learned to help each other — or else to keep our own counsel. Actually, she had tended to ignore me; it was always obvious, in little, subtle ways, that she preferred Jamie. It used to upset me, but I suppose I got used to it.

I thought of her fleshy arms and frequently-displayed deep cleavage, and the way she always touched people, the little intimate-seeming gestures, the overt hugs and enfolding arms. She was, undeniably, sexy, and could be a flirt. There was the way she threw back her head when she laughed, so that the inside of her mouth was visible and her throat and chest exposed. An open invitation; but, apparently, one that was unaccepted. Or unacceptable? And then I saw all too clearly the half-empty chest, the one remaining shrunken breast, and I felt great pity, because I could see now that her strength and the joyousness, even though it had rarely been directed towards me, had then also begun to shrink.

I could imagine her sitting in the garden, staring at the smooth shape of 'Bob' and seeing the likeness, seeing an areola in the concentric pale-grey markings, and holding the sun-warmed white stone against herself, perhaps tucking it inside the sagging, unpadded tee-shirt (for she had never been one to resort to subterfuge, to attempt to show something that wasn't there) and laughing at herself, showing the gulls on the roof and making her solitary joke: 'Just look at Babs! Double 36D again.'

I must have been staring vacantly at the suitcase. I realised what Matt had said, and I looked at him and shrugged.

'Men? There was a man around when we were in our late teens — Andy, he was called, but he was younger than her, and Jamie and I hated him. He was really wet, and I expect we were horrible to him. He didn't last long.'

'Perhaps she had secret lovers after you'd both left home?'

That made me smile. 'Can you imagine her doing anything in secret? No, I think she was just too strong a character — perhaps she even intimidated men.'

'Hmm. I dunno.' Matt had put the paper back into the case and was fidgeting with the books. 'Hey-ho. Didn't you know about this Anne Church business, then? I suppose it's fairly typical of Barbara not to have mentioned it, she'd probably forgotten all about it. History! I haven't forgotten about the hidden treasure, if you sell those books for stacks of loot. You've still got to promise to share it with me. Do you want a coffee? There doesn't seem to be any beer.'

I had resolved to leave the notebooks until morning; but curiosity kept nagging at me until I gave in and took the books up to bed with me.

Matt was now upstairs, playing snatches of some of my old jazz cassettes. Themes I knew so well that my mind followed without thinking were abruptly halted and rejected, causing me physical shock as the waited-for phrase never came. But Billie Holiday had apparently found favour, *Autumn in New York* seemed to be fitting in with his mood.

Before I went to my room, I knocked on Matt's bedroom door and peered in; he was sprawled on the rug next to his CD player and the radio cassette player that he had appropriated from the kitchen.

' 'Night, Matt. I'm off to bed.'

He looked up at me consideringly. 'Okay.'

'Quite an interesting day.' I made it sound like a question rather than a statement.

'Yup. Are you going to look at those notebooks in bed? That woman looked to be quite good at drawing seashore beasties — perhaps you should show the books to that Elizabeth Wilson character over at Nancarrow, she might find them interesting.'

'That's a good idea. She might, at that.'

'And then, if she really liked them, you could swap them for Granny B's painting and I could put it up in here.'

Matt's expression was tense and I wanted to go to him and hug him, to try to comfort that deep hurt. But his legs were stretched out and his back was against the bed; he was inaccessible.

All I could do was smile, kindly, and say, 'Oh, Matt' and 'We'll see what we can do,' and keep on smiling as I closed the door.

It was probably true that Dr Wilson would find the notebooks interesting, but I had no intention of giving them to her, for Mummy had left them for me.

The Ilfracombe notebook was essentially an exercise book, containing annotated sketches and descriptions of marine animals and algae. Anne Church must have tried to be scientific and methodical: a drawing on the left-hand page, with clearly-labelled features indicated by straight ruled lines; notes on the right-hand page, on colour, size, locality, and where possible, some elements of the animal's biology.

There was a double page given over to an exercise on shells. Dr Wilson would definitely have enjoyed this. I looked at the drawings of cowries (and was reminded of Matt and my mother), the tiny curled cylinder of a *Bulla*, the large round spiral of the Beaded Nerite. No notes, merely drawings: perhaps it wasn't then known that the predatory Nerite, *Natica*, bored holes through the shells of bivalves, then digested and sucked out their tissues? If Anne had searched the shore she might have found an empty bivalve shell and seen the single hole, with its neat bevelled edges. She should definitely have found them, I knew they were there, for these were 'Shells collected at Barricane Bay. See Mr Gosse's Seaside Pleasures, Chapter III'.

I thrust my feet out of bed and ran down the spiral staircase. The only light came from the upstairs landing, and I shuffled through the case in the dimness then hurried upstairs again. By the time I had regained the comfort of my bed I had already found Chapter 3 with its engraving of the cliffs at the top of Barricane.

'A few weeks ago I took a ride along the coast to a little cove called Barricane, about six miles from Ilfracombe ... The peculiarity of the place is, that it has a beach entirely composed of shells, many of which are of rather rare kinds, and found nowhere else ...'

I impatiently scanned through the details of Philip Henry Gosse's donkey ride through the Devonshire lanes, his descriptions of the plants and animals that he saw and of the boys that guided the donkeys. *'And thus we came to Barricane.'* There they were: magical, nostalgic words.

'And thus we came to Barricane. A steep footpath leads down to an area of what you would suppose to be minute pebbles; but which, when you come down to them, you find to be almost entirely composed of shells. ... A group of women and girls may always be seen, raking with their fingers among the fragments for such specimens. They usually lie at length upon the beach, to work with greater ease; but when a visitor comes down, they throng round him like bees; and he must be a skilful tactician if he be not at least sixpence the poorer when he leaves the cove. Sometimes they offer the shells for sale just as they are found; but more commonly they make with them ornamental baskets, inkstands, &c., by gluing the smaller shells on the pasteboard or stone-bottle, in some kind of regular arrangement, scattering pounded glass upon the work to give it a sparkling appearance.

Among the shells found in great abundance here there are several which I have not met with in any other part of this coast. Besides two or three little kinds of whelk, and the common *murex*, and *purpura*, which are everywhere abundant, and the beautiful little cowry, which cannot be considered rare, there is the elegant wentle-trap (*Scalaria communis*), the elephant's tusk, or horn shell (*Dentalium entalis*), the cylindrical dipper (*Bulla cylindracea*), called by the local collectors "maggot", and the beaded nerite (*Natica monilifera*), a large and beautiful shell, to which the local women have given the euphonious appellation of "guggy".'

'And thus we came to Barricane.' More than twenty years ago I, too, had been to the sandy cove of Barricane, and had lain at length upon the beach, raking my fingers in the sand to search for shells. There had been twenty or thirty of us (I couldn't remember the details now), on a marine ecology course, and we had taken over the laboratories and dormitories of a girls' boarding school at Bideford, setting out each day to work in different habitats and shorescapes. We had seen the torn vertical reefs of Hartland, so exposed as to be almost devoid of littoral life; the oozing, wormcast-studded mud at Appledore, and the rich sheltered corners of Croyde Bay. We had searched and poked, and filled our plastic bags and Breffit jars with living

specimens, and had hunted through the Collin's Guide, and the pages of dichotomous Keys, to identify our haul.

In the evenings the school kitchens had provided us with marvellous meals and, on our last day, a huge cream tea. It had been an unforgettable ten days. But what now came most strongly to mind was neither Devonshire cream nor Devonshire cup corals — but David.

I had met David only three weeks before. He had written to me, at Bideford, and I had lain on the shelly sand at Barricane with his letter in the pocket of my jeans, and had day-dreamed about love and sex, and a safe haven from the war-torn rutting grounds of college life.

CHAPTER 9: ELIZABETH

EDITED TRANSCRIPT OF RADIO THREE INTERVIEW
(Interviewer) *Elizabeth Wilson, you have written a large number of very important papers and books on your ideas on the evolution of species, but you are not at all a desk-bound thinker, you still like to describe yourself as a 'hands-on' biologist. And of course many of your ideas have necessarily derived from your fieldwork on the ecology of snails and other molluscs. You are unusual in this respect, for several reasons, and I'd like to ask you why so few women have taken up fieldwork? Why have so few been prepared to go out into the rain-forest or the desert or outback, to search for new species in new ecosystems?*

(Dr Elizabeth Wilson) I think there are two reasons. Firstly, there is, as one might suppose, the predominant question of gender-based upbringing and the natural gender-associated attributes — women might worry about their supposed vulnerability and hold fears for their personal safety. With this comes the inherent anxiety that the presence of local male assistants might actually be more of a liability than a help in allaying these fears! Unfortunately, although one might like to surround oneself with a trusty band of female assistants, a 'sisterhood', in many countries it would be impossible to employ them, even if they were keen to help.

However, these days it isn't politically-correct to acknowledge this gender-based prejudice against ability. The present-day woman is supposed to feel empowered to do almost anything she wishes. So, returning to your question as to *why* there are still almost no female field-collectors, setting out with notebooks and bottles and pith-helmets — I suspect the answer is due entirely to the modern reductionist approach to biology, which deems that ecological and evolutionary studies are not 'sexy', but are in some way inferior to the so-called 'hard' (is this another example of male-orientated sexual imagery?) sciences of molecular biology and genetics. Consequently, grant money — the all-important financial support — is practically unavailable and no-one, male or female, can afford to do science in the field without the backing of some sort of approved body. My own work, on the distribution and speciation of snails that were potential hosts of schistosome parasites — was given credibility because it derived from the interests of the Experimental Taxonomy Unit at what was then called the British Museum (Natural History). And note the clever use of 'experimental' in the Unit's title — even in the '60s, science that could be moved forward by the use of controlled experiments was perceived as more worthy than uncontrolled, observational fieldwork! But if my *project* had credibility, my own credibility, as a female fieldworker, had constantly to be fought for.

Are you saying that the skills required by fieldworkers are found in both males and females, but that the skills fail to be exploited by females, with the obvious exception of yourself?

I've already explained why women fail to take up the challenge of exploratory fieldwork — and I emphasise exploratory, for the female successors of Fossey and Goodall are ethologists, rather than pioneering ecologists. But you're right, of course — the skills are not gender-specific. For example, it is necessary to have the skill to perceive the interesting questions in what you see around you.

To give you an example from my own work — when I first arrived in Addis Ababa, in 1958, the university authorities lent me a Land Rover and, I think very generously, the help of an experienced driver. Naturally, I asked advice of the local zoologists, but of necessity my first step was to get into that vehicle and drive out on one of the roads to look at the terrain. To 'get my hands dirty', both literally and metaphorically. The roads radiate from Addis like the spokes of a wheel, and I well remember that I chose the road to Debre Markos, heading North-West, and we drove out into highland countryside, into a type of landscape that was very unfamiliar to me, where the trees and plants were also unfamiliar. Although, having said that, many were surprisingly European, too, honeysuckle and wild roses and St John's Wort. And I knew that somewhere, somehow, I had to start looking for, and finding, snails.

So there was, at once, the immediate question — I'm afraid it was probably a slightly panic-stricken question! — of 'how do I make sense of my surroundings?'

(Laughter) Quite so.

But of course there are maps, of a sort, and local knowledge, and you go out and find the water-courses and start to search. And after you've collected many specimens, of different species, and made careful notes on habitat and distribution, you are then in a better position to decide on your most important question; it may not be the necessary one at that stage, but it may be the most intellectually-challenging, such as 'What kind of selection pressure has led these snails, which are normally found in still water at low altitude, to live up here on the plateau?' That's just one example.

Or, if you go to Lake Tanganyika, as I was fortunate enough to do on another occasion, you can look at the astonishing diversity of the thalassoid Thiaridae. These snails were first known to science after shells of two species were picked up from the shore by John Speke in 1858, and they were subsequently prized as rarities by Victorian conchologists — you can marvel at them and then you can ask yourself the question as to why there are so many species in that one freshwater lake. Another question you could ask is why the shells of these freshwater species are so heavy, and often very ornamented, more like marine shells in appearance. These are very big questions — and, as a fieldworker, you must have the skill and ability to choose a *manageable* question, that is both intellectually stimulating and answerable. That's not a gender-specific skill — it may come to anyone, male or female, partly through training, but also through ability.

Even to molecular biologists?

(Laughs.) They would require quite a lot of training! But another, very obvious, skill required in a fieldworker is the power of observation. Put a molecular biologist by an Ethiopean stream and tell him or her to find some snails, or put them in an English wood and tell them to point out five species of bird, and they would probably, in the majority of cases, perform very badly! Yes, I admit I am showing my prejudices, but allow me to use them as an illustration. There's a skill in knowing where to look, and a skill in knowing what you see — a recognition that what you are looking at is slightly awry, or that a slight movement wasn't merely a pebble shifting in the current, or a leaf shivering in the wind.

Perhaps it comes down to a perception of pattern, symmetry where you expect none, asymmetry where everything should conform.

And then of course there is the absolutely necessary skill in bringing together and synthesising information from the very wide range of disciplines within the life sciences. That's not true of the lab-based experimenter, and certainly isn't true of the ultimate reductionist, the molecular biologist who pursues the structure of the gene. It wasn't true of the Victorian shell-collectors, either, the conchologists who collected shapes and colours. The questions of ecology and evolution — and, for me, these are the basis of epidemiology — are answered by synthesis of knowledge from geography and topography, physiology, botany, palaeontology and so on. This synthetic ability is a requisite skill.

How do you think this ability to see the broader picture has helped you in your own work on the snail intermediate hosts of schistosomes?

Supposing we wandered along the shore of Lake Awasa in the southern Rift Valley in Ethiopia. Of possible schistosome-carrying snails, we might find the flat coils of *Biomphalaria sudanica*, the tall slender spires of *Bulinus forskålii*, and the squatter spires of *Bulinus truncatus*. But one of the characteristics of the *truncatus* species complex is a great variation in the appearance of the shells, so some of the specimens that we find might be bluish-grey rather than greenish-brown. So we look more closely at these *truncatus* snails, and carry out morphometric analyses of their shells and reproductive appendages (and yes, we do have to measure the size of snail penises — which always provokes a great deal of ribald comment!). We can count the number of chromosomes in their cells and, back at the lab in London, can isolate certain enzymes and egg proteins and separate these by electrophoresis and compare — between different snails —the pattern of bands formed in the separation gel. We can isolate the snails' DNA and compare the banding patterns.

So you're talking here about using biochemical and molecular biological techniques?

Yes, but using them as tools. We also look at the laboratory and field data on the susceptibility of different 'types' of *truncatus* to parasite infection. We have data on snail population biology — the reproductive and growth rates — and data on parasite development rates. We collate the geographical data such as temperature variation and rainfall, because these affect the snail host and the parasite. At warmer temperatures the snails develop faster and so do the parasites but if the temperature becomes too high, the snails may die of dehydration or lack of oxygen before the parasite larva can become infective. If the temperature is too low, the parasites may not reach the stage at which they can escape and infect humans before the snail dies of old age. It's a fine balance.

And then, most importantly, we must consider the demographic data, the size and age range of the local human population, and human social behaviour, to get some indication of the proportion of the population who will often be associated with the water, and therefore at risk.

A lot of different pieces of information.

Yes. So, to go back to Lake Awasa. We need to be able to decide whether or not it might become a focus of urinary schistosomiasis and thus, whether or not preventative measures should be concentrated there. Because it all comes down to money in the 'real' world! Think of the money and effort that were spent on widespread mosquito eradication before people realised that malaria was carried by only some species within the anopheline species complex. To make our decision we need to synthesise information from a variety of sources. And, in fact, what we find is that the bluish-grey snails are the diploid form of *Bulinus truncatus* — they have the normal double set of chromosomes — and they are not susceptible to infection by the schistosome. The browner snails, however, are tetraploid — have twice as many chromosomes as normal — and they *do* act as intermediate hosts.

So — what does this little piece of information mean in terms of the broader picture? Back to Awasa again — and actually, you would probably enjoy visiting Lake Awasa, especially if you are a romantic. Are you a romantic? But perhaps we don't have time to discuss that! *(Laughs.)* The lakeside is a beautiful place to watch the sunset — imagine sitting on the short grass on the banks, watching fish rise to the surface after insects. You're listening to the evening calls of flocks of waders, and hearing the small waves gently lapping on the shore as the sky darkens and turns deep crimson in the West. And fortunately for sunset-watchers and other humans who use the shore for more practical purposes, it's the diploid, non-susceptible snail that lives there. The brown snail that allows the parasite to develop within itself lives a few hundred yards away, where there's papyrus swamp and reeds and almost-impenetrable marsh. They live in a place where no-one is likely to go and they're not very active, they live on the underside of waterplants such as lilypads.

So you see, that's just a very tiny example of the importance of synthesis, and I haven't even mentioned aspects such as the effect of infection with other parasite species on snail susceptibility, or the effects of drug control on the schistosome population within the human population.

I'm beginning to suspect you are the romantic! But what you are actually saying is that it is impossible for one person to look at anything more than one small aspect of the problem?

But that person, that *scientist*, can read and talk and attend conferences — can communicate — with other scientists. Because that's what science is all about, isn't it? My point is that, because of this fragmentation and compartmentalisation of research, it's crucial that scientists with the overall view, the synthesisers, are funded and given credence. Because what is so exciting is that we can now fit all these pieces of the picture together mathematically, so that everyone working on the problem, on whatever aspect, plays an equally important part. I really do want to give hope and encouragement to biologists who have been put off fieldwork because it has been portrayed as 'soft' and out-of-date.

Everyone should be made aware that some of the most important biological questions today, that will have global relevance for our society, are questions about the biological environment and the epidemiology of disease.

I get the strong impression that you feel that science — biology — is the key to life, and is something that everyone should try to understand, and be excited by. As regards yourself, do you find that science is an obsessive pursuit and takes over your life?

That's very interesting. Yes, I think you may be right. I'm also very interested in music and art but yes, even when I'm doing those things, there are ideas and questions probably simmering away beneath the surface. And sometimes the answers or the insights bubble up and explode into consciousness at inappropriate moments — and then, of course, one wants to go off immediately and put them into practice. Or discuss them with someone.

A little difficult if you are sitting listening to a concert in the Purcell Room.

Exactly. Slightly frustrating! During those periods of intense thought or insight, anything else — domestic chores, normal conversation, even the weather forecast —

becomes a distraction.

Let me ask you something. Going back to those early days, camping in the wilderness — weren't you frightened, for example lying there in your tent at night? Did you ever feel very alone?

No — and I've thought about this a lot, actually, it's interesting. I think it's because external noises are not really *external*. In that situation you are part of your environment, you recognise the sounds. I find it much less frightening to lie awake in a tent out in the field than to lie awake in an empty house, because in a house external noises assume a greater significance — you are dependent on your house to create your own environment, which then may be under threat. I remember that even as a child I felt safe in a tent, but I needed a night-light in my bedroom!

So that's the secret! - it was a love of camping which turned you into a field biologist! Did you ever think about following any career other than biology? Was there a particular event in your life, a particular moment when you realised that biology, and more particularly, fieldwork, was the most important path for you to follow?

I don't think I ever made a conscious decision to choose one path and not another — it didn't even occur to me that there might be another path to follow! *(Pause.)* I suppose I was always a biologist, from a very early age, even without realising it at the time. It was so obviously interesting. What else could fire a child's imagination in the same way? I grew up in a house at the edge of a small town, with fields and rough ground just over the wall and — I was an only child, you see, so I suppose I learnt early on to be fairly self-sufficient — and so I spent a lot of my time wandering around and looking at things, insects, birds, finding nuts that squirrels had chewed, and so on. There were even lizards and slow-worms, too, though I'm ashamed now to have to admit that I kept the slow-worms captive in a box.

And snails?

Yes, although I wasn't interested in them at first. I'll tell you why I became interested in snails. They were brought to my attention by a farmer-friend. I suppose I was only about eight or nine at the time. He kept cattle and a few sheep in the nearby fields — I was allowed to go and 'help' with the milking, he let me use a special scraper and a brush to clean the muck off the cows. One time, the vet had come over to look at some of the sheep that were sick and I was told that they had 'liver fluke'. Of course I wanted to know all about it — and I certainly knew what liver was like, full of 'pipes', because we were made to eat it at school — and it was explained to me that flukes were worms, parasites, that found their way into the sheep's liver and destroyed it, making it hard and gritty so that it couldn't function. So you see I learnt about parasites very early on, too! *(Laughs.)* And the sheep caught the fluke infection from tiny snails that lived in the marshier parts of the fields. Of course, I had to go and look for these little snails, and once I started looking for snails, well, that was it! And I've been very fortunate, I've always been able to work on the topics and animals that interested me.

Perhaps fortune didn't come into it too much — you clearly had great ability from an early age.

Well, I do also think that it may have been easier for us in those days, don't you? There was not so much competition and perhaps people were prepared to work for rather less money than they were actually worth, just for the love of the subject. I think, too, that scientists had the opportunity themselves to be more free-thinking. One was less stultified by having to work merely as a 'pair of hands' in a team on a narrow project. One was able to think and not just be a — a 'handle-cranker'.

There are still rather few females in senior scientific positions these days — I think the figure is 4% of professors are female. You must have been thought very unusual when you started a career in science, perhaps even treated with suspicion? Do female scientists tend to stick together, to be supportive of each other?

Well, I ... I still remember — quite vividly, in fact — going to a wedding, and the bride's sister introducing me as "This is Elizabeth, she's *terribly* clever, she's a scientist and studying for a PhD" ... and that rather put paid to my attempts to socialise. Almost everybody my age then avoided me!

But now you live in Cornwall. You and your late husband moved there when you left the Natural History Museum. It's a county that's become something of a haven for artists, hasn't it — I wonder how a scientist fits in? Do you have artistic leanings yourself? Can you envisage a time when you might stop being a scientist and do something completely different?

You asked just now about female scientists being supportive — both male and female scientists have friendships and jealousies within their own subjects, they are ordinary people after all, they are not alien beings. I am very lucky to live in a house right by the sea which friends and colleagues like to visit — they come to talk and work. I've also been fortunate to have close friends who are non-scientists and artists — I enjoy drawing and painting and I'd like to have time to become more proficient. But no, I don't think one can ever stop being a biologist.

CHAPTER 10: ANNE: JULY 1855

July 15. Low Water at just after 11 o'clock; sea calm, light south-westerly breeze. Conditions perfect for collecting from the rocky promontory beneath Capstone Hill (although rocks treacherous <u>underfoot</u>, necessitating many offers of help from the gentlemen of the party). Dresses are so impractical. S. suggested designing a 'collector's uniform' for ladies but we all agree it is unlikely to sell well and might occasion ridicule.

Another picture that I wish I could have drawn: all 15 students scattered across the rocks, bending and poking in pools — such a wielding of lenses, waving of nets and jars; such consultations and disputations (Mr W pontificating as usual!); Mr G, so dark and <u>serious</u>, ancient black coat and broad-brimmed black hat — collecting-basket in one hand, his staff in the other. Someone shows him a specimen, probably quite common — then his boundless enthusiasm breaks thro' his severe expression. (I found a polychaete worm, a Harmothöe: kind old Mr Causley told me of the Greek nymphs and goddesses, Aphrodite, Euridice, who have also given their names to other many-legged worms; I like his gentle humour.)

At the water's edge a forest of large olive-green Laminaria fronds, half-floating, contorted like large seasnakes. Mr G and some of the gentlemen leant out and cut off fronds and we used our lenses to look at the encrusting colonies of the <u>membranipora</u>. Later examined them under Mr G's microscope. His explanations are so poetic: each animal folded within its cell is 'like a person lying in bed with his knees tucked up' (It occurs to me what a very different picture would be conjured if he had said 'with <u>her</u> knees tucked up'; I should see him in a very different light!) When the animal wishes to expand, the membrane around it 'turns inside out, just as we draw off a stocking'. Sensuous image! And the animal is 'very beautiful, as clear as —

'Sarah? How did Mr Gosse describe the beautiful *Membranipora* animal? "As clear as" what, can you remember?'

Sarah was reading my copy of Mr Gosse's little book, *Seaside Pleasures*, and she looked up with a puzzled frown.

'I'm not sure I want to go to the Valley of Rocks,' she said, 'it sounds so very gloomy. What did you ask me?'

'Mr Gosse said the *Membranipora* animal was "as clear as something glass". What was it?'

'Crystal? I don't know, does it matter? Are you quoting all his Great Sayings in your journal? You've been writing for ages.'

'No, not crystal. Oh, I remember, it was "spun". *Spun* glass. What *is* that? I know nothing about the making of glass, is that how they make windows?'

'How should I know, Anne? Do let me read ...'

I shrugged. 'All right. But do not be too long for I wish to read it too.'

There was so much to write about that day's class, so many impressions — but perhaps the drawings and notes in my notebook would serve as an *aide mémoire* for those more private reflections. I would instead write about the events of this evening, when I nearly took an evening walk with Mr Gosse up Capstone Hill. But there was almost too much to record, I hardly knew where to begin: even as I went over the events in my mind, my heart started beating more quickly and my hand grew too warm to hold the pen.

Miss Shipton and Sarah and I had dined early because — in anticipation of the distant views afforded by the clear air— we intended to take a walk to Capstone Hill. It is a favourite promenade for townspeople and visitors to Ilfracombe alike — the hill, which is almost conical, has a broad road on its seaward side and several steep tracks, from which the view out to Lundy Island, on a clear evening, is said to be excellent. Naturally our promenade was slow, Miss Shipton leaning on her stick and stopping occasionally to bid passers-by 'good evening' and make some slight conversation.

'How has she come to know so many people in such a short time?' Sarah whispered to me, when for the third or fourth time we stood behind our chaperone and waited.

'Through her acquaintance with Mrs Gosse, surely — you must have seen how Mrs Gosse approaches and converses with so many people on the shore. And because our dear Miss Shipton accompanies her, she imagines she is acquainted with them too!'

Thus we made our stately progression from our lodging and through the Tunnels to the Hill. Already, since the summer evening was so fine, there were many people thronging the walks and benches or sitting on the short turf amongst the sea-pinks and the sheep. We met Mr Causley strolling with his quiet little wife upon his arm; and the handsome dark-haired Mr Jonathan Truscott, of florid face and aquiline nose, who is also a student of Mr Gosse — and who is now paying a great deal of attention to the younger Miss Meredith (he cannot be aware that she must be at least five years older than he!). He was on his own and merely nodded politely, as befits the wounded dignity of a gentleman whose advances to Miss Sarah Nisbet have been spurned. (Sarah's cheeks, as customary, turned a little pink despite her attempt to appear cool and unflustered; in the classes she manages to avoid him — and I have no inclination to tease her in the manner in which she has — until recently — teased me about the odious, even malodorous, Mr Worthington.)

Miss Shipton expressed the wish to sit for a while upon a bench and we could only comply; however, the seats that remained were on the shadowed side of the Hill. Sarah and I were becoming somewhat desperate, and suggested to Miss Shipton that she should seat herself upon the low parapet that protected the edge of the path from the steep drop; but fortunately a gentleman of middle-age, sitting nearby with his wife upon a seat that had been cut into the rock, must have understood our plight, and came over and most graciously offered us the seat.

'We are on the point of leaving, and we should be happy if you were able to enjoy the view as we have. We have been admiring the various colours of the sea.'

His wife, who had already arisen, laughed and said, 'And we have also been much entertained by watching the other admirers!'

Miss Shipton collapsed, somewhat breathlessly (*how* she overplays it!) on the rocky bench and seemed to be gathering herself to hold our benefactors in conversation, but perhaps the lady sensed this for she took her husband's arm and hastened him away, bidding us a warm 'good evening.' So instead Miss Shipton permitted us to reflect on how the good Lord had seen her distress and had provided for us all, etcetera etcetera, Sarah and I fretting and exchanging frowns behind her back, both impatient to be on our way.

'Look, there is a dredger — do you see its sail? In line with that pale triangle of rock on the far cliff. I wonder if it is the famous "Turritella" that Mr Gosse talks about?'

'Surely that is at Weymouth? The "Turritella" is Jonas Fowler's boat —Mr Gosse says Jonas is very proud of the unusual name, Miss Shipton, for it is a species of mollusc with a tall shell. He also takes out Dr Church's esteemed friend, the Reverend Kingsley!'

'And Jonas is the self-acknowledged expert at finding *Ophiocomina* — quick now, Sarah, tell me what *Ophiocomina* is!'

'It is a type of sea star, no — a brittle star. And the boat Mr Gosse uses here has a skipper called Pen-something, a name like a dragon.'

'Penhaligon! Mr Penhaligon who is the expert at collecting the burrowing anemone, *Peachia*.'

'Named after Mr Peach the well-known anemonizer!'

'And not after Mr Turton, the well-known marine naturalist who is so much addicted to —' I lowered my voice theatrically and rolled my eyes, causing Sarah to giggle, '— to opium!'

'Miss Church! How can you bring yourself to repeat, or even know, such a terrible thing? Who told you such wicked gossip?'

'I cannot remember, perhaps I misheard.' But I distinctly recalled Papa regaling Mama with this piece of information which Mr Kingsley had let slip. 'Oh, Miss Shipton, look! Is that not Mrs Gosse coming our way?'

'Emily? Why yes, so it is!'

Mrs Gosse had paused to look out across the bay; her coiled auburn hair was escaping in wisps from beneath her bonnet, and her dress was plain in colour and style, but despite her somewhat unfashionable appearance she seemed quite unselfconscious and composed.

'Surely she cannot be out walking on her own — where is Mr Gosse? Who is she speaking to now, I wonder? She will no doubt see us in a moment and come and join us.'

Miss Shipton sounded quite put out, for Mrs Gosse had indeed exchanged a few words with a young woman who was passing; even from where we were sitting on our cold stone bench (the three of us in a row, staring intently back down the path!) we could see how the young woman responded with warm smiles.

From above us came a momentary cacophony of barking dogs and bleating sheep, causing Mrs Gosse and her companion to look in our direction, so that Miss Shipton seized the chance to raise her hand and wave. For Mrs Gosse there could be *no escape*; she waved back and then apparently excused herself, and hurried up the slope.

'Anna! Good evening, Miss Church and Miss …'

'Miss Nisbet.'

'Do excuse me! Of course, Miss Nisbet. Is it not a delightful evening? Henry was most insistent —'

'Is Mr Gosse here too?' I asked quickly, and then felt certain that I must have turned bright scarlet.

'But of course. Our little son is with him — he has been granted a special dispensation to stay up late and accompany us, because he loves to see the sheep. But he and his father stopped to talk to a cat.' She laughed softly. 'Willy misses his own little cat, which we had to leave behind.'

'There they are! And your son seems to have found the easiest way to mount Capstone Hill.'

'Mr Gosse is a willing beast of burden where his son is concerned.'

'Mama! Mama!' Young Master Gosse was sitting astride his father's shoulders, holding his father's hat in place with one hand and his own bonnet with the other. Mr Gosse (in smarter black suit, not his aged collector's garb) was clutching his son's pantaloon-ed legs and, despite the rider's urgings to go faster, was labouring up the slight incline.

'Henry, you will let him quite exhaust you! Do put him down.'

'Willingly, willingly. He is an imperious driver.'

'I want Miss Church to help me down.'

As Mrs Gosse and I lifted the little boy down from his perch, I was clumsy in my embarrassment and my arm touched Mr Gosse's shoulder. The contact ran through me like a bolt of lightning through a tree. But naturally no-one noticed, as Master Gosse was claiming his Mama's attention and momentarily all was confusion with a milling around of persons, and interrupted greetings.

'So, you have been talking to a cat, Master Gosse? Did it talk back?' Sarah asked.

'It was a … a … *marmalade* cat. Papa, tell them our poem. We made up a poem. "There was a little cat —"'

'Oh, please do tell us!'

Miss Shipton held out her hand to encourage the boy but he spurned it and remained silent and I could see that his father was retreating into the severity that he assumed in public.

'Tell the poem to your Mama and we shall listen secretly,' I suggested.

He wriggled his shoulders. 'Papa, you must say it with me.'

'Come, Henry — do let us hear it.'

So, father and son (although mostly the father) recited, with pauses at the end of each line to emphasise the rhyme,

'There was a little cat
'And she sat upon a wall.
'We gave her some meat —'

'We didn't — because we didn't have any!'
'And she ate it up all.
'We gave her some milk —'

'We didn't do that either!'

'For she wanted to drink.
She drank it all up —'

'For she liked it, I think'. (This said in a rush by Willy, before his father could speak.) *'The old puss —'*

'What comes next, Willy? You have already forgotten, I think.'

'The old puss ran into —'

'No. *"The old puss jumped down*
And ran into the house
And looking about
She soon caught —'

'*A* mouse!'

'She ran back into the garden
Without saying a word
Climbed into a tree —'

'And caught a young bird!'

Sarah and I applauded, but Miss Shipton put her hand to her mouth.

'Oh dear, the poor little bird. How cruel!'

'There is a certain lack of sentimentality in the poem,' Mrs Gosse observed. 'And naturally a great degree of zoological observation and accuracy.' She smiled at her husband.

'We have not yet completed the lines referring to "fish", have we, Willy? But it rhymes satisfyingly with "wish" and "dish" so we shall surely think of something appropriate.'

'We shall think very hard ourselves and try to help you,' Sarah said.

'Mama is allowing me to stay up late,' Willy interrupted, already moving on to more important matters, 'and we are going to walk to the very top of this hill. Will you and Miss Church come with us? Will you swing me again like you did on the beach?'

(The previous day Sarah and I had taken his hands and swung him, squealing, across the small stream that trickled down the shore. Mr Gosse had heard him and had interrupted his discourse to watch: I hope he was favourably impressed that I was amusing his beloved son. His 'little naturalist in petticoats' as he has called him on occasion.)

'I am afraid, Master Gosse, that I should find the climb quite too fatiguing.'

'We must allow the young ladies some peace after their gruelling day of learning, Willy.'

Miss Shipton and Mrs Gosse had spoken together, before Sarah and I had a chance to answer. I had not realised that we were to be denied the extra views that come with height, that we were to remain below, attendant on our chaperone, as the world passed us by. My heart truly *sank*, but Sarah, with her usual outspoken sense of what should be permitted, saved us.

'We would be delighted to accompany you, Master Gosse — and see, I have already thought of a new rhyme for you. "*She ran down to the shore, to bathe was her wish, fell into a pool, and caught a fat —*" '

' "*Fish*"!'

'Miss Nisbet is clearly a talented poet.' Mr Gosse's voice was dry, but there was a hint of a smile on his face.

'Henry, why do you not take Willy, and allow Miss Nisbet and Miss Church to accompany you both to the top of the hill? And I shall remain here with Miss Shipton. We shall happily occupy ourselves, shall we not, Anna? Miss Shipton is also a poet, Henry — she has been composing several hymns.'

Miss Shipton was making little noises of protestation although she was clearly delighted at the prospect of having her friend all to herself, but I hardly listened. Sarah was a 'talented poet'! I was not envious of the attribute: it was one to which I did not aspire. But it had suddenly become clear what I should do. Suddenly everything made sense and the future seemed brighter — I tingled with excitement, I wanted to throw my arms around Sarah and embrace her and laugh aloud. I would become truly knowledgeable about the natural history of the shore. Then he would notice me! He would call me a *'talented naturalist'*.

I was so enthralled with this idea that it came as a shock to perceive that some sort of unspoken communication was taking place between Mr and Mrs Gosse, that possibly he did not wish his wife to remain behind, possibly did not wish his two young female pupils to walk with him; his eyes were fixed firmly on his wife and his somewhat heavy features were quite lacking in animation. Indeed, it occurred to me (and this idea was something of a revelation) that he was perhaps a little *afraid* of being asked to accompany two young ladies such as ourselves — on a social occasion, where he would be required to make conversation rather than be expected to discourse on the delights and marvels of God's marine creatures. And this revelation caused me to feel great awkwardness on his behalf, and to sense that our projected walk would not be easy.

I was momentarily confused, especially because Mrs Gosse had now seated herself beside Miss Shipton (those of us who remained standing quite filled the narrow track), and Willy was holding my hand tightly, and insisting in his rather serious manner, that I should 'look at the kittiwake, Miss Church — it *is* a kittiwake, is it not, Papa?', while Miss Shipton was already clasping Mrs Gosse's hand and preparing herself to ask about the young woman to whom she had been speaking earlier.

'I think that Miss Nisbet and I should stay here with Miss Shipton,' I broke in. 'Mrs Gosse, it would be unfair of us to keep you from your family.'

I looked hard at Sarah, trying to convey something of what I wished; she was clearly surprised, but must have seen that I had a reason, for she quickly agreed.

'Yes, please do not let us detain you. We were going to sit here and point out to Miss Shipton where we had been collecting today, were we not, Anne?'

'But — Mr Gosse — before you leave us, would you indicate to us the pool where you found the Scarlet Madrepore?'

I was certain that as I spoke directly to him he responded with a look of gratitude.

And so order was politely restored, despite Willy's protestations that he had already forgotten the verse about the fish. The Gosses proceeded upwards and we soon returned along the valley to our lodging house.

My mood that evening was a mixture of anticipation at the task I had set myself, and despondency at the evening's lost opportunity: but as we sat together in the small sitting-room and took a late-evening cup of cocoa, the doorbell rang — and shortly thereafter our landlady's maid brought to us a note. It was from Mrs Gosse, inviting the three of us to accompany her family and two friends on an outing to Linton and the Valley of Rocks. Mr Gosse would arrange transport for us all, and we must leave at dawn on Saturday.

'Is that not the journey which is described in their little book, *Seaside Pleasures*?' Sara asked. 'How amusing — we shall re-enact a famous journey. We shall be able to entertain our guests with tales of our adventures when we return home. We must accept, Miss Shipton!'

Fortunately Miss Shipton was sufficiently flattered by the invitation to agree with something approaching alacrity (making only two or three protestations about the length and possible difficulty of the journey).

When we retired upstairs Sarah had immediately seized my copy of the book and had curled up in the chair, a shawl across her shoulders (for we had opened the window in a vain attempt to remove the musty smell from our room, and also that we might be awakened by the cries of the gulls in the morning). She said that the Valley of Rocks sounded very gloomy. But I shall not care: for in two days' time I would spend a *whole day* in Mr Gosse's presence, under circumstances which would surely lead to more intimate intercourse.

'To Miss Anne Church, with kind regards, Ph. H. Gosse July 17 1855.' He had written the dedication on the fly-leaf in pencil because, naturally, there had been no pen and ink to hand. One day he would write, 'To a talented naturalist' (or even 'To my dear talented naturalist'. I could but dream; and dream I shall!)

I turn to Chapter Four. Above the heading, *The Valley of Rocks*, Mrs Gosse — the author — has also signed her name. She borrowed her husband's pencil. It was Miss Shipton who discovered, earlier in the day, that Mrs Gosse had written the chapter; it seems that, in the SPCK's journals where the articles were first published, the authors remained anonymous — and the book itself is published under Mr Gosse's name. Would I, in Mrs Gosse's situation, be content to remain unknown, allowing my husband to claim all the glory? (For the little book sells well.) Yet she does not seem modest; her evangelical habit requires her often to be courageous. I have overheard her; she can be too forthright in pressing her attentions on those who shy from them. There is occasionally an awkwardness in her manner. Her chapter is also of a somewhat evangelical nature, that perhaps does not sit so comfortably with those that Mr Gosse has written.

She has emerged from anonymity for me! I am very privileged, and also confused. How I wish I understood them. Perhaps there is a flaw in their relationship that is hidden from outsiders, perhaps even hidden from themselves? Oh, Mr Gosse, Mr Philip Henry Gosse — I would write for you as an equal if I could. If you should desire me so to do!

'Do you think it was Mr Gosse's suggestion that he included the Valley of Rocks chapter under his own name?' I ask Sarah, dispassionately.

'Are you *still* puzzling about that? Does it really matter so very much?' She is standing in front of the open wardrobe, fretting about what to wear to church; we are both a little tired and querulous after yesterday's adventures. 'I thought that he was surprised that she agreed to autograph the work, if you wish to know my opinion.'

'Its content is so different, is it not? Although there are similarities in style. She is so very interested in *people*, and their stories, as well as the countryside. He is more particularly interested in the tragedies that befall people, the drownings and suchlike. Which is perhaps strange.'

'I expect she offered him her writings out of wifely subjugation.' Sarah bent forward, proffering the imaginary manuscript on outstretched hands. ' "Take it, my darling Henry. It is yours to do with as you wish." Here, let me show you, I am almost sure it is "darling Henry" that she quotes at the start. Pass me the book.'

She takes it from me and reads aloud in a high-pitched and mannered voice (*how I dislike her in these moods*). ' "To quote the words of a lively writer, 'The sun rose as brightly as if no pleasure party had been arranged.' " I wager that the "lively writer" is her own much-esteemed husband. She is probably as besotted with him as you seem to be. I am sick of the way you watch him secretly — yes, I have seen you! — and bring his name up in conversation. And all of yesterday you were trying to impress him, it was quite nauseating, and he cannot fail to have noticed and is probably greatly embarrassed. What *can* you see in him? He is old enough to be your father and is not in the least good-looking.'

'I was *not* trying to impress him!' I am so shocked that my face grows instantly hot and tears spring to my eyes. 'How can you say such things? I merely want to take every opportunity to learn, while we are here. And what about *you*? Where did your enthusiasm for natural history disappear, please tell me!'

'If you wish to know, I am quite bored with all this wandering around draughty shores and dabbling my hands in salty water. I do not wish to examine minutely even one more stinking animal! I want to go home, to comfort and friends — and be rid of the tedious Miss Shiptons and the righteous Mrs Gosses and the ... the interminably boring lectures of the Mr Gosses. And as for learning anything about marine zoology — I could not care less!'

With that, she sits down on the bed and bursts into tears.

'Sarah! What is wrong? Dear Sarah, please don't cry.'

My own tears are now flowing, too, and when I sit down next to her and put my arm around her, she turns towards me and presses her face against my shoulder.

'I wish we could go home. I am so tired,' she sobs.

And suddenly I wish so, too. Life is too *complicated* and my own happiness seems unattainable. We hug and weep together, although we are also half-laughing at ourselves — and when Miss Shipton knocks at the door and to collect us for church, we leap up in a panic of haste to finish dressing ourselves.

'Whatever is the matter? What has caused you both such distress?'

'Poor Sarah is feeling unwell. Perhaps she should remain here, Miss Shipton.'

'Let me feel your forehead. You must surely have caught a chill yesterday in that draughty leaking carriage.'

'No, no, Miss Shipton, I shall be all right. Give me a moment to bathe my face. I cannot bear to stay here in this dingy room with no-one to talk to.'

'Miss Church, your face would perhaps benefit from some cold water also. But pray do hurry, or we shall be late.'

Mercifully for us today the skies must have already used up their weekly allowance of rain for although the sun is absent, the clouds form a high unbroken layer against which gulls wheel and spiral. A stiff sea breeze causes pieces of dried seaweed and paper to eddy in the corner by the sweet shop, and catches at our balloon-skirts and the ribbons of the mushroom hats that we are wearing this summer.

Sarah's pale complexion is still blotchy from her crying, although I assure her otherwise. She observes, in return, that my nose is red and shiny. Miss Shipton is managing to keep up a fair trot, despite her stick, for we are late and the streets of the little town are emptying of church- and chapel-goers. The Gosses will already be enclosed within a meeting room with their own band of believers — studying the Word, giving thanks, or whatever it is the Brethren do. Telling Jesus.

There is a half-empty pew near the back of the church but Miss Shipton whispers (loudly) that she will be unable to hear the sermon, so we follow her echoing walking-stick up the aisle towards the front. Sarah directs her gaze at her own feet so that her face will be hidden but, despite the abundance of local townspeople in the congregation, I notice Mr Worthington sitting with the Causleys, and he smiles in a most ingratiating manner, even though his eyebrow is raised extravagantly in query at our late arrival.

I try to concentrate as the service gets under way, try to take heed of the vicar's words (delivered in softly unctuous tones) about the need for humility and self-chastisement. But the gulls are laughing raucously outside; the warmth of the packed church is oppressive and yet familiar. Do I really wish to go home? In three days' time the classes will end. Sarah and I will part, there will be no more of the ready companionship in learning, or of the varied, sociable, open-air life that we have been leading.

There will be no more Henry Gosse! Will all this become nothing more than a half-remembered dream, a cause for secret despair? Why has it been my grave misfortune to *fall in love* with a man who is hopelessly unattainable? I think about him all the time, it is like a nagging pain, I look for him on the shore, register his position in a room, listen out for his voice; I am *ill* with jealousy of his wife. I look for signs of discord between them. What am I to *do*? It is wrong, it is utterly stupid. I should not be thinking about this in church.

Chords from the organ: we stand to sing. We labour through the hymn and as it grinds to a close a horse clacks by on the cobbles outside. I kneel — and think of donkeys.

' "If I had a donkey that wouldn't go, Would I beat him —?" ' He sang it as he walked up the hill beside the carriage; he has a fine singing voice. Willy joined in the chorus, ' "No, no, NO!" '

'When we go on the donkeys the ladies beat them with sticks,' Willy told us. 'It is very cruel, Papa must tell them to stop. Our donkey was called Flower, I rode with Papa.'

'They do drive them with sticks, it is true,' his father agreed, 'for the beasts are very recalcitrant — although very sure-footed. You will be quite safe.'

For the Valley of Rocks is best seen from the back of a donkey. The Gosse family had made the trip before, some three or four years previously, and we were full of anticipation, having heard their stories. Miss Shipton was certain she would be unable to ride such a beast, but Mrs Gosse persuaded her (with a certain cunning, I thought) that it was the only way: 'For did not our Lord Jesus —' and so forth.

On the steepest hills we all (except Miss Shipton) got out and walked to lessen the horses' burden. The Pollards, who lived locally, were both knowledgeable about the countryside through which we passed. Mrs Pollard was stout but a sturdy walker and had many entertaining anecdotes to tell about people in the area; she and her husband had adopted the amusing habit of cross-checking the veracity of their statements with each other. Mr Gosse (who was rarely without his notebook and pencil) occasionally asked them to repeat some details and wrote the story down, even as he walked. Mr Pollard was also very informative about the rocks along the way; it seemed that was his speciality.

'Bless you, no,' Mrs Pollard replied, when Sarah asked her if they had become acquainted with Mr Gosse through his earlier visits to the area. 'My husband travels frequently to London, and I believe they first met at a meeting of the Linnaean Society. Is that not so, Thomas? It was an occasion when Mr Darwin was present in the audience,' she added, with obvious pleasure that her husband mixed with scientists of such eminence.

'Yes, my dear.' (Mr Pollard has a very pleasing way of prolonging his 'rrrs', so that his voice is made warm and comfortable.) 'Our good Mr Gosse was giving a lecture on the zoophyte *Peachia — hastata*, was it not, Gosse? A new species he has recently described. We had occasion to speak to each other after the talk and we have been correspondents since that day. That is so, Mary, is it not?'

'Indeed,' Mrs Gosse added, 'You can claim much of the credit, Mr Pollard, for introducing us all to the delights of the Devon coast — aided and abetted by Mr Kingsley, of course, who wishes to convince us that there is nowhere to equal the collecting possibilities of Bideford and Weymouth.'

'Poor Mr Gosse was quite unwell — with severe headaches — some years ago,' Mrs Pollard explained to me, *sotto voce*, 'and my husband happened to be visiting him at Islington, and suggested that the family should move to St Marychurch at Torquay, for the air there is very bracing.'

I stopped, so that she was forced to pause also, and whispered, 'Is he quite recovered now?'

'I believe so, my dear — although of course the poor gentleman works far too hard.'

Whenever the road became more level, we returned to the carriages, and there were then opportunities to change sets.

'Should you like me to sit by you, Master Gosse?' I whispered and he obliged loudly — my unwitting ally! — by demanding that I sit in his carriage 'with Papa and Mama'. The Pollards insisted that they had been longing for a chance to enjoy Miss Shipton's company, so Sarah and I were free to move.

We were a happy and relaxed company, admiring the foxgloves, the red cinnabar moths upon the golden ragweed, the boats on the distant Bristol Channel. How else will I remember that brief quarter-hour in their company? The *merriment*, the quotations — religious and secular — that poured from their prodigious memories ('Mr Gosse knows the entire Bible by heart.' 'Ah, but Mrs Gosse has lines from the Latin, Greek and German locked inside *her* head!'); the discussion of the crystalline shape of snowflakes that Mr Gosse had studied in Canada — and Mrs Gosse's laughing mention (as swallows and housemartins swooped low after insects in the lane before us) of the 'famous green swallow'. This swallow was clearly a joke between them that she was happy to explain.

'You must guess how Mr Gosse ranks his interests, Miss Church. His diary for September 21st 1849 records the arrival of our dear little son, in just five words, and then, of equal importance, he has noted, "received green swallow from Jamaica" .'

Sarah and I laughed, although I was a little astonished at the freedom with which she had revealed this information.

'What has become of the birds that you collected in Jamaica, Mr Gosse?' I asked. 'My father has seen your book of illustrations and he says the colours of the plumage are very bright and dazzling.'

'The majority I gave to the British Museum, Miss Church, where some have been placed on display, although most are stored away for reference only.'

'Including the green swallow?'

But he merely smiled and drew our attention to some particularly fine ferns growing in the hedgerow.

It was then that I produced my copy of *Seaside Pleasures* and requested the authors' autographs. The sudden lurching of the carriage on a rut did not improve Mrs Gosse's signature — and she protested that it was not a true likeness and if the pencil had not been indelible she would have wished to erase it and start again.

Clouds were starting to gather and soon heavy drops of rain began to fall; as we passed a village, the women were running hither and thither to gather in the white linen which they had draped upon the hedges to dry. The carriages were halted so that the covers might be raised, and Sarah and I returned to Miss Shipton's side. We consoled ourselves with the thought that it would only be a summer shower and soon the view would be restored. But fortune was not with us: the clouds piled on each other and the rain increased to a torrential downpour, that turned the edges of the road to torrents and gave concern lest the horses slip or the brakes not hold.

We continued to our halfway point, the country inn made somewhat famous by Mrs Gosse's writings, and here the horses were rested and we were glad to partake of warming drinks and other refreshments. The temperature had plummeted from summer to chilly autumn in the space of less than an hour. I looked for the head of the broken doll that, on the previous visit, had rested on the chimney-piece but, unsurprisingly, it was no longer there; and Master Gosse — having reached the grand age of five years — would not this time have been attracted to that sad little memento of the landlady's dead child.

Indeed, it seemed that the proprietors of the inn had changed, which occasioned Mrs Gosse some relief and, as we warmed ourselves at the fire which had hastily been lit, our discussion how to proceed was concluded for us by the landlady, who assured us there would be no donkey-rides that day, for the steep paths would be too treacherous from the rain.

Thus was our expedition curtailed. We returned to Ilfracombe within the draughty yet steamy confines of our carriages, the Gosses and the Pollards in one, Miss Shipton and her frustrated charges in the other. I was also fretting, consumed with a new worry.

'Miss Shipton, has Mrs Gosse mentioned to you that her husband suffers from severe headaches? You have a potion, do you not, that you find very helpful in easing the pain? Perhaps you could, privately, give Mrs Gosse the recipe.'

'I hardly think it would be suitable for me to enquire about Mr Gosse's health, Miss Church. Although I do know that Mrs Gosse constantly fears for her little boy's health — she confessed to me that she is always convinced that he will be taken from them, and she wishes him to be dedicated to our Lord Jesus, so that he may be taken amongst the saints.'

The saints! Not those that *I* think of as saints, that are depicted above me here in the church in their long robes and golden haloes, elevated because they loved animals, or were pierced with spears, or flayed alive ... no, the saints of the Brethren are apparently much more prosaic and ordinary: they number those people who, as Mrs Gosse puts it, have been 'washed in the Blood of the Lamb'; that is, are true believers. Judging by the number of Quakers (of whom, incidentally, Miss Shipton is one — although she accompanies us, out of duty, to this church), Brethren and related bodies, Jesus will find Himself surrounded by quite a crowd.

Miss Shipton is fidgeting beside me and searching urgently in her bag; her stick clatters onto the floor. She gasps softly and covers her face with her hand in an attempt to stifle a most un-genteel sneeze.

'Miss Church, do you have a handkerchief you could lend me?'

I do — although it is rather small and not entirely clean — and I avert my eyes to concentrate on the saints in the windows as she hastily mops her nose. The vicar's sermon is punctuated by the unquiet sniffs from a pew near the front and when the service finally ends and we escape into the bracing air, Sarah asks, so very innocently,

'I wonder if our Lord Jesus ever caught a cold?'

CHAPTER 11: HAZEL

I ate a bowl of muesli, wondering as always whether it was anything more than an exercise in chewing — and worried away at the niggle in my mind. Eventually it came to me: David. I'd fallen asleep thinking of David and our trip to Venice.

It was time to be decisive. I cleared away my breakfast dishes and then sat at my table and wrote him a letter, agreeing that he should start divorce proceedings at once. I congratulated him and Gail on their pregnancy and wished them well. There was nothing else that I could say, that chapter of my life was now closed. It was strange how calm I felt, as though this was happening to another person entirely.

I walked down the hill to post the letter. The tiers of slate roofs glistened in the grey drizzle and the damp stone walls smelt comfortingly normal. An intermittent moo-ing sound came from the unseen foghorn on the pier.

But of course I knew that the chapter wasn't closed: I had been avoiding thinking about Matt. Starlings were squabbling noisily over some chips flattened on the pavement, and three gulls awaited their turn on a roof top. Matt would have kicked the greasy cardboard carton, and it would have probably landed in an open doorway or hit someone on the head. I snorted with laughter, so clear was the image, and a woman entering the bread shop glanced at me distrustfully. Matt would have sworn and ducked away, trying for a nonchalant expression, his hands in the pockets of his shorts. Large but fine-boned hands; who did he inherit them from? David's hands weren't like that. Jamie's were, though. It must be my father's genes. Jamie and Matt both had the same mannerisms, more pronounced in Matt because he was taller, of ducking their heads, avoiding your eye, when they were forced to talk about something personal; a certain shyness — which Matt had managed more successfully to overcome. Matt hid behind his hair, that gorgeous shaggy mess that I loved but nagged him about.

Suddenly my head was full of pictures of him — slouching round the house or garden, filling up far more space than he should with his noise and physical presence; the times when we had shared a joke and he had, momentarily, made eye-contact with me — contact that was like a blow to the heart.

I must have posted the letter without realising. I found that I had reached the fish quay, so I sat down on a bollard, shuddering slightly as its smooth metal surface sucked the warmth out of me. Beyond the glistening estuarine mud the opposite quay was already busy with early-morning shoppers and vans delivering goods. Behind me, the morning's fish market had already finished and open crates of fish and crabs had been stacked on the backs of lorries; I could see the drivers in the tiny office, drinking mugs of tea. An old man wearing a yellow oilskin swept crushed ice into the gutter and left a trail of silver scales. He broke off his whistling when he saw me watching.

"Morning, me lover. 'Ow are you, then?'

'Fine, thanks,' I smiled at him.

But I wasn't, really. I stared at the mud and tried to recall pictures of Matt as a little boy or a teenager, but so few came to mind. We had seen so little of each other over the years. Mothers were not supposed to desert their children. What had I been thinking of? I watched the gulls poking disconsolately in the mud and wondered whether a different person had inhabited my body in those days: some sort of automaton. Unaware of what I had been doing, I must have trained myself to banish this love for my son from my mind, so that a shutter had slammed down automatically. *Matthew, begone!* Now, understandably, Matt scarcely knew me, probably couldn't care less, perhaps even despised me; he had come to the Shell House because he had nowhere else to go.

If only Jamie was here to help us sort things out! But I knew I was going to have to sort it out myself, and that would mean talking to Matt, actually talking and listening ...

By the time I'd hurried up the hill I was hot and breathless and still no clearer what I should do, so I sat on the wall for a few minutes to catch my breath. There was no sign of life in the house, no sound of raucous music.

I swivelled round and examined the house's façade. Many of the old shells had grown powdery with age. The painted mortar that held them in place was flaking and finely cracked. I wondered how I would ever manage to restore it, once the façade began to fail: alternatively, I could admit my uselessness, chip it all off and cover the whole lot in a weather-resistant coating. But my mother had managed some repairs, she hadn't been defeated. I examined the pattern of concentric circles near the drainpipe; tiny speckled shells, conical and close-packed, formed the braided boundaries between the rings. The outermost ring contained one scallop, just one, unbalancing the pattern, but at the very centre there was a large, spiky, heavy shell. It wasn't a local shell, she must have bought it in the shop on the quay that sold exotic shells, dried sea-horses and mother-of-pearl wind-chimes. I found it hard to imagine her patiently placing and embedding each shell. Out-of-character, really; I bet she swore a lot.

Suddenly a terrible howl came from above my head, a wailing cry of '*Oh shit!*'

Matt's voice, echoing out of the window like a gull's scream.

Startled, I called up, 'What's wrong? Matt — are you all right?'

He stuck his head out of the window, tangled yellow hair like a ragged halo. He was clasping his nose and his eyes were streaming.

'What are you doing down there? My *nose!* I caught my nose-ring on the button of my shirt. I thought I'd ripped my bloody nose off!'

He took his hand away and looked at it, then stuck his head even further out.

'It's *not* bloody, though, is it? Can you see? God, the pain! I think I'm going to die.'

'It looks all right to me. Don't fall out of the window, that would be even sillier.'

'It's not funny,' he said crossly as I began to snigger, and he pulled his head back in, like a snail withdrawing into its shell.

I sat at my desk and fiddled around with the pages of a manuscript, waiting, while Matt clattered around in the kitchen getting himself something to eat. At last I couldn't wait any longer, there was never going to be a 'right moment'.

'Matt?'

'Uh-huh?'

'Matt, I've just written to your Dad to tell him he should go ahead and file for a divorce. It's only right, especially for the baby.' I looked at him anxiously; he'd stopped spreading margarine on his toast and was staring at me. 'I hope it's going to be all right for you — I just can't see any other option. Can you?'

'Have you posted it?'

I nodded, and was suddenly appalled. Why hadn't I waited and discussed it with Matt first?

'What I think doesn't count, then, does it? Unless you want me to phone him up and say, "Hazel doesn't mean it. What she really wants is for you and her to get back together again and play happy families with little Mattie." Sure it's going to be okay for me. Carry on, just carry on. Don't mind me. I'm just the sad product of your long-dead marriage.'

He paddled the tub of soft marg with his knife, chopping and smoothing its surface.

'Mattie, I'm really sorry.' I was, but I knew he wouldn't believe me. 'But you knew that was what I intended to do. And there isn't an alternative, is there?'

'How come you suddenly went ahead and did it?'

'I suppose it sounds silly … something reminded me last night of when your father and I started going out together — and so I started thinking about him. And then I woke up this morning with a strong feeling that it was time for us to make the separation legal.'

'What reminded you of Dad last night, then? I'm surprised anything *can* remind you of him, it must be fucking years since you last spoke to him properly, let alone saw him.'

'That's just not true, Matt. And it was something I read in that book, *Seaside Pleasures*, about Barricane Bay.'

'Oh yeah. Right. Was that a beach where you had it off together, then?' Matt got up and loudly scraped the toast crusts from his plate into the bin. When his back was turned I closed my eyes and held my breath; I deeply regretted starting this conversation.

'No, I was at Bideford on a field trip and your Dad — David — was in London. It was in the vac and he had a job there, in a bar I think, though I can't remember now. We'd only just started going out and he wrote to me and … Gosse went to Barricane to collect shells, and I went there too, on this field trip. It's a shell beach, you see — and I remembered lying there pretending to look for shells, but actually reading David's letter.'

Matt came through into the main room and sat on the floor with his back against the wall, staring at the ceiling. He had long toes, too; I suddenly remembered how he had hated me cutting his toenails when he was small. I would have liked to have reminded him, but the memory wasn't very appropriate at that moment.

'Reading about Barricane reminded me of something else,' I said, instead. 'I found a beautiful shell when I was there, called the Common Wentletrap, though it's not very common. We each had to collect as many species of shell as possible and glue them onto white card, then identify them. I found thirty-six species, though I think the record was fifty-two — strange how these numbers stick in the mind. The Wentletrap has fine ribs like white porcelain, twisted around a delicate spire — it's a shame there isn't one on the front of the house to show you.'

'So?' He wasn't interested: why should he have been? I was wandering away from the point.

'Anyway, the Wentletrap is called *Clathrus* these days — I remember that, too, because it was such a special shell to have found — but Gosse calls it *Scalaria* in his chapter, the staircase. When David and I wandered around Europe we went to Venice. We were just meandering around, enjoying the little back streets and the canals, and we went into a courtyard, just by chance. It was small and fairly dark — and there, opposite us, was this dazzling building, just like a Wentletrap.'

How could I explain it to Matt? It had spiralled up in front of us, its white pillars and balustrades glistening where they rose up out of the darkness into the sun: the Contarini's snail shell, Palazzo Contarini del Bovolo.

'That was before you got married, right?'

'Yes. It was the summer we graduated.' David had gained an Upper Second in maths and had been due to join a London-based accountancy firm in the autumn.

'The summer you made a mistake and made me. What a bummer, eh? Hazel got pregnant and David had to "make an honest woman of her" or whatever you called it in those days.'

Matt had done the calculation years ago: parents married in January, Matt born in May ...

'Oh come on, Matthew. We're not that antique. You know it wasn't like that in those days, couples didn't *have* to get married any more. We wanted to get married, you know that, we told you that, over and over.'

Matt drew his knees up and rested his chin on them; he pulled at loose threads on his denims.

'Did you ever think of having an abortion when you knew you were pregnant?'

'No! Of course not. We were both really excited.'

'What would you have done if you hadn't been pregnant? What sort of a job would you have got?'

He was interrogating me, and I was lying. I knew I couldn't play that game much longer without making a mistake. I stood up and walked through to the sitting room end, and picked up the newspapers from the floor.

'I'd had a vague idea that I'd enrol on a secretarial course —' I spoke loudly from the other room and then walked back with the papers, so that he wouldn't think that I was avoiding him. '— to gain some "marketable skills". But fortunately these days, with word processors, you can pick up most of that sort of thing as you go along.'

'Yeah.'

I took the papers into the kitchen and we were both silent for a few moments. Of course I had wondered about an abortion. I had dithered, hoping that the disruption in my menstrual cycle had been caused by the travelling. Naturally I hadn't confided in my mother, but I had eventually told David, uncertain of what he would say. I think I'd probably been uncertain what I wanted him to say, but he had been delighted and completely unfazed by the changes it would mean to our lives, and had immediately proposed that we should get married. It had been so easy to agree! Everything had seemed easy: even conception had been easy, an easily-made mistake ... if only the Channel had not been so rough, if only I had not been puking up my guts in the ladies' loo, if only I had remembered the small print that noted the probable lack of efficacy of contraceptive pills after a bout of vomiting. Some couples try for years to produce a child; even Jamie and Lynn had resorted to adoption. Hormones are so unpredictable; it's not your parents, it's their hormones that 'fuck up your lives'.

But David and I had been contented, in our own uninspired, mutually-undemanding sort of way; and soon we had our son, our own little twiglet on the family tree, to claim the attention we should have been paying to each other. Mummy had been quite prepared to let us get on with our lives without any interference from her; I've always assumed she was relieved to be able to hand over responsibility for me to someone else. She and I had never been very close, Jamie was always her favourite.

I peered round the corner at Matt. He was still sitting in the same position, completely motionless.

'You know, Jamie was thrilled when you were born! He and Lynn were trying to have a child, they'd been trying for a year or two — that's why they adopted Suzy. And then of course they had another one of their own! Jamie's always been really fond of you.'

'He's a good bloke.' Matt stood up and wandered over to the French windows, then pressed his nose gently against the glass. 'My nose hurts, I need to cool it. He seems like he's always known what he wants from life and everything has just turned out the way he wants it.'

'Reading about Barricane reminded me of something else, to do with you and Jamie.'

'Bloody Barricane, why did I ever get that case down?'

'It was about the tooth fairy.'

'Oh God, what next?'

'I was thinking about the tusk shells at Barricane, they're very white and curved, a bit like a canine tooth, and I suddenly had such a clear picture of you losing your first tooth when we were over at Jamie's. You were really horrified that it had come out and kept going to look in the mirror because you were worried about the bloody pit!'

'I always hated that bit about losing teeth, the thought that something would get jammed in the hole. Ugh!' He shuddered, and I could see that he was interested despite himself.

'Lynn found a matchbox and some cotton wool and we put it under your pillow at bedtime. But when Jamie and I tiptoed in to swap the tooth for some money you immediately woke up and started shouting for us to go away because we'd scare the fairy away. The trouble was, Jamie had both the tooth and the money in his hand at the time!'

'Did you have to distract me, then?'

I laughed. 'He pretended that the tooth fairy had phoned to say she'd been held up and was sending an assistant who wasn't very reliable — Jamie was to call her back if the assistant hadn't delivered the money. So Jamie told you that he was just checking.'

'And I believed him? Gullible, or what?' Matt shook his head, a quiet smile on his face. 'Are Jamie and Lynn coming down this summer?'

'I doubt it. Summer's his busy time with the pheasants.'

'Perhaps I'll go up and see them for a few days.' Matt opened the French windows and the smell of the garden seeped in; damp, vegetatious, overlaid with salt and a hint of woodsmoke.

'Matt —'

'Yup.'

'You know what you were saying last night, about not having any of Granny's pictures — and wondering whether Dr Wilson would let us have the one she's got? Well, I found a hand-written extract that she might like to have, about Gosse's "naturalist's workroom" in Jamaica. Jim told you that she was a field biologist, didn't he? It might appeal to her. You could give it to her if you're going over there to see Jim. You could try buttering her up a bit.'

'I dunno. I'll see. I have to be at The Anchor in an hour or so.'

He drifted out of the house, into the garden and round the corner. A few moments later I saw him padding past the front windows, heading towards the steps.

CHAPTER 12: MATTHEW

'You may as well take it up to her,' Jim says. 'You should go meet her.'

I get a helluva shock in the dingy hallway because I think there's a person pressed against the wall by the front door; but when I look more closely I see that there are coats, macs and things like that, hanging from pegs, with wellies lined up underneath. They look dead, somehow, as though they haven't been used for a long, long time. There are umbrellas and walking sticks in a barrel, except that it isn't a barrel, it's the emptied foot of an elephant. Also dead.

'I don't know — I might get scared. Did she shoot that herself?'

Jim looks puzzled until I point out the umbrella-stand and then he pulls a face.

'It's pretty gross, isn't it? I can't imagine why she keeps that thing, she told me someone gave it to her husband. Apparently he didn't like it much either. Isn't it illegal now, anyway? She certainly won't shoot you, though — probably want to preserve you as a unique specimen.'

'Okay, then. But you go in first.'

Actually, I do want to see what she's like, and I don't know what to expect. We go upstairs — there are things like rails along the wall on one side, and Jim explains they're the remains of what used to be a stair-lift. There's music coming from an open door, piano, on its own, and Jim stops outside and calls, 'Elizabeth? I've got Matt Myers here — you know, the one I told you about, who's coming to help me with the boat? He's got something to give you.'

'Really?' She sounds kind of startled, which probably isn't surprising. 'Well, yes — come in.'

She's sitting at a huge desk by the window, but turns to look at us. She has thick grey hair, cut short, and her face is not exactly thin, but bony — obvious cheekbones, narrow nose — and she is wearing glasses, which catch the light from the window so that I can't see her eyes. It is cool in the room, a bit dim, and she is wearing a navy cotton jumper and a dark red skirt of some thick material, thick cotton perhaps. I notice this at once because of its colours, the colour combination is good and strong and surprises me.

She doesn't say anything, just stares, and I feel a bit stupid, but I go right over and stick out my hand.

'Hi. I'm Matt Myers. I think you may have known my grandmother, Barbara Lewisham — the artist? I'm staying at the Shell House at Polkenna.'

She just keeps on looking at me — looking up at me, now, and I put my hand in my pocket and step back, thinking that I'm towering over her. The piano carries on playing, very cool, very precise.

'Yes.'

She just says 'yes', that's all; and I wonder if I should go away and dig a hole in the sand and hide myself in it. But Hazel will be mad with me if I don't hand over the paper. So I pull the envelope out of my back pocket, straighten it out and hand it over to Dr Elizabeth Wilson, which is what Hazel has written on the front.

'It's a copy of something Hazel found when she was sorting through some old family things. She thought you might find it interesting and asked me to bring it over.'

I raise my hands and lift my shoulders, to show that, if the 'something' isn't interesting after all, we should just excuse Hazel for her temporary dottiness, it's nothing to do with me.

'Don't shoot the messenger,' I add, perhaps unwisely, but obviously the memory of the now-legless elephant is still with me.

'Hazel is your mother, is that correct?' Elizabeth looks at the envelope quickly and puts it on her desk, smoothing it and pushing it around until it's neatly lined up with the edge: just so. 'Please thank her for me.'

'Oh, okay. Sure.' I am really surprised because she acts as though she knows what the envelope contains. 'It's a description of a naturalist's laboratory, something to do with Gosse. She's got a thing about Gosse at the moment because she's just discovered he's a relative or something.'

Well, I know that isn't quite the truth of it, but I can't remember the details, and anyway it might wake her up a bit before she goes catatonic on me.

'Is he?' She sounds very disbelieving! But right enough, the exciting news seems to stimulate her and she slips her finger under the flap and opens the envelope. I grin at Jim, who has been lounging around by the door, watching, and he raises his eyebrows but doesn't move. I wander around the room as Dr Wilson reads all about negro youths in Jamaica.

This is another room that is full of books, even more than are in Jim's workroom downstairs. It must have been a bedroom at one time, there is still a big wardrobe in one corner, but the beds have gone and now, apart from her desk and filing cabinet, it's full up, with another table and an easy chair and loads of bookshelves everywhere. On the shelves near the desk (which has a clutter of papers, a red plastic box for file cards, a tin of pens and pencils, a stapler, anglepoise lamp and so on) are cardboard box files and folders, labelled *Biomphalaria, Snail Susceptibility, Pulmonate Cladistics, WHO reports*, and all manner of other strange titles that I have to spell out to myself to make sense of them. Reading with my lips moving — very grown-up! And below these are several books, hard-back and paper-back, author E.A. Wilson — *Speciation in Snails, The Worm Turns: Host-Parasite Evolution* — all titles that really grab you by the throat. And there are books on molluscs, and medicine, parasitology books, immunology books, atlases, dictionaries, books on evolution, genetics, a whole load of paperbacks by people even I had heard of, trendy popularizers; new books, old books with battered covers, and a shelf of maps. And smaller shelves with music cassettes and CDs: I wander over to look at these, and they are all classical, Bach, Handel, Telemann and so on. There is an empty Chopin tapebox by the music-system, so I guess that is what the piano music is. There are shelves of fiction paperbacks, too, and hardbacks, all sizes; and encyclopaedias, biographies — everything.

'Quite a library,' I say, and she looks up from the Gosse thing and smiles; for a second, I think she has put on a different face, she looks so relaxed.

'Yes. Books can become an addiction.' She puts the paper down and takes her glasses off, and rubs one of her eyes. 'Your — Hazel was very perceptive. This piece about Gosse's workroom is delightful. He sounds very well-organised. Do thank her.' She smiles again, then she stands up, suddenly quite brisk. 'And now — I understand Jim has persuaded you to help him restore the dinghy. I'm afraid it's not in very good condition — the sails have probably rotted away completely — but it's quite possible that you will be able to use it as a rowing-boat.'

That didn't sound very exciting. Jim puffs out his lips and waggles his head from side to side, and the thought that perhaps he was a mongoose trying to hypnotise a snake makes me splutter with laughter. Elizabeth glances at me and there is a real twinkle in her eyes.

'Not quite your style? I have a suspicion, from what Jim has let slip, that there might be an ulterior motive in renovating the boat. That it's not purely for fresh air and exercise? Your rationale is a little more related to young women, perhaps?'

This time the smile was so quick it was almost subliminal, but I caught it, and I think that she is okay. Jim and I both laugh aloud.

'Yeah,' he says, ' something like that, Elizabeth. And maybe we'll go look out for a small motor.'

'Or even a large one,' I add.

'Well, I think your priority is to make the boat sea-worthy, and then we'll see what can be done.'

'Did you and your husband use to sail it? It's a Redwing, isn't it? Hazel said they need two crew.'

'No, it was here when we bought the house, Matthew. The previous owners no longer had a use for it, so they left it behind. And I'm afraid my husband was disabled so it was too difficult for him …' Her voice trails away and she looks instinctively (or perhaps pointedly) at a framed picture propped on the filing cabinet, a red chalk drawing of a man in a wheelchair: an unusual subject for a drawing, except that it was probably her own work and the man had been her husband.

'Is that your husband? May I look?' I step across the room. 'Did you draw it?'

'Yes. How did you know?'

'I saw some of your snail drawings downstairs when I was in Jim's workroom looking at his computer. And Hazel said you drew portraits — that was where she and Granny met you, at the Polkenna art exhibition.'

The husband's legs are covered by a rug but his arms are resting on the sides of the wheelchair, his hands curving over the ends. The drawing is fine-lined, detailed, like an Augustus John.

'It's really good. Is it like him? Are you pleased with it yourself? He looks — kind.'

Perhaps I was a bit outspoken because her face goes sort of still.

'Can you really see that? You know, I am very glad, and I think I should be flattered, too. He *was* a kind man. He was very — thoughtful.'

This should be the time to ask her about Granny B's painting: but I don't have the nerve. Instead, Jim and I say that we'll see her later, and she says she might even come down and see how we are getting on.

But when we are downstairs again I ask Jim if I can go into the big sitting room, where we were yesterday, because Hazel said that one of my grandmother's paintings was there. Roger is in there, too (I'd almost forgotten about him in the excitement of meeting Dr W) and we have a bit of a chat, and he asks how Hazel is, I say 'Fine', the usual sort of thing. And we all look at the painting — but I am really disappointed because although the colours and execution are good, the subject is really quite boring. I'm glad that I didn't mention wanting to reclaim it, after all. I suppose Hazel gave me the Gosse photocopy instead of her precious notebooks to try to appease me and keep me quiet. No need now. It's a bit depressing: I tell the others that the painting isn't anything like Barbara's usual work.

Jim asks if I want jelly sandwiches again, but I tell him I've remembered to have lunch this time, so we grab a couple of cans and go out to the boat. Actually, I don't know too much about boats, and it isn't a great day to be working on it, the sky is grey and overcast, not exactly blazing sun, off-with-your-kit weather. But we drag out the bucket and stuff from underneath — a metal paint scraper, sandpaper that has gone soft with damp, a couple of chisels and a rusty old Stanley knife, really useful odds and ends like that — and have a look.

Jim shows me what he was doing yesterday, when we first saw him. I don't know why he had been varnishing, the whole boat looks as though it needs scraping down first — the old varnish is peeling and blotchy, some of the planks are bashed and splintery. We turn the boat over and look inside and I poke around with a chisel between the planks. In one place there is daylight showing through.

'Shiver-me-timbers! Ar-har, Jim-lad, we need to caulk the plank. Arr.'

Then I remember that he *is* called Jim, so I have to explain about *Treasure Island* and Captain Hook. Except that I don't think it was Captain Hook, that was something to do with crocodiles and ticking clocks. Then somehow the conversation gets around to Captain Kirk, and Spock's ears, Moby Dick, Peter Pan and so on, and we both get into the boat and pretend it's out at sea in a typhoon. Jim lurches around, pretending to bail, I have the lager can to my blind eye like a telescope, like Nelson looking for whales, and conversation is getting a bit silly and obscene, the way it does, each trying to outdo the other, and we're pissing ourselves with laughter and being incredibly childish, when there is a horrible cracking noise, not loud, from the hull.

Jim starts yelling, 'We're gonna drown. Pray, goddam you, pray! The water's pouring in. May Day, May Day, May Day!' and I beat out 'Dah-dah-dah, di-di-di, dah-dah-dah' on the side with the can.

'You'll break that boat.'

Not a loud voice, more a sort of quiet statement, but we both hear it, in spite of the racket we are making, and look up. He's just standing there, at the top of the jetty, staring at us; he must be in his seventies, bent-backed and wearing a flat cap, jacket with leather elbow-patches, and baggy trousers with turn-ups — even though it's summer. Everything brownish, tweedy, even his face looks kind of brown and tweedy. He's holding a squashed-looking rollie, and I'm surprised it's not made of brown paper, too. He's not smiling, but not exactly disagreeable either: just looking at us.

I'm surprised to see that Jim is looking embarrassed and has definitely quietened down.

'Oh, hi, Peter. Yeah, I guess we should take more care. We were just saying that we need some help with this thing, you can see the gaps in the planking. Do you know anyone could help? Matt, this is Peter Pascoe, Elizabeth's gardener. Peter, Matt here has come to help, in case you see him around and wonder who he is. He's staying in Polkenna.'

Peter Pascoe is now looking at me, pretty hard, and I wonder if he's against long hair or nose studs or something, but he just says,

'Aye, I know.'

'Do you?' I'm really startled. 'How do you know who I am?'

But he doesn't explain, just nods a couple of time (which makes him cough) and says, 'Billy Martin. He can help,' and then off he goes, back to the house, quite dignified but a bit bandy-legged as though he's wet his pants.

'Phoo!' Jim pushes out his lower lip and blows, so that his hair puffs upwards. I raise an eyebrow at him, and we both climb out carefully and, with a lot of heaving and groaning because it's bloody heavy, we get the boat turned upside-down again. We stow away the bucket and chisels and stuff, and the empty cans, because it's obvious that there's nothing much that we can do. We look to see what made the cracking noise, but there's nothing to see, probably just that bit of driftwood that shifted on the pebbles underneath, and so we decide to wander along the shore.

'Wonder how he knows who I am?'

'I dunno. An old guy like that, lived around here all his life ... I guess he gets to know most things. You know how he travels around?' Jim gives me his big white grin and shakes his head in disbelief. 'He's got an old motorbike, an old Bantam would you believe? And he chugs up and down these little roads. Jesus!'

'I bet he has a leather helmet and leather goggles, then.'

'Nope. That's the funny thing. He's got a real high-tech helmet, that looks like one of those virtual-reality headsets!'

The idea of the little old bloke with his huge helmet on his little old bike sets us off laughing again as we walk down the shore.

The tide is on its way out and the sand is grey and shiny. I like the way, when you tread on it, you squeeze the water out and leave a dry, sharp footprint — and then the water creeps back in and makes a foot-shaped puddle. The sea is grey, too, and the small waves just roll in, trying to cover the sand but being sucked back out again. There is a line of dirty froth and bubbles marking the edge, but the line soon gets left behind and another one forms, further out.

'Does Oregon have a coast?' I try to visualise the map of America. 'I suppose it must.'

'Sure! All the way down the left-hand side. You can drive down to the ocean from Corvallis, it maybe takes a couple of hours. The coast is not too different from this — longer beaches, yellower sand, I guess, but cliffs like these, too. But one thing I've really noticed here — especially in Polkenna, with all those fishing boats against the wharf — here there's a massive tidal fall. Compared with the Pacific Ocean. Hey — when I was a kid, around ten or so, my dad took me down to the ocean to camp, because he wanted to be there for the lowest tide of the century. Can you imagine that? We camped up in a forest back of the beach someplace, I don't now remember where, and he'd bought fish and we broiled them over a fire while he told me stories. The real Boy Scout, wilderness experience! And then he made me get out of bed real early, about five am or thereabouts. It was cold and dark, although I do remember it was summer, and we drove down to the shore. I was expecting something real dramatic — perhaps being able to walk for miles over uncovered ocean floor or suchlike — but there was a fog, and we couldn't see anything very much. And then there was the water, looking not much different, as far as I could tell! My dad said there were more rocks uncovered, and we climbed down onto them. But I don't remember I was too impressed!'

'Hmm.' I try to imagine my dad doing something like that when I was a kid, but fail; we stayed in holiday cottages, once in a caravan, and Hazel cooked.

'Was your dad a biologist, then?' I ask. A plastic carton is half-buried in the sand; I excavate it with the toe of my trainer and throw it in the sea, but it fills with water and sinks.

'No, not at all. He just liked to go to the beach — and he liked the idea of being there for the lowest tide for a century. It sounded important. Kind of romantic, I guess.'

'Yeah.'

We jump and splash across the freshwater stream that flows down the beach and spreads out over the sand, and clamber up onto the rocks. There are barnacles and the whitish-yellow snails that I recognise from the shell-lady's arms. The wet rock is smooth, the brown weed slippery, but the barnacles provide good grip for our trainers and we leap from ridge to ridge, heading towards the cliffs on the right side of the bay. A couple of little birds have been rooting around in the pools and they fly off twittering, skimming over the rocks. Easier than walking.

'We have brown pelicans. And dolphins. Do you have those?'

'Not pelicans. I don't know about dolphins around here. There are sharks, though.'

' "Jaws" '

'Not quite. Blue sharks, I think. They catch them off Looe. Barbara told me how you could go down to the quay when the shark boats were coming in and count the yellow pennants on the rigging. That showed how many sharks had been caught — sometimes there would be half-a-dozen, she said. And the biggest sharks were hung up on hooks to be weighed, then left for everyone to look at. It would go on day after day, several boats every day, in the tourist season. Then suddenly there weren't many sharks left. And I bet all the poor buggers did was eat a few fish!'

'Huh. Not good.'

Jim bends down next to a rock-pool and picks up an empty yellow-and-brown striped shell and passes it to me.

'Your grandmother used to own this Shell House that you live in, right?'

I nod. 'She died about a year ago. I was really fond of her — I still can't believe she's not there. It's kind of odd, staying there without her, I keep thinking she'll come in, or shout to me, or something. Still, I've only been there a few days, I'll just have to get used to it — that, and living with Hazel. I live with my dad and his partner when I'm not at college. In Thame — that's near Oxford.'

I crouch down and poke at some pink weed in a pool because I don't want Jim to see my face; I have this horrible feeling that I might just say something about Gail, might brag about it, for Christ's sake. And that would be sick, and stupid — and very, very pointless. So I dabble my fingers in the pool, stroking an arms-out sea anemone to feel its tentacles grab me. A round yellow shell lifts up and dashes across the bottom of the pool to hide, its crab's legs scrabbling; I pick up another yellow shell but it's empty, so I keep it.

Jim has sat down and is staring out to sea. Water has splashed onto the leg of his jeans and made a dark patch shaped like India or maybe Africa.

'What did she die of?' he asks.

I stare at the watermark trying to identify Madagascar or Sri Lanka, but they're not there. I want to add an island with my wet fingers, but that's the sort of gesture that gets misinterpreted.

'She had cancer,' I say eventually; and I do *not* want to remember the frightening non-person in the bed, so I ask him quickly,

'What did Elizabeth's husband die of?'

Jim looks at me. 'Allan just wasted away, I guess. I don't know what was wrong with him. It's not the sort of thing you ask.'

'You just did. You asked me.'

'Sorry. I guess I shouldn't have. But, well, Matt, it's kind of easier to talk to you than Elizabeth. She's okay, but — well, you know …'

'Sure. That's okay. Don't worry about it.'

I squat down next to him, and we just stare out to sea for a bit. There's a yacht motoring into the bay, with its sails down, and towing a dinghy. A man walks along the deck and there are shouts and instructions and arm-waving as the boat slows down. He throws an anchor overboard and waits to see if it will hold, and the woman who is steering bends down and turns off the engine. There are kids on board and their voices are loud across the water. The sun shows, flat and yellow, through the grey cloud and is hidden again. Everything misty-grey. Like Turner, but closer. The yacht's anchor is holding, which is nice for them but not so interesting for Jim and me. There's nothing like a bit of incompetence at sea to keep the watchers entertained.

'Don't you get bored here?'

Jim laughs, once. 'Hah! You think I should?'

'I suppose I thought they might not be very exciting company.'

'I'm here to work, Matt. What we're doing is real good. We're synthesising all this data — we're getting data from the lab in the States, and from London, as well — and it's already beginning to show some real interesting things. But it's kind of frustrating, too — there are gaps ... I don't have too much time to be bored.'

'You have time to sit on the beach and play shipwrecks.'

'Sure, but that's necessary time-out. I need to take a break, right? When you have to work in this concentrated way, with a time-limit set on it, as I've got here, you become — how'll I put it? — immersed in the work. Drowning, almost. My graduate tutor used to say that you know when you're really thinking about your project when you start dreaming it at night. But there are only so many hours that I can spend at that damn' keyboard ... and I need to get out and clear my head. Open the flaps and let the wind blow through.'

'Do you think Elizabeth dreams about snails?'

'Not every night but I'll bet she has done many times in her life.'

'And Roger?'

'Probably not. I guess Roger's more a "do-er" than a thinker.' He looks sideways to see my reaction

I picture Roger, and smile.

'Yeah, you may be right. Well then, I won't ask you what I was going to, which was "If you're bored, why don't you come back to Polkenna for the evening?" I start work at the pub tonight — training session, so I'll likely be pretty busy — but we can ask around for this Billy Martin character, and you can go and check out the scene at some of the other pubs if you get bored. But of course, you don't get bored!'

'I guess I could easily get bored staying here tonight, now you mention it. If the offer's still there, sure, I'd love to come. Ah — but if I drive in with you, how will I get back?'

'You can stay the night with us, no problem. And I'll run you back tomorrow. Or Hazel can. Whatever. We can sort something out.'

Jim thinks for a few moments, then nods.

'Okay. That sounds good.'

'Cool.'

A sharp pain is growing at the top of my thigh and I remember the two snail shells that I put in my pocket. I stand up and take them out: plain yellow, and yellow-and-brown striped. Squat and round, not like dogwhelks; a smooth, pleasing sort of shape. I've seen others on the seaweed, other colours, and empty shells piled together in pools and on the beach. Shell-drifts. Jim and I wander along the rocks, just talking, and throwing pebbles into the pools and at gulls that are giving us the evil eye. And I pick up more of the shells from here and there, brown, red, yellow — and two more with stripes, prizes. They are uncomfortable in my jeans pockets and I tell Jim to wait, and leap back over the rocks, to find the plastic pot that the waves have left behind again, again half-buried in the sand. The shells rattle in it like sweeties, and we collect as many of each colour as we can, to see if we can fill it.

'Why do you want them?' Jim asks; an obvious question. But I can't tell him because I don't yet know.

The boat-people have rowed their dinghy ashore and the little kids are tottering around with their buckets and spades. They won't stand still so that Mummy can take off their life-jackets. Daddy is pulling up the dinghy and trying to find a rock to tie the rope around. I've been trying to remember a rhyme about pelicans, and now it comes back to me. I tell it to Jim.

' "What a wonderful bird is the pelly-can. Its beak can hold more than its belly can." '

Back at the house we sit at the kitchen table and snack on jam sandwiches and orange squash. Second childhood! I'm about to tip out the shells onto the table, but they're still sandy and I know how Barbara would have grumbled, so I fill the plastic pot with water, and then tip it out, holding the shells back with my hand; wash and tip, wash and tip, trying to flush the sand down the plug-hole out of sight. There isn't any paper towel (remember, Hazel looked for some yesterday?) but Jim pulls down the teatowel from the rails above the sink and we make a bag of it and tip the shells in. I hold the ends and swing the bag around my head outside the door. I didn't think about holes, but there aren't any and I scrape the less-wet shells onto the table. The deep red ones, wet, glow.

'That's *real* pretty,' Jim drawls, and he sits back in his chair, arms dangling, snorting when I give him the two-finger sign; watching as I sort out blocks of colour, grading, finding transitional states. The banded ones rebel. A few shells still contain snails, a mistake: I throw them out of the open door because they'll stink.

While I sort shells I ask Jim about Corvallis and he tells me that the campus has lots of space and trees. The street where he lives (he rents a house with another guy, there are blueberry bushes in the garden) is long and straight and lined by other single-storey houses. On summer evenings when he goes out running he has to watch that he doesn't skid and rip a muscle because there are so many cherries on the sidewalk and, later, plums. He pumps iron, too. He asks how I keep in shape and I say I jog a bit and play a bit of football, but that's an exaggeration. I don't want him to know that I'm basically a slob!

'I push shells around,' I say.

I'm still pushing shells around when Elizabeth comes in. She sort of smiles and goes to put on the kettle.

'So the sea was too stormy to carry on repairing the boat, was it?'

Jim and I look at each other quickly.

'Er, hmm. You saw us? Of course.'

'Of course. That's why that room is my study, because it has such a good view.'

I see that her eyes have that twinkly look again, even though her expression is almost dead-pan.

'The boat began to sink,' I explain. 'It's full of holes. So we had to abandon ship.'

'Peter Pascoe wasn't too pleased. But he said that someone called Billy Martin could help — do you know him, Elizabeth? As a matter of fact, Peter Pascoe often is not too pleased — I get the impression that he's not keen on having us around.'

'That's not entirely true, Jim. He got on very well with Allan — they spent a tremendous amount of time discussing the garden. Peter's a very good gardener and a very knowledgeable plantsman, particularly for this rather warm, salty climate. And he was also very good to Allan, acting more or less as his general factotum. He's just a little insular in his outlook. Do you have an interest in *Littorina obtusata*?'

I assume she's talking to Jim because I don't understand the question, but she's looking at me. I realise my mouth is open so I use it to ask, 'Sorry?'

'That's what all your shells are. You have been busy.'

'Jim helped. Even though he said it was childish.' I glance at him and he grins, as usual. 'But they can't all be the same thing, surely?'

'Not like your damned *Bulinus*, Elizabeth — they all look the same and yet you and Roger are always telling me they're all different!'

'They don't all look the same, as you well know, Jim. You're just trying to be controversial! But you're right, the differences between the *Bulinus* are fairly insignificant compared with these *obtusata*. Look at that beauty!' She picks up one of the three yellow-and-brown striped shells. 'I see you've found a *fusca*, too — that's one of the least common morphs. *Fusca* is the dark brown variant. And these are *citrina, aurantia, rubens, olivacea*.' She points at the yellow, orange, red and greenish-yellow shells that I have arranged in blocks of colour. 'Lovely poetic names!'

Roger Trenton comes in at that point.

'Did I hear you filling the kettle? Funny how the sound of the kettle brings everyone running — even our American friend. Aha! Now there's a fine example of colour polymorphism.'

He starts picking up the shells, too.

I feel possessive about the shells and wish everyone would leave them alone. I have this feeling about the colours and patterns, that there's something important there: a block of yellow (*citrina* — like a lemon?), a block of yellowish-green, a single row of orange (bright orange), two dark red and one dark brown. And at the right-hand end of the row, the banded shells. Something is nagging at my mind. There is no gradation, they don't gradually change. They jump: there is a jumpiness. I'm only half-listening to the others, but I don't understand what they're on about, it's like they've switched to a higher level of language.

'Some of the other littorinids have colour morphs,' Elizabeth is saying, 'but it's much less common. In *obtusata* this type of intrapopulation polymorphism is the rule. You can see that these morphs are completely discrete, too, completely lacking in intergradation. There is some variation in shell thickness but, as you would expect, that's ecophenotypic — thinner-walled, smaller shells on exposed shores, where they can creep into crevices, and thicker-walled shells on sheltered shores like the one here at Nancarrow, possibly as protection against crab predation. As far as I can remember, the reason for the colour polymorphism is not at all clear.'

'I'm groping a bit here, I'd have to check the literature, but I seem to remember that the allozyme frequency shows a surprisingly high diversity.'

'Well, I think you would expect that, Roger, wouldn't you? *Obtusata*'s slightly unusual, compared to the other littorinids, because the larvae are non-planktonic, so there is limited dispersal over the range. And therefore the likelihood of a high degree of genetic variation within the population increases.'

(It's like a dance, I think. Or a game. That's it, they're playing a game. Now Roger's hitting back but I can't tell if he's on the ball.)

'But isn't there a linear distribution on the shore? — different colour morphs found on different algae? There's an element of cryptic colouration.'

'There's some evidence that *olivacea* is most common on *Fucus vesiculosus* at the top of the tidal range, and *citrina* lower down on the yellower *serratus*. So it's likely that the colour polymorphism is selected for, rather than neutral, perhaps by visual predators such as crabs. If the crypsis is important, I suppose the morph ratios could be maintained by a frequency-dependent selection.'

Jim has been sitting silently, but now he starts to mutter something about allozyme frequencies and phenetic clustering and molecular clocks, and they all burble on a bit more, so I give up and start putting the shells back into the plastic pot. All the same species: hard to believe. 'Morphs'!

'Perhaps they change from one colour to another as they get older,' I say. 'Metamorphosis, like tadpoles.'

That stops them rabbiting on and they all look at me, sort of in surprise. Roger jumps in with, 'Oh no, the shell colour is determined genetically, laid down right at the start — that's what we've been talking about.'

I smile and nod, because I had at least understood that they were talking about genes, not jeans, but I was just stirring things up.

But 'metamorphosis' stirs me up, too, because it was a game that Barbara taught me to play: 'to stop you turning into a vegetable,' she used to say.

'It's a game. Metamorphosis,' I say aloud, and look around for two examples.

'Teapot and shell. How do you get from one to the other? Anyway, we need to get going, Jim. Do you want to grab a toothbrush or something?'

'Do you always talk like that when you're together?' I ask Jim as we drive towards Polkenna.

'Sometimes. But it's fun, don't you see? Sometimes it's genuine, because we're really trying to figure something out and kicking ideas around. Or genuinely wanting the information. Other times it's kind of point-scoring —'

'I bet Elizabeth always wins.'

'Yeah, mostly. Against Roger, any rate. He's got tunnel vision, she sees all around, thinks laterally, pulls in data from all over the place. It's exciting —'

'It's exclusive.'

'I guess. But only amongst the initiates, when they're talking shop — it doesn't *have* to be exclusive. But also, you never stop questioning because you never know all the answers. And one answer raises another question, or two questions. It's a way of thinking. You have it naturally — but you can learn it, too.'

I swing Hazel's car round a sharp bend and there's a car coming towards us, filling up the road. We both dither, and look over our shoulders, but eventually the other driver backs up and I squeeze by. I hate these narrow lanes.

'So — going back to my question, have you thought how to metamorphose a teapot into a shell?'

'Nope.' Jim thinks for a while. 'How about "teapot, porcelain, clay, limestone, shell"? Shells are made of a type of limestone.'

'Not bad at all for a beginner. Then how about this for lateral thinking, or whatever it's called? I don't know what the hell this means, but what about "teapot, watch, molecular clock, shells"?'

I glance at him, but he looks blank, so I just laugh and keep on driving. Ignorant Americans!

CHAPTER 13: ANNE: SUMMER 1856

The Nisbets' house is quite grand, in the modern style, built of a pale yellow sandstone and with a pillared portico placed between the bow-fronted windows that look towards the Frith of Clyde. I have been given a room at the rear and, although I cannot see the sea, I look out onto the walled kitchen garden (and watch the snatched conversations between the gardener and the little kitchen maid!), and the newly-planted stand of trees where, Sarah confides in me, she hopes that her own children will eventually find sufficient cover to play hide-and-seek. Sarah is engaged to be married to a Mr Gordon Armstrong, who is as tall and handsome as herself (for she has grown in stature and elegance during the past year).

Despite the diverging courses of our lives since our shared time at Ilfracombe, and a geographical separation that exceeds the length of England, we have remained friends and correspondents. Sarah has apparently learned to curb her more outspoken outbursts, at least in public, but with me she remains as injudicious as ever: her views are wicked and hilarious and, in the safety of our own rooms, no-one is spared from analysis — nor does she spare me from her *intimate* thoughts!

Thus, in April, she summoned me here to Helensburgh: 'I am so happy, dearest Anne, and so full of excited anticipation for our married life. I had not imagined that "love" should also create so profound a sensation in the body! — such poetic nonsense about "beating hearts" and pathetic sighs! My darling Gordon provokes such profoundly <u>physical</u> sensations within me (and, I believe, these are reciprocated!) that there are times when we can scarcely bear to <u>touch hands</u> in secret! And when I think of you I cannot bear that you should be thus deprived — I shall be your matchmaker, you must trust to my great experience in these matters! Gordon has several friends — possibly even endowed with a little intelligence, such as would appeal to you — any of whom would, I am certain — and especially with my guidance! — fall immediately in love with you (how could they fail to do so, seeing your sweet good nature and your calm demeanour?).'

This description of me came as a surprise: do I appear confident to others? It is true that I attempt to remain calm even though my mind is seething with ambition and ideas for new projects — in all of which it seems I must be frustrated. I am rather prone to tears; but if I were a man I would not be so. I would not consider myself 'sweet' (and neither would Mr Worthington, nor his successor Mr David Thompson, both of whom I successfully rejected — thus incurring Papa's great displeasure and, possibly, a certain measure of desperation in Mama). Furthermore, why should this array of handsome young Scotsmen be attracted to a 23-year old *spinster*, of medium height, who is not strikingly attractive (although neither is she entirely plain) with a round face, a somewhat broad nose (my eyes are good, they are brown, and my eyebrows are well-shaped), and unruly brown hair — and, moreover, who is not always dressed in the height of fashion and has some difficulty in persuading her garments to remain uncrumpled and neat?

'How could they fail to fall in love?' Sarah had asked. I could think of many reasons: but the only answer to that question was to test it out in practice!

Thus, in the last week in June — with notebooks and a variety of probably inappropriate clothes in my trunk (what *does* one wear in Scotland?) and a copy of Miss Emily Brontë's *Wuthering Heights* in my handbag (and a determination to re-acquaint myself with the details of that dark *passion*) — I took the train from London to Edinburgh and thence to Glasgow. There I was met by a middle-aged couple, who were neighbours of the Nisbets and returning home, and we were conveyed by carriage (for the railway was as yet incomplete) between rolling hills on sometimes precipitous roads, and finally, *finally,* reached the fashionable resort of Helensburgh on the banks of the Frith of Clyde.

Life here is certainly very gay, and there is much coming and going, and picnics and other outings. Sarah's fiancé is indeed dark and handsome and they are both clearly strongly attracted to each other (sometimes, in the absence of the parental presence, a little too strongly!) so that on occasion Sarah almost seems to forget my presence. I have spent several hours in the company of the various 'handsome' (and, indeed, even 'intelligent') male friends, and we get along tolerably well — but there has been no mutual *plunge* into love (or even passion, hidden or otherwise).

The difficulty lies in myself, I am certain, for they seem so … immature; moreover, I feel a certain resistance within myself towards being drawn into intimacy with any one of them. I feel so *old*, and this frightens me for then I think that I shall never be loved and married. I have long accepted that I myself can love no-one but Henry Gosse.

Two days ago a handsome yacht sailed up the Frith, tacking to and fro to show its style, its sail glistening in the early-evening sun; it moored at the easterly end of the town near the entrance to the Gareloch. Mr Nisbet watched from the steps of the portico, his small telescope to his eye, and then announced with apparent satisfaction,

'That's Ballavich's boat, I'm sure of it.'

'It is likely. I had heard that their house had been opened,' Mrs Nisbet agreed.

It seemed that the Laird of Ballavich and his lady had a summer house here in the town: the estate of Ballavich, much of which comprised rough heathery hillside in the Highlands, had been partially sold off and thus greatly reduced in size, and its owner now spent the greater part of his time in Glasgow or travelling abroad (as does Mr Nisbet himself, who holds an important position in a shipping firm — indeed may even own it — that is based on the Clyde). Mr Nisbet is a *daunting* man, perpetually busy and with a head full of business, who has little time for other people in a social context — but he was clearly pleased that the Ballavichs were about to grace Helensburgh with their presence. Mrs Nisbet lost no time in sending a servant round with a card.

Thus it was that Mr Duncan Robertson came to call. His uncle and aunt sent their apologies, he explained, but his aunt was not entirely well. Presently, after some direct questioning by Mrs Nisbet, he provided the information that he, like Mr Nisbet, was in the shipping business (although naturally not in nearly such an elevated position) and that he had spent several years in his firm's office in New York: but he had now returned to Glasgow, where doubtless he would remain.

'Is this your first visit to Helensburgh, Mr Robertson?' Sarah asked. 'You will find it rather quiet after the excitement of New York.'

'Indeed, it is the first time that I have set foot here, Miss Nisbet — and I am sure the alleged 'quiet' will suit me very well. Although my aunt assures me that the inhabitants occupy themselves very fully with every conceivable activity during the summer months!' He smiled at her. 'But I have been exploring the waters of the Frith whenever opportunity and the weather have allowed.'

'So do you sail frequently in the Laird's yacht? That must be wonderful, she is such an elegant boat.'

'I hope you do not suffer from sea-sickness, Mr Robertson. And there are some very contrary winds in this region, so I am told.'

'I am afraid, Mrs Nisbet, that I turn a most unpleasant green.' He lifted his hands slightly and smiled self-deprecatingly as he caught my eye. I liked his smile, and the way the skin round his eyes crinkled; he must smile very often for the crinkles were pale in the unfashionably weather-beaten tan of his face. His manner was quiet and unassuming, but not at all deferential or perturbed by Mrs Nisbet's relentless questioning.

'And as for the use of the Laird's yacht — no, it is too swift for my purpose. Even should he permit me its prolonged use! My explorations are usually from the decks of fishing boats and dredgers — whose skippers naturally are hardy souls, so that I am obliged to go out in all kinds of uncomfortable seas. I swear several of the men are willing to take me only because my discomfort causes them such amusement!'

'Sarah and I very nearly had the opportunity to sail in a dredger last summer — but on the agreed day the sea was deemed too rough for the lady students, so two of the gentlemen went instead. I still wish that we had been allowed to go.'

'That was in the Bristol Channel, Mr Robertson, not here. We were attending Mr Gosse's shore classes — in the days when his marine aquaria were all the rage. Although Anne remains quite fascinated by polyps and prawns, do you not, Anne? It is all we can do to drag her away from the shore!'

The old, mocking Sarah could not remain hidden for long! I felt myself grow confused and inarticulate to have my *raison d'être* thus paraded and derided. But I was also somewhat relieved, as well, that she had decided not to pay the role of matchmaker: Mr Robertson was neither young (he was perhaps in his early thirties) nor handsome (he was of only medium height and stocky, rather than slim, his face broad about the cheekbones, his eyebrows thick and dark).

'Indeed?' He was looking at me (his eyes were strange, a curious hazel-green).

'But I, too — ah, I shall lay myself open to your scorn, Miss Nisbet! I, too, have been making observations on the local marine fauna. Most recently I visited the Isle of Arran in the company of the Reverend Donald Landsborough, who is himself a collector and —'

'What is it that persuades vicars and preachers to devote so much energy to studying the life of the sea-shore? There was that odd little curate who lived at Ilfracombe, Tug-something — do you remember, Anne? Whenever he saw Mr Gosse on the shore he would scurry down to offer his help in identifying "critturs" .'

'Tugwell. The Reverend George Tugwell. He was writing a *Manual of sea-anemones*. I thought he was very informative and good-natured.'

'And then of course there is the Reverend Charles Kingsley, with whom Anne is well-acquainted.'

'Is that so, Miss Church? I have a copy of his *Glaucus* in which he extols the moral virtues of examining the "Wonders of the Shore". I seem to remember — although my memory is probably inexact — a phrase about "the young London beauty amid all the" ... oh, let me see ... yes, "amid all the temptation of luxury" ... something ... ah yes, "her heart pure in a boudoir of shells and sea-weeds". That conjures up quite an image, does it not? And further phrases about remaining immaculate, "unspotted", by considering how the lilies of the field grow ...'

Poor Mr Robertson. He must suddenly have realised the implications of his words in the present company, because his face turned quite pale and he floundered to a halt. I felt so sorry for him that I attempted to change the subject, calling attention to the name that sprang so readily into my mind.

'Our tutor, Mr Philip Henry Gosse, is also mentioned in the Reverend Kingsley's book. Indeed, the very shore class that we attended is advertised in its pages. But it is my father who is slightly acquainted with the Reverend Kingsley — not I.'

'Gosse? Yes, Miss Nisbet mentioned him earlier, did she not? I believe I have heard the name, but I must admit to being unfamiliar, as yet, with his work.'

'Of course! Mr Gosse is another case in point,' Sarah exclaimed. 'He may not be a curate or a bishop or a member of the established church, but he is much given to preaching — not only in his books, but in actuality. To the Evangelical Christians, or Brethren, or whatever their little group of the "Saved" is called. And did not Aunt Isabel mention he wrote religious books and tracts as well? That dreadfully prim Miss Shipton sent you some, did she not, Anne?'

'Sarah, a little more piety in your demeanour would be beneficial,' her mother said, but without any great sense of weight in her suggestion.

'Miss Shipton included three of Mrs Gosse's tracts when she wrote to tell me that there was not to be another shore class this summer. Have you discovered any unusual species, Mr Robertson?'

'I have been conducting some small experiments — no doubt you would think them amateur, Miss Church! — with the cloak anemone, *Adamsia palliata*. And I am sufficiently unsure of my skills at identification as to be always on the verge of claiming a specimen unknown to man. Only to discover that it is the Common Beadlet!'

His broad smile was so good-natured and unaffected that I could not help but laugh aloud.

Sarah, too, must have been amused by his candour, for she exclaimed, 'I think Miss Church and I should act as your tutors, do you not agree, Anne? We shall find our notebooks and identification manuals, and take you in hand.'

'Would you? I should be a very willing and studious pupil. Mrs Nisbet — I am promised a trip in the "Betty Blue". She is a small vessel, owned by James MacKenzie — no, you probably do not know him, why should you? We shall sail from here via Kilcreggan, to drop a trawl in the mouth of Loch Long. Would you give your permission for Miss Nisbet and Miss Church to accompany us on the trip? That is, if you would find such a trip entertaining?' He looked at me then at Sarah for confirmation. 'We shall of course wait for a perfectly calm sea and we shall take all manner of provisions. Please do permit it!'

'*Yes!*' I wanted to shout it out. 'Yes, yes!' But of course I could only put on a pleased, expectant air and hope that my hostesses would agree. I was fortunate.

'Why not?' Sarah was laughing. 'What fun! What an adventure it will be. Of course we shall come, shall we not, Anne? Mama, of course you will agree. We shall be out of your way, enjoying the fresh sea air. Perhaps we shall even bring home some oysters for Papa's breakfast. Mr Robertson, you are a marvel! And by the end of the day Anne shall have taught you to be as *expert* in marine zoology as we are. But beware — Miss Church is a very dedicated task-master.'

'Indeed?' He ducked his head and looked at me from under raised eyebrows; he was unsmiling but there was a glimmer of humour in his eyes.

'Indeed, yes.' I nodded, seriously, but I could feel the happiness welling up inside me.

I can point exactly to the moment when I knew that I would marry Duncan Robertson if he asked me. It was not on that exhilarating trip to Kilcreggan, when the wind strengthened and the bow of the sturdy boat smashed into the waves, sending gusts of spray back over us as we huddled further astern. I was almost overwhelmed with the drama of the trip, at the closeness of the water, our closeness to the *depths* — depths that were peopled with medusae and fish, worms and burrowing molluscs. We were out upon the sea! The heavy boat raced and bumped across the waves, pointing its nose towards the distant hills, its canvas sail taut and salt-stained. I clutched the side, bruised and wet, yet wanting to shout at the excitement of it all. But Sarah and Duncan succumbed to *mal de mer* amidst the ropes and tackle and empty dredge, the clouds became a solid grey mass and the wind showed no sign of abating — so we returned to Helensburgh before we even reached Kilcreggan.

Nor was it on the occasion when we were examining the catch brought back by two fishermen from Loch Long. They had thrown the flatfishes, which had been caught in the turbot net and were now dead and glassy-eyed, into boxes but, in expectation of reward and knowing of Duncan's interest in the creatures of the deep, had set aside the animals of other kinds which had been trapped in the net. Father and son, bearded, ruddy-faced and inscrutable, they stood and watched as we searched carefully through the bucket.

'What *is* that?'

Duncan rummaged amongst the scallops and the elongated coils of ribbon worms and then freed a startling creature.

'What a beauty! It's some sort of actinia — this is a very interesting find.' He picked up the rock to which it was attached, and then placed it gently in a collecting jar but, as he straightened up, his expression as alive with expectation as a hunter chasing his prey, he suddenly checked and lifted the jar and handed it to me.

'Miss Church is an expert,' he explained to the watching men. They did not appear especially impressed although the older man pursed his lips and nodded once.

'You take it,' Duncan said to me. 'You should draw it and make the descriptions.'

How I valued it! I set it in the small aquarium tank that Sarah had asked the maid to retrieve from amongst the discarded objects in the cellar, and I watched and watched the actinia. It changed its shape; sometimes it was constricted like an hourglass, sometimes it became a short thick pillar like a dice-box. I had seen nothing like it before and there was no description in any of the books that Duncan and I had obtained for our use. With my magnifying lens I watched as it discharged a multitude of globular ova, each the size of a mustard seed. I drew it and annotated the drawings, then mixed my water colours to catch the flaked carnation red of the column, the white tentacles with scarlet bands. The drawings I made were the best I have ever done (for I am not skilful — Duncan's sacrifice was all the greater because his drawings of animals are very accurate and fine).

No, I did not think of marrying Duncan then (even though I liked him and was very happy and comfortable in his company): my thoughts were only of Mr Gosse — and how I would send him my drawings and descriptions of this possibly hitherto unknown species. I would send it to him *with a letter*. My mind churned with my dreams and hopes: I would arrange to meet him in London to describe the species further; I would also show him my observations on the plumose anemone, *Actinoloba*, that I had found at low tide on the shore of the Clyde; I would discuss, knowledgeably, the other marine creatures on which my studies now filled several notebooks. Surely, *surely*, I would become his 'talented naturalist'? And even as my thoughts ran in this manner and I yearned for Mr Gosse's attention, I knew that I was doing Duncan Robertson a wrong.

Duncan was so attentive; and all the while a gentle mocking humour lay within him. His intentions towards me were soon obvious to the Nisbet family as well as to myself.

'But he is so *old*!' Sarah said. 'Shall you mind? And will your Papa agree?' And, being Sarah, she voiced aloud my own unspoken worry. 'Why is he still a bachelor, at his age? Perhaps there is something wrong, or unpleasant, that is as yet hidden from us. And,' she added wickedly, 'will not be revealed until the first night of your marriage! I shall ask Mama to speak to the Laird's wife.'

'No, Sarah, you will not! It would be most presumptuous. And what if he discovered that we had been spying behind his back?'

I was horrified: but *very* relieved when the report came back that Mr Robertson had been engaged to be married to a young lady of good family, who had professed herself unable to wait for him whilst he was working in America — and had accordingly broken off their engagement and married someone else.

'So he stayed in America for several more years. Who can *guess* how he occupied himself in that time?' Sarah stressed the words suggestively.

I knew I *would* marry him that day when we all — Mr and Mrs Nisbet, Sarah and Gordon, Mr Robertson, several other friends and myself — took the steep and hilly route from Helensburgh to Loch Lomond. The carriages were laden not only with their human cargo but also with provisions for a picnic and a day on the loch-side shore; the horses laboured and we walked frequently and, despite the steepness of the hills, still had breath remaining for conversation.

Mr Robertson had — no doubt to please me — managed to purchase or otherwise acquire several of Mr Gosse's books, and professed himself delighted with their easy and informative style. We had stopped to admire the gorge beneath us; despite the steepness of its walls, a rowan and two silvery-barked birches, as stunted and twisted as hobgoblins, had found footholds amongst the jagged rocks; their leaves dripped constantly from the accumulation of fine mist that the burn threw up as it tumbled between the mossy boulders. A sudden liquid stream of birdsong burst out from below: a small dark bird, with a white chest, bobbed up and down upon a stone and then flew off, barely skimming the surface of the water.

'A dipper!' Mr Robertson exclaimed. 'We were fortunate to hear it sing. Look! — there it goes, wading in the water.'

'Dipping.'

We watched the little bird, delighted with its behaviour.

Sarah and Gordon, who had been lagging behind around the corner, caught up with us; they were both a little flushed, but perhaps not from the walk.

'What are you discussing so eagerly?'

'The good Mr Gosse's works,' Mr Robertson replied, without a moment's hesitation (like me, he must have felt that the dipper was *our* secret). 'And I think I agree wholeheartedly with you, Miss Nisbet, that Gosse is occasionally somewhat exhortatory in tone. However I suppose that these men of God who are also naturalists must be allowed to set forth their wares in equal measure. Would you agree, Miss Church?'

I was taken unawares: I sensed at once that this question was perhaps a test to see where I stood, and I wished he had not asked it so publicly and that I were not so confused about such matters. It is not in my nature — I am not like Mr Gosse! — to extol openly the benificence of our Lord and offer prayers of thanks for His wonders. Even the mildest evangelical approach makes me uncomfortable. I wish Mr Gosse were not so outspoken because surely these are matters between oneself and the Lord, private beliefs not necessarily to be displayed. (But perhaps Mrs Gosse has encouraged this aspect of his character?) My own opinion was much closer to Mr Robertson's than he realised, but what could I say? My answering question must have hinted at my own lack of steadfastness.

'Perhaps one "measure" nibbles at the edge of the other, so that the overall result has less than double the effect?'

I felt a traitor to Philip Henry Gosse.

'Goodness, this is far too serious for us! Come, Gordon, we shall leave them to their theological debate.' Sarah pulled her fiancé's arm and they set off up the hill.

Mr Robertson gazed at me a moment and I endeavoured to hold his stare; then a delighted smile lit up his face and he nodded a few times.

'Yes indeed. There is a *diminishing* effect ....'

We walked on in silence for a little while and I had the curious feeling that the narrow space between us prickled with a force that attempted to draw us into closer contact.

On the shore of Loch Lomond, where the pebbles were pale and fine, rugs were laid out and the hampers unpacked. Champagne corks popped, and little brown-flecked birds started up from the water's edge in alarm. Tiny waves hissed softly and repetitively, and the light wind that caused the birch leaves to flicker also kept the biting midges at bay. Mr Armstrong showed us how to skim stones along the water's surface so as to make them bounce, while a floating branch made target-practice for the gentlemen. The island of Inchmurran and the other smaller islets were lent added enchantment by their inaccessibility.

'I wish we had a skiff so that we might reach the islands — I think you would not be seasick here.' I was walking slowly with Mr Robertson along the narrow shore. 'I would like to learn to row, and then I would be always out upon the water.'

'I think you would be in — or perhaps *on* is more appropriate — your element,' Mr Robertson agreed. 'But I shall not be conquered by the waves. How can I allow myself to be? Miss Church — may I call you Anne, at least when we are privately together like this? The formality is so tedious.'

I nodded, without looking at him and he glanced around quickly and, seeing that we were unobserved, took my hand and held it for a moment. I did not draw it away.

'Anne — I shall never advance far in this shipping business. I am good at what I do but my heart is not in it. I want to travel across the seas and search out plants and animals that have not been seen before. I want to explore, and describe, and perhaps have a species named after me, something-Robertsonii.'

His grip on my hand was tightening as the intensity of what he was saying increased. I nodded, because my throat felt constricted.

'I want to do what Mr Alfred Wallace has done, travel up the Amazon. And Gosse — have you read his book about Jamaica? I will copy it out for you, his description of his "workroom" in the jungle. There is so much to do, Anne. There is so much that is unknown — *how* can I allow myself to be beaten by the fact that we live on a small island surrounded by the sea?'

'You must not.'

I freed my hand, bewildered. When he first took my hand my skin had felt alive with anticipation, I was waiting, trembling inside; but now my throat was so tight that I could hardly speak. Yet speak out I *must*.

'Why ... why do you pay me so much attention ... Duncan? Why do you act as though —? I am sorry, I am much younger than you and inexperienced — but why do you lead me to believe that you have an interest in me, and then tell me that the future you most wish for is to go far away?'

He put his hand to his forehead, and then rubbed his face, hard, so that the flesh on his cheeks was furrowed and dented.

'I am so sorry,' he said, simply. 'I have made a fool of myself and I have not yet made my meaning clear. Anne, my dear, dear Anne, I dream of us, the *two* of us, having our own "workroom in the jungle" — or on a foreign shore or river-bank. I want to be a naturalist and so do you. I have watched you, dearest, I love your enthusiasm, and your dedication. We would make a partnership, we would work together. We could be together *as husband and wife* ... if you so wish. But you must think it over.' He turned away, suddenly agitated. 'There are many, many implications. Oh, I have been so inept! Forgive me.'

We remained like that, silent and apart for several minutes. I was too much taken by surprise to be able to make an answer. Marriage, yes: Mrs Duncan Robertson. I had thought about that, although I had not yet formed a definite response in my mind. But marriage founded on partnership and foreign adventure? That was too sudden and surely, to my mind, impossible? It did not seem possible that a woman could do what Duncan had described. But why should I not? (Did I have sufficient courage? Could I bear to leave the relative safety of these shores?) And what should we do about children — surely Duncan would want sons and daughters? (But did *I*?) I had been uncertain until now whether I would marry him, and now he had confused me with this further great decision.

The water made soft poppling sounds in the breeze and I looked at Duncan's sturdy figure, the back of his rather square head, as he stood staring up the loch towards the great mass of the mountain. He seemed so solid, so *safe*. Did he love me? I could not tell; but whatever happened he would take care of me, of that I was certain. For a moment I felt like a child again, wanting the comfort of a parental embrace. And then I knew that I would accept his proposal: I would cherish him and tend him on the sea, and he would cherish me on land.

'Duncan.' My shoes crunched on the pebbly sand. 'I am afraid you will have to come all the way to Winchester to ask my Papa.'

He turned around slowly, and then reached out to touch my face. 'Winchester is so much closer than New South Wales.'

He was about to take me in his arms when we heard Sarah calling, and we moved apart. But when next we were alone he held me and kissed me — and I began to feel something of what Sarah had described.

In late September, after many letters had passed between Glasgow and Winchester, our tones of endearment and intimacy increasing with each communication, Duncan came to our house to meet my parents and ask Papa's permission for our marriage. Having observed my happiness (and no doubt all too conscious of my age and status as the eldest daughter) both Papa and Mama were both delighted to agree, and our marriage was set for the following Spring.

Three weeks later I received a letter from Miss Shipton informing me that Mrs Gosse was ill, and living away from home, in Pimlico. Perhaps I would wish to come to London, Miss Shipton suggested, and we could go together to visit Mrs Gosse and her little son?

That night I awoke from a dream in which I was being fitted, over and over again, for a wedding gown: and the shocking thought came to me that, in agreeing to marry Duncan, my decision had been premature and that I had made a grave mistake.

CHAPTER 14: ELIZABETH

Chopin was younger than Jim Steinberg when he composed the *Études*! The pianist's hands were surging up and down the keyboard: the lyrical melody seemed to be floating in a mist of spray above the waves.

It was the early afternoon: a time for contemplation — except that it's impossible to use Chopin as musical wallpaper because the ear and inner eye over-rule the thinking brain, determined to follow the intricacies of the patterns and polyrhythms. His patterns are not merely aural: there is also a visual elegance, waves of black notes surging across a page, delicately ornamented notes embroidered around a trelliswork; the complexities are intriguing and demanding of attention.

So I concentrated on listening to the music, but I knew that I was fooling myself because I was also listening out for Barbara's grandson. I didn't expect to meet Matthew Myers: he and Jim would go about their business, in the way young men do, and would leave the 'old woman' in peace (thereby avoiding any danger of interrogation — I could easily imagine the stand-at-ease posture, so awkwardly polite). I didn't need to meet Matthew, I didn't want to meet him, but I would be extremely interested to observe him from the window.

The B minor sonata was now playing, and I tried to distinguish its partly-hidden homage to Bach but now I could hear that Matthew had arrived. The voices were in the kitchen, but soon they were in the downstairs hall, the young men were coming upstairs, Jim was knocking at my half-open study door — and Barbara's grandson was here, inside my room, with jeans, bushy hair, nose-ring and all. And tall, as they all are these days, brought up on healthy diets and plenty of exercise. He held out his hand and was slightly awkward and ungracious, and I could see that he was not like Barbara at all.

As I stared at him, he pulled a brown envelope out of his back pocket. He handed it to me; it was warm and slightly curved. It was from his mother, he said: to 'Dr Elizabeth Wilson'. I was quite unable to open the threatening envelope, and I placed it on the desk, trying to avoid it. Matthew was waiting: the contents were something to do with the naturalist, Gosse, he said. Matthew remained in the room, I read the spidery handwriting. Matthew peered and touched, and cleared his throat, and Jim lounged by the door, a caricature of one of the subsets of American youth.

The article was an extract from one of Gosse's books, a delightful description of his 'field-station', and I thanked Matthew for bringing it to my attention. We talked briefly and he surprised me with his percipient comment about my drawing of Allan, but then I remembered that Jim had told me that he was an art student of some sort. His appearance certainly conformed to one of the current student 'types', and his initial gawkiness diminished as his confidence increased. He was a few years younger than Jim, but they seemed to have struck up a friendship. I was pleased for my American lad, who must surely find this Nancarrow backwater all too quiet — but I was very disturbed about the implications of Matthew's visit on my own peace of mind.

More shocking, though, was Hazel Myers' gift. Why had she sent it? I assumed she had learnt about my fieldwork through conversations with Roger Trenton; Hazel's hayfever and her visit had initiated seemingly endless comment and discussion between my visiting scientists. But I was the only one who would speculate, privately, whether her visit had really been unpremeditated and coincidental. Did she have an ulterior motive in sending the Gosse extract? Those were questions I could only ask myself, and she was the only person who could provide the answers. We were barely acquainted with each other; we had met only once, at the hanging of the summer exhibition four years ago. I remembered quite exactly how she and Barbara had helped to carry Allan's wheelchair down those difficult steps. Hazel had hardly spoken, but Allan had later remarked in private that Barbara had been wrong to say that her daughter had a placid disposition.

Adhering to the photocopy was a yellow 'Post-it' on which Hazel had written, 'Thank you for the Disprin (given in your absence). I thought this might interest you. Best wishes, Hazel Myers.'

After a while I realised that the Chopin had ended, quite unheard, yet I had been subconsciously aware that the lads had left the house. From the window I could see that they were now strolling along the sea wall towards the dinghy. I changed the disc for Bach's *Musical Offering* because I needed the intellectual challenge of its precise logic. 'Old Bach'. Chopin plays games on the page, Bach plays games with one's mind and ears, *trompe l'oreille*.

But yet again the music began to slide past, heard but not analysed, as I re-read the Gosse piece and admired his own logical progression around his laboratory, his exactness.

'Let me describe a working naturalist's laboratory. Suppose the time to be 2pm, after a morning's excursion to the mountain. In the room are 3 large tables, one of them against the window, at which a Negro youth is sitting. Before him lie half a dozen <u>birds</u>, one of which he is skinning; beside him lie scissors, knives, nippers, forceps, a pepper-box of pounded chalk, a jar of arsenical soap, needles and thread, cotton-wool, and other apparatus, with several cones of paper ready to drop each skin into, when finished. Across the room are strung lines in various directions, from which are suspended some hundreds of similar paper cones, each tenanted by a bird-skin; they are thus placed in order that they may dry out of the reach of rats, which nevertheless sometimes manage ingeniously to scramble along the slender lines and gnaw the feet and wing-tips of the specimens.

On another table is a large bowl half full of water, in which are thrown the <u>land shells</u> collected in the morning. The animals in the dry season withdraw themselves into the recesses of their shells, covered either with their operculum, or, - if this be wanting, as is the case with the numerous Tribe of snails, - with an epiphragma of hardened mucus that serves the same purpose. They are thus difficult to extract; but a few hours' immersion in cold water stimulates them to action, and they crawl about freely. A boy sits at this table with another vessel containing boiling water; into this have been put the shells collected on the previous day, after having been all night in the cold water. The hot water kills them immediately, and the lad takes out each in succession, extracts the animal with a needle of suitable size, and separates the operculum if there be one. He then takes a soft toothbrush, and well cleanses the shell from earth, mucus, and all other defilements, rinses it in a basin of clear water, and lays it on a cloth to drain, with its operculum in it. When thoroughly dry, each shell is wrapped in soft paper separately, (the operculum having been confined in its cavity by a bit of cotton wool,) and carefully packed with others in boxes.

In one corner of the floor a third youth is engaged in laying out the <u>botanical specimens</u> brought in... The new plants are taken from the large portfolio in which they were placed when gathered, and added to those in the press; while such specimens as are sufficiently dried are successively removed to the store-box.

Perchance the curious visitor might see the naturalist himself busy with his <u>insect-spoils</u>; immersing the beetles in boiling water, subjecting the Lepidoptera to the vapour of prussic acid, pinning them in the setting-boxes, and fastening down the wings of the butterflies with little braces of card-paper. Or he might be recording the facts observed in the morning's tour, before their freshness had faded from the memory; or taking sketches of forms and colours that death would destroy; or occasionally glancing a master's eye over the operations of the subordinates.

But other than human tenants occupy this room. The visitor would see hanging against the wall a long low cage containing a dozen or so of the native <u>Columbadae,</u> among which the noble Baldpate and gentle Peadove are conspicuous. Another large cage is inhabited by the more gaily coloured fruit-eating birds ... and in a gauze-fronted box on one of the tables are half a score of Lizards of different species.

Beautiful Orchideous plants growing on clumps of wood are hanging from pegs in the wall, some throwing out their fantastic spikes of blossoms, others in a state of rest. On the trunks of the trees around the dwelling house are placed specimens of some twenty or thirty species of epiphyte Orchidaea, fastened in various ways, partly that I may enjoy the beauty of a race which has always been a favourite of mine, and partly for a more practical purpose, that of identifying them. The watching of the daily development of the plants, and the pleasant suspense and expectation of what the flower may turn out to be, are enjoyments that will be readily appreciated by every one who has ever cultivated a flower-garden.'

So clearly — 150 years later — could I picture how he had been engaged that I had a strong urge to re-experience for myself the excitement that he would have felt. Almost nothing that he collected had ever before been described, and so was full of promise. I, too, had known that excitement, in Ethiopia; so much of the snail fauna had still been unknown to science, despite the work of early pioneers like Blanford and Jickeli. There are only a few people in the world who have had that, the privilege of first description: until a species has been described, it is unknown.

A species, an *object,* is unknown until humans are made aware of it. If an object impinges on my awareness, it becomes known to me — and through me, to others. It is as though I had created it. For a few moments I am God!

Except that I don't accept the existence of God or gods. But, for Gosse, every new species was testament to the creative skill of the Lord, for did not God create even Adam's omphalos?

The copyist had noted that the extract came from *A Naturalist's Sojourn in Jamaica*, published in 1851, so Gosse himself had probably been in Jamaica in the 1840s. Without looking it up, I didn't know when Gosse was born, but he was certainly Darwin's contemporary. Indeed, I well remembered coming across their respective obituaries in the *Proceedings of the Royal Society* for 1889, in which I had been consulting a paper on cuttlefish. Darwin's detailed obituary took up about 25 pages, but the plaudits for poor discredited Gosse merited slightly less than two! So it was entirely plausible that he was a young man when he had sojourned in Jamaica. Expeditions were being mounted to seek the North-West Passage and to find the source of great African rivers like the Niger, and young Gosse too was setting out on an expedition by sea and land: travelling across the Atlantic, and then down the American coast, under sail, not knowing what he would find; aware that he would be, in essence, exiled in a strange land for many months with the aim of collecting, recording, preserving and classifying — 'stamp collecting', to use Rutherford's pejorative term. Perhaps there was a small amount of truth in that, the philately, but Gosse had been a true naturalist, he had been an observer, of behaviour and the development of the living things that he found.

A few years ago, shortly after Allan died, I was the subject of a radio programme, one of several in which senior scientists were interviewed about their work and beliefs. Needless to say, amongst the twelve people interviewed, I was the only woman. My interviewer, himself a scientist and latterly a 'media guru', asked me why there had been so few female field-workers, women who were prepared to go out into rainforests or deserts or uncharted back-country, to establish camp and search for new species. It was an interesting, if obvious, question, and naturally was one which I myself had often debated. During the course of my argument we had an enjoyable bout of sparring for he was, and still is, a staunch adherent of the reductionist dogma, believing that our understanding of biology, of life itself, will only advance through the reduction of every process to its simplest molecular level, to investigation at the level of the gene.

But he was a clever interviewer, he didn't interrupt to take up the holistic gauntlet that I threw down; he smiled and nodded soundlessly as I was speaking, and I knew he was thinking that this would come across well and wouldn't require much editing. There were only a couple of minutes left, and he was going to round off the interview, and bring it to a neat conclusion. I had already begun to relax and was sitting back from the microphone when he dropped in another question, in a quiet and conversational tone, immediately bringing the interview onto a different and more personal level. My long pause was, of course, edited out, but when I listened to the recording afterwards, the change in my voice was very obvious: no-one had ever asked me before what it was like to be alone in the field, or about my childhood. The producer retained those answers, and cleverly edited the beginning of the interview so that it fitted into the allotted slot.

Now, as I thought back to that interview through a train of thought that had arisen from Hazel Myers' gift of the Gosse extract, I suddenly wished — no, wish is not strong enough — I *desired*, strongly and hopelessly, that I could discuss it with Barbara. I wanted to explain to her why I had needed to be 'out there', in the field: that I needed to be continually reminded of the things that are good and important in this world of ours, the beauty and elegance of the complexity of nature. A romantic idea, perhaps, but one that she would have understood. Yet she would also have told me that it was human relationships that were important, that they were real, complex, 'of the here-and-now.'

But if I had explained the scientist's passionate need for enquiry, the almost sexual excitement of chasing that elusive insight that is nearly within grasp, and which, suddenly, astonishingly, you finally hold — would she have understood? Probably not.

Why did she and I never discuss this? For art and science are both creative acts. The artist and the scientist both express themselves in their creations, whether it be a painting or a neat hypothesis or well-devised experiment. We both communicate and speak to others, through our different media. Even da Vinci understood that: 'Truly painting is a science, the true-born child of nature. Whatever exists in the universe, the painter has first in his mind and then in his hand.' Thus with a scientist, although first in the hand then in the mind.

If I'm honest with myself, though, I know exactly why I did not discuss this with Barbara: because of the fear that she would have laughed. She would have deprecated my need for analysis, not because her own ideas were facile, but because they only found expression on her canvases or remained shut away inside her head.

'That's just the way things are,' she would have said.

It's an interesting anomaly that she could be open about her feelings yet jealously secret of the rationale behind her work, while for me, paradoxically, it is the complete opposite. Even in our intimacy, we closed off certain compartments from each other. We found each other too late in our lives, when it was too late to change our habits of thought.

Someone once asked me if I would write my autobiography because, he said, tritely, I had 'been to so many places, done so many unusual things, and produced so many stimulating ideas.' Yet what a wonderful obituary those words would make! My immediate reaction was to say 'no' and later, having had more time to analyse my reasons, I knew that was the correct response: my ideas, and the events, places and reasoning that led to them, are well-documented in my research papers and reviews — and it is those ideas that I wish to be remembered by, not the edited details of my personal life.

But while I was reading Gosse's description of his workroom, an urge grew in me to write something similar. I wished I had written it for Barbara. It would have been pointless to write for Allan since, of course, he had seen my workrooms; and I would not write anything for Barbara's daughter.

As for the grandson, I could see from the window that he and Jim appeared to be playing pirates or shipwrecks in our poor old dinghy, unaware that Peter Pascoe, like a rheumatic panther, was prowling towards them along the wall. Peter walked carefully, like Frederick's theme through the six-voiced Ricercar: but he walked in a unenigmatic straight line, without the inversions and superpositions that Bach required. Peter Pascoe as acrobat was an intriguing idea, and I was still smiling when the young men climbed out of the dinghy and walked away down the shore.

' *"The malacologist's workrooms in Ethiopia."* '

Unlike Gosse, I had more than one: there was my tent and also a small amount of space on a bench in the Institute of Pathobiology at Addis Ababa. Sometimes there were hotel rooms and once, for three wonderful weeks, a room of my own in the Anderssons' house in Asmara.

' *"The malacologist's work-tent."* '

'Suppose the time to be mid-afternoon after a morning's excursion to the highlands. The work-tent is of mould-spotted, khaki canvas with a separate groundsheet, and in it is a folded sleeping-bag, upon which the naturalist is sitting. Before her lie several plastic bags and small glass Universal bottles containing live snails; beside her are forceps and Petri dishes, and a wooden box that contains spare dishes, Universals, stoppered bottles of alcohol and menthol and Carnoy fixative for preserving tissues, callipers and a rule, boxes of glass slides and coverslips, pencils, erasers, and paper labels that are adhering to each other in the damp. Several of these supplies are also in a canvas satchel that lies open on the ground. A front-opening wooden box, at present locked but with its key dangling from the handle on a piece of string, contains a black metal microscope.'

There is also, of course, my bag with a few clothes and personal possessions. If Musa, the Somali driver, and I have planned our excursion well, we have previously stopped at one of the cafés or petrol stations run by Italians, where we have feasted on pasta; but if we have been unable to adjust our plans in order to be at the right place at the right time, we will soon have to inspect the contents of the locked wooden box that is kept in the Land Rover, to decide which is the least unpleasant of the options of processed cheese, Spam, tinned beans or — our favourite! — canned meatballs. But at present, since it is late afternoon, the rain pours down and there is no possibility of brewing our usual strong, sweet tea.

Consequently, Musa dozes in the vehicle and 'the malacologist is busy with her *snail-spoils*.' But, unlike Philip Gosse's assistant, she does not place the snails in boiling water because she wishes instead to keep their bodies intact and in a relaxed, not cooked and contracted, state.

'Some of the specimens are placed in menthol solution to relax and narcotise them overnight: in the morning, she will wash them and immerse them in fixative in small, carefully-labelled bottles, so that the tissues will be preserved. But this is a precaution, for the malacologist intends to keep the main proportion of her specimens alive.'

So much of the sorting and examination of the specimens had to be done when I returned from the collecting expedition, usually at a weekend. It was often exhausting, a race against time. We would drive back to Addis on the Friday, our clothes, equipment and the vehicle dusted red with laterite: if we were unlucky — and this was often — we would puncture a tyre, and then a crowd of children would appear from apparently nowhere, bringing with them clouds of flies, to watch as Musa and I struggled with the wheel.

The air around Addis was filled with a haze of smoke that smelt of burning eucalyptus and charcoal, from a thousand cooking fires, but for me there was no time to eat, for I must busy myself in spreading out the tent, with its own sharp fungal smell, to dry; in sorting the snails, returning some to water in the aquaria in the lean-to shed at the back of the Institute, setting some specimens aside for measurements and drawings, some for tissue squashes to count the chromosomes and check for parasite infestation. If I managed to finish early there might still be time to socialise with the other Europeans and Americans who were working at the university; but not for long, because I'd need to get up early on the Saturday to take the live snails to the airport's Post Office, so that they could be flown to London on the next plane: 'snail sandwiches', live snails held tightly between layers of damp, squeezed-out cotton wool, in plastic boxes. Back at the Museum the survivors would be cared for until they could be used for further analysis and identification work.

Gosse wrote about botanical specimens: there were plants in my workroom too. Mary Johnston, the American botanist, now returned to mind with unwelcome clarity. She was about five years my senior and had appointed herself as my guide, using her intention of botanizing in the highlands as an excuse to accompany me on the early expeditions. It made for awkward travelling in the Land Rover, the two of us in intimate contact next to Musa on the front seat, and he clearly felt that driving two white women was undignified and implied a loss of status. It was also unfortunate that, despite Musa's obvious experience and knowledge of the countryside, Mary was a nervous passenger and repeatedly warned him about pot-holes and ditches, admonishing him to be vigilant for the *shiftas*, who reputedly hid beneath bridges, like horseless highwaymen, ready to prey upon unwary travellers.

(Allan, who never once saw a *shifta* during his five years in that part of Africa, explained to me that they were not local thieves at all, but were disappointed Norwegian trolls, who continued to lie in wait for the characteristic 'trip-trap, trip-trap' of the hooves of the Billygoats Gruff. Or perhaps for Swedish missionaries.)

I eventually found Mary to be a tiresome and demanding companion; but it had been a comfort to have her with me at the start. I had thought our liaison had been born out of loneliness, but with time I recognised that her percipience and experience had been the initiators.

Ethiopia. Thinking about Ethiopia makes Nancarrow stifling and too cosy. I miss the space and emptiness of the highlands: the flat plateau stretching endlessly into the distance with the wind hissing in the yellow grass; the heather and juniper and lobelia trees; the abrupt plunges of the gorges and scarps; the striped and weathered rock pillars and needles that rose shockingly vertical from the flatness. I miss the strangeness and thrill of cold nights in the highlands, when I curled tightly in my sleeping-bag and listened to calls of unknown birds outside the tent; the hyenas' distant, eerie whooping that would set Musa, rolled in his old army greatcoat in the Land Rover, to muttering and groaning.

Mary hated the nocturnal sounds. In the highlands imagined lions or marauding baboons, in the lowland valleys imagined marauding tribesmen bent on rape and robbery. She wanted to be my teacher and protectress, but I soon became the protector — and discovered that it was not a role I wished to play. I persuaded her to remain in Addis, that she had enough botanical data to keep her busy at the university for several weeks, and thus Musa and I settled down to a workable relationship, enhanced by growing mutual respect. He soon became an enthusiastic snail collector himself — as long as there was no chance of being seen by anyone other than myself. On the southern Rift Valley lakes and along the more populous stretches of the Lower Awash, he preferred to retreat to the Land Rover, where he would lounge in the driver's seat, occasionally deigning to speak to the small groups of men and children who came to stare.

As for me, I learned to look cold and intimidating when the need arose, and gradually I lost the fear that my personal safety might be endangered by the hands of other humans. My greatest worry was that illness and careless accidents would incapacitate me and use up valuable time. On one occasion I frightened myself and, I think, Musa, and if it had not been for his proximity and quick reflexes, my precious specimen-bag would have tumbled into a ravine.

The adventure occurred by a rock-pool at the side of a torrential stream in the highlands. A few yards away, the stream poured over a lip of rock, flinging itself down a series of cataracts, down into the impenetrable and thickly-vegetated ravine below. Amongst the vegetation in that pool was the small flat spiral shell of *Armiger crista*, more usually found in European marshes. Another snail, similar in appearance, but twice the size and with a smoother shell, was jerkily moving beneath the surface of the pool, hanging, held by surface tension — *Ceratophallus*, later identified as *natalensis* (a species in which one of Jim's former Oregon colleagues had subsequently found eleven species of parasite in Tanzania!). And then, on a rock, I found an unusual specimen, the little prosobranch *Valvata nilotica*. Extraordinary treasures, all in one small pool; a microcosm of paradise for a malacologist! My collecting bag was strapped around my waist, and I rummaged in it to find the forceps and a bottle in which to store the *Armiger*, but the stitching that held the strap suddenly parted and the bag and its already precious contents fell into the stream and was rapidly swept away, bumping and dragging against the rocks. I snatched at it, and fell, banging my ribs against a rock and grazing my knees and hands. But immediately Musa saw what was happening, he leapt across the slippery rocks to the extreme edge of the waterfall, seized the bag before it was flung down the falls and then, grinning broadly, he scrambled back and helped me to the bank. When I pointed out how close he, too, had been to the edge, he merely laughed and opened his clenched hand. Somehow he had managed to pluck a very fine specimen of another tiny, flat-spired species, *Segmentorbis angustus*, from a backwash by the waterfall's edge!

I had wanted to travel much further North, to reach Eritrea, but on that first expedition, when I was still learning about the country and its possibilities, there was no spare time. The journey to Asmara would take several days, and I needed to find out more about the terrain. Not only was I eager to carry out fieldwork in that northern province, but I also wanted to explore as much of the country as possible; and not only the countryside, either, for I was eager to see the rock-hewn churches of Lalibela and the falls of the Blue Nile at Tis Isat. Hearing of my future plans, one of the Americans at the Institute introduced me to the Lundbergs, missionaries sent by the Swedish Evangelical Church and based in Addis Ababa.

The Lundbergs had already lived in the country for some time, moving between different missionary outposts. I was excited to find that they had met the students of the Cambridge University expedition of the late 1950s — the unusual specimens collected by that expedition were part of the reason that I was here. Some of the Swedes' compatriots were also to be found in Eritrea, not only in the lowland area around Cunama, but also in the capital, Asmara. The Lundbergs were certain that I would be welcome, and gave me names and addresses as contacts.

Thus it came about that on my second collecting expedition — again with Musa and with the now ageing Land Rover — I moved firstly to the wide Rift Valley East of Addis, to collect snails along the hot and sticky Awash valley, and then we headed back up into the hills and North to Asmara. It was a tough, difficult drive on unpaved roads, physically-demanding as well as uncertain in terms of our own safety. Our route took us through small towns (where men sat almost motionless in the bars, in front of small cups of coffee or tea, and the women sat behind piles of bright fruits and spices in the market place; a common enough sight now in travel brochures or on television, but for me, in those days, something new to be noted and marvelled at) and forests (that even then were being cut down) and mountains. We stayed at small and basic hotels, where we were offered pasta, or oily-red, chili-laced *wat* to be mopped up by *injira* bread, and we stopped for an extra day at Lake Tana from which the Blue Nile arises. I would have liked to have had time to be a tourist; to linger in the ancient capital of Gonder, exploring the ruined castles rather than visiting the Health Centre, and I would have liked to draw the huge carved granite stelae at Aksum. But there was work to do and not much time, and so we drove on to reach the faded Italianate beauty of Asmara, where the Anderssons warmly welcomed us.

I used their fine red-brick house as my base throughout that period and I revelled in their modern bathroom, and the good food that came from their modern kitchen (no Spam, no grey sheets of *injira*). Their two small blond sons, who had been pushed together into one bedroom to allow me a room to myself, would come home from school or from their games of football with the native Eritrean children, and would stand silently in my room, watching as I unpacked my daily collection of bottles and boxes and Petri dishes.

And it was there, in the warm Asmaran night, as I lay sleepless on a real mattress, listening to the roaming packs of dogs and the occasional donkey, that I began to understand where my intellectual curiosity might take me.

Gosse, Lyell with his rocks, Darwin and Wallace — they had all minutely observed and described, categorised and classified. Their enthusiasm for that essential primary task of collecting, identifying and placing organisms and inorganic objects in 'the scheme of things', flows out from their writings. The three biologists all struggled to understand the natural history of organisms, but only Darwin and Wallace were beginning to understand that the inter-relationships and adaptations had been tested by the natural laboratory of time. They moved on from observation to theory and hypothesis, but that was a path down which Gosse could not, dared not, follow. I knew nothing of Gosse on my trip to Asmara, and had no more than glanced at the Victorian prose of Darwin's *Origin;* but I could already see how I personally could move on and as I lay awake, thinking and planning, the excitement began to grow inside me.

Linnea Andersson was a midwife, and her husband, Olle, taught at the local school in addition to leading religious services in the local and surrounding churches. It was 1962, and the Eritreans were no longer willing to have their affairs organised and dominated by Haile Selassie's Ethiopian government, so our talk at meal-times was of rumours of small-scale uprisings and attacks on police stations and military installations North of the city, as well as of the more pressing local concerns of health and food. Olle's assistant at the school was Allan Galbraith, a somewhat gaunt young engineer in his mid-twenties, perhaps two or three years younger than myself. He was a Scot with a quiet, dry sense of humour, who seemed content to sit and listen, and occasionally to raise an ironic eyebrow at the independent-minded English biologist. Allan was recovering from a debilitating attack of malaria, and was pale and clearly weak, but he professed an interest in accompanying me on a three-day trip during my second week. He proved a knowledgeable companion, for he knew much of that north-west area well, not only through assisting Olle with administrative and educational work in some of the villages, but because he had spent several months in villages near the Sudanese border. Musa, who did not know Eritrea, nevertheless liked to pretend that he was an expert, and I was impressed at Allan's tact in persuading him to take the correct tracks or find a more suitable campsite or hotel. Allan was responsible for educating me about the peoples of Ethiopia and Eritrea; he encouraged me to look away from the ground (as did Barbara much later and in a different manner) and try to understand the habits and interactions of the human species around me. His discernment and the acuity of his vision surprised and perhaps even humbled me, for he seemed to understand the local peoples in a way few Westerners do.

North-West of Asmara, in a rocky stream near Mekerka, I found the tetraploid *Bulinus* that have four sets instead of two of the normal chromosomes, but although we know it is a potential host for *Schistosoma haematobium*, there was no urinary schistosomiasis there, only the gut form, *S. mansoni*, and its snail host, the flat-whorled *Biomphalaria pfeifferi*. But earlier, in the Awash valley, I had found another *haematobium* host, *Bulinus abyssinicus*, and had been delighted to be reminded of the ancient name, that was redolent of rich princes and Prester John. (When I spoke to Allan Galbraith about the name, he told me of a Scottish farm that lay at the bottom of a fine, bleak, glacial valley to the North of Loch Long and whose name, Abyssinia, had long puzzled him: until he read that the great eighteenth-century explorer, James 'the Abyssinian' Bruce, had been born and had died — 'of a fall downstairs' — at Kinnaird, nearby.)

I made more trips to Africa, to Tanganyika and Rhodesia, before politics and tensions made visits impossible. I went back to Ethiopia for a final expedition and spent some time at the university at Addis Ababa. Mary Johnston was still there, but by then Allan Galbraith was in Addis, too, and he and I were both happy to enlarge upon our acquaintance.

At the end of the Gosse extract there is a passage that Allan (and Peter Pascoe) would have liked: 'The watching of the daily development of the plants ...' Another testimony to the Glory of the Lord, an aspect of Gosse of which Allan, in his Ethiopian days with the missionaries, would have approved.

CHAPTER 15: MATTHEW

Shit! I couldn't believe it was already after 10am! I clawed my way slowly out of bed and struggled around with my eyes still half-closed, looking for a clean tee-shirt in the clothes-heap on the floor. Hazel usually got up quite early and she'd surely have disturbed Jim.

Jim and I hadn't got back until after midnight (I'd helped wash up glasses and then we'd sat and chatted with the woman who runs The Anchor) and then of course we stayed up late, sitting and drinking a few beers that we'd brought back as carry-outs. Discussing our lives, the Universe and all that, and coming up with the answer 'forty-two', pretty much on cue, at about two in the morning.

We'd met Billy Martin. Or, rather, Jim had met Billy Martin — and neither of us had plans to meet him again. We'd have to look for some other help with the dinghy.

Jim had been sitting at the bar, idly chatting to me (when I wasn't too busy serving) and other people. We both occasionally asked around to see if anyone knew Billy Martin, and mostly they said 'nah' or looked round a bit and said he wasn't in yet. Then, at about ten o'clock or so, Jim asked some guy standing next to him and he said yeah, Martin was sitting on that table over there with his mates. Martin was a big, bearded bloke, you could tell he wasn't tall but he was beefy, muscle-y arms with tattoos; helped on the fish quay and mended boats and went gig-racing in his spare time, so Jim's informant said. Well, he looked pretty busy talking and Jim didn't want to go over; but eventually Martin came up to the bar to get more drinks.

Jim told me later that he'd spoken to Martin, kind of said where he was staying and that we'd been told that Martin might give us some advice about mending a boat. Martin had sort of stared at him, then taken his mates' beers back to the table and had come back to sit next to Jim at the bar. Jim introduced me as I was passing, but then I was sent off to the store to get more crisps and stuff, and by the time I got back, about ten minutes later, they'd both gone. 'Though Jim hadn't finished his beer.

Next thing I knew, Jim was coming back fast looking kind of fired up, sort of excited and shocked, both together, and hissing at me that I should come over.

He made me pretend to polish the bar and look busy and whispered, 'Shit, man, is there somewhere safe I can hide behind the bar? I went to the john and next thing I know, Billy Martin's followed me in and tried to proposition me. He was real persistent — but I don't fancy him at all, he's too mean. Watch out, he's coming back.'

I sure as hell hoped Martin wasn't going to come back to the bar, I didn't know what to do, this was a bit outside of my experience. But he just stared at Jim and me, and then went back to his friends. I wondered if they were all the same and would guess what he'd been up to, and if there'd be any lewd comments, but I managed not to look.

'How did you get out of it?' I whispered.

Jim sort of twitched and pulled a face. 'I said — sorry, Matt — I said I was already spoken for.'

It took a while for the implication to hit me, and without thinking I glanced across at Billy Martin just as he was looking our way. He didn't smile but he just raised his beer glass at me, and then carried on talking.

'Sorry,' Jim said again and he looked really young and worried.

'Hah!' I said. 'Great! There goes my street cred,' and I tried to grin. 'Oh well! That's cool — if it got you out of trouble.'

Someone called me from further down the bar, and when I got back to Jim a few minutes later he was looking puzzled.

'I have this idea that Peter Pascoe set me up,' he said. 'What beats me is how he knew.'

'Knew what?' Again I was being a bit slow on the uptake but then I got it; and of course it was something I'd wondered about all along. 'Oh. Are you?'

'Yeah, if you mean am I gay. And so now I guess you'd like me to piss off and walk back home — to Nancarrow.'

'You can't be serious! Of course I don't want you to do that, don't talk such crap.' Then the funniness of the situation got to me and I grinned.

'See those girls sitting along there? The two blondes in the little bum-freezer dresses? I'm putting all this effort into chatting them up, and then it's just my luck to pull a gay bloke! What's that going to do to my reputation with the women? But I'm joking, man. It's cool, no problem — just you sit tight. Martin and his mates are leaving, anyway.'

Jim didn't look round but, since I was the bar-man, I saluted the tattooed man as he left and he nodded, sourly I thought, and went on his way. I hoped he wouldn't jump us in some dark alley!

'I guess we're going to have different priorities for passengers if we ever get that boat mended.'

'If.'

'Uh-huh.'

We were both sprawled in the chairs, music on low with the bass turned down, talking quietly even though Hazel's bedroom door was closed. Jim was kind of relieved that we had things clear between us and that I wasn't frightened off, and he wanted to talk about homosexuality in a kind of general way. I let him ramble on for a while, he was really unwinding. I know quite a few gay men — and women — at college, some of the men outrageously camp, some quite dull and quiet. It wasn't a novelty, they weren't threatening, they were all just people. So what? Strange, listening to Jim made me feel quite old.

But Jim was rabbiting on about the so-called 'gay gene'.

'If you think about it, gays ought to be a biological dead-end. We're the "also-rans." '

'How do you mean?'

'The whole point of having two sexes is for them to get together and produce offspring, right? Gays can't produce kids — if they only have gay partners — and there's evidence that says their ability to reproduce is in any case lower. So if our behaviour is determined by a gene, why doesn't the gene die out? Sexual success is supposed to be at the core of evolutionary theory. Only the fittest survive.'

'Er — yeah. Tell me.' I lay back with my eyes closed, trying to co-ordinate the position of the open bottle with my open mouth.

'Have you noticed that women like gay men? Not the aggressive ones like Billy-the-Prick, but the prettier ones, who —'

'Are you a pretty one?' I opened one eye.

'Beautiful. I'm a Beautiful Person.' He leered; he was a bit pissed by now.

'You have a lovely smile. No — down, boy! Down!'

'As I was saying. Gay men who don't camp it up too much and aren't aggressive are good companions, they're attractive to women. Suppose the so-called gay gene provides these traits, then if it was expressed in an otherwise really virile man, he'd be charming, sensitive, warm, caring —'

'Sounds too good to be true!'

'Oh, so you would fancy him too?'

'You know I didn't mean that.'

'Call him a homosexually-enhanced male — he'd certainly be an attractive mate for a woman. And he'd have enough of an evolutionary advantage to keep that gay gene in the gene pool. There wouldn't need to be much of a selective advantage … Elizabeth would know. She knows about evolution.'

'Does it really matter?' I was getting bored. 'I thought all that business about gay genes had been shown to be garbage, anyway. Why worry? Just do it! Do you want another beer? Oh hell, I'll have to keep staggering down in the night for a wee if I drink much more.'

I did, too — bloody spiral stairs! I didn't wake Jim, he was snoring in a sleeping-bag on the sofa, but Hazel made some crack about the noise when I finally wandered down in the morning. She was sitting at her desk with the computer switched on, talking loudly to Jim who was in the back extension.

Jim was obviously in the toilet but the door was open, and he came out holding the small picture frame that normally hung above the loo. He'd taken a shower and he had a towel draped round his shoulders under his long wet hair.

'Hold it in front of the mirror in the bathroom,' Hazel said.

'Hi,' Jim said to me. 'You look a bit rough. You can come in here when I've solved the puzzle.'

'Thanks.' I yawned and went to fill the kettle. 'Anyone else want coffee?'

'So, what's all this about then? Okay guys, let's take a look.' Jim wiped the steam off the mirror, wiggled the picture-frame around close to it and slowly read out the printed words:

' "Look at walls splashed with a number of stains, or stones of various mixed colours. If you have to invent some scene, you can see there resemblances to a number of landscapes, adorned with mountains, rivers, rocks, trees, great plains, valleys and hills, in various ways. Also you can see various battles, and lively postures of strange figures, expressions on faces, costumes and an infinite number of things, which you can reduce to good integrated form. It should not be hard for you to stop sometimes and look into the stains of walls, or ashes of a fire, or clouds, or mud or like places, in which you may find really marvellous ideas. Leonardo da Vinci." That is really amazing. Leonardo was the artist who painted that doughy-faced Mona Lisa, right?'

'And a few other things besides. He was okay at science, too.' I shook my head in disgust. 'Ignorant bum!'

'Okay. Now tell me why it's printed backwards. That's interesting, by the way — how do you get to do this backwards?'

'My mother said something about photographing the typed page and inverting it — the negative, I suppose — and then copying it again,' Hazel said. 'But I'm not sure she really knew. Apparently someone gave it to her after they'd seen the walls, or something.'

'Mmm. It would be quicker to scan it in to the PC and then reverse it. Or print it onto acetate sheets for an overhead projector and copy the reversed sheet. But why *is* it reversed?'

Damn! I should have thought of all that myself.

'Da Vinci was left-handed, he wrote everything backwards because it was easier for him. Why are Americans all so ignorant?'

Knowing that I hid him from Hazel's view, Jim gave me the finger, and I pretended to shriek and waved my hands and ran backwards, saying 'No, no! Leave me alone!'

Hazel could now see that both of us were laughing, and she laughed too.

'What on earth is going on? You're like a couple of children! Matthew, find something for Jim's breakfast — I've got to finish these letters.'

My bladder was about to burst, so I made Jim wait outside the toilet, then we both looked at the drawings on the walls and on the inside of the door. The pine planks of the door had remained unpainted and the wallpaper had been that gruesome mess of blue, brown and yellow swirls and splotches ever since I could remember. Hazel said it had been here when Barbara bought the house and that by now it was a bit of our family history so she didn't like to change it. (Our *family* history. What the hell is that?)

'It was Barbara's idea,' I explained to Jim. 'She said it would sharpen our perceptions. The more you stare at the patterns in the wood-grain or on the wallpaper, the more objects you start to see. Whenever I came to stay I'd rush in here to see what had been added! She was very strict with me — you know what kids are like, they want to draw all over the place — and I was only allowed to draw one thing at the end of each holiday. That way, even if I could see lots of shapes, I had to decide which would be best.'

'And which would stand up to the scrutiny of history,' Hazel added from the other room.

Jim looked at the pencilled outlines of animals and faces, and mundane and exotic objects.

'It's like the walls are alive! Which are yours, then? It's a pity they aren't initialled, because when you get famous your biographer can show how your talent evolved. What's this? A girl, no, a mermaid, I guess, on a swing. How about this camel-like thing?'

'Could be.' I was doubtful. 'I can't remember now. The "metamorphosis game" grew out of this, too. At least, I think it did. One shape can develop into another one by looking at it a different way. But that was too difficult or too messy to draw so Barbara made us stick to words.'

'That's really cool. She sounds like she was really something, your grandmother.'

'Yeah. Hey, do you fancy a bacon sarnie? Hazel, is there any bacon?'

I fried up bacon and bread and the kitchen filled with smoke and Hazel grumbled. Jim had put on his tee-shirt but had left his hair loose so that it was still dripping on his shoulders, and he was staring out of the kitchen window, busy thinking about something — I'd noticed that before, that he suddenly gets all oblivious to what's going on around him.

'Scientists as a group have a higher proportion of left-handed people than the rest of the population,' he said. 'Does that mean that being sinistrally-oriented prediposes towards a scientific mind-set, or that science pulls in deviants? Didn't I read somewhere that Leonardo was gay? And he's left-handed *and* a scientist, you say!'

I stared at him. 'What are you going on about? This is all garbage.' I handed him a plate and a couple of greasy sandwiches. 'Here, eat that.'

'Yeah. I know. This looks disgusting! Is this the famous English breakfast? But it's fun to mess around and pretend there are correlations.'

'What's that famous example?' Hazel called from the other room. 'Something about umbrellas and heart-attacks in men.'

'Something to do with eating high-cholesterol sandwiches in the rain?'

Jim wandered through to her, chomping on his sandwich, and they both nattered and laughed as they thought of other daft examples..

'Hazel, can I borrow the car to run Jim back to Nancarrow?'

'Now? Well, I don't know, Matt, it's not very convenient. I'm trying to get these letters finished because I've got to go across to Bodmin to the office suppliers. I'm nearly out of paper for the printer.'

'Well, it's not raining or anything,' Jim said. 'I guess I can walk back over the cliffs, if you point me in the right direction. Left or right, can't be that hard.'

We had started debating the best way for Jim to get back when the phone rang. I grabbed for it and listened, then put my hand over the mouthpiece and said, 'It's Roger. He'll come and collect you.'

I gave him some instructions on how to find us.

'Yeah, that's great. Yeah, Hazel's here.' I raised an eyebrow at her. 'No, she's fine. Quite recovered, minus the red nose, back to her usual stunningly beautiful self. Yeah, right. See ya!'

I put down the receiver and grinned.

'Well, that solves the transport problem. He "finds he has to come over to Polkenna", and thought he'd kill two or three birds with one stone, or something like that. Wants to see the famous Shell House. Will collect Jim at the same time. Perhaps you're one of the birds, too, Hazel — you can't go rushing off to Bodmin now.'

'Matt! Don't be so silly! And why did you tell him to leave the car in the public car park and walk up the hill, instead of telling him about the back road? That was a bit unkind.'

I just grinned and shrugged. 'Must have forgotten. Bring your bacon buttie outside, Jim — we'll go and sit in the garden and leave Hazel in peace. She can give Rog the guided tour when he comes.'

Much later that morning, after Jim had left with Roger, and Hazel had gone off to do her shopping, I got out the coloured winkle-shells that Jim and I had picked up at Nancarrow. I pushed them around on a tray in my room, trying out different patterns, messing around with a few sketches. The idea hadn't come to me yet, but I knew it would, I recognised the kind of tingling feeling that told me that something would happen, a pattern would emerge. It was frustrating, but I also quite liked the anticipation.

My bum had gone to sleep from sitting on the floor and I got up to look out of the window. There was an old woman with a shopping bag plodding up the hill, but she didn't look nearly as out-of-breath as Roger had!

I could just see the estuary, half-full of water. On a roof lower down the hill, half-a-dozen gulls were fighting over something that looked sickeningly like a dead white rat but was probably a shredded burger-bun. For some reason I was thinking about Jim reading out the Leonardo thing, thinking about looking for pictures in stone walls, and then I suddenly had this brilliant idea that perhaps there was something hidden in the stones of the quay, by the ferry steps, that had caught Barbara's imagination. That would be why she'd done that out-of-character painting.

I was about to trot down the hill to look until I remembered that the tide would need to be right out. I'd have to wait.

So I went down after lunch — a couple of baked potatoes done in the microwave, better than nothing I suppose, and soup that Hazel had bought (feeling guilty, she said, didn't want to starve me) — and sure enough I could now get down the slimy steps and onto the slip to have a look. I looked this way and that, from the distance and close to, so that people must have thought I was the local idiot; but I couldn't see any obvious shape. I hadn't seen anything in the painting, either, so it was just a daft idea and I had wasted my time. Though not entirely, as I'd chatted to a good-looking German girl who wanted to know about the ferry. Ah well, *'c'est la vie'*, as they say somewhere-or-other that isn't Germany. But I did have an idea about those shells ...

CHAPTER 16: HAZEL

Roger Trenton was one of those drivers who travels in a time and space of his own, perhaps even in his own private dimension. Improbably, he succeeded in avoiding physical contact with other drivers who were quite clearly on the same road. He drove through country lanes, speed-limited urban developments and on dual carriageways at a steady 40 mph, and then relaxed into the middle lane of the motorway at a boring 65 mph. The little Fiat was noisy and bumpy, but he explained that he had left their larger car, the Vauxhall Estate, at home in Croydon, for his wife to ferry the kids and their friends. In any case, it was probably old and full of sweet-wrappers and tape-cassettes without their boxes. I wished now that I'd offered to drive in my car instead, but Matt had persuaded me to accept the offer of a lift; partly out of mischief, I was sure, but mainly because he wanted my car for himself.

I had already been planning to visit the publishing house in Oxford for which I freelanced, so this arrangement had seemed sensible. The latest manuscript that they had sent for copy-editing had proved to be a real problem, and was going to need considerable revision by the author, far beyond what I could be expected to do. The editor had phoned me beforehand to warn that it was 'a bit of a dog's breakfast', but I had already put in many hours, and had only succeeded in reducing it to a cat's-cradle of lines and comments. It was a technical text, on a physiological subject, but what with the non-matching references, the incorrect listings of obscure journals, and the bodged figure legends, it was clear that the editor and I needed a serious discussion about the manuscript's future. Or my rates of pay.

I had been pleased (I suppose at the author's expense, and that was probably unfair) to be able to use the manuscript as an excuse to get to Oxford, because I had wanted to visit the Bodleian library and see what they held of Gosse's books. I would stay with my brother Jamie and his family, and take a few days' holiday at the same time. I had told Matt that I was going away for a week or so and that he would have to look after himself. If he needed to go anywhere he would have to walk or take public transport.

'You'll manage,' I had said. 'After all, you've got a job, a friend, and somewhere to sleep. What more do you need?'

Matt had still been grumbling about being stuck in Polkenna when Roger had telephoned. Roger had visited the Shell House a couple of days previously, ostensibly to collect Jim and to look at the shells, and he had stayed and talked to me for a couple of hours. He was now 'phoning to ask if I would like to go to one of the moorland pubs the following evening, for a drink and a meal. He wanted some different scenery, he'd said; he wanted to see heather, and dilapidated mine workings. I wasn't all that keen, so I rapidly decided that I would have to leave for Oxford the next morning. Unfortunately the excuse had delighted him: he was himself intending to drive back to London in a couple of days' time, so if my business in Oxford could wait an extra 24 hours, he'd be happy to give me a lift. It wouldn't take him far out of his way, only an hour or so extra. Matt had been hovering in the room and must have caught the gist of the conversation, because he had waved his arms at me and started mouthing instructions.

'Could you hold on a minute, Roger?' I had asked. 'I think Matt's trying to tell me something important.'

I had switched the phone to 'mute', and raised an eyebrow at Matt.

'Okay, listen. You go — you get a lift with him. It'll save you the hassle, you know you hate motorway driving.'

'Do I?' I hadn't realised this was the case.

'Yeah, you're always grumbling about lorries and spray and stuff. It'll be great. You'll have company, no hassles, chauffeur-driven limo.' He had snorted with amusement. 'You can get him to wear a peaked cap. And if you wear trousers it won't matter if he puts his hand on your knee.'

'*Sshh*!' I had checked hastily to make sure the phone was muted. 'And of course, you get to keep my car. Quite so.'

'Quite. Then you can get the train back. You like that, too — it's a nice ride.'

'Well ... I don't know ...'

But there would probably be no harm in accepting Roger's offer, and Matt was right, it would be quite pleasant to have company on the drive. Unwanted hands I could deal with: if I wished.

'All *right*,' I had hissed at Matt, and he'd punched the air and shouted 'Yeah!' like a kid, so that I was laughing when I switched the phone back to 'Talk'.

'Roger? Yes, that's fine. It's very kind of you. But in that case I think I had better say no to the drink tomorrow. I need to get all this paperwork sorted out to take with me.'

The excuse had made no sense, but I had guessed rightly that Roger would not insist.

Roger Trenton is not exciting, but I suppose he is pleasant company. Excitement is not a necessary requisite during a drive on motorways in any case, but I worked hard at maintaining a relaxed state, pushing my seat back as far as it would go and letting my body sag into the tiny, uncomfortable space. We seemed to find enough to talk about to help the miles slip by, even though the wind rushing over the open skylight made talking a little strenuous. We'd talked about my job, and now we were talking about his. I thought about the difficulties of going straight into biochemistry from school, and I asked why he had chosen that route. Roger just shrugged, and rubbed his beard and moustache with one hand. The little car veered erratically.

'I suppose I must have been keen on that side of things at school — especially the names. It was rather like belonging to a secret society, being able to rattle off "glucose-6-phosphatase", "succinic dehydrogenase", "ribosyl transferase" ... Pull up your trouser leg at the same time and you could almost belong to the

Freemasons!'

His pleased grin made me laugh, too. He looked sideways at me again and reached up, seemingly to pat me on the head.

'Did you know your hair was blowing out through the roof?' he asked, and when I reached up to feel if this was true, our hands touched briefly. I pulled the skylight shut.

We drove past the sign that advertised the Cheddar Gorge, and for want of something to say, I mentioned it.

'Have you ever taken your family there? David and I took Matthew to the caverns when he was quite young, and we were really impressed with the shapes and colours of the stalactites. Though I do remember feeling slightly claustrophobic in one of the caves — there's one that's much smaller and narrower than the rest. Matt had to hold my hand — he was being very brave and looking after Mummy.'

(Matthew used to hold my hand and call me 'Mummy'! Once upon a time our lives had been like that, but it seemed that we had moved on. I had moved us on.)

Roger didn't answer my question immediately, and I felt that he was staring at me again. But eventually he replied, 'No, we haven't been to Cheddar. Paradoxical, isn't it, but we did visit some caverns much further afield, in Virginia. There was a conference in Washington a few years back, in the Fall, so I saved up and took the family. The children were in their early teens and Alison — my wife — kept them occupied for a couple of days while I was busy. Then I took a few days off, too, and the children and I went to places like the Space Museum while Alison went off to look at the art and sculpture. We touched the moon-rock.' He smiled. 'It sounds corny, doesn't it, but if you make yourself think about that little bit of rock — where it came from up there in the sky, how it ended up in a museum in DC — that's quite something. Quite amazing.'

It was almost unbelievable.

'Do people wish on it? No doubt it's supposed to have the power to change your future — being part of the Moon and all that.'

'Probably. The Japanese were all taking photos of each other touching it. But I suppose everyone will be going to the Moon in a few decades, quite a tourist route. Look at all these rich folks paying for a trip to the International Space Station ... Where was I?' He paused.

'Stalactites,' I reminded him. 'We were talking about caverns.'

'Well now — we hired a car and drove along the Ridgeway to see the Fall colours, which were just as spectacular as the hype leads you to expect. On the way back we stopped at Great Organ Caverns which, again as you would expect, are reputedly bigger and better than any other system of limestone caves. And I have to agree that they were extraordinary. There's a really naff thing there —' he snorted with laughter. 'They've set up hammers to strike the stalactites and play a tune, like an organ. In such bad taste — amplified music and lurid lights! I told Elizabeth about it once — the "well-tempered cavern", she called it. That was rather clever, wasn't it? But the scenery was amazing. You wouldn't imagine, would you, that a few simple ingredients like water, calcium carbonate and a few metal ions could take up such fantastic shapes and colours ...'

His sentence tailed off again.

It was so easy to guess what he wanted to ask. He wanted the information, and he would ask the question now, while the topic was still floating in our memories.

'What happened to — David, you said — Matthew's father?'

I told him the situation, and used the word 'divorce' in conversation with an inquisitive male for the first time. He grunted once or twice but made no comment. There were no hints as to the happiness or otherwise of his own family life, no attempts at hand-on-knee, no casually-held elbow when we stopped for coffee at the service-station and walked across the car-park. I suppose I was mildly disappointed.

He seemed to know his way around Oxford's complicated traffic system, and we drove through the diesel fumes and the parties of sight-seers to the back of the Bodleian Library. He parked the car on a double yellow line near the Radcliffe Camera and helped me get my suitcase and briefcase out of the boot. Engraved on the archway above our heads was the Latin demand or prayer that the Lord should enlighten us. Instead, Roger seized the day and kissed me on the mouth. It started with his hand on my shoulder and an attempt at a friendly peck on the cheek, but at the last moment he swung his head so that his glasses hit my cheekbone and his beard grazed my chin. Our lips made contact.

'I could give you a lift back to Cornwall,' he then suggested. 'If you give me your brother's phone number, I can call you in the next few days and find out your plans.'

So I wrote down Jamie's number for him. He kissed me again, more forcefully and, because the telephone number apparently indicated a pact for the future between us, he furtively slid his hand between us, and pressed it against my breast.

Thus, it seemed, the inevitable was set in progress. I had no intention of thinking about whether I was insulted or amused, but I certainly didn't feel fired up with passion. Edward had been so very much more adept! But here in Oxford, I didn't want to think of Edward, in case even the memory of his name conjured his appearance in the flesh.

I wheeled my case across the uneven flagstones to the library office, and endured the subduing business of renewing my lapsed membership. Then, using the credibility of my new plastic-coated card, I was able to leave my case in the cloakroom and go upstairs to sit at the computer and order my books. It might take a day or so for them to be delivered to the desk and since the business at the publishing house could only be stretched to fill one day, I wondered if I could really be bothered.

Jamie, Lynn, and their children, Suzy and John, all look remarkably similar, despite their differing ages and sexes. The straight brown hair and the healthy complexions must have something to do with it, but the similarity of their mannerisms and ways of speaking must contribute. The similarity is all the more surprising because Suzy is adopted — at seventeen, she's a very good mathematician and wants to be an accountant and to get rich — but I've noticed before that adopted children often grow to resemble their parents. John wants to be like his father and become a game-keeper, so he's planning to go to the Agricultural College.

'Keeper's Cottage', where they live, comprises two small houses that have been knocked together, in a terrace of three. The estate's tractor driver and his wife live in the third. The terrace is a couple of miles along a single-track road on the Downs, South of Oxford, and the chalky arable land sweeps away into the distance. I wonder if this isolation has also contributed to that branch of the Lewishams becoming such a close family unit. It's so different from my own 'family' circumstances that it always takes me some time to adjust.

The children had been ferried to the bus stop and Jamie was already outside, exercising the dogs, by the time I came down to breakfast. Lynn and I were a bit quiet, mainly because we both had hangovers.

Lynn, with her shoulder-length hair and long fringe, looks — even in her forties — like a stocky schoolgirl. She's quiet, but she's determined, and after a couple of glasses of wine she becomes very talkative and very funny, and we both remember how much we like each other. She works part-time as a receptionist in a doctor's surgery, and at breakfast she offered to give me a lift to the bus on her way to work. However, Jamie had already said that he'd run me to the nearest station when he'd finished checking the birds and, since I was looking forward to a couple of hours alone with him before I went to the publishing house, I said I'd stay.

When I walked by the kennels, the liver-and-white Springers barked and whined, leaping at the wire, their tails wagging ecstatically, but the old labrador was silent, and merely curled her lips in a grin and lay on her back submissively. Jamie had cats, too, and a parrot, and a barn owl that he was nursing for the local Barn Owl Trust. He also had what seemed to be thousands of pheasants.

There were eight of the large tent-shaped wire cages in the field next to the house, and I stopped and looked into each one as I walked by. Two cages of partridges and the rest of pheasants, each cage containing a different age-group. The youngest birds were rushing about, but the older ones pecked at the grass as well as the chick-crumbs, and jumped onto perches and flapped their stubby wings. They scurried away, 'peeping' loudly, when I came close — but in seconds had forgotten that they'd been frightened and dashed off on some other important business.

Jamie was crouched half-inside a wooden coop at the back of the furthest cage. There was a gap between his old check shirt and his khaki working trousers so I ran my finger lightly over his bare skin. He started, and hit his head against the door and swore foully, then he backed out and rubbed his head as he stood up. There were quite a lot of grey hairs mixed in with the brown, and his face was crumpled in pain. Some of the stubble on his chin was silvery, too.

'You made me jump,' he said, unnecessarily. 'That really hurt.'

I reached up and stroked his head.

'Sorry. I thought you heard me coming. What's wrong with that one?'

He held out the limp body of a brown-and-yellow chick.

'Dead. Squashed to death. These are the two-week-olds — you see how they dash away when they're frightened? Quite the opposite from domestic chickens, it makes sense in the wild — mum shouts "scatter!" and they all hide so there's less chance of them all being caught together. Trouble is, in the coop they all pile into the corners and don't care whose head they're stepping on. Doesn't happen very often, luckily. Poor little soul.'

I smoothed the soft, stiff little body. '*Soul*? If you think of them as having souls how can you bear for them to get shot? That's completely illogical.'

He looked at me in alarm but saw that I was teasing.

'Got me worried there, Haze, thought you might've joined the anti-this-and-that brigade.'

'I like eating pheasant as much as you do. But *do* you think the birds have souls, Jamie?' I really wanted to know what he thought.

He put the corpse on top of the coop to collect later, and smiled slowly as he shook his head. 'Ah, Hazel ...' He thought a bit and then shrugged. 'Buddhists do. They think that.'

Jamie has such a slow, deliberate way of speaking that some people might think that he's also slow of thought. But that's not so: he thinks a lot about matters and events that touch his life. He once told me that whatever opinions he might have about political matters, for example, he wouldn't be able to change the situation: his duty was to his family, and to the animals in his care and to his employer. In that order. That was probably more than enough for any man, he said, if you were going to put your love and care into something other than yourself. He was quite matter-of-fact about it, he wasn't being belligerent or trying to make a point. That truly is what he believes — and I love him for it.

I stood around and watched while he finished feeding and watering the birds, and then we walked over to the small deciduous wood where he had set up two woodland pens for the young poults. When I walk in the countryside with Jamie I realise how blind I am on my own. He pointed out where a muntjac had marked its territory by thrashing its antlers against the bark of a sapling; some droppings and slot-marks of a roe deer; he picked up a great spotted woodpecker's feather and found a few badger hairs snagged against a wire fence. He's a man of the land, he understands and works with its rhythms. I often wonder how he became like that, if it was a conscious effort or if the wiring of that behaviour was always in him, ready to be switched on. After our father died, Jamie always took care of me. He protected us both from our mother's wilder whimsies. He still does take care of me, even though I'm nearly forty-two. 'Jamie'll fix it.' Not that there's anything broken.

The pens were enormous and were full of trees. The trees were fenced in by ten-foot-high chicken wire, double-thickness at the bottom and buried deep — I looked round, remembering the details — to keep out foxes and rabbits (and deer, so perhaps the trees didn't mind being fenced in.) On the outside of the wire was a low electric fence, at fox-chest height; the fox could only sit and yearn while the birds ate and drank and gyrated their bodies in the dustbaths.

'I envy your pheasant poults, being able to live like this. If they had any intelligence in those bird-brains they'd stay here for ever instead of flying out into the wide world.'

'That's teenagers for you. Don't know when they're well off!'

Because it was still July the pens were empty, but one time I came here in late August when they were full — two thousand birds, resting in the trees or scratching in the undergrowth. And sun-bathing, lying relaxed, wings part-spread, like humans with their eyes half-closed with pleasure. Today, as then, long-tailed tits flitted through the trees and beech leaves were transparent green against the sun.

'Forest glades,' I said to my brother. 'Sun-dappled forest glades. It's like a fairy-tale, isn't it?'

'Until the wicked uncle comes with his big shot-gun.'

'That sounds obscene!'

We both snorted with laughter.

'How about you, Haze? Are the wicked uncles keeping out of your way these days?'

He was serious now, not quite looking at me. I wondered if he was referring to Edward.

'David and I are getting a divorce, so he can marry Gail. We've started proceedings.'

Jamie nodded; he was clearing last autumn's leaves from a wire-netting pop-hole that led into the pen. He finished and stood up and came over to me.

'Is that all right? Does it upset you? I'm not quite sure how things stand — after all these years. Will you go across and see him?'

'It's fine. David and I haven't seen each other for years. And no, I'm not going to go and see him now.' I hesitated. 'I don't know about Matt, though. You know he's staying with me this summer? He's got a job at the Anchor, down on the quay.'

'No, I didn't know.' Jamie's eyes were anxious. 'Is it working out? I'd be so happy, it would be great for you — for you both — if you could both get along. He's been over here a few times, not often ...'

'Has he?' I'd had no idea. 'Has he said anything? About whether he'll stay on living with David and Gail? Though I don't suppose it will be for much longer, anyway, he's almost independent now.'

'No. You know what Matt's like — he comes over and drifts around, tries to impress Suzy.' Jamie wiped his bent arm over his face, and his cheeks creased with a slow, warm smile. 'And then drifts off again. I like Matt, Haze. He's a good lad, he's turning out all right.'

I thought about that. 'Mmm.'

'*Could* he stay with you? There's space isn't there — he's sleeping in Ma's old studio?'

I thought about that, too, the dirty clothes and dirty plates, the loud music and interminable phone calls that tied up the telephone for hours. The discontent. But Jamie had to put up with some of those things, too. Suzy and John were not so different from Matt. I just wasn't in the habit of sharing my space any more, especially with someone so much younger. Even if he were my own son. I sighed.

'I don't know. I haven't really thought about it.'

'What about this bloke that drove you up to Oxford, then? Is he your new man? That could be a complication.'

('This bloke'. Roger. The business with Roger needed some thought, too, and I didn't even want to consider it. Not when the sun was dappling through the trees onto the undergrowth and beechmast-covered floor of the pen.)

So I just laughed. 'Oh no. He's a scientist who works at — oh, of course, you'll know the place, Nancarrow House, just along the coast — and his family lives in London. It was convenient. He goes up and down all the time.'

'Nancarrow. That was where that snail-woman lived, wasn't it? Wilson, she was called.'

'Yes. Still does live. Dr Elizabeth Wilson. Roger's working with her this summer. Do you know her, then? I've only met her once, I think, years ago, when she and Mummy were both exhibiting at the Art Show.'

We sat down on one of the large logs that Jamie had placed as a perch for the pheasant poults, and I scuffed my feet in the leafmould and sniffed the smell of earth and bark.

'Ma took us all there, to Nancarrow, it must be several years ago. Suzy wanted to go to the beach, as usual, and it's a good beach there. Ma had to drop something in at the house so I must have met Dr Wilson then — to talk to — but only briefly. But I recognised her at the funeral service, she came over and spoke to me, offered condolences and that sort of thing. She didn't come home for the tea.'

'No. Did you meet her husband? He was disabled and had to go around in a wheelchair. He's dead now, though.'

Jamie stared across the pen, and then chuckled. 'Yes, that's right. He was quite a pleasant chap, grey beard, and when we saw him he was being pushed round by an aged old fellow who must've been the gardener or handyman, something of that sort. Going quite fast, they were, then they'd screech to a stop by a plant and discuss it, or so it seemed. Then off they'd career again. I seem to remember the old gardener pushed the wheelchair along the pier — yes, that was it, he left the husband there for a bit, to watch the beach.' He chuckled again and rubbed his head, but then winced. 'Hell. My head still hurts. So how come you've met this scientist who works at Nancarrow but haven't met Dr Wilson? Have you been pubbing and clubbing in Polkenna?'

'Ha ha. Basically, Matt and I were out for a walk, and we had to call in at

Nancarrow because I needed some aspirins for my hayfever.' I shifted my position on the log. 'Yes, I know it sounds daft. Anyway, the thing that I wanted to tell you about Nancarrow — Elizabeth Wilson has got one of Mummy's paintings. There are only two left at the Shell House and Matt's really upset about this. I don't suppose you know who else would have one, do you? Matt would dearly like me to buy one or two back — though I'm not sure I could afford it, even if we could find them. You haven't got any tucked away in the loft, have you?'

Jamie stood up and went over to look at an empty feed hopper. When he turned around his broad face was creased and frowning; for a moment I reverted to being his anxious little sister and I wanted to smooth his forehead, smooth the ridges and furrows away so that everything would be all right.

'No. I haven't got any. That's a strange thing, isn't it? — why have we never thought about that before? That Ma didn't leave us any of her paintings.'

'Perhaps she thought we weren't interested. Actually, I suspect she didn't think of us at all.' I felt rather uncomfortable at that idea. 'She was fond of Matt, though, so I'm sorry she didn't remember him.'

'But come to think of it, she wasn't like that, Haze, was she? She didn't think about possessions, certainly not the business of handing them on. Look at her Will — it wasn't exactly complicated. Money to me, Shell House to you. Full stop.'

'Yes. "You've got your own lives to lead" and so on. I suppose you're right. And all that destiny business. Jamie, that was awful.'

'Yeah.' He stared at his earthy hands and then rubbed them together with a sound like sandpaper. 'You really got lumbered with all that, didn't you, at the end? I felt bad about that, that I couldn't help more.'

'Of course you couldn't. You have all this to keep going — and there's Lynn and the children. I was so much freer. At least you were able to get there a couple of times... You should come down sometime and see what changes I've made — if you can get away from the birds for a day or two later on.'

I stood up too, and we walked slowly back to the house together. On the way to the station we passed a field of linseed flowers that were, in response to the sun, as blue as the Cornish sea on a bright summer's day.

That evening, as we sat around talking in a desultory way over the low background noise of the television, I explained that I'd finished my business with the publishing company, and that I intended to spend the next day in the Bodleian Library, browsing through a few books by a Victorian naturalist, Philip Gosse. I couldn't be bothered to go into details, I was beginning to lose interest myself.

Jamie was sitting yawning and apparently on the verge of sleep, but when Lynn and Suzy began telling me about a film they'd been to see, he suddenly said, 'I'm sure I've got a book by that Gosse chappie. Ma gave it to me. Do you know where it is, Lynn?'

'Well, if it's anywhere it'll be on the bookshelves on the landing. That's the only place we've got books.' She rolled her eyes at me. 'I suppose you want me to go and look for it, since you're half asleep.'

'No, you sit there, I'll find it.'

I was so astonished that I must have had my mouth open. 'Shall I come and look, too?' I managed to ask.

'If you want. You'll probably recognise it before I do.'

He went up the stairs two at a time, and I hurried after him. The bookshelves were not large, and the books were obviously not often consulted, judging by the dust. Some of the green *Countryman* magazines jumbled amongst them dated from ten years before. The Gosse book was easy to find because its black leather binding was so much older and stronger than the others. Jamie blew the dust off the gilt-edged pages and opened it, then showed me the title page.

'There — *Life in its lower, intermediate and higher forms, or manifestations of the divine wisdom in the natural history of animals.* That's why Ma gave it to me.'

'She thought you needed some divine wisdom?'

'No, of course not! When she knew I was serious about going into 'keepering, she thought it might help — the "higher" part is about birds and deer and so on, as far as I remember. But I haven't looked at it in years.'

'Hmm.'

I wondered why our mother hadn't given me the *Actinologia* when I went on the university marine course, but then I realised that she would either have forgotten about the book, or more probably (and here I felt a brief spasm of superiority) hadn't understood what the title meant. Or — and this was a much more interesting rationalisation — perhaps she understood the importance of the book to the 'family archive', and recognised that I would not yet be able to appreciate the significance. But no, that was unlikely, too; in her estimation, the significance would have been insignificant.

I took the book from Jamie, and then I showed him the name written inside the cover.

'Look at this. It belonged to "A.B. Robertson". Anne — she was a relation of ours. She was a naturalist — you see how you're following in her footsteps, I suppose our dear mother didn't explain that? — and she knew Philip Gosse. I found some of her old notebooks amongst Mummy's things.'

I flipped through the stiff pages, looking at the pictures.

'It doesn't look very interesting.'

'No. But I think there was another book. Robertson rings a bell. Robertson. I'm sure she gave me another. Here, this could be it. We should put in a stronger light bulb, the light's hopeless, I can't read what it says.'

He held the brown cloth-covered book up to the light.

'*Nature's Survivors* by D. Robertson, Esquire. Ah — it was "AB" in that other book, wasn't it? This is "D" and a male at that. Any good?'

'Duncan was Anne's husband. I cannot believe you just put these books away and forgot about them.'

I took the two books and clasped my hands around them, gripping them.

'Why not? Just old books.' Jamie shrugged and looked at me consideringly, watching my expression. The light above his head made shadows of his eyes and throat. 'Hey, I was just teasing, Haze. If I'd known you were interested in them I'd have given them to you long ago, you know that. So tell me what's so fascinating about them, anyway.'

'Oh ... I don't know. Just that these books have been passed down through the family for nearly 150 years. That's quite something, Jamie. We may not have any of Mummy's paintings worth speaking of, but we have at least got some books from our ancestors.'

'You should keep them, Haze, they obviously mean a lot more to you. You look after them.' He yawned hugely. 'Anyway, time for bed. I've got an early start tomorrow. Lynn'll take you to the bus.'

He took the books from me and put them on the chest at the top of the stairs, then put his arms around me. 'You know, Haze, that's the first time I've seen you so agitated in a long while. And all about some old books!'

He hugged me gently, and for the second time that day I felt like a child wanting to be comforted. We stayed like that for a few moments; Lynn and Suzy were clattering and talking in the kitchen, laying out the things for breakfast.

'I'm glad you're here for a few days,' Jamie said into the top of my head. 'Sometimes I worry about you living at Polkenna, in Ma's house. I often wonder — "How does your garden grow?" '

It was an old joke of ours, a chanted taunt from our teenage days, when we pretended to be on the lookout for 'talent': 'with silver bells, and cockle shells, and pretty maids all in a row.'

I pushed him away and grinned, noticing how the overhead light made the stubble on his chin glint.

'Oh, plenty of pretty young men. There's Matthew, and his handsome American friend, Jim — and quite a few cockles around, as you'd expect. But I'm fine.'

Before I went to bed I looked at Duncan Robertson's book. He had written, 'To my dearest darling Anne, my never-reproachful assistant and constant friend. From your ever-loving husband DR. March 1861.' Was the handwriting the same as on the extract copied from Gosse's Jamaican book? I was almost certain that it was, but I should remember to check.

I found it hard to get to sleep. Jamie's hug had reminded my body what it needed, and although one can be quite inventive on one's own, there's no substitute for a real, live man! Roger Trenton's body was apparently on offer. But he was married: what was he playing at? I sighed, and rolled over, pulling the cover more closely around my shoulders. I decided that I would probably let events with Roger take their course. I sighed again, but it turned into a yawn.

I spent most of the next day in the Bodleian and then the Radcliffe Science Library, browsing through some of Gosse's works. He had written several religious books, too, but I avoided those. I preferred the books he had written about places and the animals that he had found there — *The Canadian Naturalist, Letters from Alabama, Tenby, A Naturalist's Rambles on the Devonshire Coast.* The last two held plenty of insights into his family life; they seemed to have had a jolly time, lots of picnics and excursions. I quite liked the sound of the man and wondered if the young Anne Church had liked him too. The catalogue also referred to a book by an Emily Gosse, *Abraham and his children: parental duties illustrated by scriptural examples.* Was this his wife, the woman with whom he'd enjoyed the jokes and walks? Was she of the same religious persuasion?

Then my request for Stack material delivered up a thick book by Edmund Gosse ('He's the one who wrote *Father and Son*,' the librarian commented helpfully.) *The Life of Philip Henry Gosse.* The son's biography of the father. Time was running out on me, my eyes were sore with reading and the heavy hushed atmosphere was making my head feel fuzzy. But Emily was listed in the index and she was, of course, the wife and mother. I hadn't time for details, I skimmed the pages. Suddenly, Emily was ill — and then Emily was dead. She had died of breast cancer.

I closed the book and sat for a while, elbow on the desk, forehead hidden by my hand. Eyes closed. Mrs Gosse had chosen the wrong treatment. My mother had chosen no treatment. I had thought that I had got over Mummy's death.

We drank the two bottles of wine that I had bought, and Jamie fell asleep in his chair. Lynn said it was lucky that I was leaving in the morning because her head and liver needed to recover.

Roger telephoned, wanting to know my plans. I explained that I now needed to go to Cambridge, to the library, and there was a long silence before he spoke again, but he sounded very pleased.

'You'll need to get the train to London to do that, won't you? Why not come and have lunch with me and Elizabeth? She's going to be at the Natural History Museum for a couple of days before she goes to Amsterdam. You were only saying the other day how you would like to meet her — now's your chance.'

'But I can meet her in Cornwall! And I can get a bus directly from here to Cambridge without coming into London,' I pointed out.

'This will be much more interesting. I'd like to show you backstage at the NHM, it's a fascinating building. You'll love it.'

He was so pleased with his plan (and, as a plan, it had its attractions) but I would not be dissuaded. It was quite clear to me that I needed to go to Cambridge: Gosse's *Memorial* to his wife was there. And various letters. I had telephoned ahead, and because I'm a graduate of that University, I could be issued quickly with a library card. I would be able to sit in the Manuscript Room, and books would be delivered to me within the hour. I wanted to get there soon.

'Where will you be staying in Cambridge?'

'At my old college. They have guest rooms that are very cheap, if you're an old student. Why?'

'Well —' he hesitated. 'I need to visit Cambridge myself, to see the schistosome people in the immunology department. I could ... I could come up to Cambridge the day after tomorrow. We could meet up — if you would like that.'

I tried to imagine him at the other end of the telephone line.

'Rog?' I hadn't meant to address him like that, it just slipped out. 'Are you wearing your glasses?'

'What? Now? Yes, of course!' He sounded mystified, but then he laughed, rather suggestively. 'Oh. Well — I can take them off if ...'

'That might be more convenient.' I began to laugh, too. 'Why don't you leave a message at the College Lodge to say when you will be coming? We could meet by the back gate of King's, the one nearest the library, at, say, two o'clock.'

We chatted a little while longer, almost inconsequentially, but I'm sure the line had a little extra buzz as it transmitted our unspoken sexual anticipation.

'There's nothing like sex for clearing the mind,' Edward had once said. I think my mind had been an empty attic with the wind whistling through, during the time I had spent with him. I would go to Cambridge, and then 'Rog' could clear my mind. In fact, I needed him to do it right now.

I called the Natural History Museum in the morning and asked for Dr Elizabeth Wilson. The man on the switchboard could not find her extension number, and I had to explain that she was probably now only a visitor; as I waited, my palms were surprisingly cold and wet with nerves. Finally, she was found.

'Hallo. This is Hazel Myers — from Polkenna. But actually I'm in Oxford at the moment.'

'Of course. Hazel. You're coming for lunch, aren't you?' She sounded brisk and unsurprised. 'What can I do for you? Are you trying to contact Roger?'

'Oh no, not at all. And I'm afraid I can't meet you for lunch as I have to go to Cambridge this afternoon. But I wanted to ask you something, to see if you could help. You remember the Gosse extract that Matt brought you, the one about the workroom in Jamaica?'

'Yes. It was intriguing. And I do hope your son thanked you my behalf.'

'Yes. Gosse was collecting those birds and other specimens for the British Museum. And I wondered if there's any chance that his birdskins are still in the collections somewhere. Though I suppose they might be rather moth-eaten by now.'

'I'll find out for you.' She was positive. 'There's a reasonable chance that they are, not much gets thrown away here. He described collecting snails, too, didn't he? It might be interesting to see if the shells are in Malacology's collection, too, from my own point of view. But it might take a little while to track them down. Where can I contact you?'

I gave her, too, the telephone number of my college, and explained that I might visit the Museum in a couple of days' time, on my way home, if there should be a chance of looking at the specimens.

She didn't find it curious that I wanted to look at Gosse's bird-skins, nor did she ask me why. I suppose it was the sort of thing that people were always wanting to do at the Museum, to burrow through the past. She was pleasant, and brisk, and she was on her way to the Netherlands for a conference. She did not suggest that we should try to meet in Cornwall.

CHAPTER 17: ANNE: 1857

On Wednesday February 25th 1857
A Lecture
will be delivered by
P.H. Gosse, Esq., ALS, FRS
Subject: —
The Natural History of Sponges and Zoophytes
Illustrated by coloured drawings
To commence at 8 o'clock precisely

The hall smelt of damp wool, and wooden chairs scraped on the floorboards as local naturalists and also, I suppose, the merely curious, arranged themselves comfortably amongst their bulky garments. The sound of polite conversation grew louder; the lamps spluttered each time the door was opened and an icy draught swirled around our ankles. My nerves seemed extra sensitive, every sound was a blow to the ears, each small object required my visual interrogation: the folded umbrella that stood with its nose in a pool of water; the great-coat decorated with a line of dust where it had swept across the floor; the colours of stained glass made muddy by lamplight. There was a blackboard on an easel. Two wooden chairs with arms and padded seats. A table, rectangular, with turned legs. A carafe of water with two glasses. In my imagination I poured water for him, held out the glass, allowed our fingers to touch...

'Anne darling, do please sit still.'

Mama's voice made me start, I had forgotten she was there. We had travelled over to Edinburgh for the lecture: Mama and I, Duncan, and the Laird of Ballavich and his lady. Mama had only been persuaded to make the journey because she was tiring of Glasgow, and I think both she and I were anxious to return home to Winchester, for we had become exhausted with so much visiting and planning.

But Duncan and I had found a house, our future home — a terraced house, not long built, in York Street running down to the Clyde — with space for a maid, and perhaps for a housekeeper, should we be able to afford one, and Duncan would be able to walk down to his offices on Broomielaw each morning. But one requires furnishings for a house, and all manner of other goods must be purchased or received as gifts — and our deliberations had been endless and enervating. Mama and I had also been entertained frequently, and most hospitably, by Duncan's relatives; we had visited museums, glass-houses and exhibitions and — as far as the wintry weather allowed — all nearby viewpoints and sights of interest.

The weather was cold and damp in Glasgow: in Edinburgh, where we were to stay the night, it was even colder, and the wind was cruel and piercing. The grey bad-tempered skies, and my increasing anxiety about the new life upon which I was to embark in less than two months' time — in this *foreign country*, amongst people who spoke with such a broad tongue as to make our common language almost incomprehensible! — had combined to make me secretly depressed and apprehensive. But now, although I sat, outwardly calm (although apparently fidgeting!) between my dear Mama and my fiancé, my mind and heart were a turmoil of excitement and nervous anticipation. How would he look? Would he talk of the North Devon coast? Would he talk to *me* after the lecture?

A gentleman appeared through the door at the front of the hall and held the curtain back. As the rustlings and murmurings of the audience died away Mr Gosse, accompanied by Professor Kerr, entered and mounted the steps to the daïs, then sat down at the table. Such was my shock that I almost exclaimed: the *gauntness*, the lines of weariness or pain that marked his face! Exhaustion was so apparent in his demeanour! I hardly recognised the man (oh, beloved man!) whom I had seen, so briefly, last October. My heightened anxiety and the flood of pity — and love, such an overwhelming *rush* of love — that I felt for him made tears spring to my eyes. His wife's illness was clearly taking its toll on his own health; for a moment I felt resentment not only against her that he should be made to suffer so — but also, fleetingly, against the Lord.

Yet when he stood up to speak, and turned to the blackboard upon which an assistant had now pinned a large, beautifully-coloured drawing of the orange sponge, *Halichondria*, his voice resonated as strongly as I remembered it, from those magical days at Ilfracombe. He moved from species to species, drawing to drawing, with all the assurance that lecturing had always seemed to give him. (Is this perhaps because with lecturing, as with preaching, there is no need for *intimacy* with strangers?)

Only once, when he was describing a species that he had found at Tenby last summer, and the circumstances in which he had found it, did he pause in his fluent monologue. For *they* had been at Tenby last summer, the whole family. Even at that time Mrs Gosse had been ill: when Miss Shipton and I had visited her at Pimlico in the autumn she had attempted to be light-hearted, to tell me about Willy's adventures on the rocks, and the caverns that her husband and brother had explored, taking with them candles and lucifers and a ball of twine. She had used her own name for him, perhaps forgetting for a moment that I was not an intimate friend, merely a former pupil.

'Henry persuaded my brother to crawl on his stomach, like a worm,' she said. 'Henry explores large spaces by seeing minute detail.'

She had tried to laugh but this had brought on a fit of coughing.

While Willy and I had absented ourselves to take a walk, she had told Miss Shipton (who had of course disclosed the information later) that the Lord had ordained that their time at Tenby should be a time of great trial for her, and that she prayed that she had not been found wanting for she had brought several souls to Jesus 'while Henry conducted his work on the shore.'

Had he found the scarlet sponge of which he now spoke on a day when his wife persuaded a new sinner to repent in the Lord? Is that why he faltered momentarily, remembering Emily's fortitude? 'God moves in mysterious ways' indeed: one may 'tell Jesus', but His answer may be a riddle. I remembered Mrs Gosse's wasted frame, and I shuddered, so that Mama glanced at me questioningly.

The Laird was leaning forward, hands crossed on the ivory handle of his cane; I wondered if his wife was asleep for she was apparently staring at something in her lap, and her head distinctly swayed. Duncan sat bolt upright next to me, seemingly enraptured by the details of encrusting growths that were to be found upon the bladderwrack. Mama, having observed Mr Gosse at length, was now covertly observing the audience. I heard nothing of the lecture: I watched and watched him — and for a while there was such a *confusion* inside me that I thought I might cease to breathe.

At the conclusion, Mr Gosse was almost besieged with questioners and those who wished to have their copies of his books inscribed, so our little party waited until the hall had almost cleared and then, as was only proper, I approached him with Mama and my fiancé. Of course, he must have remembered that I would be present, for I had written to tell him so, but I was secretly relieved that his lack of surprise passed unremarked by Duncan. Indeed, his greeting was cordial and polite and, on being introduced to Duncan, congratulatory.

Duncan somewhat diffidently told him about his own collections from the Frith of Clyde and Mr Gosse gave the appearance of being most interested.

'It is my intention to put together a work on the actiniae and corals of the British Isles,' he said, ' and your observations would be of great value to me. Do please write to me with the details, Mr Robertson. And Miss Church — I beg you to forgive me for failing to respond to your interesting description of that most unusual specimen. It is quite unlike anything I have seen before, but I —'

Duncan glanced at me in surprise and I looked away.

'— am afraid I have not yet had sufficient time ...'

'How is Mrs Gosse?' I interposed quickly, and then was aghast to see his great brown eyes fill with unshed tears. Duncan, too, must have seen them, for he turned hastily and spoke to Mama, contriving to take her to join his aunt and uncle in the group around Professor Kerr.

I could not move: I could *not* take my eyes off him, although I could see how he struggled to compose his face and voice.

'My dear wife was committed to our Lord's care two weeks ago. She has gone to be with Jesus.'

Emily Gosse was *dead*? I had not thought her quite so ill. For a moment I was unable to reply, so great was my agitation. Then, as I saw his glistening eyes and hollow cheeks, I reached out and touched him, touched his hand. I really could not help myself.

'It cannot be! Mr Gosse, dear Mr Gosse, I am so sorry. Forgive me, I cannot comprehend ... she was such a *good* person .' There were tears in my eyes, too; tears for this poor hurt man.

'The Lord granted that she was able to spend her last days with us at home.' He withdrew slightly, so that my hand was left unsupported.

'And Master Gosse — is he travelling with you?'

'No, it would not be suitable.' There was reproof in his voice, but as he spoke of his son, a sort of desperation crept in. 'He is staying with my cousin's family, in Bristol ... The lecture tour had already been arranged. My darling boy. How I *miss* him, Miss Church. You have met him, you can understand that. I write to him daily. I pray constantly that Jesus will keep him safe. What will he do, without his Mama?'

I gazed at him, helplessly, for I knew exactly how I would wish to answer. But that answer was unthinkable, and premature. Instead I replied,

'He will care for you, as he cared for his mother. And you will care for him likewise. He must know how you love him.'

'He was a little ministering angel.' His lips tightened, making his heavy features severe as he tried to stop his eyes filling once more.

'Yes. And he will be your helpmeet — he loves to assist you, I have seen him. Especially on the shore.'

'Mrs Gosse was my helpmeet, Miss Church ... I think we will leave London. There is much that needs to be written.'

'Your work on the actiniae.'

'And other work.' He was in control of himself again. 'You may be certain that that I shall draw heavily on your own notes and description. I congratulate you.' Was there even hint of levity when he added, 'And on Mr Robertson, too'?

There was nothing more, at this time, to be said, and for a moment we stood awkwardly together.

Duncan (he is a kind and tactful man, so tactful that sometimes I wish he would assert himself more strongly) was not far away and came to save us both.

'I expect Miss Church did not tell you, sir, that we intend to travel after we are married — to collect and study the creatures in rather more remote parts of the world. I have it in mind to go to South America.'

Mr Gosse looked at me in surprise. 'Do you also wish to go there, Miss Church?'

'I believe so, yes. Although I know that this would be somewhat unusual.'

'Some years ago I wished very much to return to Jamaica but, in the end, I saw it was not possible. Perhaps you would like to go there instead? —there is a great deal that remains to be done. Please write to me if you decide to go there and I will provide you with some notes and introductions.'

We thanked him and, conscious that we had taken up much of his time, left to find the others.

The Laird, who found omnibuses uncomfortable, had ordered a carriage, and as we returned to the hotel I was quizzed by Duncan and Mama, both of whom wished for an explanation of what had taken place. There were many exclamations of sorrow and, from Mama, of surprise, for she had been privy to some of the details of the meeting in Pimlico.

'Have you then sent Mr Gosse the description of the anemone from Loch Long?' Duncan asked softly, after a while. 'I hope you made a copy, dearest, for your drawing was very fine. I had hoped you would give it to me as a memento of our first day anemonizing together.' He took my hand, squeezing it gently, then carefully straightened the fingers of my glove; he smiled as though to soften the hurt behind his question. 'Why did you think to send it to him without telling me? I had hoped we might track it down together.'

'I sent it on a moment's impulse. I had thought that as he was parted from his wife at that time, the arrival of a new specimen, perhaps a new species ... that is, the *drawing* of a new species, might perhaps offer him some cheer.' My explanation sounded feeble. 'I am certain Mr Gosse will return my papers just as soon as he has finished with them — and you may then take them and frame them. And hang them prominently in your study.'

I smiled back at him reassuringly, but I was terrified by what I had done. I had sent the details to my adored Henry Gosse to ... to *remind* him. To remind him of my existence, in the knowledge that he would be vulnerable in his loneliness. I had not known (dear Lord, please forgive me) that Emily Gosse had returned home and was on the point of death. My letter must have reached him less than two weeks before she died. It was small wonder that he had not read it closely.

The carriage rumbled over the cobbles and the air inside was close and damp, and smelt strongly of fumes from the lantern. All I could think of was Henry Gosse. The agony of indecision, the jealousy, the giddiness and loss of appetite — all those had beset me as my visit to Glasgow had approached. One moment I would be dreaming of Duncan, of the kisses and embraces that thrilled and excited us both — and then, within seconds, I would be remembering every detail of my encounters with my beloved, and my heart would seem ready to *burst* with pity and longing. There were times when I was so desperate to be with Henry that I could scarcely carry out any task in hand; I would imagine myself in his arms, imagine myself as his friend, and helper — and *lover*.

It had become a sort of madness within me! Yet he did not even notice me, in the hall he had taken away his hand. There were too many obstacles.

No, there *had been* too many obstacles. Now there was one less. Suddenly, I felt quite sick and faint. I could not breathe and I gasped with fright.

'Anne! What is wrong, child? She must have some air — Mr Robertson, please open the window.'

The Laird banged on the roof with his cane and ordered the carriage to stop, and they all fussed around me with *sal volatile*, and fanned in the cold, (such bitterly cold) night air. There was a buzzing in my ears, I could not comprehend what they were saying, but I managed to sit upright again and wave away their concern, and I hugged my sweet, anxious and long-suffering Mama.

After our return to the hotel in Glasgow, we finally began to make the preparations for our journey home. Duncan arrived whilst Mama was supervising the maid in the packing of our bags; amongst the various purchases that we had made there was, I regret to say, a preponderance of heavy woollen cloth in the chequered tartan pattern made so popular by the Queen's husband (whom the Laird, otherwise so cosmopolitan in his outlook, still refers to as 'the German Prince'!)

I picked up the tartan beret, or 'bonnet' as it is called here, that I had bought for my brother, and perched it on Duncan's head.

'Do you really think little Tom will consent to wear this? He will be horribly embarrassed!'

It was, of course, far too small for Duncan's square manly head, and made him look ridiculous, with his dark curls sprouting out at each side. He grimaced, but laughed good-naturedly as he removed it, and then placed his hands on my shoulders and examined my face intently.

'You seem to be recovered, darling — you gave us all quite a fright.'

His close scrutiny would have unnerved me, except that his tender concern was so genuine and his own face appeared quite *crumpled* in his anxiety; my heart felt torn in two yet I could not help but laugh, and kiss him lightly on the lips.

'Come, we still have arrangements to make. Mama, we are going down to the morning room to make a list!'

There was a large gilt-framed mirror on the stairs and I made him halt, so that we stood side-by-side. How similarly unhandsome we were as a pair!

Duncan placed his arm through mine. 'Thus shall we stand on our wedding day. But better-dressed!'

He attempted to set his crumpled waistcoat to rights with his free hand, and I straightened my back to stand taller, and noticed how the blue taffeta petticoat now hung loosely about my waist. I rubbed my cheeks, hoping to restore some colour to them: I did not look my best.

My fiancé, yet again, was regarding me intently, this time in the mirror, and I could not meet his gaze but urged him to continue down the stairs.

'No more carriages,' he said. 'When we travel abroad we shall travel in the open air. You shall learn to ride on horseback, or we shall go on foot or in an open cart! What do you think? You shall wear "clothes that will not spoil" — let me show you what I have found here in *Maga*.' He showed me the cover of a pamphlet called *Blackwood's Edinburgh Magazine*. 'You will enjoy this.'

The morning room was, to our relief, empty of other guests, and Duncan seated me on a sofa next to the fire, then opened the magazine.

'*New facts and old fancies about anemones.* The latest, apparently, in a series of articles which were called *Seaside Studies* — we may assume that the author thus intended to point out that its contents were more studious than those in Mr Gosse's own book of *pleasures!* The new facts concern some simple experiments which the author carried out last summer when he and his companions were at Ilfracombe.'

'*Ilfracombe!*'

'Yes indeed. But I thought you might also be interested that one of his companions "has taken the precaution of wearing clothes that 'won't spoil' " — and I have it on good authority that this companion was a woman. However, I am afraid the author is also somewhat disparaging about some of Mr Gosse's opinions as to the function of the "stinging cells" in certain anemones, but I would tend to side with Gosse. Ah yes — read this! Do you think this could be true?'

I read the passage aloud. ' "If the monotony of the anemone wearies you, you can eat it! Mr Gosse describes his frying them in butter, if I remember rightly: and although he felt a little difficulty in swallowing the first mouthful, yet, having vanquished his scruples, he ate with some relish!" '

How strange that the author should refer to that.

'Yes,' I said, wonderingly. 'Yes, it was *Actinia crassicornis*. Mrs Gosse told me about it — there was a time at Ilfracombe when I shared their carriage. She told me because she knew I had some slight connection with the Reverend Kingsley, and it was he who sent the *crassicornis* to their house in Islington.'

My memory of that day was so strong that I had to look away, into the fire; there was a lump in my throat, too.

'You see, Mr Gosse had read in the Abbé Dicquemare's work that the anemone was good to eat — so he must test this for himself, and cooked some in a saucepan. I do not think he used butter. He presented some to Mrs Gosse and Willy to taste.'

'And did they eat it too?'

'Mrs Gosse told me that she could not. She said ... what were the words she used?' I frowned, trying to remember: she had been laughing as she told the story, teasing her husband. It had been during our failed expedition to the Valley of Rocks; they had both been very light-hearted for it was a holiday. 'She said it was as though a *sentinel* stood at the entrance to her throat and would not let the morsel pass.'

'A sentinel. I like that. And her son?'

'Mr Gosse told us that he himself had had difficulty with the "sentinel" but eventually he overcame it and ate several portions. He thought it tasted very good. So did Willy.'

They had prompted Willy: 'Tell Miss Church what you thought of the *Actinia crassicornis.*' It had clearly long been a family joke.

'I said "More 'tinny. 'Tinny tasted good". But I was very small at the time and couldn't speak very well. I meant "actinia".'

'Our little Oliver Twist, holding out his plate for more!'

'I am afraid we dined on several of Mr Kingsley's offerings, Miss Church — did we not, Henry? There was that dish of cockles.'

'Indeed. The excellent *Cardium tuberculatum*. Leaping and clattering in their dish of sea-water in the drawing room. They had been making quite a disturbance with their shells!'

'Your "Signor Tuberculato"! Perhaps you should not have given them names before we killed and ate them.'

'We "killed them to save their lives"!'

'I preferred the taste of the 'tinny, Mama, didn't I?'

'Yes, my darling one.' Emily had laughed merrily, and had caught the boy up in her arms, hugging him to her. 'You shall become a connoisseur as well as a naturalist.'

(The *manner* in which Mr Gosse had looked at her and his son!)

'Will you tell me, Anne?' Duncan leant forward to see my face but I kept it turned towards the fire, and shook my head.

'Please. You have been so withdrawn ever since you spoke with Mr Gosse. Tell me about Mrs Gosse — if it will help.'

'I cannot.' My throat was tight again, and I swallowed.

He reached out and turned my head gently to him, and then, hands against my cheeks, kissed me on the mouth. He was too gentle: if he had been rough or matter-of-fact I would not have burst into tears. Great sobs shuddered out of me, they seemed to come from so deep within me that I was struggling for breath. If Duncan was shocked, he did not show it; instead he held me tight and rocked me, stroking my hair as though I were a child. After a while he released me to bring out a handkerchief, and I tried to dry the shoulder of his jacket, and my face.

'You have a little more colour now — especially around the nose and eyes! Ah! Was that a little giggle? I love your giggle! Oh, hide your face quickly in this book, here comes the maid.'

Clever Duncan! We both pretended to be engrossed in an article in *Maga* while the hotel maid, very correct in her little lace cap and pinafore, poked at the fire and piled it high with coal, and Duncan smiled and thanked her as she bobbed and left.

'Do you feel more able to tell me what is worrying you now? Tell me about Mrs Gosse, if you wish, for it may help to … oh, exorcise her ghost. If I may put it so bluntly.'

'Alright.' I sighed. 'I'll tell you about the time I visited her when she was so ill — with Miss Shipton. You remember, she was the lady employed to chaperone me and Sarah at Ilfracombe.'

'Mmm. Some sort of evangelist or Quaker, was she not?'

'Yes. Miss Shipton had struck up an acquaintance with Mrs Gosse. Their love of the Lord brought them together, perhaps when Mrs Gosse was handing out tracts. It was strange, Ilfracombe seemed to attract such people — there were Mormons, too, preaching in the street … Anyway, they seemed to become good friends very quickly. Although I think Miss Shipton presumed often on Mrs Gosse's goodness, or perhaps tolerance. Mrs Gosse could be very sympathetic.'

I paused for a moment, remembering Miss Shipton's long tales of woe or complaint, and clicked my tongue in irritation.

'Miss Shipton once stayed with the Gosses in Islington, and she told me that they spent a very happy evening discussing the Scriptures — and Mr Gosse explained some point by reference to modern life, "like a parable", she said. And I recall now that she extolled Mrs Gosse's kindness in arising early to light her fire and bring her breakfast — she had apparently been awakened by Miss Shipton's restlessness.'

'Poor Mrs Gosse — it sounds as though this Miss Shipton was something of a trial.'

I blew my nose on Duncan's handkerchief, and then stood up to put the screen before the fire, for the heat was making my already-hot face burn even more.

'There was also the instance of Miss Shipton's jewellery,' I said, as I returned to the sofa.

'Your eyes are looking better now. I am not sure the same can be said about your nose.'

'You are such an *honest* man, Mr Robertson. I need never fear that you will dissemble!' I leaned against him, with one arm across his chest, breathing in his warm smell, soothed by his comfort. He lifted his arm to hold my shoulder, pulling me closer to him, and his chest rose and fell with a large sigh.

After a while, although we were silent and unmoving, I knew he was as conscious of me as I was of him; our bodies were heavy against each other, I felt every inch of their contact. Duncan moved his hand slowly (I thrilled in anticipation, my skin sensitive to the slightest pressure) until it rested lightly on my breast. We were both breathing fast, quite silent, rapt in these sensations, not wanting them to end ... but it was mid-morning, in a public room in an hotel ...

'I am very impatient for us to be *united*.' His tone was dry and controlled, when he eventually eased me away. 'I think you had better tell me about Miss Shipton's jewellery. Had she not renounced all worldly goods?'

He kissed me lightly, and we avoided each other's eyes as we straightened our clothes.

'Miss Shipton had several fine rings and necklaces — Sarah and I were quite surprised.' My skin was still tingling, and I moved a little way off and sat up straight. 'Apparently Mrs Gosse suggested that Miss Shipton — Do you *really* want to hear about this, my love? I cannot ... I cannot think straight!'

'It will benefit us both if you will tell me. I have an inordinate curiosity to hear the details.'

'You are mocking me. So I shall tell you as a punishment. So — Mrs Gosse suggested that Miss Shipton should indeed put away all earthly riches, but Miss Shipton found herself unable to do so — this is her own account, by the by. But one day, when she was praying, a beam of sunlight came in through the skylight and shone upon her rings, where they lay on top of the chest — and she interpreted this as a sign that she should give them up for the Lord. Mrs Gosse's advice had been sound.'

'So she gave them to the first poor woman she met in the street?'

His dry humour made me smile, and when he saw it he leaned forward and kissed me on the mouth.

'Anne, I love you so much.'

'But *why*?' How could he be so certain when I myself was so confused?

He shook his head, then suddenly gave a boyish chuckle. 'I really do not know. Although your antagonism towards the poor Miss Shipton amuses me. Well — now you have told me about Miss Shipton rather than Mrs Gosse. I am still trying to reach the point where it seems that the lonely Mr Gosse requires cheering with the news of an anemone unknown to man — although presumably very well-known to its Creator. Or am I being very callous and insensitive?'

'Oh.'

The switch in tone and subject startled me. I glanced at him quickly, aware that I had misjudged this man that I was soon to marry. I would have to reassure him that my action had been reasonable; I would have to provide an explanation that lacked embellishment or feeling, that was a straightforward recounting of the facts.

'I shall tell you. I heard these stories from Miss Shipton last October, a few weeks after I returned home from Helensburgh. She wrote to me and asked me to meet her in London, so that we might go together to visit Mrs Gosse, who was apparently very ill — and staying in lodgings with her son. I am not certain why she wanted me to accompany her, perhaps she was a little afraid of visiting on her own. I do not know.'

'Perhaps. But perhaps also, to do her justice, she thought that, since you were both acquainted with Mrs Gosse — and, in your case, also with her son — such a visit from the two of you might be beneficial. Master Gosse must surely have been lonely and in need of companionship.'

'She probably wished merely that I would take Master Gosse away and leave her in private conversation with Mrs Gosse — which of course I did.' I knew I was being overly critical and censorious. 'So — they were staying in lodgings a few doors from the doctor's surgery in Pimlico. He was an American doctor who professed to have a cure for her illness. I do not know what her ailment was, but it was in the upper part of her body and clearly caused her very great pain. Miss Shipton knew but would not tell me. Mrs Gosse was staying in Pimlico because it was too far from Islington to travel every day — she told us that Mr Gosse had a great deal of work in hand, so it was necessary for him to remain at home, although he tried to come down to see them every day.'

'It must have been very distressing for the family to be parted like that. And you say that the boy was there with her? Could he not have remained at home with his father?'

'I think she must have wanted him to be with her, to keep her company. Perhaps she had not realised that she would become so incapacitated. It was terrible to see,

Duncan! She lay there in her bed ... When we arrived, Willy had been reading to her from Newton's *Thoughts on the Apocalypse*! He told me that they sometimes sang their favourite hymns together. There was nothing for him to do but *watch* her — and she had become so thin and pale. I took him out for a walk and when I came back she was out of bed and standing by the fireplace, just leaning against the chimneypiece and *rocking*. Trying not to ... to moan.'

'I had no idea, my darling. I should not have asked you to explain.' He ran his fingers over my temple, tucking some stray hairs behind my ear. 'But nevertheless, it seems you must have thought that she would recover.'

'*She* seemed so certain! She said that she and Mr Gosse were optimistic, because they had asked the Lord. She had been ill for several months, even at Tenby in the summer, and when she came back — thus she told Miss Shipton — the doctor had decided that a more severe treatment was required. But every time she visited his surgery, she took it upon herself to cheer the other patients and bring them to Jesus. In spite of her own hardship! What I cannot comprehend is — if she was working so hard on the Lord's behalf — why He should then not see fit to help her to recovery?'

'It is very hard. There is an argument that the Lord takes His own — you must talk to a cleric to attempt to understand.'

'The *jealous* God. I cannot ... oh, I cannot believe that.'

'What did you talk about with the boy?'

'Nothing of great importance, as far as I can remember. Poor little boy! I wanted him to have some freedom and entertainment, albeit briefly. We watched the street sellers, and I bought him some hot chestnuts — but they were burnt and not a success. We talked about our time at Ilfracombe — and he told me about some "fat ladies" who were cut off by the tide on an island at Tenby, and had to be carried to safety by the bathing women. That had made everyone laugh, apparently, he and Mama and Papa too. And Papa had collected some *Purpurea* and squashed them, so that he and Willy could write their initials on a piece of cloth — the extract from the snails turned purple. They made purple letters ... He wanted me to buy an orange for his Mama because he said she did not care for grapes. Miss Shipton had brought grapes ...'

'That is a wry smile. Tell me.'

'Mrs Gosse was, I think, quite *saintly* about the grapes, Duncan. Miss Shipton had brought water-grapes, arranged on leaves in a basket — and when the landlady showed us up, there were already some grapes on the table. Miss Shipton made a fuss — "oh, she had so wanted to bring something special — but you have some grapes already, Emily dear." Etcetera, etcetera. And Mrs Gosse at once told her that the grapes on the table were inedible and sharp, and Anna's grapes were *beautiful*, she should lay them on the bed. A few moments later she took one of Anna's grapes and held it up for a minute — and closed her eyes. I didn't know what was the trouble. Then she said, "My dear Anna, I have been praying to the good Lord that He will never deny you grapes — as long as you live"!'

'Extraordinary woman. I wonder if He has?'

'I wonder.' I sighed. 'I was so dismayed to see her in that state, and the situation was a terrible ordeal for Willy. We were just on the point of leaving when Mr Gosse came running up the stairs — we could hear him — and burst in. He was quite taken aback to see us.' (His face had closed, for a moment he could scarcely speak our names.) 'Willy rushed up to him and jumped about, hugging him and kissing his hand. He had been writing, he had been preparing papers for the Royal Microscopical Society. We did not stay much longer — I think Miss Shipton is perhaps a little in awe of him. And he is awkward in her presence. Mrs Gosse gave Miss Shipton one of her tracts — *The poor man's penny* it is called, I have it still. It recorded something that happened to her on one of her earlier journeys on the omnibus between Islington and Pimlico.' I sighed again, I could not help myself, for I felt very weary. '*The poor man's penny* ... I would like very much to go to Jamaica, my darling. Do you think the voyage is very long?'

'That is a dramatic change of subject! We shall read Gosse again, on that subject, although it must be more than ten years since he was there. I have it on good authority that Mr Darwin consults with Gosse about Jamaican doves.'

'How *can* you know that?'

'Hah! From my uncle, Ballavich, who is a friend of Professor Harkness the geologist, who is naturally acquainted with Lyell and Huxley — for they are all Fellows of that august body, the Royal Society, where all the very important figures of the scientific establishment know everything about each other!'

'I suppose they do.' The thought of all those busy gentlemen for some reason filled me with unease.

'Shall I tell you something else? The author of this anemone article is a George Lewes — and he and his wife were persuaded of the merits of Ilfracombe for hunting sea anemones by the very same Professor Huxley — who had been there for his honeymoon!'

I joined in his triumphant laughter at this morsel of gossip; but there was a little idea flowering in my brain, wondering if my beloved, bereaved Henry would try for Jamaica once again. The well-being and education of his son would present him with a problem, but if there was a cousin in Bristol ... I pushed the idea into the deepest recesses of my poor, over-taxed mind.

Some weeks after I returned to Winchester I received a letter from Miss Shipton. She had been travelling in warmer climates and so had not known immediately of her dear friend's death. It was a curious letter, a mixture of sadness and jubilation. Emily was now amongst the saints — and she, Anna, had foreseen it. She had had a vision, which she had told to Emily:

'My dear Emily, on perceiving the inevitable outcome of the disease, wrote to me and asked, "Anna, is this the meaning of your vision?" I have spoken to Mr Gosse, and he has told me that, at the end, she called aloud for the doors of Heaven to be opened, to let her in. I had written out my dream for her, and I enclose a copy so that you too may rejoice in my darling Emily's eternal happiness.'

'I had a remarkable dream. I beheld a chamber, dark with clouds. In the centre stood Emily. Angel hands clothed her in a heavy purple robe, the weight of which bent her body, pale and emaciated, almost to the earth; in their hands they bore her up, lest she should dash her foot against a stone. The darkness passed, and her feet were set in that 'large room', that lacketh neither light nor freedom; it was open to the sky. Beneath the angels' ministering hands, the heavy purple robe gradually disappeared, and more and more visibly shone another robe, of surpassing beauty, in which they clothed her. Her attitude was that of a happy, innocent, obedient child.'

We must all die, we have no choice in the matter: but Anna Shipton thought she had foreseen the manner of her beloved friend's early departure. Only Emily's spirit could tell us if the details had been exact.

CHAPTER 18: ELIZABETH

I have just received a telephone call from Roger Trenton, who was apologetic and, I am certain, disappointed that Hazel Myers would be unable to join us for lunch. I am not a little relieved that she has gone across to Cambridge, but I try to reassure him.

'You will surely have an opportunity to introduce us at Nancarrow — although you must know that we have met before.'

'Yes, that's what she said, too. But I had especially wanted to show her the labs and the tower.'

That is understandable, because the building is full of surprises for the first-time visitor. Waterstone's glorious architecture, warm blue and honey-gold, the elaborately-moulded terracotta animals, barleysugar twists, gargoyles and climbing monkeys — every surface reveals some little delight.

'Why have I never been here before? How did I miss all this?' Allan kept asking that first time, as I showed him round the galleries.

That was in the late 'seventies, before the evolution of push-button interactive displays and moving models of dinosaurs. Natural light streamed in and Allan stroked polished mahogany cases and traced the details of moulded trilobites and ammonites on gingerbread pillars. The light, the echoing space, the tiled and mosaic floors all entranced him, and he made me see the building anew, through his eyes.

When we passed from the upstairs galleries, through the tall, polished double doors and into the silence of 'backstage', he was amused by the abrupt denial of overt ornamentation; the plain stone stairs with brass handrails, the painted doors and locked cupboards, unpeopled space with nothing on display. It still remains the same: the science moves on, as do the ideas and techniques, but the habitat is not much changed. It's a metaphor for our own evolution, the unchanging façade behind which the human brain leaps forward to form ever-greater connections, reaching further and further into the unknown. No longer does it seem that anything is unknowable.

I brought Allan here, to this office, which is now Charles Hetherington's but which was then mine. We came through that door down there, stepping onto the plain wooden boards, into the institutional, pale-green, cupboarded space, and I showed him my eyrie. He laughed at it! We had been awkward with each other in the galleries but he now became elated. (It must have been early in the year, because he wore a scarf and tweed coat, and the air was crisp and clear. He was dark-haired and clean-shaven, his face rather fuller, cheeks less hollow, than they had been in Addis. My hair was brown, and longer; I think I had pinned it up.)

'We have walked across the sky to find your tower,' he said, in his hinted-at Edinburgh accent. 'And now I find that you live in half a threepenny bit. A penny-ha'penny princess!'

He wasn't quite right, the old threepenny piece had twelve facets, and the room is an octagon — but the small rooms at the back, and the windows, confuse the pattern; a type of Victorian mezzanine, conceived as a store, a half-floor across the tower. The cut edge is fenced with a wooden balustrade, which now, as then, prevents the desk from toppling to the floor below. As I sit here and look South over London, I'm distracted from my final preparations for the Netherlands visit; distracted by memories of Allan and also, once again, by Hazel Myers.

I think I have been — *ambushed*, by Hazel Myers. Always this Gosse business; she forces him upon me, re-fashions him into a species of Trojan Horse so that she can slip in and break down the flimsy palisades behind which I have tried to imprison my memories, of both Barbara and Allan.

Surely she cannot know, or even suspect? We were so careful, Barbara and I. Hazel cannot be so cynical and destructive as to want to remind me of what I have lost. What I have lost of myself, too; that strange, joy-filled, besotted creature for whom the world took on a different perspective. I could scarcely, in that brief period of our lives, recognise what I had become. Barbara re-fashioned me! Barbara, my darling, my true love. Who showed me, so late in life, the ecstasy of love. Who made me look upwards, away from the ground, and outwards; who made me laugh and do childish things, and put aside, in her presence, the persona of the inhibited and serious Dr Wilson. What was it that made her find me worthy of pursuit, and so certain that if she were to bore deep into my mind she would find my little core of warmth, and would fan it into life? Cherish it, and make it hers. So that when she died, and was no longer here to light my love and life, that spark — that changed perception — spluttered out. And now, as before, I have returned to the outside, merely an observer trying to understand.

I have to suppress those memories. If I acknowledge them the memory of love fades and its place is taken by guilt; always the guilt, just beneath the surface, ready to pounce and destroy and take on its own enormous importance.

So why do you do this to me, Hazel Myers? What significance could Philip Gosse possibly have, for you — or for me?

Do you aim to use Roger Trenton as yet another Trojan Horse? Poor kind, weak Roger, who casually slips your name into conversations and tries not to sound petulant when his transparent attempts to woo you fail. If Roger had brought you here today you would, unknowingly, have visited the place where Allan proposed to me.

On the day that Allan proposed marriage, the rain and wind were beating against the tower. I was sitting at this desk, working. I heard footsteps outside on the metal walkway. The door opened and the noise of the wind burst in, but whoever had entered then stood still, waiting, perhaps listening.

'Elizabeth?'

I can still hear his tentative voice, very quiet.

I stood up and looked down over the balustrade, wondering what was wrong. Oh, that rare and beautiful smile, transforming his serious face, opening up his expression ... There was rain on his face and hair.

'Elizabeth!'

He held up an enormous bunch of red roses, and a gust of wind made the cellophane rattle; held them up towards me with both hands, and was full of courage and determination.

'Please will you marry me?'

I couldn't reach the bouquet, and he made some remark about Rapunzel before he climbed the stairs. (If we had ever had children, he would have been a good raconteur of fairytales; he would have been a good father.)

His face was cold and wet against mine. He had hurried through the downpour, hurried because he had to know my answer, and when I said 'yes', I think his courage left him, because all he was able to say was 'Are you really sure? You must be certain, because you know I don't have much to offer.'

You see what you have unleashed, Hazel Myers? You see how I remember those words? It would seem that there was a hierarchy in our perception of our worth, in certain aspects of our behaviour.

I would be interested to learn where Roger Trenton places his wife relative to Hazel Myers. My remembered perception of Barbara's daughter is of a certain calm languorousness, an impression of an uncluttered life; and that image might hold appeal for a middle-aged man who notes his own time passing.

Gosse's shells are not here. His bird-skins are not here, either, but are stored at Tring. However, when I was downstairs I found a copy of his book about Jamaica: 'Let Natural History be compared to a room-full of valuable objects and curiosities, thrown promiscuously in a heap,' he wrote. 'The objects themselves are almost unavailable until they are arranged in the shelves and drawers appropriated to them; yet it is obvious,' — and so it is, but it required an author's moment of inspiration to recognise the obviousness — 'yet it is obvious the *shelves are for the sake of the objects, not the objects for the sake of the shelves.*'

Thus we classify and arrange the objects in the compartments that we ourselves have devised. We know their co-ordinates, and can retrieve them after they have been stowed away. We rationalise; and remember the reasons for the rationalisation. We learn the system's geography. And when we find a certain drawer we know what category of object it should contain. As with objects, so too with memories.

When I returned from the Collections, I climbed the spiral staircase that led up to the roof and opened the doors onto the metal walkway, where Allan and I had 'walked across the sky'. The walkway is short, but fretted with holes, so that one may look down and see the roof below. Day after day I had crossed and re-crossed this drawbridge to the tower, occasionally stopping to glance at the view, but it had of course been Allan who had shown me the detail. The bright sun and sharp shadows had created illusory, shifting frames of reference and Allan, a man by then committed to the fine-focussing of electron beams to create a two-dimensional image, was captivated. Whenever he came to visit subsequently he would always spend time on the walkway, usually with the binoculars that he carried specially in his case; it wasn't so much the panoramic view of the city that had astounded him, but the intricacies of the Museum itself, so recently cleaned and restored to all their glowing detail.

But after he had become a regular visitor and had come to know the tower better, he and several of my colleagues had devised a scheme for constructing a *camera obscura* in the tower. Perhaps fortunately, the scheme had never come to fruition, partly because the risk of discovery was too great, but mainly because Allan had become too ill. The idea and design had all been part of his burgeoning interest in microscopes and image-capture, whether through the focussing of electrons or photons. He had already started to collect old microscopes, whenever he could pick them up cheaply, and now he collected old books and manuals about microscopy, and rummaged through boxes in street markets and dark little corner-shops to find spare parts. There was a table in the corner of the sitting-room in our flat where he would sit, patiently oiling, cleaning and re-assembling pieces, or attempting to re-centre an unaligned condenser. He found a man who would re-silver mirrors and, through him, someone else who had an interest in prisms and polished glass.

Apparently, when he was a young boy, eleven or twelve years old, his parents had taken him to the *camera obscura* in Edinburgh. He described to me how he had climbed the stairs to a darkened circular room; there were about a dozen people there, he recalled, shadowy figures who stood around a central table that was in fact a shallow white bowl. An elderly lady — or so he thought then — with grey hair and a gentle voice and accent, had explained the principles of the optical device, and had advised them what they would see. She had opened the shutter at the top of the room — and her prosaic explanation had not prepared young Allan for the astonishing living picture that had appeared on the table in front of him. Buses moved erratically along Princes Street, people walked the pavements, darted in front of cars, and flowed in groups in and out of shops. And it was all in colour! *Red* buses, a person in a bright blue coat, the bank of yellow daffodils in Princes Gardens! For several minutes, the watchers in the tower had pressed forward, pointing and exclaiming, and then suddenly the picture had dimmed and the colours had faded.

'A cloud has covered the sun,' the lady had said, precisely.

The captured Edinburgh scene was now little better than a black-and-white film, poorly focussed. But, my dear Allan told me, those few minutes had been enough!

Now, as I stood on the walkway and rested against the metal handrail that prevented one from falling to the roof below, a haze of heat and fumes partly hid the distant view. I could hear the buses and cars on Cromwell Road, but they were hidden by the bulk of the long South Building.

Below me stretched a landscape of ridges, peaks and intrusions: steep slopes of grey-purple slate, garnished with lead; tilted rectangles of frosted glass; warm red brick, and honey-coloured tiles; and the iron railings, incongruously punctuated with brass balls, inverted exclamation marks, that marched across the main ridge like a boundary fence along a scarp. I tried to see the roofscape again with Allan's vision, but the lighting was too diffuse, my vision blurred, and I was on the point of returning to the tower when the door opened and Charles Hetherington stepped out.

'Hallo, Elizabeth. Are you coming back in? I thought we might go and look at Douglas' results on those Senegalese worms, if you're interested.'

Charles was an old friend, only a few years senior but suddenly grown white-haired and stooped, yet still full of humanity despite his dry, somewhat brusque, manner. He stopped beside me and gestured at something above my head.

'Have you seen the buddleia?'

I looked up, surprised: a small buddleia bush had sprouted from between the slates of the corner turret, and its single blue flower spike wobbled in the breeze.

'No, I hadn't. How on earth does it obtain any sort of nutrition?' (Allan would have noticed the plant, and its incongruity, at once.)

'Pigeon droppings?' Charles shrugged, and leant against the rail beside me. He was silent for a few moments, then said quietly, 'Allan always raved about this view, didn't he? How long is it since you both left London — ten years? Twelve?'

He gave me a long look, then, his lined face creased further by a frown.

'Ten years or so. I was just thinking about Allan, too ... Did you know that it was the spiral staircase that finally convinced him of what was happening to him? They phoned from Reception to say he was on his way up to my office, but he was taking such a long time that I went to look for him. It's odd, isn't it, that some small delay — a small change in a behaviour pattern — should trigger an alarm? I opened that door, and there he was, still on the staircase, *sitting* on the staircase ...' (And weeping quietly, although that remains a secret between Allan and me; weeping and helpless.) 'It seems to be a day for memories. When I was sitting at your desk, I remembered how he came bursting in and proposed to me —'

'And Sidi had to hide in the boxroom, he didn't dare come out!'

Charles and I both laughed, remembering the Lebanese student's embarrassment.

'Yes, I never did tell Allan that Sidi had been in the office when he arrived. Of course Sidi thought we were far too old for those sort of antics. If you were in your forties you were really past it!'

'You had a good few years together ... It was a tragedy that no-one could pinpoint what was wrong. With the concentration of experts on unusual viruses and tropical diseases that we have in central London, you'd think *someone* could have come up with a diagnosis.'

'But there are so many exotic viruses with neurodegenerative effects — and who can ever predict how they'll interact with other strange infections? We would have had a lot more time together if we hadn't, well, lost sight of each other for so long after he came home from Ethiopia. As you know, we didn't communicate for years

— I was very involved with things here, and he was busy re-training.'

'Electron microscopy was an exciting new technology then, of course — it desperately needed its specialist engineers. Oh dear, look at that poor creature there.' Charles pointed to a particularly scrawny pigeon that was limping along the nearby ridge. 'Is it my imagination or is there indeed a higher incidence of sick birds these days?'

'I don't know, Charles. Maybe there are more pigeons around. Did you realise that was how Allan and I met again? Over the new scanning EM at Imperial College?'

Charles gave a pleased little snicker of amusement. 'No, I didn't. It sounds like Mills and Boon. "Lingering looks in the darkened room, two heads bent over a single viewing-plate ..." Sorry.' He pulled a contrite face. 'Forgive me, that's inexcusable. You know I'm not mocking.'

'It's all right. It does have aspects of soap opera about it — the place, the coincidence. I was over there with Jill Rotheram — do you remember her? — we were using the SEM to see if the microspines on the cercarial tegument might be used as a defining characteristic, to help us to distinguish hybrids. Actually, it was a marvellous excuse to play around and look at the images. What an eye-opener it was then, to see the three-dimensional representation of structures we'd only previously seen in section!'

'Do you remember those extraordinary scanning EM photographs of *Lymnaea* cells that the Dutch group showed, quite early on? Beautiful cells, with those lovely rippling pseudopodia. You could just imagine them reaching out and crawling over and engulfing something they didn't like ... I did rather wish then that I was a cell biologist. Oh, of course, you're going over to see some of those people tomorrow, aren't you? But excuse me, I interrupted you yet again, it's becoming a bad habit of mine.'

'There's nothing more to tell, really, Charles. It took Allan and me another couple of years after that meeting to decide to get married.'

'Hmm. And what about Nancarrow? Will you stay there, Elizabeth? It's a charming place — if a little isolated. Although I suppose its very isolation allows you ample thinking-time, assuming that's what you still want.'

'Where else would I go?' His question had startled me. 'It's my home — and lots of people come to visit, there's a stream of scientific colleagues. And I'm still perfectly capable of travelling on my own! But you're right about thinking-time, to some extent — solitude allows time for weeding out ideas, rather than creating them, I think.'

'Quite. Quite so.' Charles nodded. 'You know, this really is a very draughty spot. I hope you'll forgive my inquisitiveness — but we've known each other a long time, haven't we, Elizabeth? And I had the impression that you were in the mood for reminiscing. I was taking advantage of you, because it's rare for you to relax that guard. I suppose I'm just becoming a nosy old man.'

He held the tower door open for me.

'That's what we are here to do, isn't it? To be nosy. You can't escape your scientific training.' I smiled at him, and stretched my shoulders as we went back inside. 'And yes, we are old friends. I think my "guard", as you call it, has been relaxed because I had a phone call from the daughter of another old friend, a friend who is now dead — and she seems to have stirred up a whole mixture of memories. In fact, this girl wanted to know whether the specimens that Philip Gosse collected in Jamaica were still in the Collections. That's where I've been, down in Malacology.'

'Gosse, eh? He was a much under-rated man, you know. He had the misfortune to be around when Darwin and all that crowd were stealing the show, and everything had to be in black and white. You were either a Believer — in natural selection — or you weren't. Of course, Gosse was also a chum of Soapy Sam Wilberforce.'

He waited for me to pick up the allusion.

'Wilberforce? Oh, Bishop of Oxford. British Association meeting, eighteen —, let's see, eighteen-seventy-ish.'

'Hmm.' Charles nodded. 'Good. Very good. Eighteen-sixty, actually, and T.H. Huxley firing off broadsides all round, "rather be descended from an ape than a bishop." And so on. Hmm. Now, if you'd just wait down here a minute, I need to pick up a couple of reprints.'

Charles carried on talking as he went upstairs to the office.

'I always had the feeling that — given time — Gosse might have come round to the view that there could be a Divine Guiding Hand in evolution. There are always compromises to be made.' He peered down at me over the balustrade. 'He was very aware of the subtle gradations between the different Classes of animals, snakes as lizards without legs, and so on ...'

'I didn't know you were such an expert on Gosse. Why is everyone suddenly so interested in him?'

'I'm not an expert. But one can't fail to know something about him in this business. He was a taxonomist, to some extent. And we taxonomists are all evolutionary dead-ends, you know. A bit chilly out there, wasn't it?'

He stopped to put on his jacket over his thread-bare dull-green pullover, and then came cautiously down the stairs.

'Is it next year that you retire?' I asked. 'Have you and Rosemary made any plans what to do with all that spare time?'

'Hah. Rosemary's got all her bits and pieces of committees, and the grandchildren. She won't want to be shifted. No, my dear, I expect I'll find a corner and stay here, if they'll let me. And when I die they can embalm and varnish me, like dear old Jeremy Bentham — bless his philosophical soul! — and put me in a cupboard in the dinosaur gallery. Then I can be wheeled out to frighten the children when they're more than usually brattish.'

'I didn't realise you had been harbouring dreams of auto-iconism all these years, Charles. And I would have thought you would have preferred to haunt the Men from Clades and send them to an early grave,' I teased him, as I followed him along the narrow corridor to the labs. Charles still held out against the classification techniques of cladistics, the quantitative assessment of difference and similarity between species and genera. He joked about the 'numerical taxonomists', but I knew he felt threatened and bitter.

We had reached the door of the lab and he stopped for a moment.

'I haven't been able to compromise on that, have I? Old dinosaur, you see — making me old before my time. But you've done all right, though — you're still active, ideas flowing, internationally known and giving lectures all over the place, several books to your name. FFRS. It obviously keeps you young.'

'F-FRS?'

'*Female* Fellow of the Royal Society. A rare species, but on the increase, all of three percent at the last count. The RS became enlightened, if that's the word, rather earlier than the MCC, at any rate!'

He snickered again, but his eyes were tired and sad. 'You'll be on "Desert Island Discs", next, with Ms Lawley quizzing you about the luxury item you'd like to take.'

I smiled at him and took his elbow. 'I've been asked already. And I refused. Let's go and see what Douglas has got for us.'

Douglas wasn't in the lab, but his Research Assistant, Angela, was sitting at the bench, looking down a dissecting-microscope. She had obviously been perfusing hamster blood vessels, because there was a tray of plastic petri dishes in front of her, each numbered and labelled, and containing pink saline solution. She looked over the top of the binocular eyepiece and grinned at us.

'Hi. Look at these! Hybridising pairs. And just look at these livers!'

She lifted the lid of one of the dishes to show pieces of hamster liver, speckled pink and white with granulomata, the inflammatory lesions which had formed around schistosome eggs that had become trapped in the hepatic tissue.

'Isn't that great? We should be able to get loads of F1 eggs out of that one.'

'What are these — *haematobium* males and *mattheei* females?'

'Yep. Do you want to look?'

Angela shifted sideways off the stool so that I could sit down at the microscope. She knew quite well that I had looked at hundreds of schistosomes in my time, but she would also know that the sight of live worms never failed to thrill a parasitologist, or even a malacologist. Schistosomes are not like other parasitic flukes, they are not hermaphrodite and therefore capable of self-fertilisation, but instead there are separate sexes and somehow the males and females manage to find each other in the enormous dark warmth of the body. This is particularly surprising considering that, initially, the minute larvae migrate in through the skin and into the underlying tissue and are then swept around the body in the bloodstream to the liver, all the time growing and developing, and employing their cunning molecular trickery to avoid being attacked by the cells of the immune system. Then on again, from the liver to the blood vessels around the gut or bladder, there to brace themselves against the stream, to hang on and find a mate. The *improbability* of the life-cycle never fails to astound me.

They mate for life: the male captures a female and folds the flanges of his body around her, keeping her close until they die, parodying the metaphors of constancy and fidelity but in the baser interests of sex, of procreation. The two of them become a machine for producing fertile eggs, and propagating their genes.

And here Angela was showing me something rather special and unusual, in that worms of two different species were forming egg-producing pairs. Flushed out of the warmth of the bloodstream into the light, the coupled pairs, about two centimetres long, were writhing gently together in the medium in the dish, each long slender female projecting from the male's embrace — 'like a frankfurter from a bun', as I once heard Douglas incautiously tell an Asian student. Some pairs had become uncoupled, and the dark eggs were visible in the female's almost transparent body.

It's difficult not to be impressed by such beautifully-adapted and deadly organisms, even though they are responsible for causing great human suffering and economic loss. But if such hybridising pairs occurred naturally — and there was increasing evidence that they did — they might be capable of changing the pattern of human infections in the areas where they were naturally found. Another factor in the multifactorial complexity of the host-parasite equations.

'Roger Trenton's coming over from King's to collect a sample for analysis, isn't he?'

'Uh-huh. He wants the males and females separated, so I'm doing that just now.'

I stood up. 'That's really very exciting. Well done! Is Douglas around? He wanted to talk over some of the results with us.'

'He's just in the snail-room with Tim — they're setting up to do the single-miracidium infections this afternoon. But he'll be up in a minute — he said you were to go through to the seminar room. He's quite excited. He's going into one of his manic moods — you know what Doug gets like.'

Angela grinned again, and I laughed.

Charles and I spent an hour or so with Douglas discussing his results, sitting around the Seminar Room table with photos of DNA gels and tables of comparative data spread in front of us. It was an interesting story, as yet predominantly experimental and lab-based, but with some corroborating data from the field. *Schistosoma mattheei* normally only infected ruminant animals, but wherever it showed sympatry with *S. haematobium* (and they both had the same geographical range in South Africa, for example) it appeared to be able to infect humans as well. What was so very interesting was that results from laboratory experiments suggested that the F1 hybrids — the first-generation offspring produced as a result of mating between the two species — were more infective to both the snails and the mammalian hosts than were either of the parent species. This heterosis took the form of more rapid growth and maturation of the worms, and a greater output of eggs. If this were also to occur naturally, in the field, it would have important implications for the epidemiology of bilharzia in that region.

There was also the absorbing question of how this hybridisation between the two species would affect the gene pool. This was the question to which I always returned: it was the intellectual puzzle that had, perhaps, become my obsession, whether it concerned the gene pool of schistosomes, or snails, or species X or Y.

Douglas had been called to the telephone, and Charles and I, as so often, were discussing speciation, how one species could ultimately give rise to two.

'The problem, as we know, is that during the earliest stages of their divergence, there may be less difference between them than there is variation within them,' he was saying, 'and they can still interbreed.'

'I like to imagine the original species as a pebble thrown into a pond. A wave of divergent forms spreads out in a ripple, further and further apart, until the outermost ones cannot interact — breed — with the point of origin, and they become new species. The same applies to the diametrically-opposed variants, they can't interact either. The reproductive isolation that results is the point of no return, the *only possible* outcomes are new species. Of course, if you're going to use this as an analogy, you also have to postulate local differences in the water or in the way the ripples spread — there have to be selection pressures in the environment that act locally on the spreading ripples ...'

I paused for a moment, staring out of the window, momentarily surprised that there was no rippling water in sight, only roofs and haze. The potential danger to the snails, the pathological threat, seemed so obvious.

'So, if you transfer that analogy to the case of speciation of snails, one new selection pressure could be the threat from a new parasite that is itself becoming more infective to the snail. As might seem to be the case with Douglas's F1 worm hybrids.'

'Of course,' Charles interposed dryly, 'The differences arise as adaptations to the environment, not as devices for reproductive isolation. Or devices to help the poor old systematist sort out his species. That's the trouble with us classifiers, we're always looking at the hierarchies, and searching for the dividing lines. And wanting clear-cut answers. So we can say definitively that this is species A and this is species B — as though the process of evolution ended with Darwin and wasn't carrying on all the time.'

'Charles, stop pretending to be so archaic.' I laughed at him; this was his familiar stance. (Shelves for objects, or objects for shelves?). 'Did you ever meet Jim Steinberg? He's staying with me at Nancarrow at the moment — a population biologist, but a mathematician by training. His greatest pleasure is in thinking about the *dynamism* of the speciation process — its fractal nature, as he calls it, the splitting and bifurcation of species into other species. The chaos that gives rise to order.'

'That's your strength, Elizabeth — like a mighty Colossus, you bestride both camps. Concerned with populations and not merely individuals.'

'That sounds unhappily like a criticism.'

Societies of people versus the single person? I hoped not. I wondered if that was how I was perceived. When Allan had quietly and despairingly commented on his biological uselessness, I had been uncharacteristically glib, had tried to console him with a joke. It was unimportant, I said: the human gene pool is large enough without us needing to contribute. 'Gene pool': a term that was bandied about, a useful shorthand for the effects of fertilisation, that was quite divorced from the sexual act, or love, or need. That was the only occasion on which Allan had become angry with me and, consequently, the words we spoke then had been locked permanently, and painfully, in our memories.

But Charles seemed to have ignored my comment, and was apparently still considering speciation.

'The trouble is, the generation of biological diversity requires enormously long stretches of geological time, and I'm not sure —'

'I wish I had lots of time,' Douglas said, as he erupted noisily back into the room, with a box of transparencies for the overhead projector in his hand. 'I need to stand still so I can catch up with everything that's got to be done.'

'No point. Might as well give up now, before the next asteroid hits. Did you know that our own great Richard Owen coined the word "dinosaur"?'

'Yes,' I said. 'I did. And our Great Founder also briefed Bishop Wilberforce for the Oxford debate. Against "Evolution". Did *you* know, Douglas, that Charles wants to be embalmed like Bentham and put in the dinosaur gallery?'

'Huh. Better to get that Damien Hirst to pickle you in a glass tank. He stole the idea from the zoologists, so it would be appropriate to bring one of his so-called sculptures back here.'

'Hah. With little paper labels pinned to different parts of my anatomy, I hope. But I think that on balance I'd prefer to keep my clothes on.'

When I pointed out that he had wanted to frighten the children, his wheezing laugh echoed down the corridor.

CHAPTER 19: HAZEL

'My own love, How lonely you must feel tonight — and how much I am sure you must wish me back.'

'My own sweet boy — Now that beloved mamma is gone to be with Jesus, you are all that is left to me.'

I cannot get their words out of my head. I had gone there to read Gosse's *Memorial* to his wife, Emily, but I had been sucked in; had delved deeper; had requested folders of letters, and diaries. I had been unable to leave the Manuscript Room. I'd known Roger was waiting, possibly afire with sexual anticipation — but I hadn't cared.

I had held letters that Gosse and his wife had written to each other; their hands had touched that paper, their pens had traced those words. I had intruded on their love, and the horror of her dying.

****

A woman across the aisle from me swore briefly and sucked her hand as hot coffee sloshed from her plastic cup. I grabbed my briefcase before it hit the floor and braced my elbows against the arm-rests, waiting for the crash. But the train settled back into its former breathless rhythm and galloped on towards the West. I opened the briefcase and pulled out my notebook, now half-filled with pencilled notes.

Emily Gosse had taken nearly ten months to die: every day, as she massaged the ointments onto her breast, treated the wound and changed the dressings — every day she would have been aware of what was happening. And at the end, opiates. Homoeopathy. A century and a half later and we still used the same painkillers and witch-doctor methods. But would she have survived if the cancer had been excised?

The pointlessness of my question hit me. My own mother had undergone that surgery, the total removal of her right breast. And she had still died.

I rested my head against the window and thought of those two women, dying slowly, knowing that they were dying. Accepting it; even, in Emily's case, happily awaiting death, longing to be with her Jesus. The Lamb.

I could remember when my mother had, apparently, acquiesced. By then — it was about three weeks before her death — she was receiving morphine injections. She alternated between clear thoughts and abstract ramblings, and she was often imperious; she frequently frightened or upset me, and I tried not to panic because I didn't know what to do. She had asked me to read her horoscope, one of the full-page kind in a magazine devoted entirely to that silly business, and she had made me repeat certain sections, several times throughout that day. She told me to put the magazine under her pillow, so I lifted her shoulders and slipped it beneath her head.

She was gaunt and skeletal, almost weightless. Her heavy body had become so thin that sometimes I could scarcely recognise her. Matt had come down a couple of days previously — but he had been frightened, and he'd fled.

(Back to Gail, I was certain. The soft enfolding body of Gail, who had known how to comfort him as a small boy, and would have known how to comfort the grown-up lad. The comfort of sex. I could see Matt's tanned young body, imagine him with Gail. Not just Matt, though — my son's body. The picture made me inhale sharply. Roger. Imagine Roger. Pale fleshy torso, a little flabby, sparse dark hair on his belly and chest? I shuddered a little, and said in my mind, 'Sorry, Roger.' I would have to do some explaining there. And groped for my previous train of thought, surprised to find tears on my cheeks.)

That horoscope, the one that I put under her pillow, had calmed Mummy and made her happy. I hadn't understood why, I'd never understood the language or the nuances. I don't know what happened to that magazine, I suppose I burnt it with the others. She hadn't explained the meaning. She had smiled occasionally, and sometimes she had said, 'Yes' or 'It's all right' or 'I understand.'

'That's how she died.'

I had whispered it aloud. Who had I been talking to? I startled myself for a moment and glanced across the aisle; the woman had made a little pile of sodden brown tissues on the floor.

That was how Mummy had died. It was unusual in her, to be so calm, to have so little to say; I wondered if the calmness had been latent in her, if her exuberance had been a disguise. I am the calm one, so they all say. Jamie, too, now that he has found what he wants in life — his family, his birds: they have no great expectations, they allow him to be what he should be. My mother's calmness arose from something deeper than the chemical effect of opiates. She seemed at peace.

'At peace.'

I whispered this, too, trying it out, but I didn't know what it meant. I had a suspicion that it was a cliché, a rationalisation.

I suddenly felt very lonely. I would have liked to talk to someone about Emily's death, and about Mummy. But there was only Jamie, and what would I have said? I closed my eyes and drifted in and out of a fitful doze.

****

Last night a dog had woken me from my dream. The small college room was stifling, and a dog had been yapping in my dream, except that as I came awake I realised that there really was a dog, barking down below in the quad. I got out of bed, feeling the damp sweatiness of my neck and hair, and looked out of the window. A small white Yorkshire terrier was scuttling along the gravel path, and it lifted its leg against the stone fountain in the centre. Why was there a terrier in the quad in the middle of the night?

I wiped my face with a cold flannel and went back to bed, and as I drifted towards sleep again, fragments of my dream came back to me. Mummy had been rubbing cream on my sunburn. I was a child again, naked; and I had run away from her, I didn't want her to do it. I seemed to be running along a path that led through a field, an endless path that led to the beach. I was running, but my movements were jerky, in snap-shot stills, a Muybridge sequence. In the distance was the beach, Mummy was there in a kaftan, somehow she had leapt ahead. Jamie was there, too, wearing dark clothes, heavy dark clothes, and he was lying face-down on the sand. What had Jamie been doing in my dream? I tried to remember. He'd had a cape, he'd covered me with the cape but it had hurt my sunburnt skin. Perhaps it wasn't the dog that woke me, I think I was crying out to Jamie, but the words were Emily's: *'I do not like to go to bed, I shall be so lonely.'*

****

At the College Lodge, the porter had handed me two notes. One was a telephone message from Elizabeth Wilson: 'Gosse's birds at Tring Museum. No shells in the collection here. Sorry.' The information had seemed irrelevant, and I hadn't been disappointed.

Roger had left a hand-written note. 'What happened? I waited until 2pm. Are you all right? Phone me tomorrow at the lab if you can.' He had included his telephone number, but I had crumpled both notes into a ball and had asked the porter to drop them in the bin.

In 1852 Emily had written to her husband:

My best-beloved, ... How I wish I could see you and know what you are looking at and thinking of this morning. I have just dined and wished I could have divided my cutlet with you. I hoped to have Baby's company at least but he sleeps on still... The day seems very long, the evening I suppose will be more so... Every tread that sounds like yours out of doors makes me sad to think it cannot be you. But I pray for you that you may be kept from all harm and greatly enjoy your journey, and may you find it conducive to your health.

How much I love you, and how unlike the house is, without you, to what it was and will be again, with your dear presence.

****

A penny bun. *'The blackened lump dropped out ... the size and shape of a penny bun.'*

****

The 'whoof-*thump*' of a passing train, startling me awake near Plymouth. The River Tamar; a curving metal track; the huge grey railway bridge. By pressing my cheek against the window I can see the words 'I.K. Brunel. Engineer. 1859'. In November 1859, Darwin's *Origin of Species* was published.

February 1, 1859. P.H. Gosse to his son:

Montrose, Tuesday evening. My beloved Boy, You see I have just got to the extreme point of my travels, 650 miles from Torquay. I have just dined with some agreeable friends, and expect to deliver my first lecture in about an hour. Montrose is a pretty little town, and the coast is said to be pretty good for zoology.'

Poor Isambard Kingdom Brunel knew nothing of all that. He had his own worries. At the opening ceremony, his bed was pulled across the bridge on a flat-bed truck, so that he could experience the results of his engineering before he died.

****

Matt is waiting for me on the platform as the train pulls in. I'm surprised, because I thought he might make a point of being late. I realise I've been looking forward to seeing him, but I'm not sure if he is entirely pleased to see me. He looks relaxed and casual as he chats with a railway official, but his grin is less natural and his shoulders are tensed after he catches sight of me. He'll have enjoyed having the Shell House to himself. He'll have liked the independence.

He greets me warmly enough as he takes my case. I would like to hug him, but he walks on ahead.

CHAPTER 20: MATTHEW

I'm so *pissed off*! Hazel's in a funny mood, Jim's in a sulk or brooding. And Caz has left, her holiday's over. End of affair, not that it ever got off the ground properly, with weedy Sue hanging round all the time.

Caz and I really fancied each other, straight off. The two of them were in The Anchor one night and I chatted to them quite a lot from behind the bar, bought them a drink and so on. They were here on holiday, staying in one of the flats in West Polkenna, and next day I wangled them a free ride on Mick's speedboat trip round the bay. Mick comes into the pub a fair bit, and we get on okay; he lets me hang around and help out on the pier, selling tickets when things get busy. Slips me the odd tenner for helping. It's not much but he reckons I do pretty well for myself anyway, checking out the talent, helping the girls into the boat, stuff like that. Right enough!

Caz and Sue certainly liked that boat ride, shrieking their heads off whenever dollops of spray came over and caught them. I hung around with them on the beach and in the town, and Caz and I soon kept trying to go off on our own, but then she and Sue kind of fell out. Sue said they'd come on holiday together and she didn't want to be left on her own. Well, fair enough, I could see her point. Caz asked if I had a friend who could look after Sue, but there's really only Jim.

Anyway, I even asked them up to the house for a cream tea. (Hazel was in Oxford or Cambridge, maybe she'd even sneaked off somewhere with Roger, I didn't know.) Domesticated, that's me! Bought all the stuff and a bottle of white wine. They really liked the house and the shells, and we sat out in the garden and ladled jam and cream onto scones. Caz came and helped me in the kitchen and we had another good snog, and things began to get a bit exciting. So Caz took Sue some of my CDs and my Walkman, and told her to carry on sunbathing in the garden for a bit, we'd be inside. We went up to my room, and I shut the back window in case we made too much noise — but it wasn't much good because she was too nervous, with Sue being there and so on. It was really annoying, in fact it was bloody frustrating — and we both felt really bad about being so useless. Caz said we needed peace and practice!

And then of course Hazel decided to come back the next day. She rang in the morning to ask me to pick her up from the station, and so I couldn't meet up with Caz for a little more practice, as planned — we'd arranged to go back to her flat. So, now she's gone home. But though she's nice-looking (nice eyes, cropped blonde hair) and funny, and we got on really well (we even like the same music, which is cool but quite weird), I guess we both know we probably won't keep in touch. She's a year older than me and a nursery nurse, and works in Birmingham.

Then Jim's all moody because he got this letter from his partner back home. This bloke was supposed to be coming over next month and they were going to spend a few weeks going round Europe together; but now he can't come. He's being sent off on some course to do with his work or something, and Jim's really sad. I can see why, it's a real bummer for him and, as he says, it's hard to talk on the phone because there's eight hours time difference, and anyway, you can't communicate properly if you can't see the other person's face. Jim and his partner have been together for two or three years, he says they're quite an old married couple

But part of his problem — my problem! — is that he's also very pissed off with me, mainly because I asked him last week if he'd like to come and keep Sue company, lay on his famous charm and all that. After all, I said, you're always going on about women liking gay blokes — and she's quite a sweet kid, it'll be someone for you to talk to other than me and Elizabeth, for a change. He got into a really bad mood and said that was a helluva thing to ask, it wasn't as though we were that good friends, and so on and so on. Yeah, well, it was pretty dumb of me, I can see that, but I was getting desperate. So I said I was really sorry, but things have been a bit cool between us since.

And as for Hazel. Well, she came back on the train in a really funny mood, all preoccupied. I asked, kind of casually, if she'd met up with Roger at all, and she acted surprised and cold, and said, 'What on earth has Roger got to do with anything?' So I don't know what went on there, I hope *nothing* went on because I sure as hell don't want our lives complicated by Roger Trenton. Anyway, she's been working like crazy since she got back, these big manuscripts arrived by courier. (Couriers are supposed to be quick, aren't they? He should have run up the hill. Heh heh!)

I was talking to Mick the speedboat man about the dinghy at Nancarrow (he used to know the people that owned it before, said they were useless at racing, always lagging at the back and capsizing). He thought he knew how to fix it, with the fibreglass stuff you put on cars, and he gave me some to try out. He's a good bloke, he and his wife used to run the fish-and-chip shop until they got sick of the stink of hot fat. Now their daughter and son-in-law run it, and Mick's wife does the ice cream kiosk and sells shrimping nets and postcards as well.

It was great having the house to myself, even though it's not my house. I had a good snoop around, but there was nothing much to find — though I did get out Barbara's paints and brushes and the other stuff. Most of the acrylics have gone hard, I wonder if Hazel will buy me some more because I can't afford them myself. 'Educational expenses'? But I don't seem to find the opportunity to ask her, and now that she's working, I feel I'm in the way. There's nothing much to do. I even wondered about going back to Dad's. But I'd really be in the way there, too. And I've got the job here, I need the money.

Actually, my life's a fucking mess and I'm feeling pissed off and sorry for myself. So I've taken the car and Mick's magic boat-repair stuff, and — well, what the hell! — I'm going to Nancarrow to mend the boat. With or without Jim's help. Maybe after that I'll row off into the sunset and drown myself. Hah! Then they'll be sorry (if they even notice.)

What was that about killing myself? Nearly got killed by a fucking tourist caravan, filling up the whole fucking lane and couldn't reverse. If they can't fucking learn how to manoeuvre those things they should stay on the fucking motorways! God, it gave me a fright! I can hardly believe I've got here in one piece. Elizabeth's car's here, so is Peter Pascoe's bike, his helmet sitting on the seat, watching in case anyone comes too close. It's got an evil glare. No Roger, but then he's not due back until tomorrow.

I go round to the kitchen door. It's open, as usual, and Elizabeth's inside; she's heard me coming and smiles her brief eye-crinkling smile.

'Hello, Matthew. Would you like a piece of this excellent old howdah?'

She points the little sharp knife at a big old cheese with yellow warty skin, that she's hacking bits off. It's mid-morning and seems a funny time to be eating cheese, but I say yes and she gives me a sliver. It's hard with little white crunchy bits in and she explains that she brought it back from the Netherlands, and that it's a good one, nicely matured. I eventually realise that it's probably the cheese I call 'gooduh', but I don't want to show my ignorance; so I ask if she had a good time, and she tells me that it was interesting and worthwhile. And that Jim's working on his computer if I want to go on through.

I'd already seen Jim through the window as I walked past and he lifted a hand but carried on tapping at the keyboard. However, he looks up as I come in. He seems quite tired and strained.

'Hi, Matt. How're you doing?'

'Fine. Look, I can see you're busy but —'

'Yeah. I got a load of data yesterday from the Oxford group.'

'Right. I was wondering if you'd like to work on the boat a bit? Mick gave me some goop which he thinks will fix the holes —'

'Matt, I'm right up to here right now. This isn't a good time, okay?'

'Okay.' I can see it's not. 'I'll just leave the stuff then.'

'Sure.' Jim looks up at me, and raises his shoulders then lets them drop with a sigh. 'Maybe later, okay? Give me an hour?' He sighs again, sort of in exasperation, but I don't know whether it's at himself or me. 'Hey, man. Look, I'm sorry, I don't mean to sound like a bastard, it's just that things have been getting to me a bit, you know?'

'Yeah. I'm sorry. And I'm sorry too about asking you to help out with the girls last week, I'd no right to do that, it was kind of insensitive. Especially with your own plans falling through, and everything.'

'Yeah. Well. I guess we'll work something out. But let's you and I be friends again, hey?'

He smiles at me and holds out his hand. There are bags under his eyes, and his hair is loose and tucked behind his ears; it makes his ears stick out.

'Sure.' We shake hands, kind of formally. 'That's great.' But he holds onto my hand for a moment and looks sort of serious. 'It's a real shame you're not gay, Matt.

You and I could have some fun, we'd make a great couple.'

'Ah no. I don't think so. It's just not my scene.'

I let go his hand, a bit nervously, and Jim laughs out loud.

'It's okay, guy, don't look so scared, I was just giving you a line. I wouldn't want to compromise your heterosexuality.'

'Sure. Silly me!' I laugh, too, but even though he was joking he'd shocked me for a second or two.

'Right. If you can find something to occupy yourself I'll join you just as soon as I've got this glitch sorted.'

So, I wander back outside, taking an apple from the bowl on the kitchen table as I go. Elizabeth is in the garden at the back, up at the top where the wood comes spilling over, talking to Peter P. He's smoking and coughing, as usual, and I get the feeling that he's staring at me, though he's too far away to see his eyes.

The tide's half in or half out, I don't know which; and it doesn't depend on whether you're an optimist or a pessimist, the sea's not like beer. There are big waves rolling in and the wind's whipping the top off them as they curl and spill, so that spray's blowing up the shore. A couple of boats anchored, a few families sitting among the rocks or behind stripey windbreaks; some sort of little poodle-thing dashing about and yapping ... I sit on the seawall for a bit and stare out to sea. I guess most people who are hetero must wonder what it's like to do the other thing. There are guys who do both sexes, but I couldn't hack that. I mean, how do you know who you are? You could lose track of yourself. At some stage you'd have to decide which side you batted for. At some stage you'd have to settle it, and settle down — or you could die pretty lonely. A butt of jokes. Or a joker's butt. Hah. Choices, though: you have to choose.

After a while I jump down onto the shore. I take off my trainers and put them under the boat so that no-one will nick them. I've left the apple on the wall and have to go back and get it. The shaley pebbles are warm and smooth but I tread on some dried seaweed and it hurts like hell.

I poke along the strandline and find a tiny cuttlebone, only a few centimetres long, and a bunch of egg-cases that look like a ball of bubble-wrap, but don't pop when you press them, just stink. The yappy dog comes bossing around, little bully-boy, so I throw the ball of eggs at it, and it sticks its tail in and rolls its eyes at me, then runs away. Then I worry that its owners will come and chuck things at me, so I head over to the rocks. The barnacles are not too useful on bare feet, but I find a boulder next to a big deep pool, and sit on it and start to eat the apple that I've been saving. I'm sitting there, taking the occasional bite, staring up at a couple of vapour trails and wishing I was flying off somewhere far away with Caz, when I notice Elizabeth walking down the shore. She's wearing trousers and wellies, so she doesn't have to mind where she's walking and she's definitely heading my way.

'Matthew,' she says when she gets close, 'I'm glad I found you. I thought you might be working on the boat.'

'No, I thought I'd wait for Jim. "Waiting for Jim". Sounds like the title of a film, doesn't it?'

'Your mother phoned to check —'

'Hazel,' I correct her. 'I don't think of her as my mother.'

But I didn't mean to sound quite so rude.

'Of course. Hazel. Hazel telephoned because she plans to walk over here. She has something she would like to discuss with me, apparently — and she was hoping you would be staying here for a while so that she could get a lift back. I gather you have her car. I believe she should be here in about an hour.'

'Right. I guess I'd better wait, then. I suppose Jim *will* be out soon.'

'Poor Jim is very busy. May I join you for a few minutes?'

'Er, sure. Yes. Shall I pull you up? Oh — hang on a minute.'

My hand is sticky from the apple, and I stand up and look for somewhere to chuck the core. I hurl it towards the sea and it arcs through the air and falls onto a rock, where it bounces and rolls into a pool. Elizabeth has climbed up without waiting and she watches the apple core fall.

'Food for the crabs and shrimps. Good.'

She smiles at me and looks behind her to choose a smooth place to sit. I bend down and dabble my hand in the pool at our feet.

'I find there's something very satisfying about eating an apple out of doors, don't you? — particularly when one is out walking. You can plan when and where you are going to take the next bite. It becomes necessary to examine the apple and turn it around, to decide whether to eat it in a continuous circle or symmetrically. And the most interesting part,' she says, 'is planning how to dispose of the core. I like to throw it where I can imagine that a variety of insects, for example, or a vole or field mouse will find it. An unexpected food source for a small ecosystem! But perhaps you think that is rather fanciful? "Apple-eating as an exercise in strategic planning"?'

Her eyes are screwed up slightly against the sea-glare; wrinkles radiate out, their ends curving down. The skin on her arms and the backs of her hands has large brown freckles. If you joined the dots you might make an interesting shape. I've been staring at her, and what she has been saying has surprised me a bit.

'I like that idea. I hadn't thought of apples like that. But some people even eat the core …'

'Very selfish! When I was in Africa, it was very easy to buy ripe mangoes — I know you can get them here now but they are always tough and wooden in comparison — and eating them always required a great deal of forethought because otherwise one would end up being covered in juice. And a magnet, as a result, for insects! So it was always a question of organising a mango-eating session near some water, where one could wash one's hands and face afterwards. Moreover, it needed to be water that was unlikely to contain schistosome-infected snails. Sometimes the planning began to seem almost too much trouble!'

'Where did you go in Africa?'

She talks a bit about Ethiopia and Tanzania — Tanganyika it was called then — and I can easily imagine her trekking around on her own, with her sun-hat and tent. She must have been pretty brave when she was young. What my Dad would call 'a tough cookie'.

Slightly scary, though, and I feel she's always looking for simple ways to explain things to me. But I suppose that's okay, at least I can understand.

'I'd like to go to Ethiopia and Eritrea,' I say, 'it sounds good. Apart from the fact that they're always fighting each other. But I don't suppose there are any jobs for an unqualified artist.'

'But you have other skills, Matthew. Most people do.'

She puts her head on one side and looks at me; it's like she's almost forcing me to make eye contact, and I can't help myself. Her mouth is slightly puckered and she's frowning.

'You will realise your own potential, you know.'

'What potential is that? There's no great history of potential in our so-called family. My Dad's an accountant, always has been. Hazel — well, look at Hazel. She just kind of drifts along. Even my grandmother wasn't a brilliantly-successful painter. My uncle's a gamekeeper. Boring, all of us!'

She turns away and watches some little kids who are shrieking at the edge of the sea. How did we start this deep conversation? I see how cleverly she winkled her way in with all her talk about apples.

After a while she says, 'I don't think … You sound rather bitter, Matthew. I think that you're probably denigrating yourself and your family. And I wonder if Hazel *really* drifts? Have you any idea why she's coming to see me?'

'No, though it's probably something to do with Gosse again. It's an obsession with her just now, Emily Gosse, and some relation of ours. Bloody Gosses, who cares?'

There's that quick-flash, eye-wrinkling smile again, that comes and goes almost before you notice.

'I see.' Long pause. 'Matthew, I have the distinct impression that there is a small black cloud hovering above your head today.'

I put my hand up and feel around, and I can't help grinning. I give a little tug on an imaginary string and then snip it with my fingers.

'Yeah. Sorry. And do you think you could call me "Matt"? "Matthew" makes it sound like you're telling me off. Which maybe you are.'

'I just wonder what has caused the cloud. Perhaps life is rather unexciting for you at present? You need some extra stimulation? Goodness — I nearly forgot! I picked this up for you on the way.' She leans back and scrabbles in the pocket of her trousers, and brings out a deep ruby-coloured shell. 'Another *Littorina obtusata* for you, one of the less common colour morphs. Have you done anything interesting with the others?'

'You remembered! Thanks, that's a really good colour. Yeah, I've drafted out a couple of designs. I tried out a sort of interlocking pattern, but it's a bit difficult getting the colours right. I wanted the different colours to move towards each other so that — well, I wanted to make it like they play tricks with you, so that you're seeing one colour type and then suddenly it's the next. But of course it doesn't work out like that, they're too —'

'Disparate. In real life — with real shells — there is too great a disparity in the colours. But the beauty of art, of the artist's eye, is that you can interpret. Isn't that what so-called artistic licence is all about? Surely it's up to you to do what you wish — unless of course you want to reflect the true biological nature of the phenomenon. If you want to do that you must attempt to create a different design — because the object itself *is* the design, it interprets itself and there is no room left for licence. And in that case the artist has to learn to see the inherent qualities and depict them accurately.'

'But that's just plain illustration. Like your own drawings of different types of snail.'

'No, there is a difference. Those are factual drawings, statements, of proportion and other characteristics rather than of "character". And "character" is that indefinable quantity or entity that the artist as observer must interpret and then define.'

'So how do you tell a living snail's character? If you draw a snail shell and a living snail, surely they're still both depictions or statements? You can't "interpret" something like that boring anemone down there in the pool. But I can paint it.'

I'm sure I've got the better of her on this one and I must sound pretty pleased with myself. As I point at the red contracted blob with my big toe I notice that my feet are pale and wrinkly with the cold.

Elizabeth scratches her neck underneath her chin and looks again into the distance, then turns to me with a little nod.

'That's a very good question, Matt. I can make a straightforward illustration of a living snail, yes, but with a little more *understanding* I could also convey a lot more than obvious physical characteristics. If we go back to the idea of inherent qualities … We're talking about known aspects of behaviour, aren't we? The manner in which a particular individual comports himself, for example how he arranges his limbs and holds his head, in response to certain moods.' (I think of that portrait of her husband in his wheelchair, and how she's somehow caught his character.) 'And perhaps, also, as with the maxim of the late-Renaissance painters, that you wear on your face the evidence of your past experience. That's also true of snails, incidentally, their past experience is described on their shells. But regarding the behaviour of snails, I've learnt by observation how a certain species would behave in a certain situation. Likewise for that beadlet anemone, down there — what it is doing, in fact, is showing a very elegant response to unfavourable conditions. It is not covered by water, and water is the medium that gives it life.'

'I knew it was a mistake to get into an argument with you,' I mutter. But I'm kind of elated, too, because who else bothers to talk to me like this? I wish I was better at thinking of clever things to say.

Elizabeth gives a funny little laugh and she reaches out and sort of pats my knee.

'You're definitely going to realise your potential, Matt,' she says. 'Now —' she grunts slightly as she pushes herself up from the boulder and for a moment she looks a bit unbalanced as she pulls on her jumper. 'Now', she says again when she's got herself organised, 'Come with me. I want to show you something interesting.'

She sets off across the rocks, pretty nimbly considering her age, and I'm soon left behind because of the barnacles and my bare feet. Need to do some toughening-up exercises, walking on hot coals or something. Ouch! Oh shit!

'Wait there, then, I'll be back in a minute,' she calls, and she heads over to some rocks at the side of the bay, beneath a crumbly cliff. Gulls and oystercatchers are standing around on the rocks but they fly off as she approaches. I wonder what the hell she's doing as she bends down and picks things off the rock. She waves that I should join her at the top of the beach and my feet are glad to walk on the cold wet sand. (The poodle-thing keeps out of my way this time, though it would probably rather chance its luck with me because there's an Alsatian sniffing at its bum.) I run across to the boat and stuff my feet into my trainers while I wait.

Elizabeth has a handful of big black winkles.

'*Littorina littorea*, related to your little coloured ones. Now — we also need some seawater. Is there some sort of a container under the boat?'

I rootle around and find — embarrassingly — one of the empty beer cans that Jim and I left there a few weeks ago. 'That's all there is.'

'That will have to do. Run down and get some water — seawater, not from the stream — and make sure you wash that can thoroughly first! And then bring it up to the kitchen.'

I do as I'm told, and feel a bit of a prat as I walk carefully back up the beach. 'One pint of seawater, madam.' Bloody Alsatian's after me now, too, sniffing at my heels, so that I have to resist the temptation to tip seawater on its nose.

Back in the kitchen, Elizabeth has put the winkles into a couple of glass beakers, the sort we had in the school labs, and she tips the seawater on top of them. She clears a space on the windowsill next to the door — half-dead spider plant, dead flies — and puts the beakers there.

'We'll have a cup of tea and leave them to come out of their shells,' she says, as she fills the kettle. She digs out a packet of fig rolls from a cupboard, sniffs at an open carton of milk on the draining-board and pulls a face, and gets another carton from the fridge. Jim comes in and homes in on the biscuit pack.

'Great. New cookies. What are you guys doing?'

'It's a secret,' I say. 'She won't tell me.'

Jim raises an eyebrow and helps himself to three fig rolls, but Elizabeth just looks over at the beakers.

'Three of them are out already. Now — that looks hopeful. Do you see this large one that's already crawling around? Its foot is much darker than that of the other two.'

The almost-circular yellowish-brown object pressed against the glass is the winkle's foot. It seems to glide over the surface, the winkle's head with stubby tentacles and the hefty shell following on almost like an afterthought. The other two winkles that are moving around have pale creamy-white feet. Now several of the others are starting to move, too. Elizabeth and Jim and I are all crowding round the window, watching the shells lurch as the feet grope around and attach to the glass, then pull the snails upright. The snails have no option but to follow. Several of the feet are dark yellow or brown.

Elizabeth pours tea and milk and makes us sit at the table and wait. She's smiling to herself and refuses to tell us what miracle we're supposed to see. It's almost like she's a kid, instead of a sixty-something scientist. We talk about what Jim's been doing, and he tells Elizabeth that he's emailed the Oxford people, that some of his predictions tie in with their own. Elizabeth keeps glancing at the beakers and suddenly she scrapes her chair back and jumps up.

'Good. It's starting.' She bends down so that her eyes are level with the beakers. 'Come here and look. You'll need to get the light behind the beaker.'

Jim and I exchange glances and he shrugs, but we both squat down next to her. I can't see anything new, other than a sausage of greenish stuff in one of the beakers, which I suppose is winkle-poo.

'If you look carefully, about halfway up, you should be able to see a small white wriggling object. It's very small, it may take you a moment to fix on it. And if you watch this large littorinid here, look, at the junction between its foot and its shell... there!... you can see more of these tiny larvae wriggling out and swimming away. They move upwards and towards the light.'

She stands back to let Jim and me look more closely. I move my head from side to side — there's a distorted image of the trees outside that muddles the picture — and suddenly I see it. Very small, swimming in a jerky path. Now that I've got my eye in, I begin to see the others, coming out of the snail, and I show them to Jim. Elizabeth has picked up the other beaker and is holding it to the light.

'This one is even better, two of the snails are shedding.'

I look, and there are many more of the white wrigglers in that beaker.

'Well, are you going to explain,' Jim asks, 'or do we have to guess? They're obviously parasites of some sort.'

'Ugh!' I step back, revolted. 'I *touched* one of those winkles!'

'You won't die.' Elizabeth is quite merry, considering. 'I wanted to show you something that resembles the schistosome parasites that we work on — but which will not infect you. Those tiny larvae that are swimming around are the cercariae. We'll need to look under the microscope to check, but they are probably *Cryptocotyle lingua*, and they will swim around — in a rock pool — until they find a fish. Then they'll encyst in the skin of the fish and become dormant. Schistosome cercariae are rather different, though, in that they don't encyst, they burrow straight

179

into the body through the skin of warm-blooded hosts like humans or cows — or birds — and develop into adult worms. I certainly wouldn't be handling snails that were potential schistosome hosts with unprotected hands.'

'God, that's scary.'

'If these cercariae encyst on fish, what's the final host?' Jim asks.

'Gulls, predominantly. That's why I was collecting littorinids from those rocks,' she explains to me. 'I know the gulls tend to congregate there. They eat the fish, and the larvae break out of the cysts and develop to adult worms — and here's another difference from schistosomes which are blood flukes — and live in the gut. The parasite's eggs pass straight out in the gull's faeces, and then a miracidial larva hatches out into the water and swims around until it finds and burrows into a winkle. I'll show you what happens inside the winkle in a few moments.'

I hold the beaker up to the light to see the snails and the parasites, glad that they're safely behind glass, and shake my head. 'That's amazing! Such tiny things and such complicated lives. Daft! But the snails don't seem to be too bothered. What's that about the brown foot?'

'The parasites live in the snail's digestive gland — that's an organ with some functions similar to liver — and some of the breakdown products from the gland cells are coloured, and accumulate in the tissues in the foot. It's not entirely clear why. You can think of it as being similar to liver disease such as certain types of hepatitis in humans, where the breakdown products from the liver turn the skin yellow and jaundiced. Another interesting observation is that parasitised snails often show gigantism, they grow bigger than uninfected ones. The same is often true of schistosome-parasitised *Bulinus*, incidentally.'

'How long do these whatcha-me-call'ems —' I shuddered and put the beaker down, but I had to keep on watching, there was a horrible fascination and the things were so *bizarre*.

'Cercariae.'

'— cercariae keep on coming out?'

'Sometimes for an hour or two. Their emergence is correlated with the state of the tide, and it's affected by a variety of other factors such as water temperature, light and so on. Moving shadows make them swim more actively — which makes sense because the shadow might be a fish, and the main objective in their short lives is to find a fish.'

'All these years I've paddled around in rock pools and I never knew.' I am, in truth, amazed. 'Can you see the cysts on the fish? How big are the adult worms — are they like tapeworms?'

'No, they're not like tapeworms at all.' Elizabeth leans back against the sink, her arms crossed as she explains. 'They belong to the Class that includes the flukes such as liver fluke in sheep and the blood flukes that I work on, schistosomes. The adults are flat and leaf-shaped, probably about a centimetre long, but I'd need to check on that. They're hermaphrodite, too, unlike schistosomes where you have both male and female worms. And as for the cyst on fish,' she laughs, 'yes, you can just see them as small black spots, usually around the gills and on the fins. So — the lifecycle is a bit more complicated than schistosomes', but you can get the general idea. Three hosts instead of two. Anyway, that's enough of facts, let's have a look inside one of these *Littorina*.'

She hunts through the kitchen drawer and brings out a nutcracker, one of the old metal type with a hinge at one end.

'We'll try these. Although pliers might work better.'

She lifts the large brown-footed winkle out and, wedging it between the jaws of the nutcracker, expertly cracks the shell without reducing the snail to a nasty mess.

I wince a bit, but say, 'Not bad. I bet you're good with brazil nuts.'

Now she puts the cracked snail in a plastic dish that she's brought in with the beakers, and adds seawater. Jim and I troop upstairs after her and wait while she takes the cover off a microscope, then plugs in its flex and turns on the light. I hadn't noticed the microscope the last time I was in here, there are two of them on the big table at one side of the room. The table, which seems to be made from a door, is supported at one end on a big chest that looks as though it has map-drawers, long and shallow; or the sort you find in art-shops and studios. Elizabeth adjusts the lighting and fiddles around in the dish with two pairs of forceps.

'There you are, look at this extraordinary sight. I've teased the digestive gland apart — that's the coiled part which is normally up inside the spire of the shell.' She lets me sit down, and I look down the microscope but bang the bridge of my nose. 'You may need to adjust the eyepieces — just pull them apart. That's right. You can focus with these knobs here.'

I blink and adjust the focussing. And then I see them. Both inside and surrounding the coil of snail tissue is a heaving, pulsating and wriggling mass of orange and white shapes.

'Are all these things parasites? *Yuk!* That's *disgusting*! Pity the poor winkle. Oh, what's this small white thing flicking from side to side, is it one of those cercariae?'

'Yes. If you look carefully you may see that it's got two black eyespots. They're square, like this —,' she draws a little diagram on a piece of paper, 'although we probably need to look under higher magnification than the dissecting microscope to see the shape. And do you see the large orange sausage-like larvae?'

I nod, and bang my nose again. I could hardly miss them. Jim is leaning on the table next to me to peer into the dish, and I can feel the heat of his skin and smell herbal shampoo on his hair. It's strange how, knowing he is gay, I'm disturbed by his closeness, and I wonder if he does this on purpose or whether it's just part of his natural, in-built behaviour. I concentrate on the orange parasites.

'I see them.'

'Those are an earlier larval stage. Essentially they become sacs containing cercariae — you can see the cercariae inside them, they're recognisable by their eyespots.'

'Yeah. This is amazing! Can you see them, Jim?' I prod them with the fine-pronged forceps. 'The orange sausages seem to come in different sizes.'

'That's right. They carry on growing and producing more cercariae. There's another larval type, too, that comes before them. And everything that you see there may have developed from a single miracidium that infected that snail. By a sort of asexual reproduction, that involves a rather complex method of division and replication'

I get up and let Jim take my place. 'It's a horror movie in real life. You should have a look. One malicious little invader gets in and makes hundreds more.'

While Jim looks I get Elizabeth to write down the names on a piece of paper. CRYPTOCOTYLE LINGUA. CERCARIA. MIRACIDIA. And I add FISH-CYSTS and GULLS.

'How come nobody knows about this?' I ask her. 'It's the sort of thing that school kids would love to learn about and I bet their teachers don't even know. Hey, people *eat* winkles, don't they?'

I shove my hands in my hair and look at Elizabeth in horror, so that she laughs.

'Cooked, I think, or pickled. At least in this country, but perhaps raw as *fruits de mer* in France. But even if you ate infected winkles raw, it wouldn't matter, because the larvae would be killed in your stomach and digested.'

'I like the orange colour,' Jim says. 'Schisto isn't coloured, is it? Looking at that seething mass kinda points up the meaning of "prepatent period" and "reproductive capacity", doesn't it? And I try to describe all that,' he gestures at the dish, ' by an equation. Hey, hey. Give me a half-hour, Matt, will you?' He gets up and goes to the door. 'And then we'll go down to the shore. Right?'

'Right. See you.'

'Poor Jim, he's very down,' Elizabeth says. 'I expect you heard that Paul — his partner — can't go on holiday with him as planned.'

'Yeah.'

'It's good that he's got you for company.'

'But I'm not gay,' I blurt out, almost without thinking.

'No. But you don't have to be gay to be a friend.'

I must say her attitude surprises me, I'd have thought someone of that age would have been a bit shocked.

But she has quite matter-of-factly taken another microscope out of a wooden box and is setting it up. She has some glass microscope slides, and rummages in a drawer to get other bits and pieces.

'We'll put some of these larvae on a slide and look at them under higher magnification. That is, if you're not too bored.' She glances at me. 'Would you like to do that, or have you had enough?'

'No, let's look.'

I stand back and watch as she sucks up some of the larvae with a glass pipette, and puts them on a slide. 'We'll just put these pieces of broken coverslip each side to protect them ... and then —' she holds a small intact square of glass in the forceps and lowers it on top of the broken bits, 'we'll cover them and have a look.'

While she plays around with the microscope I glance around the room again, and see how much I missed the first time I was in here. There are all the books and tapes and so on, but there's also an old brass microscope under a glass dome on one of the shelves, and bits of rock and fossils, and photos. On this table there's a leather wallet that contains dissecting instruments, and there are little bottles and jars. It's quite dusty, too, some of the stuff probably hasn't been moved in centuries.

'This room's a bit like a museum,' I say. 'Your own personal museum of things that are to do with you.'

She sits back and has that puzzled, thinking sort of expression that she had earlier, and she looks around the room.

'Yes, you're right, Matt. A sort of cabinet of curiosities. You know, I had never looked at it in that way, but it's true. My own personal archive. I suppose one collects around oneself a series of objects that describe — oneself. What an interesting thought. A bit dry and dusty, too. Oh dear!'

'A bit dusty,' I agree. 'Not too dry, though.'

And we swap smiles. I sit down and she shows me the cercaria (I check the name again on the bit of paper) and the sausages ("sporocyst" — another big word, soon I'll be a scientist!). I can see the shapes, the moving tail, the square eyes, in detail once I get used to looking down the microscope.

'Do the coloured snails that I collected have stuff like this inside them, too?'

'Yes. I'm afraid so. They can get infected with *Cryptocotyle* and other parasites, too.'

'I'd quite like to draw these. Do you think you could lend me some paper? If I'm not in your way.'

'Of course. Can you draw from a microscope? It's quite difficult until you get used to it.'

She unlocks one of the map drawers and finds an artists' sketch block and tears off a couple of sheets of paper. I start to try to draw what I see and it is surprisingly hard. But she's rummaging round again, and from the top drawer takes another wooden box that contains a black metal tube and other bits and pieces.

'This might amuse you. I don't use it very much myself but it's rather fun. We fit it onto the microscope, and it allows you to view the object and watch yourself drawing it at the same time. It's a way of cheating, really, almost like tracing a phantom image.'

It takes a while to get the cheating device fixed up, because the microscope has to be partly dismantled, and I learn it's called a *camera lucida*.

'Not like the camera you use for taking photos, but "camera" as in Latin for "chamber". So it's a "light chamber".'

She's attached a chunky sort of eyepiece to the microscope and the black tube sticks out horizontally to one side. She puts the paper underneath it.

'There are two polarising screens in this eyepiece, and you arrange the paper under the free end of this horizontal tube. There's a special arrangement of prisms in there that enable you to see not only the parasite down the microscope but also your hand holding the pencil. The trick is to get the lighting right, not too bright and not too dim, and that's what the polarising eyepiece is for. You'll need to rotate it to cut down the light, so that the brightness is balanced between the image and the paper. Clever, but a little confusing at first. Now see how you get on.'

Soon I'm practically gurgling with happiness like a baby. 'This is really cool. This is the best fun I've had in ages!' I copy a cercaria. 'Hey, but there's absolutely no room for interpretation here.'

'No, you're right. You are being dictated to, by a mirrored image. But not a mirror-image.'

I haven't a clue what she's on about, but I burble away and she carries on chatting in a really relaxed manner while she potters around the room. I keep being amused by the fact that although my hand seems to be drawing round an image, there's nothing projected onto the paper. Magic! But bloody tricky! However, just as I'm getting into the swing of all this, Jim shouts up from downstairs.

'Elizabeth! Hazel Myers is here. Shall I bring her up?'

Elizabeth and I look at each other, and it seems to me as though her whole face closes up, shutting this chatty, enthusiastic character away inside a box.

'No.' She goes to the door and calls down. 'No, I'm coming down. Show her into the drawing room, I'll only be a couple of minutes. You carry on, Matt, as long as you like. Just leave things where they are when you've finished.'

'Thanks, Hazel,' I mutter as I carry on drawing on my own, gradually getting the hang of following the image as I move the slide around. While I draw I think of this parasite and all the forms it goes through, all its 'hosts', and I stop and quickly sketch a plan that involves coils and coloured whorls, curved tails and curved downy feathers. And somewhere the yellow-and-black eye of a gull.

The black cloud that Elizabeth said was tethered to my head seems to have blown away and I'm no longer feeling sorry for myself. I just feel very happy as I mess about with pencil and paper and the things I *see* inside my head.

Jim comes in and surprises me, I'd forgotten all about our plan. But he seems more cheerful, too, and we rampage down the stairs together, leaving Hazel to talk to Elizabeth in the drawing room. The sun's shining through a gap in the clouds, too, and I even wave to Peter Pascoe who's wandering around with a rake. I'm not pissed off any more.

CHAPTER 21: ANNE: JULY 1858

'Shark, *shark*!'

'There, look, sir! Over there — see the fin!'

'Another one there — further to the left. Two of the beggars.'

Duncan and I leapt to our feet, despite the awkward angle of the boat. Black fins, huge and menacing, stuck out of the water like cleavers, were lost from sight in the valleys between the waves, then reappeared, shockingly close.

The fins were *enormous*! I had not expected them to be so big, and when suddenly the entire back of one of the creatures — water streaming off its rough grey skin — broke through the surface of the sea I could not help but be alarmed.

'Great heaven! It's a giant!' Duncan cried, and he gripped my arm in excitement. 'Look at the size of her, Anne!'

'I'm looking, I'm looking.'

'*Selachius maximus*, rightly named indeed!'

The skipper sang out a warning and we crouched as the heavy boat lurched around into the wind and the boom swung amidships. Wordlessly, the men carried out those tasks with ropes and pulleys that were necessary to lower the faded sail, and the boat, suddenly stopped in its tracks, wallowed from side to side as the waves passed beneath her. Scummy water slapped back and forth around our feet, stirring up fragments of fish-scales and an ancient, foetid smell of fish. Viewed from this strange finger of sea that attempted to cut Britain in two, the nearby English shore seemed flat and excitingly *foreign*.

'Why have you stopped? Can we not go closer?'

'No sir, 'twould be dangerous. We might over-run her and she could lift her back and smash us to splinters. They'd be collecting us for firewood in Maryport for days to come!'

To be so close to such mighty fish — to be in possible *danger*! I clung onto the side and peered into the brown waters of the Solway Frith, willing the sharks to come even closer. Gulls gathered above the boat, perhaps hoping for discarded offal, tilting their wings against the wind to hold their positions; the braver ones descended to sit bobbing on the water, and tipped their heads this way and that, watching us with their fierce golden eyes.

'They're coming closer. Do you think they want to take a look at us? Is that another one over there?'

The basking sharks circled lazily just beneath the surface, their dorsal fins tracing their passage.

'I cannot believe that a creature could grow so big merely by sieving animalcules from the sea — you would think something like that would need a dinner of seals and porpoises.'

Duncan pointed down, almost hurling himself overboard in his excitement. 'I can see its mouth — do you see? That one there!'

And there, indeed, was the head of the shark, its mouth a huge pale cavern, jaws held agape as it scooped in the turbid water. We both stared in awe, willing the fish to approach closer still; but it must have felt that we had been granted sufficient privilege, for it swam away slowly to describe a larger circle, its long body undulating from side to side.

I could not take my eyes off them. They were magnificent, and so *ancient*! They had surely been swimming in the seas since the beginning of time! Sunlight made dazzling shifting diamonds on the water, burning my eyes, so that I closed them and breathed in the smell of tar and wood and wet canvas. Everything was perfect: I wished we could stay there for ever.

'I think I have never seen anything so *thrilling*! Blast this wind — why cannot the boat *stay still*?'

The pages of Duncan's notebook were being rattled by the wind. I opened my eyes and saw that his eyes were glimmering with excitement and that the pallor induced by his sea-sickness had vanished. His foot was propped on the crude wooden seat and his notebook held against his knee, but the uneven motion of the boat caused his writing to describe great sprawling lines. I quickly took the pencil and notebook from him and wrote 'I love you' in crooked letters in the corner.

He threw his head back and laughed aloud, and would have kissed me, except that the men were watching — strange rough men, used to fishing the unpredictable west coast waters, and not at all pleased to have a woman on board; they treated us, the 'gentry', with suspicion and barely-veiled contempt.

For perhaps a half-hour more we remained hove-to (or whatever the nautical term is for a fishing-boat that does not move of its own volition but is left to the whim of the wind and tide). The two sharks swam languorously, moving slowly westwards towards the mouth of the Frith, and we drifted with them, our course occasionally corrected by the dipping of an oar, so that there was ample time for us to observe them and the coasts on either side. On the distant horizon the Isle of Man lay, rugged and mysterious. On our right, the valley hidden from us by a promontory, lay the Scottish port of Kirkudbright whence we had set sail; close by, the gentle rounded dome of the mountain that is called Criffel or Crieffel overlooked the sea, the burly rearguard of a rolling waves of hills that led into the heart of Galloway. To our left, the southern shore, the English coast: a low green plain from which rose abruptly, improbably, the long range of peaks and valleys of the Lake District (wherein — so difficult to imagine from our vantage-point on the sea — Mr Wordsworth and his sister had found gentle places that harboured hordes of yellow daffodils). We drifted, idly, in this watery divide between two countries — and saw two seals, who stared as hard at us as we at them; and the large, brown-frilled *Rhizopoda* jellyfish that is the size of a wooden bucket; and little black-and-white birds that flew with rapid beats of their short wings, and that Duncan said were called guillemots.

'This is the most perfect day I have had in my life.' This time I spoke my thought aloud.

The skipper, overhearing, was unimpressed, and it seemed that his patience finally had been exhausted. 'If you want to make Silloth we need to get under weigh. There's nothing more to see.'

Without even waiting for us to assent and settle ourselves more comfortably, he set to and raised the sail, setting a course so that the boom swung far out to the side, its tip occasionally dipping in the waves. Thus we drove up the Solway with the wind behind us, towards Silloth on the English side.

Soon, however, it became clear that we had left our inward trip too late, for although the wind was freshening behind us, the outgoing tide was fighting against it, and winning. We ceased to make sufficient headway against the ebbing stream and, the Frith being here so wide and shallow and made hazardous by sandbanks and low rocky reefs, the skipper announced that we would be obliged to disembark on the beach at Allonby.

As we sailed parallel with the shore we regarded the little resort with interest and thought that the few houses strung out in a line looked, from this distance, bright and welcoming. We would surely find accommodation for the night; the fishermen agreed amongst themselves that there was an inn.

'Is there a quay?' Duncan enquired.

'There is not. But the water's shallow — I cannot get in close, so you'll be needing to get your feet wet.'

Duncan frowned and was starting to expostulate, but I put a hand on his knee, and leaned out to dabble my hand in the water.

'Darling, the water is warm. And we have only the one small bag.'

'I don't think I can carry you *and* the bag.'

'You don't have to. I shall wade too. We shall take off our shoes and carry them.' I laughed at his incredulous expression. 'It will be amusing!'

'Aye. Listen to your lady, sir. You can both have some *amusement*. And doubtless you can dry your clothes at the inn.'

So the skipper was paid off and he brought the boat in as close to the shore as he dared — but it seemed he was not inclined towards great daring. The water stretched for yards and yards between us and dry land, but he turned the boat into the wind and bade us hasten over the side or he would soon be stuck fast. I was tempted therefore to tarry, for the delight of effecting such inconvenience — but Duncan was already clambering over the side, causing the boat to tip alarmingly, and was now standing in water that reached above his knees. I passed him the bag, and he took my shoes, and I tried to exit the boat with some grace; but as my petticoat billowed and rose around me and the cold struck my stockinged legs, I was hard-pressed not to cry out.

The skipper, who had been steadying the boat with the oars, now curtly ordered Duncan to push the boat away and within seconds our Captain Ahab and his crew had manoeuvred the bow towards the wind, hoisted sail and were hastening away. We stood and watched, two fully-clothed humans in a near-flat sea (which had *not* parted around us) and I began to giggle.

'Look, I'm a medusa!' The hem of my skirt still floated around me, like the edges of a bell; the water no longer felt so cold, and I wiggled my toes in the soft muddy sand.

We waded and then trod splashing through the water, completely careless of our clothes, and soon laughing helplessly. Duncan was the first to reach the shining wet sand and he struck a pose.

'And thus we reached the English shore. Where shall we set up camp for the night, Mrs Robertson?'

'I think we shall be obliged to camp beneath the stars, Mr Robertson, for it is certain that none of the natives will receive us in this state.'

Now the reality of our heavily-wet and sandy clothes became apparent as we struck up the shore. Sand gave way to pebbles, then to lines of crackling seaweed, broken shells and bleached twigs. I sat down and tried to squeeze my sodden stockinged feet back into my shoes, and the impossibility of the task reduced me to near-hysterical laughter yet again.

The waters of the Solway had retreated even further and our shark-spotters' boat was a-sail on a thin blue line that was tinged with brown: the pebbles on which I sat were a mixture of shapes and colours of the most astonishing variety — eggs of speckled granite, deep-red sandstone patties, and smooth, creamy-green fragments that looked as though air had been bubbled through them. Duncan sat down beside me, his trousers caked with fine wet sand, and dropped a small rock into my lap: it was the pale-blue colour of a hot summer sky.

'What kind of rock is that? It's beautiful.'

He shrugged. 'I don't know. But the flat ovals that you are sitting on so comfortably are the New Red Sandstone that Harkness was talking about when we met him in Dumfries.'

'I liked him. It was kind of him to invite us to visit him in Dublin, I wish we could go.'

'Ballavich heard him talk at the British Association in Edinburgh in '50, did you realise that? But now you must arrange yourself decorously, my love, if not decoratively, for here comes a native — who fortunately looks friendly.'

Our unconventional progress from boat to beach had surely been observed by the majority of the inhabitants of this small hamlet, and very soon a lad of fifteen or sixteen came clattering over the pebbles in his heavy boots. He was the innkeeper's son, come to carry our bag and tout for custom, and so we put up for the night in 'The Ship', in a room which looked North over the Frith — to the benign bulk of Criffel and my adopted country. Travelling light as we were, we had no dry top garments and so were obliged to wring out hems and trouser-bottoms as best we could, and then to take a stroll along the dunes to dry our garments in the blessedly warm breeze. The sharp grasses whipped our legs and salt water dried to white tidemarks on our clothes but there were delights to be found — silver-blue spikes of sea-holly flattened in a hollow; a scattering of pink-and-brown banded snail shells cracked around a thrush's anvil; an iridescent green beetle scurrying across the sandy soil. These treasures, the mountains and the sea, the sharks, the novelty of an unexpected landing in a place where we were almost anonymous ... the combination produced a *fervour* within us both, so that we found a hollow near the shore where we might rest unobserved, and we were like newly-weds again (although better than newly-weds, because now there was no shyness or ignorance between us).

Later, as we sauntered back towards the inn, Duncan suddenly halted. His dear face was alight, his face flushed with the sun and salt air.

'Darling — we should go abroad *now*. We shall not be daunted! We've waited long enough and nothing shall stop us. It is time for the world to take notice of us.' He was animated and resolute; but then his face fell. 'But what if you become pregnant again?'

'We shall practise abstinence.'

'For a *year*!'

I could not help but laugh that he had believed me. 'Of course not! Women produce babies all over the world, Duncan, not just here in Great Britain — and with scarcely a pause in their normal labour. Why should I be any different? Why must we be reliant on linen sheets and maids with jugs of hot water and physicians with their black bags? We shall not be daunted, as you have said.'

Deep in my heart, however, the thought of the inevitable discomfort and an *accouchement* amidst the exuberant vegetation and fearsome insects of a foreign land filled me with dread. We had been married eighteen months — and already I had miscarried twice: I had been frightened by the experience, my body had hurt . Abstinence was indeed impossible, for in private Duncan was a hot-blooded, sensual man and he had early aroused in me a passion that had lain unrecognised and dormant. (Would I ever dare to question him about those years in America? How often Sarah's teasing question came to mind, 'Who knows what he did *there*?')

Sarah now had two sons and, to my astonishment, seemed to luxuriate in motherhood and all its yeowling, dribbling consequences. That the paternal instincts of the handsome Gordon were somewhat lacking mattered not one jot: she basked in domestic bliss, content to be at the centre of her family in her new house in Helensburgh. Her world had contracted around her and I did not, ever, wish to be guided by her example. I wished, secretly, *always* to be free to do whatsoever Duncan and I desired.

By now we had reached the outlying houses of Allonby and, anxious to delay our return to the inn, we stepped down onto the shore and searched along the line of dried débris deposited by an earlier high tide. The thought of rain-sodden jungles was preying on my mind; I had read portions of Mr Wallace's *Travels on the Amazon* and the privations hinted at by that intrepid naturalist filled me with apprehension.

'I am a little afraid of South America', I ventured. 'It sounds so *wet*.'

'But it is not all forest and river delta, my love. There are mountains and deserts, and I hear that there is even excellent farmland to be found, already colonised by Scots! We should not be alone.'

'But has not Mr Wallace carried out most of the work that is needed?'

'His specimens were destroyed when his ship caught fire, do not forget, so there is a great deal of collecting still to be done, if I could find a sponsor. Bates has collected extensively amongst the insects, of course, and there is that botanist fellow from Yorkshire, what is his name? Spruce. A tree, most appropriate. Spruce is there yet, searching for cinchona, so I hear. And now Wallace is busy with butterflies in the Malay Archipelago. Should we go *there* — to islands and warm seas? We are becoming practised at dealing with those conditions, do you not agree?'

'I like the idea of *warm* seas. Look how the tide is racing in now.'

There were two other couples strolling near the edge of the sea. The smooth glitter of the shore around them was marred by a rash of dark pimples, the sandy coils that betrayed the burrows of lugworms; but as we watched, the water crept in silently and smoothed away the blemishes. The couples must have suddenly observed that the shallow channel between them and the upper shore was filling rapidly with water, for they turned and hastened back the way they had come. We could hear them calling to each other, and their merriment made us smile.

I clasped Duncan's hand more tightly, and my heart was full of love for him — and dismay. For the gentlemen that he had mentioned seemed to me like giants in their rigorous approach to natural history. What could *we* do in comparison? We were not thinkers or theorizers like them, we were collectors and observers. I wanted to explain this to Duncan; but I hesitated to hurt his feelings. He was already thirty-four years of age and had scarcely set his mark upon the world and, although I was so much younger than he, I understood him well enough to know that he lacked the determination to pursue his dreams. Yet it was through the anticipation of the fulfilment of those dreams that we had been united in the bond of marriage.

There on the shore at Allonby the realisation came to me (a realisation which, I now recognised, I had long suppressed) that I would *never* fulfil my own (surely attainable) ambition to become a respected and 'talented naturalist'. It was a bitter thought, and I bent down to brush away the sand that still clung to my skirt, so that I could hide my tears.

Duncan stepped forward and he, too, reached down.

'A mermaid's purse, see. A shark's egg case — but not from those leviathans out there, for I have read that they are viviparous. More likely from a small shark such as a dogfish.'

With my head averted so that he would not see evidence of my tears and enquire the reason for my sudden change of mood, I took the black horny object and ran my finger along the dried tendrils that projected from each corner.

'*Full circle*. If God had called the world into being within this hour, He would not only have placed the shark in the sea but also the evidence of its previous development and history in the rocks and on the strand.'

'Hmm. "Prochronism". Poor old Gosse. "I do not put this forward as a *hypothesis* but as a *necessity*." You can almost hear him pound the pulpit, can't you? No wonder he has taken himself off to Devon to lick his wounds.'

'Poor man.' The tears that had been held in check now trickled down my cheeks, and I cast the mermaid's purse onto the ground.

'Darling. Sweetheart! Why do you cry about him?'

'If Mrs Gosse had been alive she would not have permitted him to write such a book.'

'Perhaps if his wife were still alive he would not have *needed* to write such a book. It is the work of a man whose reasoning was not sound. And I am certain that he will eventually recover and will return to the work that he does best — observing minutiae. For which he has earned plentiful respect.'

Duncan's capacity for discernment astonished me. Sweet, kind man! I took his hand and kissed it, a gesture which I knew always disarmed and pleased him.

He straightened my shawl and took my arm. 'Come now, we should go back and make ready — as far as we are able — for dinner. And doubtless the plump and homely Mrs Partridge will entertain us with every detail of what Mr Dickens and "the young Mr Collins" ate and drank when they graced her "humble abode" with their presence.'

I woke in the night to the hiss and suck of waves on the shore, the sound of a sea that had been excited by the wind that now rattled the ill-fitting window. I had been dreaming, a confused dream with no logic or substance, in which Duncan stood on a shore, counting. He was counting and laughing as the water swirled around him and left him isolated on a sandy spit from which it seemed there was no escape. Perhaps I called to him in my dream (I am not certain) for he called out, *'Wait for me!'* then leapt into the air and reached the foot of the rocky promontory upon which I was standing. Still counting, he bounded effortlessly up the rocks: 'seventy-two, seventy-three' … and at each number he stamped his foot upon a rocky foothold. I awoke to hear the window banging rhythmically in the wind and lay still, puzzled, unable to extricate myself fully from the dream, and yet trying to make some sense of it.

Duncan had laughed at Mr Gosse's passion for accuracy — that was surely at the root of my dream. In his books Mr Gosse tells of counting the number of seconds it took for the tide to cut off the island at Tenby; and of counting and re-counting the number of steps to a chapel in somewhere in Wales; counting and recording his *pleasures* … Emily had been away when Willy took his first steps and Henry had written to her with a record of the number of steps and the distance covered; Mrs Gosse and I had been watching a little child on the shore, tottering towards its mother's outstretched arms, and Mrs Gosse had stroked Willy's head as she told me.

When we returned to our home in Glasgow we learned that, on July 1st, two papers had been read before a meeting of the Linnaean Society of London, one submitted by Mr Charles Darwin and the other by Mr Alfred Wallace, and both putting forward evidence in favour of a new theory on the origin and mutability of species. Duncan received the news in a letter from an acquaintance who had been present.

'This will set the cat amongst the pigeons!' He chuckled with glee and leapt up and paced around the little terrace where we were taking our breakfast and enjoying the fresh, early-morning air. 'It will completely alter the manner in which we perceive the natural world.'

'Then we must search for evidence ourselves. We must devise experiments with the intention of testing the new ideas.'

'Indeed we shall, my love. You sit here quietly and plan what we should do — I must leave or I shall be late.' He gathered up his letters and emptied his cup of tea with a flourish. 'To work!'

I sat for a while and listened to the muted sounds from the street in front of our terrace. Swifts raced overhead shrieking with amazement at their own dizzy speed, and a blackbird stood listening to the teeming soil, ready to pounce and carry a worm back to her noisy brood. When Kate reappeared I ordered her to bring more tea.

A friend had lent Duncan a copy of *The Geologist,* and I picked it up and turned the pages idly, wondering at the strange vocabulary. On the page of Book Reviews a name instantly caught my eye: *Omphalos,* P.H. Gosse, Esq. A late review — the misguided treatise had appeared last summer. 'Now, Mr Gosse's book is a nice book — a good book to look at, charmingly illustrated, just a little book worthy of Mr Gosse in its appearance and address, but very unworthy of Mr Gosse, and indeed of anybody else, in its doctrine ...' The tone was savage, I could scarcely bear to read further. Phrases caught my attention: 'Mr Gosse teaches the idea of a non-existent pre-existence for every created thing and being. This is the plain English of the volume after all' ... 'we must not take up our Bibles and, with certain notions of our own, say the Bible says so and so ...'

The final paragraph thundered its condemnation: 'All that Mr Gosse does in his book to prove one idea tends, without exception, to prove another; and no greater support of the gradual development doctrine has been written since the publication of the memorable *Vestiges of Creation* — a purpose, at least, his volume does not profess to serve. We think most persons would prefer to use their senses rather than blindly to be enslaved by such wild and hypothetical speculations, alike derogatory to the intellect of man, and to the power and wisdom of God.'

Papa had told me that the Reverend Mr Kingsley had received a copy of *Omphalos* from his 'good friend, the author' — and after reading it had admitted to Papa that he had never been so shocked by a book in all his life. Would even those good friends remain estranged? If only poor Henry had a loving *companion* in whom he could confide.

CHAPTER 22: MATTHEW

<u>MORPH</u>

Morph (plasticine character on tv?) = shape, change shape

Top & bottom views of shells, arranged in tight spiral (seen from above) that mimics their own design. Superimpose brown band (see brown-and-yellow banded type).

Brown band itself to be made of really small brown shells. (Fractal? Is there computer programme that will break this down further? Ask Jim.)

Also try side view? — truncated cone reaching upwards (cf. Brueghel's <u>Tower of Babel</u>) Proportions wrong, shell too flattened?

---

crypto = hidden
cotyle = hollow, cup
lingua = tongue (of course!!)

cercaria
<u>meta</u>-cercaria (meta = afterwards?)
fluke
sporocyst ('sausage' containing lots of cerc.)

Cryptocotyle lingua — <u>why</u>? EW doesn't know, probably something to do with adult fluke's shape (in gull gut).

"METAMORPHOSIS" (for Granny B.)

Snails —» cercaria —» fish —» gulls

Gull: yellow-beak, yellow-eye. Curved feather.

<u>METAMORPH</u>

CRYPTOMETAMORPH

Chicken and egg, gull and snail, which is the start and which is the finish? Circular argument. Möbius strip; or changing perpective, convex —» concave.

Too derivative? Escher.

Aerial view of widening spiral, must rise up, <u>the snail itself metamorphosing.</u>

Central small coils filled with orange sporocysts, black eyespots — pairs of curved cercaria, <u>yin and yang</u>, long tails — small curved fish, black spots again (metacerc.) At mouth of shell, fish metamorphoses into feather, carries on the curve, expands.

<u>How to return from bird to snail?</u> Tip of feather, the side branches fragmenting at their tips, spawning tiny snails, that continue spiralling out, off the page, the different colours, deep red, yellow, green, brown, etc. Orange-yellow at the outermost point, referencing orange colour of central sporocyst.

A yellow-and-black eye, gull's eye, watching cercaria's eye.

<u>Magritte!</u> 'Ceci n'est pas mon escargot.' So whose snail IS it then?

CHAPTER 23: ELIZABETH

They were still in the kitchen talking, apparently, about allergies. Jim was animatedly describing someone's foot, which had swollen like a football so that his pants had to be cut off, and she was laughing and exclaiming disbelief.

I stood for a moment in the long, dim hall and saw them illuminated by the daylight in the kitchen, Hazel holding a glass of water, pushing her hair back from her face as Jim gesticulated towards his foot and waved a tracksuited leg. Hazel was wearing striped trousers, navy and white, and a thick creamy pullover on top of a pale blue shirt. She looked cool and neat, but as she spoke to Jim there was an appealing vivacity in her face. It surprised me that they were so relaxed with each other, but I managed to dismiss my sense of siege as incipient paranoia, and I smiled as I entered the kitchen.

'Oh hi, Elizabeth. This is —'

'Hazel Myers. I know. We met several years ago.'

'Dr Wilson.' She took my hand, and although she smiled briefly, her face had lost its brightness and had become still and wary. She put down her glass and picked up a canvas satchel from a chair.

'Right, you guys. I'll get back to work. See you around, Hazel. Oh, Matt and I are going down to play in the ocean when I'm done. We're going to look for little fishes!'

'Where is Matt?' she asked me, as Jim lifted a hand in farewell and slipped out of the kitchen.

'He's pottering about somewhere. Please do call me Elizabeth,' I answered. 'Let's go into the drawing room, it's a little more comfortable. But of course, you've been here before, haven't you?'

I led the way down the hall, and then indicated a chair near the window.

'You probably noticed last time you were here that I have one of your mother's paintings on the wall? We both used to exhibit at the Polkenna show, you may remember. Of course her paintings used to get snapped up very quickly.' I wanted to pre-empt any further discussion of the painting, to excise it from future conversation, and threw out a smokescreen of different topics. 'Do sit down. I was very sorry that we were unable to meet in London — and disappointed, for both our sakes, that Gosse's birdskins weren't held in the collection there. I did ask Roger to try to find out a little more about just what was in the store at Tring. He's due back here tomorrow, incidentally. He had to stay in Town to repeat some tests — apparently there was a problem in the lab with one of the reagents.'

'Oh. I see.'

As I sat down opposite Hazel I was pleased to note that she looked slightly bewildered. She had placed the canvas bag across her knees and had clasped her hands on top of it. I returned to neutral ground.

'Did you have a pleasant walk along the cliffs?'

'Yes, very good, actually — although the view isn't too good today. A man showed me a peregrine falcon. Apparently they've recently started to nest on the cliffs.'

There was a short silence while we both looked out of the window. Somebody was flying a kite on the headland above the wood; the yellow rectangle swooped and soared against the grey sky, and then plunged towards its hidden pilot.

'It's nice of you to see me,' Hazel said, 'and I'm pleased to be able to meet you here, even though it would have been fun to see the museum. Matt obviously enjoys coming here — not that he's very communicative.'

My study was directly overhead, and I could hear Matt moving around. With a shock that was almost like a physical blow in the diaphragm, I remembered Barbara's two small paintings that hung on my bedroom walls. But surely Matt wouldn't look in there. The door was closed. Wasn't it? I couldn't be sure.

'Hazel. Excuse me a moment. Matthew's upstairs in my study and there's something important that I need to tell him. Would you excuse me? I shall only be a moment.'

She was still looking astonished as I left the room. I hurried upstairs, becoming a little breathless in my haste and went straight to my bedroom. The door was closed, but there was no key for the lock, so I took the paintings off the wall and hid them in the wardrobe. When I came out I could see Matt, hands in pockets, staring down at the beach through one of the study windows; whether a thoughtful or vacant stare, I couldn't tell.

'Don't forget to turn off the microscope light when you finish. Turn the dial on the transformer to zero and then switch it off.'

'Okay.' He nodded briefly. 'What does Hazel want?'

'I don't know yet. I'll tell her to come and find you when we have finished.'

Hazel had put the satchel on the floor and was holding a yellow cardboard folder. I looked pointedly at it.

'Now — you seemed to think that I could help you in some way. Something biological? Or are we still on the Gosses?'

I needed to force her off-balance, to put up a barrage of questions. She appeared daunted, and I wondered where she would start; but the abruptness of her first question took me by surprise.

'You knew my mother died of breast cancer, didn't you?'

To deny knowledge would have been absurd: I had been at the crematorium. Even in death Barbara had teased me. She had decreed that 'Jerusalem' should be sung, and a psalm should be read. 'Thou shalt not be afraid for the terror by night; nor for the arrow that flieth by day.' She was not at all religious, and I supposed she must have looked up 'arrow' in a Dictionary of Quotations. The Arrows of Desire. *Sagitta*. The beautiful, ironic poetry echoed in my mind, and I spoke it aloud.

' "The pestilence that walketh in darkness, the destruction that wasteth at noonday". Psalm 91, at your mother's funeral.'

'You remember that? What a good memory you have. I don't know why she insisted on that psalm. Unless it was out of bitterness, because it goes on a lot about conquering death and disease, doesn't it? Though it did include a phrase that she used a lot when I was little —' thou shalt not be afraid for the terror by night.' I think I was often afraid at night.'

I sat very still.

'Was she good at comforting you?'

Why had I phrased the question that way, revealing my own desperate curiosity? But she appeared not to have noticed; for a moment she seemed confused, and she looked at her hands, which were lying immobile on the folder. Her fingers were interlocked and pointing inwards, like the child's game: 'here's the church and here's the steeple.' Her voice was curiously uninflected.

'Yes. She was my mother.'

'Why did you ask if I knew about the breast cancer?'

She turned her hands over, the interlocked fingers relaxed but pointing upwards ('open the door and there's the people').

'I'm not sure why I came to see you, really. I felt that you might be able to help in some way, perhaps because you know a bit about Gosse. There's a strange sort of link between his wife, Emily, and my mother. Emily died of breast cancer too, you see.'

(A herd of Trojan horses thundered across the shore.)

'But other than through a shared disease, why do you feel that they are linked? Though there was a relative, wasn't there, who had some sort of link? Matthew mentioned something along those lines.'

'My mother's great-great-aunt. This aunt and her husband were actually very interesting, they were both amateur naturalists, collectors and field-workers, I suppose you'd call them these days.'

'Did they collect snails?'

'No.' She smiled a little and sat back in the chair. 'Anthozoans. They were great anemonizers. Anne Church went on one of Gosse's shore classes, which is where she met Emily. The next spring, Emily discovered a lump in her breast, and instead of choosing an operation, she and Gosse opted for a very peculiar treatment by an American quack, a Dr Fell.'

' "I do not love thee, Dr Fell, the reason why I cannot tell." A different doctor, but the words are equally applicable.' (Another Oxonian, and Wilberforce's precursor. Who was talking to me recently about Wilberforce? Ah yes, Charles Hetherington.)

'It was awful,' Hazel said simply. 'The Gosses went to him and he showed them *photographs* of his cure. Apparently he told them that the ointment contained an extract from a root that was used by American Indians and, as far as I can make out, it was supposed to kill the tumour cells. According to him, the tumour would turn hard and dark and become separated from the live tissues surrounding it. They even saw a photo of the gruesome man's fingers pulling a dead tumour away from a woman's flesh! Can you imagine? He said he had an 80% success rate.'

'They believed all this?'

'They spoke to a woman undergoing the treatment, whose tumour was almost dead. And of course they asked God what would be best to do, and it seems that he told them to go right ahead. Poor Emily had to travel across London three times a week, to Pimlico, for her treatment. Two or three kinds of ointment, alternately on different days.'

She opened the yellow file and pulled out a sheaf of file paper with pencilled notes. ' "One of the unguents employed was attended with pain, presently causing a gnawing or aching in the breast, which at times was scarcely supportable." '

'How unpleasant.'

'Yes. But they were both so optimistic — they set off for Pembrokeshire in the summer for another of Gosse's shore classes.' Hazel read from her notes again. 'He writes about the doctor "furnishing my dear Emily with a supply of medicaments, and giving her instructions for their application." Imagine the poor woman struggling with all that in a seaside lodging.'

'I am a little puzzled about the prescription of a topically-applied ointment to kill an internal growth.'

'I talked to my mother's consultant oncologist about it. He was very interested but not much help. And then I talked to a herbalist, who had lots of interesting ideas. He pointed out that lots of chemicals could be absorbed through the skin and into the blood or deeper tissues, and of course even hormone-replacement therapy uses skin-patches in some cases. But actually, Dr Fell's treatment didn't work, and Gosse says that "we returned home" — that's from Tenby — "on the second of October, and immediately saw Dr Fell, who advised removal of the tumour; the lack of any apparent result from the five months' attempt to disperse it, had led us to look to such a course as most hopeful." Elizabeth, it was horrible what Fell did then —and Gosse describes everything. I'll just read you a little bit, but there are pages of it.'

She read from her notes and I was appalled.

' "The whole surface of the left breast, an area of four inches in diameter, was wetted with nitric acid, applied by means of a small bit of sponge tied to the end of a stick. The object of this application was to remove the skin. The smart was very trying, and continued for several hours augmenting; the effect being to blister and destroy the whole skin, exactly as if a severe burn had taken place. On the succeeding day, the doctor proceeded to incise the tumour, in order that it might be penetrated by the peculiar medicament which he used for its separation. With the scalpel he drew, on the surface of the now exposed flesh, a series of parallel scratches, about half an inch apart, reaching from the top to the bottom. When these were made, a plaister of a purple mucilagenous substance was spread over the whole. The next day, on renewing this plaister, the scalpel was passed again along the scratches, deepening them a very little; and a fresh plaister was applied ..." And so on and so on. Listen. "The purple mucilagenous substance had evidently a caustic power, killing the flesh so far as it penetrated. It had, too, an antiseptic property; for the part so destroyed had no tendency to decomposition; it was brought to a woody hardness, and a deep black colour, without the least odour." '

'Good heavens! Such detail. And about his own wife's breast. And this was *published* in a book, did you say?'

'Yes. There's more. "On Sunday, the 23rd of November, to our delight, the great insensible tumour fell out of its cavity. There it lay on the table, a hard and solid block of black substance, resembling in size and shape a penny bun, deeply scored on one surface, and on the other nearly smooth".'

Hazel began to laugh, a desperate choking sound and her eyes were filled with tears.

' "A penny bun", can you believe it? The description just goes on and on ... But the poor woman died anyway. It sounds as though the cancer had spread to her lungs, and the whole area had become septic.'

We both sat silently for a few moments; the terrible description was almost unbearable.

'My herbalist contact thought the purple ointment was probably an extract of something called, believe it or not, Indian Paint or blood-root. It's proper name is *Sanguinaria canadensis* — it's reddish-purple and was reported in a book written at the end of the nineteenth century as effective against breast cancer. And apparently there's also burdock and yellow dock, their roots were used, too, but they're the wrong colour. He also half-remembered reading somewhere about an extract of red clover being applied on poultices, which caused cancers to come away like that. He was very interested.'

I scarcely heard her. 'What an extraordinarily factual account. It is, essentially, an accurate, almost scientifically-detached, chronological record, judging by what you have read so far.'

'He even had a photograph taken, just before she died. I didn't see it, thank goodness.'

Hazel was staring at her notes, and her eyelids drooped even lower over her eyes. She was clearly very disturbed, and I wasn't sure whether she was thinking of Emily Gosse or of Barbara; it was possible that the two had become fused into one.

'Presumably he needed a last image. Probably he possessed no other accurate images and he, of all people — the great observer and recorder — must have needed the accuracy. He wanted the correct and detailed picture of his wife. It was his final chance, perhaps we shouldn't despise him for it.'

We both stared out of the window for a few moments; probably we were both thinking of Barbara.

At that moment we both heard Matt and Jim could be heard charging down the stairs, and Hazel sat sharply upright in her chair. But they carried on past the closed door of the drawing room, talking noisily.

I still wasn't clear why she had come to see me. 'What parallels,' I asked her, 'apart from the type of cancer, do you draw with your mother's death? Something has disturbed you sufficiently that you felt the need to walk over to Nancarrow to discuss it with me.'

Again she turned on me that blank, slightly startled look.

'When Emily was at Pimlico, Dr Fell prescribed her opiates. The Gosses were against it at first, but she couldn't sleep for the pain. Battley's Sedative, twelve drops at first, but she was up to twenty-five by the time she left. Opiates were used even then, to relieve pain. I didn't know that.'

'But not just for pain relief. Also to inspire, and to permit the mind to escape, unfettered. Think of Coleridge and his laudanum. Opium goes back a long time, even in England. De Quincey's *Confessions of an English Opium Eater.*'

'Yes. Hallucinations. But Emily sounded pretty lucid.'

Lucid. The word triggered a warning. What had Barbara said? If she had mentioned anything incriminatory (no, it was not a criminal offence — implicatory, anything that implied) I would say that she must have been hallucinating; lacking lucidity, no clear light shining.

'My mother was on morphine, you know. But she was quite strange sometimes, towards the end. Sometimes she went on and on about mandala and she seemed to have some sort of obsession with cameras and obscure images. I never got to the bottom of that one.'

She had waited so long to get to the point, and now she had sprung it on me from a totally unexpected direction. And she seemed to be waiting; did she expect me to explain?

'Patterns and pictures. Probably the mandala referred to one of the patterns on the wall of your house. And she was an artist, so it would make sense if she occasionally dreamt of pictures. Did you feel it was important to her?'

'I don't know, Elizabeth. I honestly don't know. And I suppose it doesn't matter now. But what you say certainly sounds plausible. I think she even replaced one of the patterns herself. Thank you.'

She smiled briefly; I had apparently helped her. Suddenly I began to doubt that she suspected anything at all, but that she had merely needed someone else to talk to. The process of coming to terms with death, and its confusions and ambiguities, takes time. I knew that myself.

The house was quiet around us. My knee cracked loudly in the stillness as I half-stood to look out of the window; Jim and Matt were walking towards the jetty, Matt swinging a bulky supermarket carrier-bag.

'Sometimes she said some awful things. The morphine seemed to make her angry, and she could be very tetchy.'

'I've heard that it may have that effect,' I said carefully.

'Oh, there's Mattie!'

Hazel came over to stand beside me at the window. Her head was slightly tilted and the bob of her hair swung forward and almost hid her profile. Her voice, when she spoke again, was small and resigned.

'She even called me a little lesbian slut. She laughed when she said it, but it was quite strange and hurtful. I'm not a lesbian. And I don't think I could be called a slut.'

'No, no. Of course not. She would have been very confused, and goodness knows what terrible nightmares she was experiencing. Morphine can do that, it's apparently very difficult to administer the correct dosage in such … such cases. You poor girl, how distressing for you. But you mustn't be upset.'

The words poured out, and I even clamped her wrist with my hand, but she gently released it on the pretext of pushing back her hair. Is that all I had been — a slut? Please no. Or perhaps that was how Barbara had finally seen herself. Suddenly I wondered how much Hazel's brother knew.

'No, you're right. She was just confused. And I suppose I did know that morphine could have unpredictable effects, the hospice nurse did warn me.'

'But you have nevertheless been worrying away at these uncertainties for — how long? — almost a year. Surely there was someone else that you could discuss this with, your brother perhaps? He seemed a sensible type.'

'Jamie just said she was rambling, too. But, you see, she could also — as I told you — talk so rationally, and sometimes, even when she was talking nonsense, she acted as though she knew what she was saying. It was quite hard to sort out the sense from the nonsense, so much of the time I didn't know what she wanted. I think I usually just annoyed her. But thank you. I'm glad I spoke to you about it.'

Hazel had turned her head away but her voice was tight and I knew she was trying not to cry.

'I expect she was reacting to the pain and unhappiness and taking it out on you because you were nearest.'

'No, I don't think we got on very well, really. She always loved my brother more than me.'

The poor girl. I should have found the courage to tell her, because the truth would, in the end, have helped. But I was still silent when she turned her back on the window and looked vaguely around the room.

'I feel rather embarrassed telling you all these things about my mother. I think I'd managed to forget most of the things she said but somehow, once I started talking to you, they just resurfaced — and then slipped out. It's almost as though they were the logical conclusion to what we were talking about earlier.'

'The Americans like to call it "closure", I think. And all from a discussion that originated with your interest in Emily Gosse.'

The latter wasn't strictly true, but it was essential to return to neutral ground before I sent her out to find Matthew.

'Yes, I suppose so.' She smiled a little bleakly. 'I've learnt a lot about the Gosses in the past few weeks — and that all originated from Anne Church's notebooks in the suitcase that my mother had kept. How strange.'

'Could that have been your mother's intention?'

'Oh. Surely not!' Hazel looked startled and was clearly trying to search out the rationale. Suddenly her eyes widened.

'Oh look, there's Roger!'

I had heard the front gate open but had my back to the window. Roger had passed out of sight by the time I swung round to look, but a couple of sparrows exploded out of the Virginia creeper that trailed around the window. Hazel was hastily pushing her papers together and stuffing the folder into the canvas satchel.

'Hallo-o!' Roger was calling from the kitchen. 'Anyone in?'

He obviously hadn't seen the boys down by the boat, although he must have seen the Myers' car.

I went to the door and opened it.

'We're in here, Roger. I wasn't expecting you until tomorrow. Hazel Myers is here, too.'

'Oh.' He looked tired and crumpled from the drive and I could see that his eyes, behind the glasses, had that far-away look that comes from motorway driving.

'I'd finished at the lab by lunchtime so I thought I might as well set off straight away rather than wait until tomorrow. I picked up some groceries on the way,' he explained to me. Then, with the same lack of inflection, he added, 'Hallo, Hazel. That's where you are. I stopped off at Polkenna — but you weren't at home. Obviously.'

He stayed in the doorway; I was blocking his entry.

'Why don't you come in and sit down?' I said as I stood back. 'I need to check that Matt has cleared up upstairs.'

I had absolutely no interest in their tedious relationship, whatever it was; I felt my irritability threshold being lowered, and did not want to be pushed above the limit. I closed the door carefully behind me — for some inexplicable reason I was tempted to slam it — and went upstairs. They could make their own cups of tea.

In my bedroom I retrieved Barbara's two paintings from the wardrobe and sat with them on the bed. They were uncharacteristically small, but painted in her characteristic style: they depicted the places we both loved — a corner of her garden, a corner of mine. As usual, the observer was placed at an unusual viewpoint, seeing the vibrant, surprising colours and the deep, rich shadows, that were Barbara's trademark. But the presence of both these pictures on my bedroom walls would have indicated too strongly — to an outsider — that we had been more than acquaintances or painting-friends.

I had several times questioned why I wanted to hide the evidence, why I was not prepared to let the facts reveal themselves. But of course it was already much too late for that, in any case; I should have told them the truth rather than risking their finding out through hints and innuendo. When I honestly appraised my reluctance and my subterfuges, I was able to admit to myself that I was disturbed at the thought of the revulsion that such revelations would bring against myself. ('Lesbian slut'. *Slut*? No, no.)

I knew now, having spent time with Matthew, that it was his disgust I feared most of all; Hazel's concerned me less, perhaps scarcely at all. I had become very fond of Matthew: he made me laugh, he exercised my thinking. I liked his mind, I liked his shambling presence. He made me wonder what it would have been like to have a son. I did not want Matthew to think badly of me now.

But in truth it was not fear for myself that was the over-riding factor: I could not be responsible for showing Matt and Hazel a Barbara Lewisham that they had not known existed. She was the mother and the grandmother, the exuberant extravert they thought they all knew. She once said to me how shocked Matt would be if he knew about her 'secret life'. (She said I *was* her life.)

And yet ... and yet ... *did* Hazel know? What was the significance of that reported remark?

Matthew must never find out. And for as long as Barbara's family continued to seek out Nancarrow, all evidence of our intimacy must be expunged.

I sat on the bed and held her painting of the Shell House's garden. The observer looked down the terraces towards the house, looking past the white stones and the gnomon, to the open French windows; bright light, purple shadows, but the room beyond was dark. A pair of red espadrilles had been kicked off at the threshold and, in the dimness, some sort of patterned cloth could barely be seen, hanging over the back of a chair: Barbara's skirt.

Jim Steinberg would return to the States, Matthew would return to college; I didn't know if Hazel would come here again. I still could not decide how much she knew or guessed at. (That poisoned dart: chance or deliberate aim?) It would not be too difficult to freeze her out, so that she had no excuse, once Roger left, to return. Matthew, though, was a different matter; Matthew I would miss.

But Matt must never know. I returned the paintings to the wardrobe and tucked them at the back behind the hanging clothes.

CHAPTER 24: ANNE:1860

I had been absent, visiting friends, when the book had arrived, and had unwrapped it. He was jubilant.

'I am mentioned so many times — he quotes my own descriptions and experiments. Listen, darling.'

He turned to the first of several pages that he had already marked with strips torn from the newspaper.

' "*Sagartia bellis*, daisy anemone, D. Robertson on Cumbrae" ... "*Sagartia miniata*, scarlet fringed ... *Corynactis viridis*, DR of Scotland" ... "*Anthea cereus*, the opelet, DR on Cumbrae" ... "*Actinia mesembryanthemum*, the beadlet — a specimen was sent to me from Cumbrae by Mr D. Robertson". And this, the final crowning glory — sit down, my love, it is a long passage.'

'Wait. What is his dedication?' I leaned over his chair and took the book from him, turning to the title page. ' "To Mr and Mrs Duncan Robertson, this book is given with my heartfelt thanks. Ph. H. Gosse." Is that all?'

It was indeed a meagre reward for our efforts.

'What more should he say? He makes frequent mention of both of us, in print, surely that is thanks enough? There is a great deal about your contribution, in fact, there is a surprise for you!'

'Oh, where? Show me the page.'

Duncan took back the book but instead of finding the page that referred to me, he turned to another of his markers and smiled teasingly.

'No, you shall sit quietly and listen to me first, and contain yourself with patience.'

'*Oh!* I shall sit but I shall not listen!' I removed myself to the high-backed chair close to the window and pretended to cover my ears: the sooner he finished the sooner would I read the account myself.

' "*Adamsia palliata*, the cloaklet anemone" — incidentally, he also notes that specimens were found by my old friend Landsborough on Arran and by a Mrs A. Murray Menzies from Oban. Who is she, I wonder? One of those "desolating agents", those who wield "the hammers of amateur naturalists"? *Hah!* However, returning to *Adamsia*, "several specimens from the Frith of Clyde for which I am indebted to the kindness of Mr D. Robertson" etcetera. "From information supplied by Mr Robertson, it appears to me manifest that the membrane is a provision for the support of the growing *Adamsia*" and so forth. Then there follows much concerning my own observations on *Adamsia* cloaked in small or broken shells ... and here, behold! A long quotation from the letter that I sent him. "Lately I dredged a small *Pagurus prideauxi* unassociated with *Adamsia palliata*. After a few days I put it into a jar with an *Adamsia* which I have had for some time" — do you remember the experiment, two summers past? — "I saw them six hours after, *Pagurus* had left his shell and was perched on the top of *Adamsia* with his fore-claws among the tentacles." Then I go on to describe how the crab *Pagurus* seems to be as dependent on the *Adamsia* as the latter is on it. You see how greatly I have contributed to this important work? Mr Darwin shall write to me yet to ask my opinion!'

His face so glowed with pride and good humour, that I had to go to him and kiss him on the forehead.

'Congratulations! And now you must show me the surprise. The pictures are so beautiful, it is a *beautiful* book.' My stomach was tight with apprehension and excitement.

'I have found at least two references. One, here, is of slight importance —the *Actinoloba dianthus* that you found "in the Clyde, near Glasgow, at low ebb". Also found by old Landsborough on Cumbrae. Here is the second mention, and I suppose I must let you read it yourself!'

Once again I took the book, and I read the name of the anemone that I had sent.

' "*Stomphia churchiae*". *Churchiae!*'

I could scarcely believe what I saw, my heart beat so fast that I put a hand to my breast and took a deep breath.

'Duncan!'

'Read on, my love, read on.'

' "The specific name is in honour of the kind correspondent to whom I am indebted for my first knowledge of the animal." *Well!* Oh — but you saw it first, you gave it to me.'

'You would have seen it in any case, I merely got there first. You were the artist and observer, the credit is entirely due to you.'

' "In the month of January 1857 I was favoured with a communication from Miss Church of Glasgow, containing descriptions and figures of this showy and undescribed species, a specimen of which she had procured in Loch Long the previous summer ... Its brilliant hues and their flaked arrangement, the protean variability of its shape, and its vivacity, attracted her notice." See how he quotes me directly. "A 'body dashed with scarlet on white and yellow ... its column sometimes constricted hour-glass fashion', and the edge of the lips a rich scarlet 'like the nectary of the Hoop-petticoat narcissus' ".'

'Did you really describe it thus? But of course you did — only a lady would refer to hour-glasses and petticoated flowers!'

Henry Gosse had not forgotten me after all. He had eventually read that intemperate letter, sent so long ago with the drawings, at such an unhappy time — and he had rewarded me with this sign.

'I have a *species* named after me. How many people in the world can claim that honour? How many *women* indeed?'

It was better than a gift of pearls. I wanted to write to him at once, to pour out my love and thanks. I had waited so long! But perhaps I need not have waited until now?

'When were the sections that refer to us published?'

'On various occasions during the past year, I believe. Perhaps even longer ago. No matter, now we are immortalised in the *book*. And you are immortalised in a name, an actinia that will forever recognisably belong to you. Naturally I shall send Gosse a copy of my own book when it is published. Incidentally, he mentions his son somewhere, you will like that. It was in connection with the Walled Corklet.'

I searched the index and then turned to the page. *Phellia murocincta*, enclosed by walls. He had written that he was indebted to his little son 'whose keen and well-practised eye detected the tiny atom, as a form with which he was unacquainted, on one of the fragments that I had brought home.' They had brought home a jar of specimens from a collecting expedition at Torquay, perhaps from the shore below their house.

'I suppose Mr Gosse and his son frequently go out collecting together,' Duncan said. 'And then they doubtless spend the evening poring over the dishes and jars and peering down the microscope. It cannot be much of a life for that little boy.'

'He must be eleven years old now. I cannot imagine how they live — they must have become very close in their isolation.'

'Did you not tell me that Miss Shipton had heard that Gosse had taken to preaching and had become most severe?'

'She probably exaggerated. She is afraid of him.'

'Hmm. I think *I* might be wary of a man who is prepared to push his son into a tank of water to baptise him. I hope the boy could swim.'

'Duncan! I am sure it was not like that. Moreover, I remember that Miss Shipton wrote that Mrs Gosse had always been most insistent about Willy's religious upbringing — so surely Mr Gosse would have wanted to carry out her wishes.'

'Do not be so sure. Fortunate for the boy that he was merely dropped into a tank and not into the sea. Those terrifying bathing women could serve a dual purpose — did you notice that Gosse refers to them somewhere as "uncorsetted priestesses of the bath"? *Phew!* What an image that conjures — those sombre priestly types are the ones to watch, he must have observed them very carefully.'

'You talk such *nonsense!*' I was cross and confused: Duncan's jesting disturbed me because there were unpalatable truths hidden within it. Yet I think I preferred Henry's comments on the bathing women rather than his religiosity: to me, the extent to which one walked in the way of the Lord was a private matter (so that one might lapse a little and remain unobserved?).

I returned my attention to the book — *Actinologia Britannica*, such a grand title, redolent of *Empire!* — and opened it at one of Duncan's strips of paper. There was *Anthea cereus*, which Duncan had found on the Isle of Cumbrae at the mouth of the Clyde. The passage dealt with the unpleasant stinging effect produced by the tentacles (a fact which had been most viciously disputed by Mr George Lewes in the *Maga* article on the sea anemones of Ilfracombe and Tenby — but he was no expert, he was surely a dilettant. And it had recently become common knowledge that his wife was the author George Eliot, who apparently had not the courage to use her own name!). Under *Anthea* there was a quotation describing how 'the whole of the back of the hand and fingers was covered with blisters as if I had thrust it into a bed of nettles, and nearly as painful.'

The evidence was provided by 'Miss Pinchard, an accomplished naturalist of Torquay'.

I wished that she should be immersed in a tank of *Anthea cereus* and not removed. She was there, in Torquay, on his doorstep.

She was an *accomplished* naturalist. I hated that unknown lady. And I saw that I had been quite deceived, for what was a 'communication' from Miss A. Church, now Mrs D. Robertson, compared to a nettle-rash on a locally-available accomplished lady? *Stomphia churchiae* — what an ugly sound the genus had!

CHAPTER 25: MATTHEW

'This boat's wearing the evidence of its past experience on its features,' I explained knowledgeably to Jim. He was scraping out the cracks so that we could fill them with Mick's magic goop. 'An alternative point of view is that it's carrying an archive of its past. I like that word, "archive", don't you?'

Jim sat back on his heels.

'What is all this shit you're spouting? You've been spending too much time with Elizabeth, that's for sure. Are you her new convert to biology, then? Her favourite new pupil?'

'Yup. Teacher's pet, that's me. Here — catch!'

I chucked him a half-bald paintbrush, but he ducked and fell over backwards onto the shingle.

'Shit,' he muttered as he struggled upright again, and brushed sand and bits of bleached seaweed off his tracksuit bottoms. 'Oh bloody hell.' But he sniggered, too, and so did I, and then we both ended up roaring.

'Anyway,' I said. 'Going back to this perfectly serious topic of conversation. I was saying to Elizabeth that her room was like a sort of personal museum — she thought that was quite a clever idea, by the way. I'm not just a pretty face. Oh no, I keep forgetting — *you're* the pretty face.'

I dodged as the paintbrush came flying back again.

'Missed. And she said that one collected a series of objects that described oneself, or something along those lines. So, my question to you, Dr Jim Steinberg, is — what does your own personal museum consist of?'

'Why? Why do you want to know?'

'Why not? I was thinking about mine, I suppose — and discovered I didn't have one. How boring is that?'

'Right. Sad person. Well, let's think this through.' Jim sat cross-legged. 'There's a lot of garbage, I guess. So I have to choose what qualifies. And I guess that means that you have to decide whether these objects describe you to other people or to yourself. That's a major criterion for selection. Also, are you selecting chronological mementoes of your life, or do you concentrate on objects or whatever that have influenced you in becoming the person that you are?'

'Christ! I thought I'd asked a simple question. This is all becoming a bit philosophical, Jim-lad.'

(This seemed to be my day for deep discussions; I was beginning to get the hang of it, but it made me realise what a feather-weight I was. Or maybe I was just starting to mix with people who were a bit above me, intellectually. Perhaps that organisation for brainy people, MENSA, ran courses, or I could go to a Mind-gym and train my mind and astound everyone by my genius.)

But, concentrating on what Jim had said, I suddenly remembered something he'd told me about camping in Oregon.

'Hey, what about that time you and your dad went to see the lowest tide of the century, and you both went camping? Perhaps there's something you collected then that would qualify.'

'Actually there is. There's a sea-biscuit — that's a flat sea-urchin like a sand-dollar. But I don't know how much that influenced the course of my life.'

'Okay. This is getting difficult. Just try to choose six objects that you'd like to put in your personal museum.'

'Right. That *is* hard. A photo of my dad, I guess — he's been dead a few years but we were real close. The first research paper that I got published. It was very mathematical and I was the last-named of six authors, but it was my first publication.'

He paused. None of this sounded very exciting, so far.

'The first letter that Paul wrote to me. Paul's my partner, I can't remember if I ever told you his name. And there's a photo of Paul and me at Yosemite on our first hiking trip together.'

His smooth face went kind of ridged and frowning, and he started picking at the pebbles by his feet.

'I can't think of much else, Matt, to tell the truth. I guess he's been the biggest influence. Our relationship partly describes me, these days.'

I was embarrassed then because I'm not into talking about relationships and all that analytical stuff. But what really embarrassed me was that his eyes were wet and shiny. I didn't know what to say. He got up quickly and moved away, pretending to be very interested in the windblown junk beneath the wall.

A little kid had been hanging about near us, a little girl, about seven or eight, dressed in one of those daft bikini-things. The top had slipped and showed her flat chest and little nipples. No different from little boys' nipples, so why bother with the top? The kid was carrying something that she'd picked up. I thought it was a burst orange ball but it was a broken fishing float. She came up to me.

'That man's crying,' she said, accusing me as though it was my fault. Perhaps it had been.

'Nah. He's just stubbed his toe. You know what it's like when you stub your toe, it hurts so much your eyes water. He's just walking round to make sure the toe's still working.'

She looked disbelieving, but wandered off towards Jim.

I wondered what it was like to love someone so much that their absence could make you hurt enough to cry. I realised that I envied him, because nothing like that had ever happened to me. Even when Hazel left, when I was a kid, I didn't cry: I was just too angry. And when you're a kid you don't really think about *loving* your parents; love is more a grown-up concept. I felt really sad for Jim because I liked the guy. I was also quite scared of showing I liked him. But Elizabeth was right, I could be a good friend without being gay. In fact, now I thought about it, it was better that I wasn't gay because that would just confuse things. This way, I was not in competition.

Jim was coming back and he was trying to look cheerful.

'Why did that kid ask me if she could look at my toe?'

'Dunno. Maybe she thought you'd broken it when you fell over backwards.'

If I'd been American I guess I'd have told him that he should go ahead and cry, that I'd like to be his buddy and I'd always be there for him, and so on. But because I'm actually an anal Brit I didn't say a thing and we just pretended that nothing had happened, and went back to working on the boat.

The other person that came back was Roger. It turned out this was a bit of a surprise to everyone, and probably not least to Roger and Hazel when they came face to face. Old Roger the Dodger had stayed on in London to get some work done, so Jim had said, and hadn't been expected back until tomorrow.

Instead of which, down the lane he came in his rackety little car. We heard him first, and we stood up and spied over the seawall to get a better view, and saw him walk in through the gate — where Elizabeth and Hazel must have seen him from the front room — and round to the kitchen. About twenty minutes later, when I just happened to be standing up to stir the fibreglass in its pot on top of the wall, I just happened to see him and Hazel come out of the kitchen door together and disappear up into the garden behind the house.

It wasn't that much later that Hazel suddenly appeared on the wall above us, on her own, and said that we should go home. Jim put his hands on the wall and did a press-up to get up to her level, but I'm not much good at that so I had to go round to where the jetty sloped down to the shore, and when I caught up with them they were being quite flirty with each other. Whatever next, eh?

Hazel let me drive.

The clouds had turned into fog higher up. It was rolling across the hills and we seemed to be driving at, rather than through, two-dimensional gloom, quite eerie.

I definitely needed to know about Hazel and Roger. I told her about Elizabeth's 'personal archive' idea (or was it mine?). She seemed a bit distracted, so to focus her mind I asked her the question.

'If you were only allowed to select six objects for your museum, what would you choose? It has to be objects that have influenced your life. Sleazy Edward's head, for example — ' (his head? What am I saying — what about his *dick*?), 'or Roger's perhaps. What else?'

'*What?*'

I'd shocked her; her eyes were wide and her face was pale. She didn't seem to know how to reply, so I prompted her again.

'What's been going on with you and Roger?'

A lay-by next to a gateway appeared on the next page of fog, so I steered the car off the road. I really did need to know.

'Oh Matt. You frighten me sometimes.' She took a breath and let it slowly. 'Nothing has been going on between me and Roger. Roger would have liked something to have gone on. And since you think you're old enough to interrogate me, I'll tell you the details, shall I?'

Hell, now I'm for it, I thought. She was quite cool, she didn't shout or do anything uncharacteristic like that.

'You can forget about hands patting knees and all that pathetic nonsense. In Oxford, Roger kissed me on the mouth and put his hand on my breast. It didn't "turn me on". In Cambridge, he planned that we should meet up and have sex — and don't for a minute think that it would have been "making love". But I didn't meet him. I have avoided him ever since, and he has been hurt and upset. And I have just explained to him why I failed to meet him, that there is no prospect of our having an affair. And that I am sorry if I gave him the wrong impression initially. He understands. He's a married man.'

I tried to imagine Roger putting his hand on my mother's breast, and I wanted to puke.

'And what about Edward? You were a married *woman*! You didn't let that stand in your way.' Suddenly the anger was there, and it scared me. 'You were my mother. My mum.'

I thumped the steering wheel and when I looked at her, I saw that her eyes were wet and shiny, too. So I had made her cry, as well. Oh *good*.

'I'm sorry, Matt.' She whispered it. 'But there's nothing I can do about it now, it was so long ago.'

We sat and stared out of the windscreen at the fog that was blowing across: a page of fog, a page of fog and cows, a page of cows, a page of fog. Red-brown cows — South Devons, Barbara had called them, proud of her wide agricultural knowledge — appearing then disappearing in the murk. Not that they cared. Could she not just touch me, even pat me on the head?

'When Roger and I drove up to Oxford, we went near the Cheddar Gorge and I was reminded of the time the three of us went there, your father and you and me. We had a lovely time. We all thought it was wonderful. And in the shop afterwards I gave you some money to buy a souvenir, and you bought a keyring that said 'Gough's cave' and gave it to me as a present. You used to call me "Mummy" in those days. And now I don't even have that any more.'

I looked at her: I wasn't sure if she meant the title or the keyring.

'What I'm trying to say is that I haven't kept any sort of a personal archive. Except the shell lady, and it turns out that wasn't even from you.'

It was true. I looked round the Shell House in my imagination and there was almost nothing that wasn't functional. She seemed to have no baggage, mental or otherwise. Was it deliberate policy, or did she really just not care?

'There's your graduation photo,' I suddenly remembered.

'Jamie made me a copy after Granny died — he still had the negative.'

'Granny didn't keep much, either, but that was because she was always looking forward to the next thing.' It had been a positive thing, with her, a sort of optimism, I supposed; not this sort of flat, negative approach that Hazel had. 'Though she did keep the famous suitcase of books. Don't you even want that any more?'

'No, I think I've finished with that.'

She thought for a bit, and I was impatient though I could see she was trying to explain something. It was almost as though she was trying to convince herself, or to make herself look at her own actions and explain them to herself.

'It's not that I can't be bothered with the past, Matt. That was Granny's attitude. I just don't want to have to think about the past because I haven't managed my life very well. So I've learned to take each day as it comes. I react to the seemingly random events and just hope that everything will turn out all right in the end. It's not such a bad approach, Matt — I get by.'

The shutter was coming down again. Calm eyes, the heavy lids curtaining them. I didn't want her to go away inside herself just yet. I risked it.

'What about me? I don't seem to have an archive either — certainly not in Polkenna. Unless you count the scribbles on the toilet wall. But I have this memory of *you* somewhere in my museum as someone that had an influence on me. I can't quite manage to discard you in the way you seem to have discarded me.'

'This personal archive analogy's getting out of hand,' she said, sharply. 'It's a silly concept. Matthew — you are my son. You are here, living with me, in what is now our house, if you'd like it to be. I would like you to stay. And I do love you, although I know there isn't a chance in hell that you'll believe that.'

I was bowled over; I hadn't had the slightest hint. 'Do you really want me to stay? To stay with *you* instead of Dad and Gail?' My mouth probably looked like the hole in a postbox.

'Only if that's what you yourself want to do. I'm not going to hold you against your will.'

There was an unconvincing smile, an attempt to lighten up, but she was breathing quite fast. I would have to think about it. But she had definitely said that she wanted me to stay. I wouldn't just be a temporary visitor. But I wasn't sure that we could ever be mother and son again; yet did we really need that, anyway?

'It would be good if we could be good friends.' There it was again, love and friendship, the deep and meaningful stuff. Oh shit. Whatever happened to me today?

'We should try to concentrate on that for a bit,' she agreed. 'We've been quite good friends, on and off, in the past few weeks. We could work on that a bit more. And you really don't have to worry about Roger getting in the way. Can we go home?'

I started the car again and a blackbird, startled out of the hedge, made a near-suicidal dive across the road.

The funny thing was that as I drove on I wasn't thinking about Hazel and living with her at the Shell House, but was thinking about Elizabeth instead. Elizabeth's personal museum wasn't contrived. It just looked like a jumble of stuff that was part of her and her past. I thought it was probably quite unselected. She didn't need to describe herself to other people, because she wasn't trying for any sort of image; not like me or Jim. I guess she just lived comfortably with herself, and the bits and pieces of her past. Nice, that. It must make life a whole lot easier. It would be quite cool to live there, with Elizabeth, at Nancarrow, with all that interesting stuff and by the beach. I tried out the idea in my mind and yet again I found I envied Jim.

I thought I might try building my own personal archive at the Shell House, and I wondered where I would display the deep red shell that Elizabeth had given me; it seemed significant somehow.

CHAPTER 26: HAZEL

'Look at these biceps, then,' Matt said.

He was sitting on the stool in the kitchen, wearing only jeans, and he flexed his raised arms in body-builder's pose. He reminded me of a picture I had seen somewhere: an early Athena poster, perhaps, in a student room?

'Impressive, or what?'

'Not bad. What's that from then — pulling pints and carrying crates at The Anchor?'

'Oh.' His pleased grin dimmed and he slumped forward over the grapefruit that he was mangling. 'Hell. I hadn't thought of that.' He tried out a pulling motion with his coffee mug. 'I thought it was from all this rowing.'

'Well, you're looking a lot fitter than when you first arrived — getting rid of the flab, despite the beer! Are you and Jim training for the gig racing, then? Or is the grapefruit-and-cereal breakfast part of some "healthy living" exercise?'

'Huh. Very amusing. We've been rowing around the bay — it's bloody hard work against the waves. I didn't know rowing was so difficult. It turned out that Jim'd never rowed before, either, so we spend a lot of the time going round in circles and looking right prats.'

'And Elizabeth's dinghy is watertight now, is it?'

He grinned around a spoonful of Raisin Bran. 'Not exactly. But we've got a plastic icecream tub as a bailer. I'm not sure the fibreglass bandage stuff was the right thing to use, but it seems reasonably okay. And Elizabeth doesn't seem to mind.'

'That's good. She seems remarkably tolerant of you two.'

'Yeah. She's okay. I've never met anyone like her before. She said she'd buy us an outboard motor if we can find a cheap second-hand one. Hey, there's the postie!'

I stretched, straightening my back, and pushed some of the papers on my desk aside, as the metal letter-flap on the porch door slapped shut. Matt was already struggling with the front door, and he came back from the porch with white and brown envelopes in his hand. One of the white envelopes was for him — he retreated to the other end of the room and sprawled on the sofa to read the letter — but the rest were for me. A long stiff envelope addressed to me contained notification that the divorce was going through, and that the *decree absolute* would be granted, if no dissension was received.

So that was (almost) that. The law had looked at our relationship and had decided that there was no reason for us to remain legally united, since it was clear that we hadn't behaved as a unit for a very long time. I looked at the piece of paper and felt neither regret nor relief for my own diminished role in the Myers' family saga. I would soon cease legally to be a Myers: would I re-assume the Lewisham name, protecting myself with it as I now inhabited the Lewisham house?

But then I remembered Matt: if I reverted to the Lewisham name, Matt would nevertheless remain a Myers. We would be divided by our surnames, and who then would know that we were biologically related? Only genetic analysis would prove scientifically that we belonged to the same twig on the tree. Only the pattern of bands on a gel would prove that he and I were kin.

When I had gone to live with Edward, I suppose that, deep down, naïvely, I must have always hoped that Matt and David would take me back 'if things didn't work out'. It was hard to believe that I could have thought that way, but lust, the thrill of the affair, whatever, seemed to have made an idiot of me, reduced my reasoning powers and responsibilities; had even swept maternal love aside. Afterwards I'd been ashamed, almost disgusted, by the basic primitiveness of the whole business, a relationship reduced to crude animal instincts.

It had been easy for Gail to take my place on a full-time basis. For a couple of years she had kept an eye on Matt in the holidays and after school; she had cooked and washed and jollied him along. A small step from there to having sex with and comforting my husband; and then also, apparently, my grown-up student son. Oh, the three of them had made a happy family unit. It had been like some awful soap-opera, life imitating not-quite-art. I couldn't have taken Matthew from them when he was younger, for how could I have managed with him on my own? In any case, it was unlikely that he would have come with me, for by then I had become 'Hazel'. But we had at least had a surname in common.

I swivelled the desk chair surreptitiously and glanced across the room at Matt. He had retrieved his bowl of cereal from the kitchen and was hunched forwards on the sofa, ladling flakes into his mouth, somehow avoiding his hair, and reading his letter again.

'Matt's turning out all right.' That was what Jamie had said to me a few weeks ago. And so he was.

Just watching him made me want to laugh aloud; he was gauche and infuriating, but he was also very amusing — and surprisingly sensitive. That side of his character must have come from my father's genes, I supposed. Jamie had it too. I realised I was getting used to having Matt around, and I thought we were getting to know each other a little better. I didn't want us to become estranged again.

He looked across at me. 'What are you grinning at me for?'

I shook my head and, folding up the solicitor's letter, said, 'Nothing much. It was just that you looked so happy yourself.'

He waved his letter. 'Caz says she's really missing me. Isn't that nice?'

'Are you missing *her*? That would be even "nicer"!'

He shrugged and screwed up his face. 'Uh-huh. Perhaps.'

An idea suddenly struck me. 'It's Thursday, isn't it? Is that today's paper next to you? Bring it over here a minute, Matt. I want to check something.'

Muttering about being nothing but a house-slave, he brought it over and wandered past me to the kitchen to search for something else to eat.

I flicked through the pages looking for the Classified Advertisements. *'Livestock.' 'Pets.' 'Farm Machinery.' 'Auctions: Household Furnishings and Effects.'* There were two of them. I reached up to the shelves above the desk and took down the local Ordnance Survey map. As I thought, 'Trelawn Barton' was only about fifteen miles away and, judging by the range of goods on sale, the farm was due to be sold off.

'Do you want to come to an auction with me? We'll have missed the start but it won't matter.'

'An auction. Why?'

'For fun! It's only about half-an-hour's drive away. Grab yourself a shirt while I get my bag. It'll be interesting. You never know what we might pick up cheap.'

Matt looked surprised but amused. 'Okay. If you don't have to work, let's do it. Why not!' and he padded upstairs to find some clothes. .

I waited impatiently — 'grabbing' a shirt obviously wasn't something to be hurried — but eventually he came downstairs wearing his smarter pair of jeans and a tee-shirt with 'Heaven or Hell?' printed on it (why?) and a stud instead of a ring in his nose.

There had been a heavy rainshower, and we drove through steam that rose up to the windows. We charged whooping through the smoking pockets. I drove and made Matt navigate, and near the farm, in deep, banked lanes where there were many junctions and unspecified crossroads, we became infuriatingly lost. Since we each swore that North was in a different direction, it looked as though we might be lost for ever.

'One day someone will come this way,' I said, 'probably by accident, and find an ancient rusting car with two skeletons in the front.'

'Food for crows.'

'What a disgusting idea.'

'Ecologically correct, according to Dr Wilson. Stop, go left!'

Twenty yards further on there was a farm gate to which was attached a printed advertisement for the auction. I drove carefully along the pot-holed track and squeezed the car into the concrete yard beside an assortment of pick-up trucks, cars and large fourwheel-drives. The Landrovers and Landcruisers were mud-spattered and equipped with tow-bars and wild-eyed sheepdogs, rather than bull-bars and golden retrievers; functional vehicles, used for crossing rough land and checking on stock and fences; their presence obscurely satisfied me.

Objects were stacked together in the yard and identified as lots for sale by numbered cardboard labels. Men stood around and discussed what they saw, gestured with rolled catalogues, prodded at wooden pallets, fingered a pair of unused metal field-gates; a mixture of people and garbs — boots or leather shoes, flat caps or bald heads, Standard English or local dialect. Swallows dived into the barn, where the auctioneer was already hectically pushing up the bids for the machinery that we could see inside. We looked into the milking parlour, with its tubes and aluminium pipes and vats, where a blackboard still held a smudged reminder of a telephone number.

'I wonder what happened. It's all so desolate.'

'Bloody government, that's what happened. Bloody DEFRA, kowtowing to the bloody EU!' The middle-aged man's face was burnt red by weather and anger. 'That and the TB from the bloody badgers. Had to kill the lot, didn't he, poor old bugger? 'Scuse my French. Had to pack it in.'

'What will happen to the land?' I asked. In common with the rest of the area, it was steep-valleyed pasture with little arable.

The man shoved his hands into his jacket pockets, which made him look even more belligerent, but he spoke more quietly. 'Stratton next door'll put in a bid. And Kivell, I wouldn't be surprised. Bloody mad, what's the point?'

He turned his back and stamped out into the yard, into the pale sunlight.

'That's rough,' Matt said sympathetically. 'I bet the farm had been in the family for ages, too. This is really depressing — I thought you said it was going to be fun.'

'Yes. Sorry. We'll go into the house. Unless you want to bid for a tractor.'

'Hey, perhaps there's an outboard motor in that barn, we could look.'

'I very much doubt it. Let's go and get a catalogue.'

There was a greater mixture of people inside the house, browsers, bargain-hunters, a high proportion of women, a few dealers, and a couple with young children who said they were hunting for a wardrobe.

'Are we looking for something specific?' Matt asked, as I opened the drawers of a huge, scuffed, oak dresser. 'That's too big, for a start.'

'Yes, we're looking for a table. No, that one's too big as well,' I added as Matt pointed at the worn pine kitchen table. 'It has to be small enough to fit in the space between the front door and the stairs. There's actually quite a lot of space there that we don't use.'

'Why do we want to put a table there?'

'To eat off. So you can have somewhere to eat, instead of on the sofa where your "*fucking*" tomatoes roll around. Remember? Or at the kitchen worktop. We are looking for a table at which you can sit in comfort — where *we* can sit in comfort — on proper chairs. Above all, I want you to be comfortable.' I smiled up at him, and hooked my arm through his. 'See?'

'You know, you're really short. Stunted! I hadn't realised that before. A table! We can sit around it with candles and everything, and hold terribly civilised conversations about politics and the latest best-sellers.'

'Politics and religion aren't allowed. But do not mock. You grumbled about the lack of a table — so now we shall get one. It is to be a symbol,' I said, firmly.

'This sounds a bit heavy. Okay, let's look for a symbolic table. Does that mean it can be an Impressionist table, or a Vorticist table? Or must it be perfectly proportioned and polished like a Dutch sixteenth-century table — ' he was grinning his head off, getting carried away, 'on which you'll arrange a bowl of perfect flowers that has a posing butterfly and snail? No, it should be a Whiteread table cast in concrete or a Tracy Emin table covered in apple cores and spit.'

'Matt, do be quiet.' I squeezed his arm more tightly and pulled him towards the hall. 'Whatever it is now, it's going to become a Shell House Dining Table — so let's see if we can find one.'

There was a table in the hall, but it was the wrong shape; there was another in the sitting room but it was too small. Matt said the search reminded him of the bears' chairs in *Goldilocks*. I sat in a white-painted Lloyd-loom chair, enjoying its bucket-shaped comfort, and wondered about buying it for the garden. We looked through the bedrooms, searched through a box of books, and checked an (empty) trunk. We went downstairs again. Matt opened the drawer of a sideboard and then closed it quickly and turned away.

'I'm embarrassed that we're doing this, poking around in the remains of someone's home. Trying to buy up bits of someone's life for a few quid.'

'What price a "personal archive", eh? Is it the cheapness or the intrusion that embarrasses you? Though there's nothing very personal about all this, the important pieces have been removed.' I looked round the dining room. 'Other than that box of knick-knacks — and those must be the ones they didn't want — there are very few clues as to the likes and dislikes of the owners. Or to their memories.'

Matt, despite his misgivings, took a few objects out of the box: a china dalmation with a soppy expression; a cheap painted weather-house in which the man and woman were doomed forever to swivel in and out without ever seeing each other; a blue glass ashtray. As he placed the ornaments on the glass-covered top of the sideboard, a picture of a shattered doll came suddenly, shockingly, into my mind. The Valley of the Dolls. No, no, Valley of Rocks, that chapter in *Seaside Pleasures*. On a day's outing from Ilfracombe the Gosses had stopped at an inn and one of the children found a little broken china ornament on the mantelpiece. What had Emily Gosse called it — 'the trunkless head of the Arcadian Flora', or was it a headless trunk? Which was worse? The landlady had apparently been very upset that the ornament had been touched because it had belonged to a dead daughter; a memento of happy times past.

As Matt stowed away the ornaments again, his head perilously close to a light hanging from the low ceiling, I knew that I had been wrong when I told him that I didn't want to surround myself with a personal museum. But what price could be put on a hand-made shell lady?

As for tables, we seemed to be out of luck, and I was very disappointed. But in a small back kitchen, where there was still a double porcelain sink and a smooth cement floor sloping towards a central drain, Matt found a small collection of tools. He picked up a Black and Decker drill.

'We could do with one of these at home. You haven't got any tools worth speaking of.'

'Do you know how to use it? I don't remember David being much of a handyman.'

'Sure. We use them in the art department at college. Look at this, though — talk about lucky coincidences! Look what the tools are resting on.'

It was a brown-varnished rectangular table, straightforward and unpretentious, with a square-sectioned leg at each corner. I took out my cloth tape-measure: the table was neither too big nor too small. I dug a finger-nail into the surface near the edge: the wood was soft, probably deal or pine.

'Perfect,' I said. 'And that drill has a sanding attachment, doesn't it? So we can bid for both and you can do up the table. Assuming our bid wins.'

Matt's face fell. 'Shit, I forgot we can't just go and pay for them.'

We checked with the woman who was preparing the invoices for successful bids and she told us that the outdoor sale was nearly over, and that we were in luck, the auctioneer would be starting the indoor sale in the kitchen.

'Lots 153 and 162? Say half-an-hour.'

We picked up the numbered card that registered us as serious contenders and sat waiting in the kitchen, on a bench against the wall. Within twenty minutes or so, a mass of people started to surge in through the back door. I grabbed Matt and we pushed our way to the front of the small crowd. But we needn't have worried, for the throng re-ordered itself, those people uninterested in the kitchen lots moving on to take up positions in other rooms.

The auctioneer was small and wiry, but had a voice as loud and high as a wren. He carried a small set of folding steps to which was attached a tall pole that acted as a hand-hold, and he set up his position in the middle of the room, pointing to each lot as he galloped through the bids. They were coming and going so fast that I hardly had time to feel nervous, although I felt my palms turn damp and my cheeks flush. Suddenly we were there.

'Lot 153. Assortment of tools, including Black and Decker drill and attachments. Who'll give me £15?'

Matt nudged me but I kept quiet.

'Two pounds,' said a man somewhere over on my left, patently unimpressed.

'Two-fifty.' I raised my card.

'Three.' The unseen man. The auctioneer looked at me. I nodded.

'Three-fifty,' he said.

'Four.'

I nodded. 'Four-fifty, the lady on my right.'

'Five.'

I made no sign, though the auctioneer looked my way. I gripped Matt's arm.

'Five pounds. Any advance on five pounds? Five to the —'

I raised my card, trying to ignore my scarlet cheeks.

'Five-fifty, then.'

My opponent kept quiet. I could almost hear him shrug; five pounds was his limit, he hadn't been that bothered, the items were probably for a market stall or car-boot sale.

'Lot 153. Five poun' fifty pee. Goin' to the lady on my right …'

Pause. Bang of his gavel on his wooden clipboard. I held up my numbered card.

'Number seventy-one,' he called to the lad who was acting as his scribe.

'So have we got them?' Matt whispered, slightly bemused. 'You were so cool — how did you know what to do?'

'Oh, David and I used to go to auctions when we were first married,' I whispered back. 'But I didn't feel very cool, it still makes me nervous as hell. Sssh. What number are we at now?'

I'd planned on £20 as the absolute maximum for the table; it wasn't worth it as a piece of furniture, but I'd be unlikely to find another of the right size. And I wanted it today! The auctioneer started at £7 and wouldn't take my bid of five, so the reserve was probably ten. Astonishingly, nobody else wanted it very much, and it was mine for £11. I felt pleased but also guilty. I put my arm around Matt's waist.

'Let's wait outside for a few minutes until the bids are registered, and then we'll go and pay and see about getting the table delivered. Then go home.'

'Can't we just take it with us? I bet we could tie it on top of the car.'

I was doubtful; but that would certainly be a cheaper and quicker solution. We went into the barn to see if any string was lying around, but a farmer, hearing what we were looking for, said he had a length of twine in his pick-up if we'd come with him. He gave us several yards of rough blue binder-twine and then, hearing that we hadn't got a penknife either, roared with laughter at our unpreparedness, and came to help collect and lift the table.

With many instructions, and much joshing from his friends, he and Matt upturned the table onto a couple of newspapers on the car roof, and lashed it through the rear windows and to the front and back bumpers. Matt wanted to stick a flag on each leg but had to make do with two lot-number labels. He insisted on driving us away.

'Not you! I can't be driven off by my mum, like some little kid.'

He stuck his hand out of the window and waved when our helpful friend slapped the car on its rump as we edged by.

I wanted to reach up and pat the table in gratitude, but my arm wasn't long enough; and it would be dangerous to rejoice at one small lapse.

We got lost again on the way home, and the table bumped and clattered on the roof, but that didn't seem to slow Matt's driving.

'You think we should sand it down and varnish it, do you?' he asked. 'That sounds boring.'

'What did you have in mind?'

'I wondered about livening it up with some sort of design.'

'*Papier-mâché* with inlaid mother-of-pearl, then lacquered deep red like a box. That should keep you out of mischief for a bit.'

'What mischief? Some hopes. No, I could paint something jazzy on it. I don't know what, I'll have to think about it.'

'You'd better paint those awful chairs to match, then. They won't look at all right, otherwise.' The four straight-backed chairs from my desk-table were scattered in odd corners of the downstairs room and landing. 'I expect I can re-cover the seats.'

'Are you serious? I thought you'd throw a fit at the idea!'

'We might as well enjoy the table if we're going to sit around it such a lot.'

As we took the sharp left turn onto the narrow road that wound up to the top of East Polkenna, Matt suddenly said,

'You realise what we're going to have to do now, don't you? Get the bloody thing off the car and down the steps. That's *really* going to be fun!'

CHAPTER 27: ELIZABETH

Allan and I first discussed the possibility one autumn evening. I brought in logs and driftwood, then lit a fire and closed the internal shutters so that the drawing room was cosy and self-contained, scented intermittently by stray wisps of smoke from the chimney.

Allan sat next to the fire, with the biography of Dorothy Hodgkin resting on the rug across his knees. I had my feet up on the sofa, and the *Independent* folded to the crossword on mine. But we certainly weren't sitting in silence, companionable or otherwise: I occasionally read out clues or spelt out the skeletons of words, and Allan replied, or not, as inspiration took him. Handel's *Solomon* was playing on the radio and Allan sometimes sang or whistled. The music reached a critical point.

'Wait for it!'

Allan raised his hand, finger pointed like a baton. And then we were off, into the *Queen of Sheba's Entry*, Allan whistling furiously and accurately, his eyes beginning to crinkle, his poor, thinning face flushing, cheeks taut, snatched breaths coming ever more frequently ... until he suddenly couldn't keep going any more and collapsed, gasping and laughing, and I tapped my fingers against the newspaper in applause.

'Very good.' I was laughing too. 'Sheba doesn't realise what she missed. But I wish I didn't always think of Greta Garbo when I hear it, Sheba can never have looked like that.'

'Phoo!' Allan was still puffing. 'Just think, Beth, if only I'd known you before we met at Asmara — we could have gone to Aksum together. I still envy you seeing where Sheba was buried.'

'Supposed to be buried. Yes, but as I told you, I don't remember being impressed.'

'You couldn't have failed to have been impressed if I'd been with you to provide the background music.'

'You'd have raised her spirits enormously.'

He chuckled. 'Oh, if only we'd —'

'Wait a minute! *Spirit*. Of course. "Ectoplasm". Yes. Blank, C, three blanks, L, A, two blanks. It fits. "The substance of ghoulish cells, perhaps?" Obvious, now. Sorry, my love, "if only we" what?'

'I was going to say, if only we could go and have a look at Asmara again. Go back as tourists. "If only".'

'Yes. At our age life is full of "if onlys", isn't it? Yours — and therefore mine — perhaps rather more than most people's.'

We looked at each other and although we were each half-smiling, I knew we were both feeling the same deep sadness and probably, in my dear Allan's case, also fear.

'I do love you,' he said quietly, and he held out his hand towards me. I went to him and took the hand that was offered to me with love and friendship, and sat next to him on the arm of his chair.

'I love you, too.' I meant it, but there was a chill dread inside me because I already knew that I loved Barbara more.

We sat quietly together, staring into the fire. The scarlet shell of a log collapsed in on itself with a soft rattle against the metal basket. We sat and we didn't speak. The Virginia creeper scraped against a window, stirred by the wind, and smoke puffed, like a wave breaking upwards, into the room. I suspended thought about the future and instead, it seemed that the air around us became heavy with a strange peace that bound us together.

Then Allan grunted with amusement. 'Do you remember that guest-house we stayed in in Scotland? The gaudy one, near Torridon?'

'What was she called? MacNally. Mrs MacNally. Yes.' I laughed, and then moved to restock the fire with logs. 'Why?'

'I was just thinking about those extraordinary mountains, and how different the sea seemed there. And that reminded me of Mrs MacNally's home-sewn mats and bedspreads, and the knitted cushion-covers. We always wondered if she saw the world in a different way, didn't we?'

'It was her apron that was the most spectacular, do you remember? All those pieces of different colours and patterns ... We had some wonderful walks along the coast.'

'We met Ralph Williams on the coast-path, coming back from Diabaig. One of those odd coincidences that always happen.'

'Goodness, yes. Striding along with a stick and what he'd have called a "knapsack". But not yodelling, or at least he wasn't when we met him. He died not long afterwards, though, didn't he? Didn't he have something wrong with his kidneys?'

'That was the reason for his death, certainly, but not the cause. He arranged to die on the night-sleeper to Edinburgh. He closed up his house to go on holiday, booked a hotel at the other end, and took some pills of some sort, knowing he had several uninterrupted hours in which they'd take effect, and that somebody would find him in the morning.'

'A very tidy suicide.'

'No. I hoped you'd note that I said "arranged to die", my love. "Suicide" implies sadness and despair to me — which isn't necessarily the case if your life is gradually fizzling out anyway, and you plan to end it a little earlier and a little more neatly.'

'I see.'

I stared into the fire, thinking about the implications, and reminded him, tentatively, 'We did talk about getting some sort of live-in nurse, when things became too difficult ...'

'Oh, come on, love. At that stage "things" are going to be very untidy, aren't they? Even messy. And you know what I'm like, obsessive about neatness.'

He gave one of his little chuckles and I couldn't help but smile, too. It was curious how, once the idea had been brought into the open, we were both able to discuss it dispassionately and with logic.

'At the moment I'm able to manage, after a fashion, with your help and Peter's, but when I become totally reliant on someone else to feed me and wash me, and do other unmentionable, degrading things — well, what sort of life is that? I don't think either of us wants that, do we?'

'I shall miss you.'

'I'd rather you missed me as I am now, or as I was, rather than as some slobbering vegetable. You know it makes sense.'

Of course it did. He deserved to choose the way in which he died; we both knew I would be hypocritical to protest, especially when it was obvious that what he said made sense. But there was a sudden coldness of fear around my heart.

'But how will you do it? How do you want me to help?'

'Oh no, it's very important that there's absolutely not even a suspicion of your implication. The last thing you want is a murder charge and all that that implies. No, I've already given this a lot of thought, and I've got plenty of time to refine it. There are ways of doing these things, people to ask who can be relied on to keep quiet. And I shall ask Peter to procure me whatever is necessary.'

'*Peter!*'

'No-one will ever suspect Peter's involvement.'

'But he'll be devastated afterwards, if he thinks he helped to bring about your death. He'll surely guess, Allan. Don't involve *Peter*.'

'No, I plan to make sure that he knows beforehand and that he'll want to help in some small way. He likes to help me, dearest, you know that, and this could be the greatest help of all. I'll find some way. And one of these days, I don't know when ... I also intend to find a way that doesn't look like suicide, either. The fewer the questions that are asked, the better. From you, too.'

It had seemed so simple, that evening. I had left it to him; he had always been a planner and schemer, and I had known that he would organise something that was best for both of us. Not long after he had shown me some barbiturates that Peter Pascoe had obtained for him (he wouldn't tell me how, merely that these things were simple once you knew), and when I had questioned whether the drugs wouldn't show up in his bloodstream ('afterwards', I couldn't bring myself to say the word 'post-mortem'), he had said that he'd thought of a way around that too, and that we should now forget all about the matter and enjoy our lives.

'I'm going to write you a poem,' he had said, mysteriously, and had refused to explain himself further.

CHAPTER 28: HAZEL

Two readers were tapping on their laptop keyboards, copying extracts from manuscripts, the rest of us used pencils. There was a barrel-shaped sharpener with a handle by the window: it smelt of wood shavings and reminded me of my schooldays.

'No portrait of my beloved existed, except one which was taken in her early childhood, and another taken in youth, which is in the possession of a distant relative in America. We had often intended to have one, and in the preceding summer had even waited for several hours in the rooms of Maull and Polyblank, the eminent photo-graphers; but the weather had become unsuitable before her turn arrived. This was a subject of regret to her, for our little boy's sake; she would have liked him to possess some means of keeping in remembrance his mother's features; she knew they could never fade from my memory. Our dear friends, Mr Hislop and Miss Georgina Long, knowing of this regret, with the most prompt kindness proffered their aid, the former to take a photograph, the latter a water-colour miniature. I thankfully accepted both offers; and on the sixth day of February, only four days before her departure, the kind artists, with the camera and the palette, were introduced into the bedroom. The circumstances were almost as unfavourable as they well could be, yet the resemblances produced, especially the first of the two photographs, are to me beyond all price. A third photograph was taken on the following Monday, about twelve hours before death. It is characteristic and pleasing, though somewhat undefined, because of the motion arising from her laborious breathing: she appears as if sleeping, but this was owing to the bright sun's rays compelling her to keep her eyes closed during the exposure.'

'Characteristic and pleasing.' Surely this must have been impossible? Mummy had been almost unrecognisable when she died.

CHAPTER 29: ANNE: MARCH 1861

It had been raining all morning: that light, foggy rain that seems to be a speciality of Glasgow and that so dampens one's clothes and mood. There is a word for it, 'dreich', that seems to describe the phenomenon and its effect entirely.

Mama and Papa were fretting indoors and comparing the weather unfavourably with that of Winchester. Mama would be glad to return home; her tasks in Scotland had been completed, she had seen Tom safely installed at medical school in Edinburgh and had reassured herself that I was happy and living in comfortable surroundings. My youngest brother had written plaintively calling for her return (Mama suspected that he was in trouble, yet again, with Mrs Jackson, the cook) so now she was ready to return to her own comforts and familiar surroundings.

My poor husband was attempting to entertain Papa in his study. When I looked in they explained they had been discussing the dangers of the sea and the hazards around our Scottish coasts, and the lighthouses that the Messrs Stevenson had therefore been building, some in very inaccessible places. Duncan was engaged in a very contorted explanation of Mr Faraday's experiments with the electric light; I could see that he was talking himself into a muddle but was unable to find a tactful way to extricate him.

And Mama? Mama was occupying herself in the drawing room, in writing her journal, and interrupted my own reading with frequent questions as to the name of this or that house or painter that we had visited or admired, so that the details she recorded might be quite correct. She was proud, with reason, that she had kept a journal without a break since she was twelve years old.

'Everything is there, Anne! From my secret thoughts about handsome young men that I met, to the date that my hair was first put up, and Papa's proposal of marriage … and the day Papa fell down the stairs and embarrassed the maid with his swearing — it was Margaret in those days, do you remember her? So very *prim*! And plays we have been to, concerts, dinners, who came and what they talked about — probably all very dreary to look back on, nobody has really had anything very memorable to say, have they, when you come to look back on it? And of course, darling, the birthdates and illnesses and little successes of all you children. It is such a pity that you did not keep up your own journal.'

'I don't think I have much to record, Mama.'

I did not intend to sound so sad, not really.

'My poor child! — for you are still a child to me, your poor old Mama, even though you are twenty-seven. You and Duncan have enjoyed so much together. Bearing children isn't everything, believe me.'

But I knew she did not mean this because she had always loved all of her children. Sometimes she pretended that she did not, that we were irksome (as indeed we were!)

and ungrateful — but she had always been generous of her time. Mama would always be our loving confidante, and she was still quite capable of teasing and cajoling us all, even Papa.

'Oh, Mama! I wish you could stay with us for ever.'

'Come here, my darling.' She stood up and held out her arms, and I went to her willingly, allowing myself to be rocked against her warm bosom, and comforted by her familiar perfume.

'There is nothing amiss between you and Duncan, is there? Is that what is making you so unhappy? It worried me, at first, that he is so much older than you.'

'No, nothing at all, Mama. He is a good, kind man. He takes care of me and loves me —' I wanted to explain, but it made me blush, 'quite passionately!'

'Then what, my darling?' She held me away a little, to look in my face, but I released myself and went to sit by the window. I noticed that even the blades of grass on the lawn were weighed down by their burden of water droplets.

'Perhaps life has not turned out quite as I would have wished. Before I was married …' I paused, and sighed in exasperation. '*After* I was married, I wanted to do so much, and to become famous.'

'Yes. I know.' Mama sat down too, and closed her journal. 'I remember quite clearly that you wanted to become a famous naturalist. You were inspired by Mr Gosse. But all children want to become a famous such-and-such.'

'But I meant it — and I was *not* a child! I wanted to travel, and collect new species, and Duncan said he wished for the same things, too. That is why we were so suited for each other. He recognised my dreams because they were the same as his.'

'But now —?'

'But it never happened. There have always been reasons, Duncan has found reasons … I cannot organise such a thing myself, I am completely reliant on him. And then my wretchedly failing pregnancies have given all the other petty reasons some legitimacy, so that we are saved from having to make plans and decisions, do you see? So you see how I occupy my days, Mama — with the trivial occupations that are necessitated in the running of a household, with reading novels, attempting to paint indifferent and uninspired watercolours, with visiting and being visited by friends. You say Duncan and I have so much to share — but it is *his* book that is there, *his* name on the cover, not mine!'

'You told me that he has included many of your own observations. And that you have had to do a great deal of reading on his behalf that has had nothing to do with novels. Perhaps you are exaggerating a little.'

'It is Duncan Robertson's book, look at the cover. All *I* have is a sea-anemone named after me, that sounds like some kind of religious dwarf!' I was shaking with frustration and anger, I clamped my jaws together to stop my teeth chattering.

Mama sat silently, pushing her journal this way and that, rubbing at marks on the table.

She eventually sighed. 'I am at a loss what to suggest. How I wish you and Duncan could have a child — then you would surely find the purpose that you feel you lack.'

I regarded her in amazement, astonished that she should so misunderstand me.

'I wish I were *barren*. I wish I had been barren and known it so, from the start. Nothing would have stopped me then. I would have gone to the Amazon — or *Jamaica*!'

Mama's expression was of pure dismay and she squeezed her mouth with her hand, so that her face looked suddenly sad and old. We avoided each other's eyes and were silent, until Kate came in to tidy the room and remind us that the Laird and his lady were due to arrive in half-an-hour.

I have grown fond of the Ballavichs: they are both in their sixties, and well-travelled and wise; similar in stature, spare in frame, it seems as though they have grown to resemble each other in both appearance and behaviour, so that they are more like brother and sister than man and wife. They live in an elegant house in Blythswood Square, that proclaims its grandeur without ostentation, being built on simple classical lines; from their windows they look down to the river, and can almost see the Broomielaw quay where Duncan's offices are situated. Apparently the Ballavich estate was largely squandered by the elder brother who (perhaps fortunately) died in his forties from an over-consumption of the *usque-baugh* (this is so frequently mentioned as the cause of demise of the Scottish landed gentry that the tale may be apocryphal!). This drunken brother having died childless (is there is an *epidemic* of childlessness in Duncan's family?), the estate passed on to the more sober brother — who was forced to sell large portions of the acreage. The Laird, nevertheless, contrives to keep a large and handsome yacht and two houses, as well as keeping fortune enough to winter in climates warmer than any to be found in these islands — even that of Winchester!

So, the Ballavichs' acceptance of our invitation to lunch no longer held any terrors for me or for Duncan, whom they professed to hold in high regard. Papa is moderately indifferent to whether or not others hold him in regard, low or high; he is oblivious and unchanging. I am afraid Mama was somewhat flustered, partly, I fear, as a result of my *explanation* of a half-hour previously, but Lady Ballavich sat next to her and conversed with her in a warm and interested manner. Poor Mama: I know I hurt her immeasurably but, selfish as I am, I was relieved to feel my own mood of despair lighten after I had expressed my views.

Even Duncan's impatience to present his book no longer irked me; I would allow him to bask in glory amongst the family.

The Ballavichs had brought an optical toy that had recently become very fashionable in London, a zoetrope which, when spun, became the 'Wheel of Life', revealing leaping figures when one applied one's eye to a slit upon the side. This, with the warm fire and a decanter of sherry, dispelled the gloom of the day, and soon the Ballavichs were warming us still further with their tales of sunny Mediterranean shores and the small adventures they had encountered thereon.

But when a suitable pause arose, my husband leapt to his feet and strode to the davenport in the corner, returning with three copies of his book, each beautifully bound in soft calf-skin.

'*Nature's Survivors: the Wildlife of the Scottish hills and coast*. D. Robertson, Esq. Published by A.B. Blackie, Edinburgh 1861.' Papa spoke the title aloud.

Ballavich was reading Duncan's dedication with a broadening smile and then he handed the open book to his wife and stood up and shook Duncan's hand.

'Excellent, my dear nephew. Your aunt and I are very proud of you.'

'Wonderful. Wonderful!' Papa leapt up, too, and joined in the back-slapping and hand-shaking. 'As good as showing off a new child!'

I avoided Mama's eyes and quickly opened my own copy so that I should not see Duncan's expression.

'To my dearest darling Anne,' he had written, 'my never-reproachful assistant and constant friend. From your ever-loving husband, D.R.'

Now I did look at him, and I wished we were alone so that I could hold him tightly and thank him for his love, and perspicacity — and friendship.

'Read the Foreword,' he said softly.

I ran my eyes over it quickly. Words sprang out at me: '*my wife*' — what had he written? What was on the printed page for all to see? 'I am profoundly grateful for the contributions of my wife, a talented and indefatigable naturalist (and who, as the former Miss Anne Church, has been immortalised in P.H. Gosse's *Actinologia Britannica* by the attribution of a specific name, given to the anemone *Stomphia churchiae*) without whose abundant knowledge and sound advice this book could not have reached fruition.'

I shook my head, almost speechless. 'You give me too much credit.'

Mama had turned to the Foreword, too, and now she read that sentence aloud to the others.

'Quite right. Well done. Honour given where it is due.' The Laird lifted my hand and kissed it gallantly. 'A wonderful book, Duncan. Amy and I are already avid to read it, aren't we, my dear? Let us hasten through lunch so that we can take ourselves home as speedily as possible!'

'No, Hugh. We shall not allow Duncan or Anne to eat a mouthful for they shall both tell us how they gathered the information.'

Mama just smiled and smiled, and said, 'Thank you, Duncan. You have made us so proud of you — and Anne.'

'We should send out for some champagne!' Papa cried. 'A celebration is called for.'

'Well, I am embarrassed to admit that I took the precaution of ordering in a bottle or two already, in the hope that my — our — book would be well-received.'

Thus was our lunch a very light-hearted and happy occasion, with Duncan being called upon to tell of ghillies and stalkers and landowners whom he had interviewed, and the fishermen and professors and amateur ornithologists. I had to recount the story of the Solway basking sharks, and other adventures in the Frith of Clyde, and to tell of our pursuit of the small ruddy pine marten in the great Caledonian forests of the Cairngorms — and of my own pursuit of elusive facts in books and encyclopaedias.

'I assume your title is a nod in the direction of Darwin's ideas?' the Laird asked. 'The animals that can live in the harsh extremes found in our Highlands must be especially well-fitted for survival.'

'That is indeed the thesis of the book. We have spent many hours debating the topic, have we not, darling?'

I nodded: we had, indeed.

'You should send copies to Darwin and Huxley. It can do no harm — I hear that Darwin is always looking for fresh evidence.'

'I thought that I might send a copy to Gosse, too.' Duncan's smile was mischievous.

'Now, that would be unkind!'

'Mr Gosse's name came up in Italy in the most extraordinary circumstances,' Lady Ballavich suddenly interjected. 'We were drawn into conversation with a most interesting and devout lady, a Miss Shipton —'

'*Oh*!'

'Do you know her, then, Anne?'

'I think so — if it is the same Miss Shipton. But please continue.'

'We would not have met her had there not been a tremendous storm — for she was expecting to sail to Sicily. But the boat would not leave in those conditions. My goodness, it was so *dramatic* — was it not, Hugh?' She looked across the table for confirmation. 'We went down to the quay to watch the waves and were nearly blown away by the force of the wind.'

'The waves were breaking over the lighthouse, right to its summit. A sight to strike terror into the heart of an old sailor! I was mightily relieved that I was not out upon that sea.'

'Well, as you may imagine, we were forced to spend most of the day indoors — we were fortunate to be occupying one of those grand and lofty rooms that are so typical of the old palazzi. Just imagine it, my dear — frescoes upon the walls, and heavy silk hangings, and every other surface hung with heavy gilded mirrors. With the fire and the candles, the room was *ablaze* with light —'

'Miss Shipton, dearest.'

'Well, this poor lady sat with us at dinner — she was a wretched sight, it must be said, suffering greatly from some form of influenza as well as an infirmity in her leg —'

I smiled. 'Yes, "suffering". That sounds very like the Miss Shipton I know.'

The Laird glanced at me shrewdly and his eyes glimmered with humour.

'She was in complete misery and despair at the thought of having to set sail at midnight, yet neither did she dare to stay in her cold, comfortless room — thus she described it — to await another boat. She told us how she longed to escape to Sicily, where she was certain she would find her El Dorado in the form of a sunny shore! So you may imagine that her conversation was not very cheerful. But I must have replied in some manner that led her to believe we had more in common than she had supposed — I still cannot remember what it was —'

'Whatever it was, the floodgates were opened!' the Laird observed wryly. 'The flow of exhortation was unstoppable. She spoke without ceasing of the goodness of the Lord — her "dear Master" as she referred to him — until her dinner became quite cold.'

'I felt sorry for her, she seemed such a lonely creature, although it was clear that her love of the Lord gave her great strength and comfort. Hugh gave her our cards at the end of the meal, and she went off to her room to prepare herself for the voyage.'

'And then, naturally, my good wife was overcome with pity — and hastened after this bearer of the influenza and invited her to pass the hours with us until her ship sailed.'

'In your beautiful salon? That would have given her great pleasure, I am sure.'

'So it seemed. She was so pleased that she sat between us by the fire and rewarded us with more than an hour's ... "lecture", is perhaps the word?'

The Laird nodded, sighing and lifting his eyes to Heaven.

'A lecture on the exceeding grace of the Lord who had previously saved her from death — some illness, we were led to believe. And then, my dear,' Lady Ballavich turned to me with a quick smile, 'she became very agitated and proceeded to rummage through her bag —'

'A most capacious handbag, almost, indeed, a small portmanteau!'

'— and produced a small package of religious tracts. I have to admit that the Laird and I were somewhat taken aback. We have never before been the recipients of religious tracts, but — and here at last is where we return to your Mr Gosse — the tracts had been written by him and his late wife. It seems that Miss Shipton was constantly in the habit, throughout her travels, of handing these to strangers!'

'She may have learnt that from Mrs Gosse. When Sarah Nisbet and I attended that shore class at Ilfracombe, it was Miss Shipton who was our chaperone —'

'Our daughter has been a model of evangelical fervour ever since.'

'Indeed I have, Papa. I have prepared a suitable discourse on the Scriptures to aid our digestion.'

'But that is so extraordinary, Anne! I had not realised that you knew her so well. That is indeed a coincidence.'

'Mrs Nisbet's sister, who is a devout Presbyterian, employed Miss Shipton to accompany us. And Miss Shipton's friendship with Mrs Gosse stemmed from that time at Ilfracombe. Mrs Gosse frequently walked on the shore and handed out tracts, so Miss Shipton was naturally drawn to her. They remained friends and correspondents throughout Mrs Gosse's life.'

'I see.' Lady Ballavich was silent for a moment, then resumed her rapid chatter.

'Now, I seem to recall that Miss Shipton told us that she was engaged — somewhat slowly — in writing a book about Mrs Gosse.'

'So she told me, herself.'

'Yes, and the Gosse tracts are translated into French, did you know? She told us that large numbers are sold in France, it seems they are very popular.'

'She gave some of the French ones away, did she not, Amy, to a poor hapless Frenchman?'

'Was he not a railway official? She was waiting for her train which — like her boat! — was delayed or cancelled, poor woman.'

'Yes, and apparently the Frenchman had a broken arm so she felt sorry for him and sent him away with a large pile of religious works. We were at great pains not to laugh.'

The Ballavichs laughed fondly at their reminiscences.

'Ah well. We should not mock her piety, almost overpowering though it was. I admire her greatly for her courage and fortitude. She seems to have been beset with disasters and uncountable difficulties, but she persevered — and I believe she still travels far and wide, evangelising as she goes. All of which must be difficult for a single lady, especially one in poor health.'

'And did she truly sail to Sicily in the height of the gale?' Duncan asked.

'It had abated somewhat by midnight,' the Laird replied, 'but I have to admit I did not envy her the voyage. I escorted her to the quay and tried to comfort her with my own knowledge of the Mediterranean — that although the waves may be rough near land, it is soon possible to escape them and reach still water. I am afraid I somewhat exaggerated the lack of danger in order to calm her fears.'

'When was this? Has anybody heard from her since?' Mama was anxious. 'I hope the poor lady is safe.'

'Back in November, was it not, my dear?'

'Yes. I confess that I feel a little guilty that I have not written to her since. We have her home address. I shall invite her to visit, as it seems from what you say that she has two other friends nearby!'

'Oh, please do not do it on my account! Or Sarah's.'

'No, Anne dear, I shall do it for her own benefit. She was anxious to meet that school mistress who is such a remarkable example — you recall her, Hugh? — Mrs MacDonald, is that her name?'

'Yes, dearest. You must invite her, if you so wish.'

The Laird adopted such an expression of resignation that his wife reached across the table and fondly patted his hand.

'Dear Hugh. You are almost a saint!'

I loved the way the Ballavichs were so secure with each other and so tolerant of each other's foibles. I caught Duncan's eye and we exchanged smiles.

'My dear wife has forgotten the other fragment of gossip that we gleaned in our Italian salon.'

'Oh, what was that?' Mama sat forward. 'Do tell us.'

'That the reclusive and partially-disgraced author of *Omphalos* is to re-marry.'

Mama looked puzzled.

'Gosse,' Papa explained. 'It was *Omphalos* that so upset Kingsley, you must remember.'

'Indeed yes, I had forgotten. I think of Mr Gosse only in connection with aquaria and sea-shores.'

I hardly heard them: I was staring at the Ballavichs.

'It is true. Miss Shipton had heard that Mr Gosse was engaged to be married — and that the ceremony would take place in December. That is three months past. He had met the lady in the town where he lives. She is a Quaker, I believe.'

No! It could not be!

'Is the lady a naturalist?'

'Why Anne, I have no idea. Is it likely? It would, I suppose be *fitting*.'

'At least the boy now has a mother, and will not be condemned to trudging on the shore with his father,' Duncan said.

'Miss Shipton told us he had become a respected preacher.'

'The scientific establishment gave him the cold shoulder after *Omphalos*. Although I hear he is doing some valuable work on wheel animalcules.'

'The Rotifera —'

'Kingsley — *Professor* Kingsley, you know he is now the professor of modern history? — still meets him occasionally, although he is much occupied with his duties in Cambridge. He teaches the Prince of Wales!'

Their comments criss-crossed the dining table, mingling with the ringing of glass and the clatter of cutlery on china, as Kate collected up the plates. The room suddenly smelt of stale gravy.

I thought only of Miss Pritchard. 'The accomplished naturalist Miss Pritchard', apparently also a pious lady; it must have been she who had ensnared the vulnerable Henry Gosse. I thought of them together: offerings of actiniae; shared moments on the shore; animated discussions over the microscope. I hoped she was fond of children; Willy would now be eleven years old and, if my younger brothers were anything to judge by, would be approaching an awkward age. I wondered how young she was. I had been *betrayed*. And — my righteous wrath grew within me — so had Emily Gosse!

Aware that my lapse into silence would be observed and questioned, I forced myself to ask the Ballavichs, 'Do you still have the tracts that Miss Shipton gave you? I wonder what their titles were. Does Mr Gosse also, like the first Mrs Gosse, take everyday events and turn them into some kind of parable?'

Duncan and Mama looked at me in surprise, but the Laird replied, 'Yes, that does seem to be the case. I recall they had strange titles such as *Stray Sheep* and *This is what I want* ... but I suspect we have passed them on to others. Do forgive us.'

I smiled and said they were not to concern themselves, and there was a short pause while Kate brought in the brose, of whipped cream mixed with whisky, which was a favourite of the Laird's; and then the conversation was steered to the Civil War in America, and President Lincoln's proclamation earlier in the year that all slaves should be released — emancipation being a topic upon which everyone had much to say.

Mama and I retired to bed early that night, leaving Duncan talking with Papa. I placed my copy of Duncan's book beside the bed so that I might, from time to time, read what he had written about me. He had instantly glanced at me on hearing the news of Henry Gosse's marriage; I had seen the consternation and anxiety in his expression. Ah, he understands me better than I know!

But he had no further reason for concern. My silly childish passion, my foolish, hopeless and one-sided love! From henceforth it would cease and I should never yearn for Henry Gosse again. A heavy weight had been lifted from me and I had a great urge to give thanks, so I knelt beside the bed and prayed a thankful prayer. When I arose my thoughts turned naturally to Emily Gosse (the second Mrs Gosse bore no further interest for me) who had prayed at any time or place. I searched in the top drawer of my chest, amongst my private letters and discontinued journals, and I found my copy of the tract that Emily had given to Anna Shipton on that dreadful day in Pimlico. Anna has the original, written in Emily's own hand; I do not know whether it has been published, but Anna had written out a copy for me, insisting that I should take it as it showed Mrs Gosse in all her compassion and courage.

The Poor Man's Penny: I turned up the lamp and sat in the chair to read it.

'*Sometimes my fellow-passengers are of an encouraging kind, and receive my tracts with pleasure. Sometimes, on the contrary, their very look repel one's advances. A company of that sort I met lately, and yet things turned out better than I anticipated. I took out a 'Torch', and after reading it myself a while, I presented it to a doubtful-looking gentleman to my right, who looked as if he would have rejected a tract. By degrees, as others came in, I presented them with what I thought most likely to please them; and as I saw some get out their spectacles, and others reading without such aid, I got into conversation with my opposite neighbour, a Christian lady, who got quite interested in the enterprise, and promised to show the 'British Messenger', &c. to Christian friends in the country, whither she was going.*

Presently my attention was arrested by a poor little old man, with an old blue bag, who had been reading. He had now taken off his horn spectacles, and put them in their paper case and, holding up a penny in his hand, he made a sign with his finger, as though he would cut it in half. Presently, when the noise of the wheels permitted, he made me understand that he wanted to know if I could give him a halfpenny if he gave me his penny. I shook my head, and signified I did not want his penny, but this did not quite satisfy him: the penny was back in his pocket, but soon appeared again.

The old man had evidently counted the cost, and ventured his whole penny. I would much rather have given him one; but I did not feel it right to refuse: it was like the widow's mite; I felt it would bring a blessing with it - a blessing to himself, and to others.

I thought, 'If I buy eight tracts with that penny, they may be blessed to eight souls, or even 800: shall I deprive this poor man of that honour? Besides, he will doubtless value the tracts I gave him all the more for having contributed to pay for sending tracts to others. Besides, this little action will lead me to pray for his soul, as I should not have done otherwise; and doubtless prayer, offered in the name of Jesus, cannot be lost.'

As these thoughts passed through my mind, my opposite neighbour, who had seen what passed, took out her purse, and offered me a shilling. Here was the first-fruit of my old man's penny. I said to her, 'I did not give the tracts, &c. away with any expectation of payment.' She said,' I know that; but of course there are expenses connected with giving them away: put that in your poor-box.' She would not have thought of it, had not the old man given his penny; many have often received tracts, and 'British Messengers', and have never thought of helping to pay for sending forth more. Many could give a penny, if not a shilling - perhaps, many will, who read this: and the old man may find, in eternity, that his penny has produced fruit a hundred or a thousand-fold.

When I had finished reading, I sat quietly for a while, wondering at her courage and single-mindedness, and trying to understand just how she had changed her husband's behaviour and hardened his beliefs. Yet again I wondered whether *Omphalos* had not been written to restore his own faith.

After a while I noticed that the room had grown cold for the coals had almost burnt away, and I reminded myself that I was never to concern myself with any of the Gosses again, so I folded the tract and placed it amongst the hot ashes, then retired to bed to wait for Duncan.

CHAPTER 30: MATTHEW

The bus doors wheeze closed and a jet of grey diesel smoke washes round my legs as I shout 'thanks' to the driver. I reckon it's only a mile or two to Nancarrow, quicker than the coast path and all downhill. Somebody's taken a herd of cows down the lane, from one field to another, and I wish I hadn't worn my sandals. Sometimes I can see the sea, but it doesn't seem to get any closer, and all this walking's starting to seem a daft idea — until suddenly I'm in luck! At least, I think I am because I can hear the motorbike revving and spluttering down the lane behind me.

Sure enough, it's the Mighty Pascoe himself, kitted up in black like the Avenging Angel. The brakes don't seem to work too well, or perhaps it's his reflexes, because he takes about ten metres to stop, and then lifts his visor and looks back.

'Do you want a lift, then?'

I've never been on a motorbike before but it's good to broaden one's experience of Life, and it should make a good story if I live to tell the tale. He just looks at me and waits. The bike is very small.

'Where do I hold on?' I ask, wondering if I'm supposed to put my arms around his waist, but he tells me to put my carrier bag in one of the panniers and to hold the handles at the sides. I haven't got a helmet and say I hope the cops don't see us, but he just gives a little bark — or perhaps it's a laugh, I can't tell — and off we go. I have this temptation to put my feet down to help us brake at the corners, and I tower over him so our centre of gravity seems to be in free fall; but it's only a few minutes before we pull up in a cloud of sand and pebbles by the house.

When Peter steps off the bike I'm reminded how small and old he really is, and I feel I ought to help him get the bike up on its stand. The bike's a bit antique, too, probably past its sell-by date; it's a BSA Bantam, but I don't know much about motorbikes. Peter takes off his black fishbowl and starts to unzip his black windproof one-piece.

'Been treating the young ladies to ice-creams, have you?'

'What?' For a moment I can't think what he's talking about. But then I remember seeing him in the distance when I was with Caz and Sue. That seems like weeks ago.

'You don't miss much.' I grin at him. 'Yeah, I make a habit of it. And if they're really nice I even treat them to a cream tea.'

'Arf!'

He gives that funny little bark again, and I know what it reminds me of: the muntjac deer that Dad gets in his garden, that bark when they're alarmed. But Peter Pascoe's not alarmed, and I'm surprised to see his face is crinkled in a sort of grimace of a smile. That's nice. I feel like barking back!

'Thanks for the lift,' I say. 'I thought I'd go out for a row. Did you see we've mended the boat. Sort of.'

'Hmf.' He nods, and finishes folding up his biker's gear and tucks it into the pannier. 'Billy Martin no good, then?' He looks up at me slyly.

'No, not my type,' I say, and then add, rather boldly, I think, 'Not Jim's either, as it happens. Nice idea of yours, though. Pretty shrewd.'

'Hmf.' He pinches the sides of his mouth with his thumb and forefinger, and white stubble glitters on his top lip. He stands still for a minute as though he's about to say something, but then seems to change his mind. The bike's been parked at the road end of the house, where there's a small gap that leads directly into the garden. I follow him through, ducking under the overgrown hedge, and then follow across to the garden shed. I'm just being nosy, I've never seen inside, but there's not much to see apart from garden tools and string, and the like; and an old chair, and a mug and plate on the wooden bench. His brown tweed jacket's on a hanger on the door, and his cap's there, and his brogues.

'The garden's looking nice — it's quite tropical with the palm trees,' I say, because it's rude to stand and stare. Peter's putting on his jacket, and then sits on the chair to change his shoes. 'It must take a lot of work.'

'It does.' His cap is on his head now, covering the scrapes of grey hair, and it wobbles when he nods. 'But it's worth it.'

He stands up quickly, and then looks a bit pink and breathless, but I've obviously said the right thing, because he wants to tell me more.

'Mr Galbraith was very keen on the garden, and I like to keep it the way he'd want it. He liked to spend a lot of time planning and ordering, and he'd rely on me, see, to get things growing proper. I've got green fingers. Anything'll grow for me. Green fingers,' he repeats, and waggles them in front of me as though they really are that colour. The grin-grimace is there again.

I look around. I don't have a clue about plants, but I try to think of something sensible to say, since he's in talking-mode.

'Is it specially warm here, then? With the palm trees and so on. I suppose the wood at the back protects it a bit?'

He starts to explain to me why it's so sheltered, being in a hollow and by the sea, never any frost, and so on; even the grapes on the summer-house do all right outside. I'm listening, still being distracted by how bent and old he is to be doing all this, when something bites my arm.

'Ow!'

There's a horsefly on the back of my arm and I swipe at it with my other hand, but it drifts lazily away and all that happens is that I slap the bite instead. The fly carries on hovering behind my back, and I flap at it again and miss.

'Cleg. 'Cause of the cows,' Peter comments. 'You need to wear a jacket or they'll get you even through a shirt. Nasty little buggers. Got good eyesight, too. Not as good as blue bottles, mind, filthy things they are. They can see a fly swat coming a mile off. It's easier to hit a cleg.'

'Yeah?' I haven't heard him speak so many words before; he's really talkative, something's fired him up for sure.

'Special eyes, you see. Mr Galbraith liked to explain it. He was interested in that sort of thing. When they look at something their eyes see lots of pictures but it makes one picture in their brain.'

'Was he a zoologist, then, like Elizabeth?'

'No.' Peter Pascoe flashes a glance up at me. 'No, he was not. He was not like Mrs Galbraith, he was very keen on plants. We have some very unusual plants.'

(Mrs Galbraith? Bizarre that he should call her that. Perhaps he doesn't hold with husbands and wives having different names.)

'Oh, right.'

I look around again at the garden, that climbs up the hill beside and behind the house; it looks jungley, all the plants elbowing each other for space, all shouting 'look at me!', but I can see that it's well-ordered, too, and I like the feel of it, and say so.

'I never met Mr Galbraith,' I add, 'though I suppose my grandmother might have met him. You said you knew my grandmother, didn't you, that first time we met? Or knew of her, I guess a lot of people knew *of* her. Perhaps she even came over here, I don't know.' I shrug and raise my eyebrow; I don't think Elizabeth could have known her very well.

Peter Pascoe's eyes are quite wide and slightly bloodshot, and I notice that he has a bit of a tremor; his head and hands are shaking and twitching. He controls his head and shakes it from side to side.

'No,' he says again, and turns away, shoulders hunched, and goes back towards his shed.

'Oh.' Oh well. No she didn't, no he didn't, no she didn't? I don't know what he means, and I'm disappointed that he's gone back into his shell. Like a little brown winkle!

There's no sign of Jim at his computer, and no-one in the kitchen; no sign or sound of anyone, the place is like the *Marie-Celeste* in fact. I leave my carrier-bag on the kitchen table and go into the hall. I can hear Roger and Elizabeth talking in the big front room, so I call out, 'Hallo! It's Matt!' so as not to give them a fright.

They're sitting at the PC with a pile of printed pages in front of them, and Elizabeth is dictating while Roger types. When they see me, Roger looks irritated and Elizabeth looks a bit vague, and I can see that I've chosen a bad moment.

'Jim is still in bed, I think,' Elizabeth says. 'You can go and wake him up if you wish — he's in the room opposite the top of the stairs.'

It's getting on for midday and I figure Jim won't mind being woken up, so I go upstairs and knock on his door. There's a groan, and a grumpy '*What?*', so I say 'It's me' and go in.

He looks bleary and the room smells of sleep and unbrushed teeth.

'Yeugh. What time is it?' He blinks and frowns at the bedside clock, and pushes his tongue around his teeth with a disgusted expression. 'Yeugh. Christ. I was working on that fucking data until three a.m.'

'I always said you were a geek.'

'Yuh, man. Very funny. How about making some coffee? Some *real* coffee. Use the cafetière. It's in the cupboard. You boil water —'

'Yeah, I know. I'm in the catering business, remember?'

I go and rummage round in the kitchen, and I'm just ready to push down the plunger when Jim appears, sucking in air in a big exaggerated sniff.

'Great. I love you, man. But where are the blueberry pancakes?'

They must all be coffee-freaks in this house because Elizabeth and Roger practically stampede down the hall, both looking a bit fraught, so I guess the dictation session or whatever it is, is not going well. I haven't seen old Rog since Hazel told him to piss off, or whatever, but he looks the same as before though his beard's been trimmed. He reaches out to take the mug that I'm holding out towards him, and I see his hand and think, 'He put that hand on Hazel's breast.' *Ugh*! I nearly drop the mug in disgust.

The three of them burble a bit disjointedly about the things that seem to be bothering them, nobody listening to anybody else, and as I fill the kettle again to make more coffee (of course there was only a dribble left for me) I say the thought that comes into my head, which is,

'Shall I ask Peter Pascoe if he wants some coffee? Or does he make his own?'

They all stop talking and look at me in surprise.

'Well yes. Of course,' Elizabeth says. 'Although he usually prefers tea, but … yes.' There's a question-mark in her voice and I explain.

'He gave me a lift down the lane on the back of his bike. I've just been talking to him about the garden.'

'Did he really? Good gracious!' Elizabeth's eyebrows are way up into her grey hair.

'I'm surprised it took your weight,' Roger says. 'It's an old Norton, isn't it?'

He's wrong, of course, but Roger starts to tell us all about Nortons, and what important bikes they were.

'He was talking to me about flies' eyes,' I butt in, speaking to Elizabeth. 'Apparently your husband was very interested in them and taught Peter all about them.'

'*Did* he?' Elizabeth's voice is clear and high, and she looks disbelieving. Then a sort of blush spreads over her neck and throat. 'Ah. Compound eyes. The multilens system, that's what he means. He's referring —' She pauses a moment, as though she doesn't want to tell us what Peter's referring to, but then must have decided it was okay. 'He's referring to the camera obscura that's in the attic. It was one of Allan's great interests.'

'Have you got your own *camera obscura?*' Roger's very interested, too. 'How unusual. Did Allan build it — well, no, I mean did Allan design it himself?'

'Yes. And Peter Pascoe helped him use it, and helped with the adjustments.' She looks at me. ' "Camera" as in "chamber" — you remember our previous use of the word. But this time "obscura" meaning "dark", rather than "lucida". It's a device that allows one to sit in a darkened room and observe the outside world.'

'On the same principle as a periscope?' Jim asks.

'Not at all. It projects the image straight into the room,' Roger answers, importantly. 'There's one in the film of *The Prime of Miss Jean Brodie*.'

'Yes, that's the one in Edinburgh, of course. Allan's parents took him to see it when he was a boy and he never forgot the experience.' Elizabeth smiles briefly. 'Apparently he always cherished the idea that he would build one of his own, one day — and this house, with its attics, was the first opportunity that he had. Though he and some of my colleagues did devise a plan for an illicit one in the West Tower of the Natural History Museum.'

I quite like the sound of Allan Galbraith.

'Could we see it?' I ask, 'Or has it been dismantled?'

I didn't mean to put her on the spot, because now we're all looking at her expectantly, and she can see it's going to be hard to refuse.

'It's still there, yes — although I'm not sure what sort of condition it's in. I haven't used it for several years. I expect everything will be rather dusty, and the handles rather stiff.'

'It doesn't matter, then.' I feel bad now about asking, but she swallows down her coffee and goes to the door.

'I'll show you. Roger and I could do with a short break. Do you all want to see how it works?'

We all troop after her upstairs, and she opens a small door that leads off the landing. The stairs are narrow and steep but, amazingly, there's a chairlift here, too, and we all squeeze past. There are three rooms at the top, one of them at least seems to be stuffed with trunks and suitcases, but the one Elizabeth takes us into is almost empty, apart from a couple of chairs, some shelves, and a circular white table near one end. Except that it's not quite a table, but more like a shallow dish. It contains a dead butterfly and two dead flies.

'If you come over here and stand round the viewing table — move the chairs aside — we'll see what sort of a picture we can get. Matt, would you turn off the light, please?'

We all do as we're told. I click the switch to darken the room and immediately a column of light links the ceiling and the table. Elizabeth has removed the corpses and she bends forward and blows so that the dust swirls and sparkles in the beam. For a moment her head touches the light, and it's like a Blake painting, God's hand sending down rays that touch the favoured one. It's good: I'd like to ask her to stay there, and to put her head and her hands into the rays. But Jim and Roger are in the way, busy looking at the table, Roger mumbling about things and pretending to be knowledgeable. Roger's such a wanker.

There's a sort of moving pattern on the table but it doesn't look like anything much to me, just dark browns and greens. Elizabeth turns a metal handle that sticks out from the wall — it's attached to a bar that goes up to the hole in the ceiling, where the light comes from — and the pattern changes.

'Jim, do you see that handle by your knee? It raises and lowers the table — would you try turning it so we can get focus the picture? I'm afraid it's rather heavy.'

He moves the table up, which doesn't help, and then down by twenty centimetres or so.

'Ah, it's the back garden,' Jim says as the picture comes into focus, and we all move around to one side to get a better view. 'What were we looking at before?'

'The trees at the top of the garden, I think,' Elizabeth says. 'They were too dark to give a very distinct image. The sharpest and most colourful images require strong sunlight.'

'Presumably there's some sort of rotating head on the roof?' Roger was looking up at the ceiling.

'Yes. It's fairly basic — essentially the turret is a rotating metal cylinder that's closed at the top and has a small glazed window that acts as the "eye". And inside the eye is an angled mirror — I can alter the angle using this other handle here — that directs the image down through a fairly simple lens system that allows the image to be focussed on the table.'

'Real neat,' Jim says.

I'm looking at the picture: it's like a silent movie but in colour, and I can see tall blue flowers bending in the breeze. And a bird on the flower-bed, a thrush I think, hammering (silently) at something.

'Do you want to try moving the turret, Matt? It can turn through nearly 360 degrees.'

She shows me what to do. It takes a moment or so to get the hang of altering the mirror angle as well as turning the eye, but I soon have Peter Pascoe's shed in view. The door's open but I can't see him, even though Jim has a go at focussing with the table, and I wonder out loud if he's in the kitchen making a cup of tea. I angle the mirror down to see closer to the house, but the picture turns fuzzy and can't be focussed properly, so I move it up. There he is, higher up among some pale-leaved bushes, standing still like a brown tree-stump.

'What's he doing?' Roger asks, and then Jim laughs out loud.

'He's pissing in the bushes!'

He is, too, and I mutter 'Whoops. Sorry, Peter,' and move on.

I glance at Elizabeth, and although I can't see her expression very well in the dim light, she looks a bit tense. I swing the eye right round so that we can see the beach, and there's the boat. There are people walking on the shore, and a very faint sound of barking comes into the attic. I look for the dog, trying to get a picture that's in sync with the sound track, but I can't find it. I bring the view back to the garden and keep it still, wanting to home in on detail.

'This is real neat,' Jim says again. 'Look at those colours — and somehow I hadn't expected to see things moving.'

'The colours fade if the sun goes in,' Elizabeth says, 'which provides an additional element of surprise.'

'Allan must have had a lot of fun planning this.' Roger's wandering round peering at bits of paper stuck on the walls. 'What are all these diagrams and photos? I can't see them properly in this light.'

'He was very interested in the history of the *camera obscura* — it goes right back to da Vinci's time — and when he was no longer mobile he kept up a correspondence with various institutions and science museums, and collected all kinds of descriptions and pictures. That framed quotation over there particularly amused him because it indicates how artists used the *camera obscura* to help them draw landscapes and figures. "How they cheat," Allan used to say. There are even scurrilous rumours that Canaletto used one! And Sir Joshua Reynolds had a portable version. Put the light back on, if you want, and you can read it better.'

'I like this,' Roger says, when he's turned on the light. He reads from a piece of red card. ' "A few experiments with a candle, a spectacle lens, a piece of looking glass, a saucer and a cardboard box would make the principle of construction perfectly clear"!'

'Yes, he found that in a Victorian encyclopaedia. And he had a long correspondence with Barr and Stroud, the engineering firm in Glasgow, who installed a new lens system in the Edinburgh instrument — just post-war, I believe. When Allan was still working as an electron-microscope engineer and travelling around, he visited Barr and Stroud to talk about lenses — that was when he was plotting to install a *camera obscura* in the Museum. He was delighted about Barr and Stroud because he knew about them from his days as an engineering student — apparently they were famous for their scientific instruments, and he used to see their name everywhere in the labs.'

Jim and I circle the walls, looking at the photos and the photocopied illustrations: there used to be desk-top forms, portable boxes — even *camera obscuras* in tents that an artist could sit inside! The attic room is pretty crowded with the four of us moving around, and Elizabeth sits down in one of the chairs and watches us; I can see that she's not at all relaxed about us being here. It's very much her husband's room.

'So it can have the same sort of use as the thing we put on the microscope — you can use it to make accurate images. But not interpretations,' I add, with a grin.

She nods, but says, 'Although sometimes it takes a little practice to resolve the image and to interpret what you're seeing because it's two-dimensional.'

'Yeah, you need to get your eye in. Hey, why was Peter Pascoe going on about flies' eyes, then, and seeing lots of images? This is quite straightforward.'

I point at the table, though of course the picture isn't visible because the light is on.

'Ah. Well. Allan experimented with different kinds of images. He designed a kaleidoscopic attachment and a multilens — they can be screwed into the cylinder in place of the simple lens system. They're in those large boxes on the shelf. Be careful, though, they're quite heavy — and it's very important not to knock any of the parts out of alignment.'

Jim and I lift the lid of one of the wooden boxes, and he helps me lift out a short metal cylinder. It's made of copper and about 20 centimetres diameter, and inside there are two long strips of mirrored glass, angled like a V. There's a lens fixed at one end and a screw-thread at the other.

'How do we fix it up there?' Jim asks. 'Oh — that's what that step ladder's for. Shall I try?'

'We'll do it another time,' I say quickly, because Elizabeth looks sort of weary and Roger's fidgeting and getting on my nerves; but Elizabeth kind of sighs and says, 'Peter is the expert. He was second-in-command up here. I'll go down and ask him if he'll come and show it to you, and then I think Roger and I had better get back to our writing.'

'Yes, we'll leave you two lads to play around while we get on with the serious work.'

Roger has the attention span of a flea, I decide, and I wave two fingers at his back as he follows Elizabeth out of the room.

We have a look at the fly's-eye attachment: no mirrors inside this one, just a bulging mass of 20 or 30 small lenses, edge to edge in a shape that domes inwards at the bottom of the tube. The spaces between the lenses are darkened, and we try to imagine what the picture will look like. Jim suddenly darts towards the door and switches off the light.

'Let's see if we can see Elizabeth. Move the mirror or whatever you do and I'll focus.'

I get the thing angled down as near as I can to the kitchen door, even though the picture's fuzzy again. Just in time, for here she comes, we're looking down on her head, and I manage to follow her as she goes up the garden looking for Peter. Strange to be in a sealed room, watching what's happening outside. She's wearing her brick-red skirt and navy short-sleeved shirt, and her grey hair looks bright. We hear her call Peter's name, but only very faintly, and she waves. They meet, they stand together, and I guess she's explaining what she wants. She puts a hand on his arm. Their faces are turned towards the house, we can see them talking but we can't hear a word. They look up, they are looking straight at us (Jim says, 'I feel we ought to wave'), they must be looking at the eye, and Elizabeth grips Peter Pascoe's wrist. Jim and I watch, fascinated, as they walk slowly down the crazy-paving path towards the house, still talking.

'Maybe I'll just leave you to it,' Jim says. 'I guess Peter and I don't get on too well.'

But I persuade him to stay and we put the light on again, and soon we hear Peter plodding very slowly up the stairs. He stops in the doorway and hangs onto the frame to cough and catch his breath.

He nods at me and speaks between wheezes. 'Clegs. Sharp lad. Quick off the mark. Hmf.'

Elizabeth has followed him and looks a bit worried.

'Will you be all right, Peter? Can you manage?'

He just nods and goes over to the metal steps and moves them. Elizabeth hovers a bit more and I'm surprised how anxious she looks, but I suppose she's worried he'll fall and break his neck. But Jim and I tell her it'll be okay, and thanks for showing us, and all that; so she eventually goes downstairs again.

Old Peter's up the ladder now trying to unscrew the bottom of the metal tube. He mutters and grumbles because it's stuck, and after a bit he comes down and lets Jim do it. But Peter insists on attaching the kaleidoscope himself, so Jim gets a chair and stands on it with the attachment and helps hold it — Jim's much taller than Peter and the roof's not so high — while Peter screws it on. He keeps getting the screw-thread jammed, and there are lots of instructions being issued, but between them they get it fixed.

'How on earth did Mr Galbraith manage?' I ask Peter as he climbs down, and I help him fold the stepladder back into a corner. 'I thought he was really disabled.'

'Mrs Galbraith and I used to help him with the chairlift, but I could help him on my own up here. I used to change the attachments for him. He called me his chief technician.'

'That's good,' Jim says. 'It's real dusty up here — I guess it hasn't been used much since he died. When was that — three, four years ago?'

'He passed away three years and eight months ago. But Mr Galbraith couldn't even manage with the lift for the last few months.'

'So I guess this is the first time you've been back up here for a few years,' Jim says, thoughtfully. 'I'm real sorry about that, Peter, I hope it's not too painful. It must have been an important place for you. I guess Elizabeth has kept this place kinda like a — a shrine to her husband.'

A shrine? I look round at the curling pictures and the dead flies. A shrine would be kept clean and neat. I don't think Elizabeth has time for shrines, it's not her style. Allan's gone; she doesn't come up here, the *camera obscura* doesn't have anything to do with her life any more.

Peter Pascoe just keeps quiet, looking down at the viewing table. He's waiting for me to turn off the light.

'Wow!'

'That's fantastic!'

Jim and I both exclaim at once. I hadn't known what to expect, but not this! A hexagon of triangles, repeating blocks of colours. None of the colours are bright, the light seems dim. Peter goes over to the wall and rotates the eye and instantly the patterns change as the eye seeks out different parts of the garden. He moves the mirror handle and suddenly there are repeating patches of bright scarlet and blue. I sneak a look at his face, that's lit only by the kaleidoscope beam; he's looking down at the table and the wrinkles have fallen out, he's sort of smiling. He reaches forward and touches a patch of blue.

'Canterbury bells.'

'Blue flowers,' I explain to Jim, though I don't know how I know. (But there's a sudden echo in my mind of Uncle Jamie, singing *Silver bells and cockle shells and pretty maids all in a row.* Why? When? Who was he singing to?)

'Mr Galbraith had me try a little experiment. He liked to experiment. He liked to find new things to do.' Peter was still touching the patch of blue. 'There's nothing special in that bed now, it's all herbaceous plants, annuals are too much trouble. But he had me plant that bed up with salvias and ageratums, and some big yellow daisies that were his favourites. Reminded him of Ethiopia, he said. He said there were places that were like a yellow sea after the rains. I had to plant them in blocks, all one colour. I didn't like what it did to the garden, but it pleased Mr Galbraith no end, when he was up here.'

'I didn't know he was in Ethiopia too. But what a brilliant idea, I really wish I could have seen that. What could we put out? We need big sheets of colour — hey, what about the sails, they're bright red, aren't they? What've we got that's yellow — and blue?'

'There's a blue plastic tarp in the garage.'

'Hey, I've got another idea! Cut out a couple of big paper lizards and paint them — then we might end up with something like an Escher graphic. Well, perhaps not, but we could have a lot of fun playing around. Would you mind, Peter?'

Peter's glance flicks up at me and he scratches his forehead under his cap as he gives a little nod. But now I want to see the insect eye and, again with Jim's help, he is persuaded to change the lens.

'This one needs a lot of sun. But Mr Galbraith was working on a way to get it brighter.'

He's right, the images are dim and they take some working out. They're overlapping circular pieces of the outside world. I'm a bit disappointed because I'd hoped the circles would all be distinct. But there's a sudden flash of movement across one section of the table and Jim and I both jump a little.

'What was that?'

'Thrush. You see — fly-swat.'

'Yeah. Point taken. Tell you later,' I say to Jim, who's looking from one to the other of us with his eyebrow raised, like 'what-the-hell-are-you-guys-on-about?'

We help put the original lens back in place and put the fancy attachments back in their boxes. Peter seems keen to go, so we thank him and have another look at the stuff that's stuck to the walls before we go down, too. I'm feeling really disappointed that I didn't know Allan Galbraith: he sounds like a cool bloke, with quite a sense of humour. What a drag for him, being disabled, he must've been really frustrated.

Jim must have been thinking along these lines, too, because as we go down the attic stairs he says, 'I bet there's something on the Internet that's to do with imaging of insect eyes. There must be a way of mimicking that overlapping fragmentation and then recombining the images in different ways. I bet Allan would have loved that stuff. 'Specially when he couldn't make it up to that room — he'd have been able to play around on the keyboard …'

'Yeah. That's really sad. I hope Elizabeth didn't mind us going —'

'Not at all,' she says. She's just coming out of her study as I come out of the attic door. 'If you're really interested in the *camera obscura* it will be a good incentive to restore the equipment to good working order.'

We follow her downstairs, talking about the 'fly's eye'.

'Do snails see like flies?' I ask. (I've never thought about snails before.)

'Creep,' Jim leans forward and hisses in my ear, and I stop suddenly on the stairs so that his face cannons into the back of my head.

'Shit!'

I grin, and Elizabeth (who is not, of course, deaf) looks back and grins too.

'Snails have rather uninteresting eyes, essentially cups of light-receptive pigment. They probably can't see much more than light and dark — they don't form an image.' She continues talking as she goes into the front room, so we follow. Roger's there, but he just carries on sitting and scribbling. 'But cephalopod molluscs — animals like squid and octopus and cuttlefish, in other words the fast-moving predators — have eyes that are remarkably vertebrate-like. Essentially an orb with a lens and light-sensitive layer, somewhat like the vertebrate retina. Which, if you think about it, is quite astonishing. In standard texts this was always considered an example of parallel evolution — a very similar organ evolves twice, quite independently, in different lineages, to have the same function.'

'Not any more,' says Roger, ' now that we know about hox genes and pax-6.'

'Not any more,' she agrees. 'Hox genes — homeobox genes — control the pattern of body form, right through the animal kingdom. Transplant a hox gene from a fruitfly into a frog embryo and it controls the development of the same part of the body. But *pax* — now there's something that will interest you in your new-found enthusiasm for compound eyes! Pax-6 is a gene that controls development of the eye in mice. If you take that mouse gene and insert it into cells that would normally make legs in a fruitfly embryo, those potential leg-cells are switched into a 'make-an-eye' pattern. And an eye grows, but not a mouse's eye — an insect compound eye! When I first read that in *Nature* I was tremendously excited — didn't you feel the same, Roger? It was such an extraordinary breakthrough in our understanding.'

'Wouldn't it have been more exciting if the fly's cells had made a mouse eye?' I didn't really understand.

'No.' She shakes her head and smiles. 'You think about it, Matt — I'm sure you can work it out.'

'I'll give you a personal tutorial,' Jim says. 'Come on — we'll go and explain it to Peter P.'

I duck my shoulder from his grasp. Flies and butterflies and things like that metamorphose. Hah.

'Hang on. If a mouse's eye can metamorphose into a fly's eye, could one of those square eyes on those parasites — Crypto-thingy — metamorphose into a fly's eye? That's what I'd like to know. Answers on a postcard, please.'

Nice one, Matt! I grin at Elizabeth, feeling very pleased with myself, while Jim raises his eyebrow and sighs, and Roger says 'Huh!' or something equally bright and meaningful.

'I don't know the answer, Matt,' Elizabeth replies. 'I think you have the last word — or the last question — on that one.'

God, I'm clever!

I persuade Jim that we should go for a row before he goes back to work. When we get outside we walk up the garden a way, trying to work out where the turret of the *camera obscura* is. Actually it's quite easy to spot, and I don't know how I've missed it before, sticking up about half-a-metre or so from the ridge at the end above the kitchen.

'Why's it got a spike on top?'

I look round for Peter Pascoe, and see him standing watching us, down by his shed.

'Peter! Why's the turret got a spike?' I call as we go down to him.

'Hmf.' His face creases. 'Because of the gulls and those blasted collared doves. When it had a flat top the birds sat up there, and if you tried to scare them away, that made it worse because they would *defaecate*. Heh heh! A proper mess, all down the glass. Made Mr Galbraith mad! So he had to have a spike put on. And a lightning conductor. Heh heh!'

Jim and I burst out laughing: not just at the picture of a gull jetting a stinking white stream all over the eye, but also at Peter's great delight.

We go down to the sea-wall, but the tide's far out, and we decide we can't be bothered to haul the boat that far. Jim finds a kid's football so we go down on the sand and have a kick around. I like that word 'defaecate.' Homeobox, defaecate and archive. Teapot to shell, find the link. Metamorphose them. 'Cryptometamorph.' How about fragmenting the picture into its constituent colours? Orange-yellow parasite, yellow gull's eye, yellow snail, kaleidoscopic symbols. Symbolic colours. Would it work? I feel that tingle, the eureka-factor.

CHAPTER 31: HAZEL

Friends of mine, a retired couple who lived in a glassy modern house on top of the cliffs, had asked me over for the evening. We would eat dinner under lush foliage in their conservatory, and would watch the light fade over the sea while Eddystone lighthouse flashed out on the horizon. Two other couples had been invited, plus a single male acquaintance, about five years older than myself. My friends were matchmaking.

I was looking forward to the evening, partly from curiosity (though I had little hope of finding a perfect match), but mainly because my friends were good company and good cooks. It would be fun. So I dithered over what to wear, rejecting one thing after another as too hot, too formal or too casual. In the end I chose the turquoise sleeveless dress with narrow straps, that looked young and sexy. I wanted to feel sexy, and lustful; I wanted to sparkle and be witty and desirable! I'd carry the little dark blue jacket with matching turquoise trim, in case it was cool outside.

I was really in the mood: so it was a terrible shame that I never got there.

I was standing by the bedroom window, holding a mirror and trying to make sure that my eyeliner was straight, when I saw Matt coming slowly up the hill. I glanced at the bedside clock, surprised. It was nearly seven o'clock. He was supposed to be at The Anchor. I knew he'd been across at Nancarrow, and I'd assumed that he would go straight to work from there. Perhaps the pub didn't need him tonight.

I finished putting on mascara and went downstairs. Matt hadn't come inside, but there was a thud against the front wall of the house, and I heard him yell 'Oh *fuck*!'. A few seconds later he came rushing and limping into the back garden, and went up the steps to the sundial terrace. He grabbed a white stone, I thought it was Bob-or-Babs, and rushed down again.

'Matt! What's going on?'

I hurried to the French windows and looked out. The front of the house shuddered to a even heavier crash, but just as I started to go round to the gate, Matt came limping through, clutching his tatty carrier bag against his chest. Two long rolls of paper stuck out of it, banging awkwardly against his ear. He looked wild and wounded, and I saw my boy was crying.

'What's wrong? What *is* it? Have you hurt yourself?'

He just shook his head and, side-stepping onto the grass, carried on past me into the house. He smelt of beer and I wondered if he were drunk. I followed, asking questions.

'Why aren't you at work — have you been sacked? What's wrong with your foot?'

But still he just shook his head, infuriatingly, and went over to our new table, that was cleaned and sanded and awaiting decoration. He pulled one of the rolls of paper out of the bag and tried to spread it out on the table, but the paper was stiff and it kept escaping and rolling itself up again, trying to hide its information. I didn't speak but fetched two books as anchors.

It was an exquisitely pencilled drawing of the façade of our house; the shabby porch and half-glazed door, the chipped windowsill to the right. All the details were there. I had no doubt that the swirls, circles and diamonds of shells were entirely accurate. Around the edges of the paper were line drawings of representative shells, some of which were tinted with watercolours to show their original beauty. Whoever had drawn this had been very knowledgeable about shells, because most of the specimens on the façade were faded and whitened with age. Of course, the drawing could have been made at the time that the façade was completed; but even without the neatly-lettered specific names and the initials at the bottom right corner, I knew that this was the work of Elizabeth Wilson.

'It's fantastic,' I said. 'What a fantastic record. Has she given it to you to keep?'

Yet even as I spoke, looking at Matt's strained expression, I saw what was wrong.

'But, she ... It must have taken her hours.'

'Fucking *hours*. Fucking days. Years!'

I looked more closely at the drawing. *Trivia, Venerupis, Donax, Ensis, Clathrus.* (*Clathrus* — where? I hadn't seen it.)

'Why didn't she tell us?'

I was bewildered, and stared at Matt. 'Perhaps she drew it from a photo for Granny? But the details are so good. She must have forgotten she'd done it — otherwise she'd have told us.'

Matt shook his head just once, and then stared pointedly at the region of my chest; he wrinkled his nose and said disgustedly, 'Where the hell are you going dressed like that?'

But neither of us was to be distracted and I needed to find the cause of his obvious misery and reticence about the picture.

'Did you *take* the picture? Matt? Come on, Mattie —' unconsciously I'd slipped into using his baby name, 'there are lots of things you need to explain.'

His eyes were screwed up, and I couldn't believe that his hands were shaking. I had never seen him in such a state. What had Elizabeth done to my son? He took the other roll of paper out of his bag and handed it to me, then he limped away and sat tautly on my chair, aimlessly fiddling with the keyboard on the desk.

Several sheets of cartridge paper were rolled together and the bundle was stiff and slippery. But as I pulled the free edge slowly outwards, a red chalk drawing began to appear. I held the curled papers open like a scroll. The drawing was so cleverly executed that, even though it was a sketch, the subject of the portrait was easily recognisable.

I looked at my mother's back as she looked out at me from the mirror on her dressing table. She sat on the stool, and was half-naked, her lower half draped in a towel, and her hair was fastened loosely on top of her head so that her neck was exposed. Her right hand held a hairbrush and rested in front of her on the dressing table so that its reflection was also in the mirror. Her left hand lay on the towel in her lap. She was a fleshy woman but not young, so that there were folds of flesh at her waist, and her left breast sagged. Her right breast was missing; there was the faintest line of a scar. Elizabeth had accurately caught one of the expressions that I remembered well, the direct gaze and slightly sardonic smile.

Matt was still sitting with his back to me, his head propped on one hand. I pulled out the other drawings; no more than ten or a dozen, different sizes of paper, some rapid sketches, some detailed drawings, and all of my mother — half-clothed, fully-clothed, naked and two-breasted, sitting or lying in our back garden, sitting in a deck chair in, I think, the summerhouse at Nancarrow. They all skilfully captured my mother in different moods.

Once more I unrolled the picture of my mother in her bedroom. My hands were cold and clammy ... the picture blurred. I began to feel odd, dizzy. I knew I was falling, I couldn't stop ...

'Hazel!'

There was a hand in my hair, someone was touching my shoulder, there was a warm male smell. I kept my eyes closed. It would be all right, Jamie was there. I could curl up and go to sleep.

'Hazel! *Wake up!*'

I opened my eyes and looked up at Matt's frightened face.

'Shit! Why did you do that? You gave me such a fright. Can you get up?'

He helped me to stand and we put our arms around each other. My ribs hurt where I must have banged them against the table. Matt's chin rested against the top of my head, and we just stood close together, comforting each other, mother and son.

After a while, he said, 'That was dramatic!' and tried to make a joke of it.

I tried to be calm. Although I felt dizzy and sick; and frightened at my response.

'Tell me how you got hold of these — we'll worry about what to do about them later. No — wait. I'm supposed to be at a dinner party. I need to telephone.'

Matt just nodded. 'There's The Anchor, too.'

'I'll sort it out.'

I phoned The Anchor and apologised, explaining that Matt was suddenly unwell. As for the dinner party, my friends seemed to have forgotten that I currently had a live-in son, and my apology and explanation took longer to deliver and convince. I would phone them in the morning to explain further, I said. (I could worry about that tomorrow.)

With the practicalities out of the way, I found I was shivering, perhaps from the shock of fainting, and my turquoise dress was an irrelevance. I told Matt to pour us each a drink and I climbed the stairs and went into the bedroom to change. The dressing table had been against that wall. I'd got rid of it to make more space. Elizabeth Wilson must have sat on the bed to make her drawing but she'd omitted her own reflection. She had been in here, in this bedroom, this house and this garden. The ache from my fall deadened into numbness. I needed to talk to Jamie.

Matt was standing in the kitchen holding a bottle of brandy and apparently staring at the open door of the loo. When he saw me he gave a little sigh and shook his head in bewilderment, then turned away to find a glass.

'I don't like brandy,' he said. 'I'll have another beer.'

We sat down at the table, with the cylinder of papers between us, and I made him tell me his story.

He said the things that happened in the morning weren't relevant, but he and Jim had eventually gone down to the beach to play footie. Then he'd decided to collect some more winkles because he wanted to look at the parasites again; that was why he'd taken over his own drawing things. I didn't understand the parasite bit, but he said it was too complicated and he'd explain it later — all I needed to know was that he was getting parasites out of winkles because he wanted to do some more drawings of them. That was what he'd been doing when I went over to talk to Elizabeth that other day.

Anyway, today was all a muddle, he said. Elizabeth was busy downstairs with Roger, and there was lots of coming and going, and the phone ringing, and Matt needed some help but didn't think he could interrupt.

'I was really pleased with myself, I managed to find two infected winkles on my own — quite the little parasitologist! Well, Jim helped me collect them and we both cracked them open. I even found the right dishes and everything. And Elizabeth came upstairs and set up the microscope for me and got out some glass slides and stuff like that. I hadn't got the knack of putting the parasites onto the slide, though — they're bright orange, by the way — and Roger came up to get something so I asked if he'd do it for me. Anyway, he made a right balls-up of it, squashed half the bloody larvae by dropping the little glass cover on them. I just got fed up hanging around in the end and said I'd do it myself. Prat!'

'Don't be unkind. He's all right.'

'No he's not, he's a right dick-head.'

'Matt.'

'Okay, okay. Anyway, he went downstairs again and I tried to draw some of the poor squashed little buggers that had their eyes popping out of their heads — I'll show you later — and then I wondered if I could set up the special drawing-tube that she has for the microscope. It's called a *camera lucida*. There's a *camera obscura* in the attic too — that's what we did this morning.'

'I know what a *camera lucida* is, but not the other. But go on.'

'You do? She keeps it in the top drawer of this special chest and she'd left the key in the lock — she keeps the drawers locked but she'd rushed off to the downstairs phone. I didn't think she'd mind, so I got it out. But then I couldn't remember how to fix it, it's pretty difficult and I didn't want to screw everything up.'

'So you put it back and then poked around in the other drawers. Oh, that was very clever, Matt.'

'Well — yeah. That's what happened. I know I shouldn't have. I just thought it would be interesting to see if any of her drawings were in there — we'd been talking a lot about drawing and so on. And then I saw the picture of our house so of course I had to look. And the others were tucked away underneath it. Once I'd seen the Shell House drawing I couldn't *not* look ...'

We looked at each other, and I nodded.

'So then you took them.'

'I couldn't think. I wanted to tear them up, but I wanted to show them to you, too. I couldn't think what to do. The bitch! She's just been playing us along, deceiving us all this time. I *had* to show you. So I rolled them up and put them in my bag. And I tidied up and came home.'

'When did you leave? Did anyone see you — will she notice that you've taken them?'

'I dunno. I don't *care*.'

But I could see that he was panicked by what he'd done.

'Tell me, Matt.'

'Elizabeth and Roger were in that front room so I didn't have to worry about them, and I just stuck my head round the door to Jim and said I had to dash, had to start work early.' He stopped and closed his eyes for a moment and clicked his tongue. 'Peter Pascoe saw me go, though. I was so angry — I saw him and I just sort of shouted at him that he must've known my grandmother came to visit. I mean — earlier this morning he said she didn't, but then I remembered how abrupt he'd been, and then it was obvious that he'd been lying. I guess he just stood there with his mouth open when I launched into him. And then I rushed off. But I sat up on the cliff for ages, trying to get my head round it all. And I had a couple of beers before I came on up here,' he added. 'I'd forgotten you were meant to be going out — thanks for staying back. And I'm really sorry about your evening.'

'Don't worry.'

'Oh shit, Hazel! I was even going to give her a copy of the design I'm doing. I really liked her.'

That was just one of the problems. There were so many different layers to this that I couldn't think straight. I didn't know what to do. Matt was so wretched. I felt such a rush of love for him. I went round, and bent down and kissed his forehead, and I pushed back his tangle of hair, and he gave a rueful smile.

'Thanks.'

I went into the kitchen to top up my drink and when I returned he'd moved to the sofa, and was sitting hunched at one end with his elbows round his knees.

'The main trouble is — it's not just Elizabeth, is it? It's to do with Granny.'

I sat down at the other end.

'How can you take it so calmly? Did you know about her already and keep it quiet from me all this time?'

'I don't think fainting — if that's what I did — is taking things calmly. Though it was a surprisingly stupid thing to do. Of course I didn't know about Granny and Elizabeth, that's all too obvious.'

'I meant did you know about Granny being a lesbian. Before.'

The pictures: my mother, naked; the laugh; a certain joyfulness. I closed my eyes. A lesbian. A lesbian slut.

'I ... don't know.'

Jamie. I need to talk to Jamie.

'How can one not know a person? Barbara was always so up-front. That's part of what gets me. And Elizabeth — I bet Elizabeth was only nice to me because I'm Barbara's grandson. She probably thinks she sees something of Barbara in me or some such crap. I thought she really liked me. She was cool, we had great conversations. It's all the fucking *lying* that gets me.'

I could see that he was close to tears again, and I felt very sad for him because Elizabeth had seemed genuinely fond of him, and to have given him something that he needed.

'You didn't know Granny that well, Matt — you hadn't seen all that much of her these last few years. And Elizabeth probably didn't say anything because she probably thought we'd be disgusted. With both of them, Granny as well.'

'It's revolting!' He almost shouted at me. 'Those pictures are pornographic! Repulsive. That's my grandmother, for fuck's sake.'

'You're right about it being your grandmother. But I think you're quite wrong about revolting. I think she's been drawn with great affection — and humour.' Although I had myself found the pictures shocking in their frankness. 'And we all grow old, Matt — you accept that? We can't help what old age and gravity do to us. It generally isn't pretty.'

I had to help Matt, I had to help him first.

'Look, Jim's gay. You don't mind that. Nor do I. We have to think about these things. And perhaps the reason why this all seems so bad is not because Elizabeth and Granny have had an affair, or whatever you want to call it, but because you feel betrayed. Perhaps that's rather a melodramatic word, but it's more or less the truth. They've lied, or haven't been honest with us, for whatever reason.'

'They betrayed you, too. Your mum.'

'Yes.'

(But not half as badly as they betrayed you, Matt, because I was not — am not — particularly fond of either of them.)

We sat there and talked, sporadically, for another quarter-hour, throwing odd, disconnected arguments back and forth. Matt, deeply hurt, and undoubtedly shocked by the drawings, was nevertheless beginning to think more rationally. I needed Jamie so much I could think of nothing else. I had to speak to him.

But first Matt and I had to decide what to do about the drawings.

'We don't know if she knows that they're missing. If she didn't, you might be able to slip them back,' I said, doubtfully.

'No. I don't want to go back.'

'Then we'll have to give them to her. Which means we'll have to show that we know, and we'll have to discuss everything. I don't see any other way out, Matt.'

'We could post them, with a note saying we're returning them and we don't ever want to discuss it. End of story.'

I thought about that option, but I knew it wouldn't do.

'No. We'll call her and ask her to come here, so it'll be just the three of us. Or two of us, if you really feel you can't face her. I suppose I can do the explaining.'

'Would you really?' He brightened slightly. 'No, that wouldn't be fair. Shit, what if she calls us? She could phone now, even. What'll I say?'

'Go and put the answering machine on — we'll leave it on as long as necessary. And go out and bolt the side gate so no-one can just walk in.'

Matt looked at me with something like respect. 'You really have thought this out. It's like being under siege. We're in a good tactical position here at the top of the hill, we can repel all invaders. Lob stones and pour boiling oil.'

'Matt, I need to find something out from my brother, in fact I think I may need to go and see him. I don't want to be in contact with Elizabeth until I've spoken to him properly.'

'What's Uncle Jamie got to do with all this? Can't we just get it all over with quickly?'

'Jamie is Granny's son, remember. And this isn't just going to go away instantly, it's not simply a matter of sending back drawings and then obliterating all thoughts of Dr Elizabeth Wilson from our minds. It doesn't work that way. Please, just give me time to contact Jamie.'

Matt stood up and stretched.

'You're so bloody rational,' he said, but he didn't say it unkindly.

I noticed that he was still limping as he walked towards the table, where he stood looking down at the still-anchored drawing of the frontage of the house. I asked him what he'd done to his foot.

'And come to that, where were you going with Bob?'

'Come and see this.'

He pointed at the drawing, and when I went across to look he showed me the section on the right-hand side that included my mother's recent repair.

'See that shell in the centre of the circles, the one that's thick and spiky? See, she's drawn it here, too. *Tiphobia*.'

'Yes.'

'There's another one of those shells in Elizabeth's shell collection in Jim's study at Nancarrow. I thought at the time that it looked sort of familiar. It's from Africa. So she and Granny probably did that pattern together.'

I remembered the thuds against the front wall of the house.

'Oh. And so you stoned it to death. With Bob.'

'*Babs*.'

'That was rather heavily symbolic.'

'It was meant to be.'

'Probably rather childish, too.'

'Yeah.' There was a trace of a smile on Matt's face. 'I tried kicking it to death but I was wearing trainers.'

'Ouch.'

'Yup.'

'Oh well.' I looked at the extraordinary picture of the façade again. 'I hope we can keep this, whatever happens. Shall we take it outside and check it against the shells? And you can show me the damage.'

CHAPTER 32: ELIZABETH

Yet another interruption! A tentative knock at the drawing room door, and here is Peter Pascoe; who surely hasn't come knocking at this door since Allan was alive.

'Yes, Peter?' I'm afraid I'm brusque.

'Mrs Galbraith, can I have a word?'

'Of course. Come in.'

He shakes his head and doesn't enter, presumably because Roger is in here with me, so I understand that I must go to him.

All day Roger and I have struggled with the final draft of this chapter, which is to appear in the book on host-parasite speciation. We have contended, delicately, over amendments to grammar, and I have tried to temper the harsher dogmas. Roger, with each further interruption, has become less susceptible to coercion, and increasingly recalcitrant and conservative. He prickles, mutters rebarbative comments. I can no longer soothe, compromise becomes increasingly unattainable — and now Peter Pascoe wants 'a word'! At least Peter's 'words' are always brief, even monosyllabic.

I suggest to Roger that he should have a break and take a walk on the shore, and he agrees that his vision would benefit from a change in perspective. (In fact, he told me that his eyes were tired, but I prefer the metaphysical implication.)

Peter Pascoe is waiting in the hall by the front door, apparently examining the elephant's foot, but when he sees me he thrusts his head forward, staring and blinking. He looks as old as a Galapagos tortoise, but not as immovable for, as he approaches, I see that his hands are shaking slightly and his head has a tremor.

'Shall we go upstairs? I don't think Matt is there any more, and I think my study is probably more private than the garden, don't you?'

The barb does not miss, even after all these years, and he makes brief eye-contact. When we enter the study I notice that Matt has turned off the microscopes and he seems to have left the table in a tidy state. But I'm rather alarmed by Peter, who is breathing quickly with shallow gasps, so I pull forward a chair and make him sit down. His complexion is grey underneath the weathered brown. I ask if I should bring him some water or a cup of tea, but he sways his trembling head. It saddens me to see how old and frail he has suddenly grown, and his cough, always frequent, has become more so.

'What's wrong, Peter? What's happened? You seem unwell.'

Why won't he speak? He refuses to look at me and stares at his knees. I rack my brains, trying to guess what might have upset him.

'Has something been damaged in the garden? Oh — your motorbike. Was Matthew's weight too much for it?'

I look at my watch; it's after four o'clock and Peter ought by now to have been on his way home. I'm beginning to feel mildly irritated, because I am too short of time and temper today for guessing games. I'd heard Matt come downstairs, but haven't seen him or Jim for a while.

'I hope the boys haven't been upsetting you. Please tell me.'

'It's that Matt. The grandson.' He speaks the last word loudly, and now he looks right at my face.

'Barbara Lewisham's grandson.' I say it carefully, so that there can be no misunderstanding between us.

'He's a nice lad, and he listens.'

'Oh? What did you talk about, Peter? I thought, when we had our little discussion this morning, that —'

'I didn't say a thing! I'm not stupid, Mrs Galbraith.' He glares at me. 'You know I wouldn't say.'

I wait.

'But he knows. He's just gone away home, running like a kicked dog, he was. The lad was *crying*.'

'Along the cliff? Did he go along the cliffs?'

I leap up and hurry to the window, but I can't see Matt. Peter says it was half-an-hour ago and that he's been so upset himself, he didn't know what to do, he hadn't come at once. I want to know what Matthew said or did, to give Peter this impression.

'He came bursting out of the back door with his bag, and he saw me and came running over and *shouted* at me, shouted in my face, waving his arms and his bag around. "My grandmother came here, didn't she? You knew all the time!" That's what he shouted. And he accused me of lying.'

Peter rummages in a pocket of his jacket and finds a large handkerchief. He wipes his cheek, then blows his nose and looks at the handkerchief.

'Why lying? When did you have to lie?'

'It was nothing much. We were in the garden this morning and he asked me if I'd met his gran, or if she'd been here, I can't remember what. But I just said no, any road.'

'Why did he ask that? Oh, it doesn't matter now, anyway, that's no longer important. But he clearly is aware that his grandmother came here. Yet that may not be too serious, Peter.'

'I am trying to tell you, the young lad was very, very unhappy.'

What had Matt discovered? I scan the house mentally, trying to guess what he might have found. According to Peter, Matt left at about three-thirty, which was roughly when I had heard him come downstairs. So he must have found something in here. I look around my study, trying to find a clue. My drawings of Barbara! But they are locked away. Yet when I sit forward quickly to look across at the cabinet underneath the microscope table, I see that the key projects from the top corner of the wooden slat that would normally fold across and lock the bank of drawers in place. There is a most curious sensation as the warmth drains from my face and hands; I can guess what Matthew has found. I suddenly feel very sick.

'Do you know what was in his bag?'

Peter looks hard at me. 'A big roll of paper, as far as I could see. But I didn't ask him to turn the rest of it out, did I? Does that make a difference?'

I am unable to do more than nod. I need to check the contents of the drawers, but I shall have to wait until Peter leaves. I massage my forehead with my fingertips, and when I look at Peter again, he is a frightened old man, because he knows that he is no longer safe.

Peter and I have a symbiotic relationship. There are positive aspects, in that we assist each other: he cares for the garden, and I provide him with an income, of sorts. He loves Nancarrow, for he has spent many happy hours here; and I respect his skill, even though it is dwindling with old age. More importantly, although with a heavy heart, I have to respect his courage.

However, he is now aware that the equilibrium has been disturbed, although he might not have expressed it in such words. Our power over each other is no longer symmetric. He is weakened because his privileged information about my relationship with Barbara is now public, and thus no longer counterbalances my own, more puissant, information about him.

Others might prefer to call our symbiosis moral blackmail, but they would be wrong because I don't think either of us is unkind. We have become united in an understanding and, in doing so, have managed to co-exist equably and in harmony.

'What'll you do, then?' he now asks me. 'What's going to happen?'

It shocks me to see him crumbling, and I slide my desk chair across in front of him, and touch his knee with my hand, briefly.

'I'll survive,' I say, although at the moment I'm not certain how. 'And you don't have to do anything, Peter. Listen to me — why should I tell anyone what you did? It gains nothing. I shall fight my own battle and that needn't involve you at all. You'll be all right, Peter, there's really nothing to worry about.'

'But I can't stay here, what if he comes back? What if he brings *her* daughter' (he never calls Barbara by her name) ' — and they start accusing me and asking me questions? What then, Mrs Galbraith?'

'They could only ask you about Mrs Lewisham and they won't do that. If any questions are asked about her, they'll be addressed to me. The horse's mouth. There's absolutely nothing else they could question you about. But look, if it would make you feel safer, why don't you take a few days' holiday? Stay away until I've sorted this out — or Hazel Myers has sorted me out! I'll telephone you in a few days to let you know what's happening. Do that, Peter.'

I take his rough bony hand and shake it a little.

'Would that make you happier, Peter? I promise you will be quite safe.'

Before we leave the room he goes over to my desk and looks at the drawing of Allan.

'I have several other portraits. Would you like one? I'll need to look through them, but if I find a good one I'll let you have it.'

He nods, and that sets off his coughing again. This has been a difficult day for Peter Pascoe and I have a feeling, as we go slowly downstairs, that he might not return, that his gardening days might be over. The thought makes me very sad, and I'm not sure what Nancarrow would be like without him. I don't want him to ride home on that old motorbike either, in his unsteady state, so I suggest that Jim and Roger should load his bike into my old estate car, and that they should drive him home. The arrangements take some time and fortunately no detailed explanations are required, because Peter is obviously unwell.

When the men have left, I return to the study and open the drawer, and find, as I had expected, that the drawings have all gone.

I climb up through the garden, through the wood behind the house, and out into the fields. Lambs, already well-grown, scamper bleating pathetically to their mothers who, with bored expressions, allow them to suckle briefly. The stone wall beyond their field has partially collapsed, and the fallen stones form a seat where, high above the coast path, I can sit unseen and rest my back.

I came here frequently when I began my love-affair with Barbara. Lesbian, gay, queer; the vocabulary of homosexuality is so ugly that I couldn't — still can't — associate it with myself, or with the love we felt for each other. Sexual love, yes, but also cerebral love, and love from the heart; all of these. It was like the bursting into blossom of a rare orchid that, in my case, had lain dormant for more than thirty years. Mary Johnston had excited and terrified me in Addis, and Allan Galbraith, my dear, good Allan, had been there to save me. But by the time I met Barbara, my poor Allan's strength had waned.

I seriously considered selling Nancarrow after his death, and moving back to London. The capital is the hub of science, its spokes radiating out across the world; I have friends and colleagues there and I would have been able to go to concerts and take in the latest exhibitions. There was nothing to stay here for, with Allan dead, because Barbara had left me, too. Using her own peculiar, twisted logic she had announced — in shock — that his death had been a punishment for what we had done, and that we were not *intended* to continue our affair. (But I am certain, although we never spoke of it, that she found it impossible to come to terms with the manner of his death.)And so, within a month, I lost the two people that I had most loved. Barbara recanted later, of course. The horrid reminder of her own mortality eventually drove her to recognise how much we needed each other, and that we were wasting precious days.

I continued to come up to this vantage point after Allan died because I needed to escape the visual reminders of Nancarrow beach. And for a while, too, I couldn't help but imagine that everyone who walked along the sea-wall or used the jetty did so with a ghoulish delight, saying to each other, 'This is where that man died in his wheel-chair, isn't it? Did you read about it? Wasn't it ghastly!'

But Allan was wise; he knew that each headline would be eradicated by the next, yesterday's story is soon forgotten. He died during one of my short trips away. He was so clever in his dying: a quiet time of year, when the coast was clear (I could imagine him saying that, pleased with the pun) and the high Spring Tide was sweeping right up to the sea-wall, engulfing the slope of the jetty.

I force myself to go over the stark facts yet again, checking what Peter Pascoe had done and said after Allan's death. He had been deeply shocked and frightened, but his shock had lent credence to his testimony at the inquest, when he described how he had, at Mr Galbraith's request, wheeled him to the end of the jetty. Mr Galbraith had often liked to sit there (and several other testimonies had corroborated this) because it provided the best view of the shore and western cliffs. Peter had then returned to the back garden, because Mr Galbraith had told him to carry on with some pruning and to come back in a couple of hours. Several times, when he had walked down to his shed, he had seen Mr Galbraith, just sitting, but he had no reason (he pointed out after close questioning) to think that anything was wrong. Mr Galbraith liked to sit still and watch the world, because he was not at all mobile in those days. When Peter had come down the garden to fetch Mr Galbraith a little less than two hours later he couldn't see him, and at first he'd thought his employer must have got a passer-by to wheel him to the house. But then he'd realised this wouldn't have been the case and so he had hurried along the wall.

He had seen the wheelchair in the water and Mr Galbraith lying on the jetty near it, with the waves coming over his head. Peter had pulled him out. No, he didn't try to resuscitate him, he didn't know how, and in any case he could see that he was already dead. All he could do was hurry back to the house to phone for an ambulance.

Poor, poor Peter. He told me later how he and Allan had said their farewells earlier and he had thought that he would come back from the garden to find that Allan had died peacefully in his sleep.

Stark facts. There had been sea water in his lungs, he had died from inhalation of water. He had rolled down the jetty, perhaps in an attempt to move the chair, and had either been thrown out or had purposely fallen out in an attempt to escape the water. As far as the coroner and the public were concerned, the official verdict was death by drowning.

The starkness. Stark images, stark terror. The blackness of it; it reaches out again and again, and I close my eyes, close my eyes and cover my head, as though the cormorants on the rocks below are attacking me. It's like a black room, no light, nothing but the image playing a closed loop. Repeating over and over in my brain, against the inner screen of my eyelids. I wasn't there, but I see him over and over, and the waves sloshing over, and over. The wheelchair, and the waves — oh, my Allan …

I was at a conference in Glasgow. The police came to me, and I drove home trying to be relieved and philosophical, as he would have wanted, for that had been the plan.

But instead, there was the jetty, and the sea, inexorably returning and retreating in diurnal certainty; and Peter, poor Peter Pascoe. Why did it have to be like that, so cruel — and courageous? The wash of the waves echoed in the empty house; I kept thinking Allan was still there, kept listening, expecting him; and nobody was there. What a terrible way to die, how could you have borne to do it that way? The images never fade. There is no-one to tell, no-one who can offer comfort. I am the only one who knows what you did, and why. I want so much to talk to *you* about it, because only the two of us could have argued it through and found an explanation. I am so bereft, so doubly bereft.

He had been so clever. He had left me a subtle clue in the form of a piece of doggerel, the *Song of the Hermaphrodite Snail*, which he had inserted between the pages of tabulated data that I had been working on the day before I left. I was certain that the verses were a clear message, to me only, that he had known about Barbara and me, and (he knew me so well!) the message had been left as the first step in a chain of logic that would lead me and Peter Pascoe to our carefully counterbalanced, interdependent state.

The wind soughed through the cracks in the wall beside me and a lamb bleated insistently for its mother. I wiped my eyes and stood up, causing the sheep to leap away in unreasoning panic, and I delved in my pocket for the much-folded copy of the poem, then sat down again to read it, for the hundredth or two-hundredth time.

THE HERMAPHRODITE SNAIL'S LAMENT

(General chorus)
'Dear, dear! What can the matter be?'
'Oh dear! Two snails with aphally.'
'See, dear - they're hermaphroditidae.
Can they have fun at the Fair?'

(The aphallic snail puts its case.)
'But I don't need another, I'm father and mother.
No sexual behaviour's an energy-saver.
A penis is silly, I don't need a willy!
I have fun on my own at the fair.

(General chorus)
Hey ho! We're Bulinus truncatus.
It's so! Our sex-life's the greatest.
Ho ho! Cross-breeders or self-maters,
We all can have fun at the Fair.

(The phallic couple's case)
We're both sisters and brothers, we're like two paired lovers.
We each can inseminate, phallus can penetrate,
Not so! I am dominant, penis is prominent.
So which has most fun at the Fair?

(General chorus)
Ha ha! Our genetics are so complex.
Ooh ah! So too are our modes of sex.
Production of offspring is one of our main objects,
So our species can go to the Fair.

(The tetraploid's lament)
With four sets of chromosomes, I'm host to schistosomes,
Humans would best avoid water near tetraploids.
A larva could bore in, through my unprotected skin –
Then I'd have no fun at the Fair.

(General Chorus)
Oh dear, this water's too fast to drowse.
Help, dear, I just want to stay and browse.
Quick, dear! Stick your foot where the rock allows,
Or we'll be washed away from the Fair.

(Exit)

(The survivor's lament)
I'm male and I'm female, but I am a lonely snail —
No-one to talk or play, they've all been washed away.
I'm alive and I'll thrive, and I hope my own eggs survive.
I'll be joined by my kids at the Fair.

A.G.
(pp The Snail)

The doggerel had made two things clear: Peter Pascoe at least thought he had helped Allan to die, and Allan knew about my affair. We both knew Latin, we had both read playscripts, and the suicide was clearly flagged as 'exit' instead of the plural 'exeunt' which the end of that verse had required. The initials 'pp' did not stand for the coy *pro persona*, as though AG was merely The Snail's scribe; PP had been involved. Allan had also left me another clue, implicating a familiar object by its absence: the small book *of Annual Tide Tables* had vanished from its usual place. No suspicious external investigator could have deduced with certainty that Allan knew that day was to be listed as the peak of the Extreme High Water Spring Tides (even though daily observation might have indicated such). As for the barbiturates, they remained untouched, in their original hiding place.

So, Peter Pascoe was to believe that he had helped Allan to die, but I would know that Allan had chosen, had planned, to drown himself at the high tide. But why try to involve Peter Pascoe at all? What was the point? The clear answer, unhappily, was that Allan knew that Peter had spied on me and Barbara: and this was Allan's scheme to block any possibility of unilateral blackmail or snide remarks from Peter implying that Mr Galbraith had killed himself because of *'them'*.

Allan had been dead for nearly a week before Peter and I had been able to have a private discussion and in all that time he had not suspected that I knew about his potential involvement. I had asked him to come back to Nancarrow, ostensibly to discuss what should be done about the garden.

We had sat at the kitchen table and I had said to him, quite gently, 'Thank you for helping my husband at the end. He would have liked me to apologise on his behalf for the final apparent act of drowning — he wanted to make sure that you were protected.'

Poor man, he had become extremely agitated and had wanted to know how I had guessed, but I had taken care not to enlighten him. I hope I managed to convince him of his own worth and courage.

'It will always be our secret,' I had said. 'I can promise you that, Peter. That's what Mr Galbraith wanted. But tell me, why did you spy on Mrs Lewisham and myself?'

Oh, how he had blushed; he had wriggled like a trapped lizard. The invective had flickered out of his mouth as his fright at discovery released itself in disgust. I had let him have his say, and had asked him what he had told my husband.

'*Nothing!*' he had almost shouted, in genuine surprise. 'What would I want to tell him that filth for? Any road, he liked her, didn't he? — took her up to the *camera obscura* and all. He wouldn't have believed me, would he?'

The process of reasoning is like a maze, or that taxonomist's tool, the dichotomous key. The path bifurcates, there are two pieces of information; if one leads to a dead end, take the other; the correct branch, in its turn, leads to another fork. So the seeker progresses, selecting and rejecting.

The hidden question had been: how did Allan discover the relationship between Barbara and myself? The possible answers are: either through Peter Pascoe's information, or through his own observation or suspicion. If the first answer is correct, then they each know that the other knows, and therefore Peter can surmise that this knowledge is a partial or major cause of Allan's suicide; and I'm left open to blackmail. Unless Allan can show that he knows but does not mind. If the second answer is correct, then it is imperative that Allan retains the impression that he remains ignorant; for the same reason as before, that there must be no opportunity for blackmail. The mental gymnastics are never-ending, like a perpetual-motion machine!

I think *Peter* knew about us because he had spied us through the *camera obscura*. Barbara and I were always very careful in the garden at Nancarrow, even though Peter's coughing could be relied on to indicate his whereabouts. But one afternoon Barbara arrived unexpectedly, on some pretext, and I was in the garden, cutting flowers. She saw me and for some never-explained reason was in a great state of excitement; she had glanced around, 'Where are they?', she'd asked, and when I had said that Allan and Peter were both inside, in the drawing room, she had engulfed me passionately, warm and exuberant in her sexuality. I was powerless, dismayed, yet was swept by her enthusiasm towards the summer house. Acquiescent; yet, out of habit, I'd glanced up behind me and had seen the eye of the turret pointing in our direction. Probably no-one was up there, but if they were, the viewing table might well have relayed the whole scene.

When Barbara and I went indoors, Allan was in the drawing room. He'd sent Peter up to the attic, he said, to fetch a notebook that he'd left upstairs; he couldn't imagine why it was taking Peter so long. Poor old Peter, he was in strange territory, and I can still understand his feelings of outrage.

And so, after Allan's death, Peter and I came to our arrangement, as Allan had known we would. I persuaded him to think it through and, rationally, we agreed that it would never profit either of us to pass on our knowledge about the other. Peter was easily persuaded to stay on to cultivate the garden as Mr Galbraith would have wished, despite its proximity to the jetty and the shore; I think we needed to be near each other, to keep each other under surveillance, or maybe we needed each other's company. Our Nancarrow symbiosis was strengthened by Barbara's subsequent absence for the next year or more, and I was free to bury myself in work. I kept expecting to hear Allan's whistling or his call of 'Beth? Elizabeth?', and I found myself listening for his laboured, dragging walk and the sticky sound of rubber tyres along the hall. Nor did I hear Barbara's voice or laughter. The house was hollow with the sound of the sea and the waves sucking at the shore. Every external noise seemed magnified and strengthened the emptiness, and so I worked hard to keep the house noisy and busy with scientist friends.

A few yards away two young rabbits are squatting, eating with busy jaws. We have been oblivious of each other's presence, and now I gently lob a small stone in their direction and they leap for cover. A rabbit's solution to a problem is so simple: run to a burrow and hide. But, little rabbits, you should beware, because the burrow may be the wrong solution — the ferrets or the fleas will get you in the end.

The facts were stark, the suspicions and surmises labyrinthine in their complexity. I shall never know whether my love for Barbara was contributory to Allan's decision to end his life. It's the *not*-knowing that is particularly hard. Until his last day, we shared the same friendship and companionship that had always been the cohesive factor in our relationship. We had shared so much, and his wry humour and sharp wit had livened my days. Marrying rather late in life, we had amused and tolerated each other, and our relationship had been sexually undemanding.

Mary Johnston, unsubtle in her anger, had shouted at Allan that he was deceived, I was a dyke. Another ugly euphemism. She was wrong, though; I *had* been a dyke and I was never to be so again for several decades. Not until his final day did Allan ever reveal that he knew of my secret 'other life'.

Matthew's theft of my drawings has potentially enormous implications, but the ramifications are as yet too unclear. Should I wait, or should I be proactive? But whatever the nature of my discussion with Matthew and Hazel, it's certain that Peter Pascoe's 'secret' will always remain just that.

CHAPTER 33: ANNE: 1863

Lady Ballavich departed, I am certain, with many secret sighs of relief. Yesterday, she took Anna to a village east of our city to visit a certain schoolmistress, a paragon of Christian virtue. It seems that visits such as these are essential to provide Miss Shipton with grist for her mill — that is, with examples which may be put to good use as moral tales. This schoolmistress has but one leg (thus making Miss Shipton's own infirmity of lesser significance.)

Anna's flood of description and praise cannot be stopped. I sit, upright, in my favourite straight-backed chair by the open window, breathing in the scent of the pink roses that Duncan planted in our first year here. Several cast skins of greenfly have drifted in onto the windowsill and I am distracted by their presence, and make a mental note to examine the rose more carefully. Anna is sitting on the sofa, her little feet neatly planted side by side, her shoes gleaming, her plain dark skirt smoothed over her knees. The period spent abroad in the past two years since she met the Ballavichs has obviously agreed with her, for she is plumper, her skin less sallow, and her face, as she talks, is almost animated. Her dress may be plain but the material is good, and although she still wears no showy rings or pearls, there is a fine dark-red cameo brooch at her throat. My memory is that she used to smell faintly of the sick-room, but now there is a faint smell of lavender-water about her.

The worthy schoolmistress, Anna tells me, was once a shop-keeper, and is now widowed and in her sixties. There is also the matter of her leg (her *missing* leg!) and this is the matter that intrigues me most.

'She had been scalded at the age of four, from her waist to her foot, and the leg had given her great trouble — so that it was necessary to have it amputated when she was in her twenties. I said to her, "It was a great affliction for you to lose your leg" —'

'Your understanding and sympathy must have comforted her greatly!'

'— and she replied, "Nae, nae, it was the best thing that e'er happened to me. It was the first step to knowing Jesus as my Saviour".'

Anna's Lowland accent is execrable!

'She sounds a remarkable woman.'

'Indeed, she is an example to us all. She teaches the little ones by day to follow in the path of the Lord and she devotes her evenings to teaching the young men who are out learning a trade by day and the girls from the mills. She teaches them to read and write and keep accounts, and —'

'How does she manage to walk without one leg?' I cannot help myself; I want to divert the flood of words, and to understand the *fundamentals* of this 'Scotch woman's' being!

Anna looks bewildered, for it is the schoolmistress' soul and not her body that has concerned her, and she endeavours to reply.

'Why ... why, she has a wondrous facility in climbing stairs ... she has a wooden substitute, it is heavy and her weight is thrown upon it, but —.'

'A wooden leg? Like one of the soldiers who returned from the Crimea?'

'Why, yes. But of course it is hidden by her skirts.'

Oh, what is wrong with me, that I so wish to laugh? I cannot contain it, the laughter bubbles out of me.

I say gaily, once again, 'A truly remarkable woman. How fortunate for you that my aunt knew of her. And now, please tell me about your journey to Sicily, after you made the Laird's acquaintance.'

Thus I succeed in diverting her yet again, and she recounts all the details of her journey from Italy to Sicily; she sailed, she said, on 'the purple sea over which the apostle Paul sailed from Melita. I landed on the strand on which he landed.' In Syracuse the inns were cold, damp and dirty, and it so happened that she had been given a letter of introduction 'to the principal family in the place.'

'I placed it in my portfolio, although naturally I had no intention of availing myself of it. But on the following morning — one of those balmy mornings of a Sicilian spring, I wish you could experience it yourself! — it was the first thing that I withdrew. I laid it before the Lord, dear Anne, and the hand of the Lord clearly marked my path.'

So, since it was the Lord's will, our dear Miss Shipton was received into the house of the 'principal family' and made a welcome guest, in considerable comfort and style, for the space of several days. Praise be to the Lord! It requires great strength of will on my part not to smile. She was taken on an expedition to the cave of Dionysius where prisoners had formerly been kept and there she sat in the 'whispering gallery' that the vaulted cavern formed.

'I proceeded to make *experiments*!' she says. 'I whispered the words that came with such power into my mind — "Blessed is the man that trusteth in the Lord" — and, lo and behold! the echo rolled back the promise from every corner, bearing a blessing on its breath.'

I profess astonishment and ring the bell. Kate brings in the tea and it is a relief to be occupied with the distribution of plates and sandwiches. Thereafter, between mouthfuls of cake, Anna tells me of similar adventures in Malta (where the Lord persuaded her to use letters of introduction that enabled her to be entertained most royally) and stories of last summer, spent — for her health — in the Austrian Tyrol (where the Lord decreed that she should find a *comfortable* hotel).

'I sat upon my balcony, with a view of the mountains, and there I composed the verses of several hymns —and completed the writing of my book about my dearest, most valued friend.'

She stops and, placing her plate on the small table in front of her, regards me, waiting.

She brought me the book, *Tell Jesus! Recollections of Emily Gosse*, a week ago. I had read it, seeking for the meaning of Emily, the first Mrs Gosse. As I read, my horror had mounted. At first it was the author's sentiments that had distressed me and her, to my mind, misinterpretation of certain events; but as the morning had drawn on and I had delved deeper into these 'recollections', I had become sickened and overwhelmed by the repugnant information contained therein. When Duncan had returned home unexpectedly, urgent in his passion for my fruitful body, he had found me in tears — and I had pretended exasperation at the story of Willy Gosse's shell.

Now Anna waits for my verdict, her narrow nose points in my direction and her hands are clasped patiently in her lap.

'I do not know where to begin,' I confess at last. I know I should praise her writing but I cannot: the style is of no consequence, it is the *content* that concerns me.

'Perhaps you cannot see why our Lord told Mr and Mrs Gosse to take that road? It seems to you misguided that they should have faith in Dr Fell's treatment rather than the surgeon's knife? But we see so clearly now that this was the manner in which Jesus would call Emily to Himself. That was His purpose all along. Her suffering was not in vain. Oh, how fortunate she is, to be gathered in amongst His Saints!' Anna lifts her hands and presses them together: she casts her eyes upwards to the ceiling as though she must see Emily floating there, bathed in a rosy glow. 'It was what He had ordained for her. Remember my vision.'

'If I were Mr Gosse I would feel only bitterness at such a mistake,' I say calmly. How *can* these evangelicals so distort the course of events to suit their purpose?

'Mr Gosse has become stronger in his determination to serve Jesus. You saw him in Edinburgh shortly after Emily passed on — surely you agree?'

'I saw only a bewildered and deeply-lonely man. Who in the following months made such a great error in his defence of the Lord that he shocked even his closest friend. Oh —' I raise a hand to fend off the expected outburst. 'I am sorry, Anna. We must consent to disagree with each other. You believe that Henry Gosse found his way after Emily's death, I believe that he *lost* it.'

Anna is fidgeting, sitting forward in her agitation, ready to interrupt with exhortations and explanations.

'I am sorry,' I say again. 'However, you mentioned that you had some other pertinent papers— please do show me.'

I have not treated her with respect. For a moment I think that I have offended her too greatly, but she sighs, a sharp little sound, and then reaches into her large handbag (the same 'portmanteau' that so amused the Laird) and brings out a book that is narrow and thin.

'Mr Gosse, knowing of my great admiration for his dear wife, most generously gave me this copy. A great deal of my description of Emily's last days is taken directly, with his permission, from this book. It is his *Memorial,* and only a few copies were printed, for Mrs Gosse's friends and family.'

She pushes herself up from the sofa and limps across the room to where I sit; the limp is more pronounced than when she arrived — I have distressed her.

'You may return it to me tomorrow. There is a photograph ...' She opens the book and holds it out to me, then returns to her seat, her foot dragging on the carpet.

I stare at the photograph. 'This *cannot* be Emily Gosse!'

When I had visited her in Pimlico, three months before she died, she had looked ill and thin, but not like this. This was an *old woman's* gaunt face; her nose angular and protruding; her eyes closed. She lies on a bed, propped up against a mound of pillows, a bonnet drawn tightly over her hair. The photographer must have placed the support for his camera at the foot of the bed. Her eyes are closed, her head turned slightly to one side. One arm lies along the cover, her hand extended from a gathered cuff. I touch Emily's hand and stroke it with my finger.

'It was taken on the day she died.'

Emily appears lifeless. She is not Willy's mother or Henry's wife. She is a stranger. I cannot see her clearly. A tear rolls down my cheek, I brush it away lest it fall on the photograph.

'Mr Gosse arranged for her portrait to be painted and photographs to be taken so that —'

There is a catch in Anna's voice, and I glance at her quickly and see that she too, is crying silently.

'It is inhumane!' I cry. 'It is grotesque. How could she bear it?'

Anna can no longer contain her sobs. 'He said ... he said there must be something for their son to remember her by ...'

I go to her, and I take her by the hand and help her to her feet. I lend her my handkerchief, as I have done before, and we embrace, standing awkwardly together (she is short and thin and I am much enlarged). Our tears flow, and her slight body shakes with her anguish. I reflect that probably, in all these years, she has been unable to *share* her grief for Emily. Despite the many differences between us, we have this in common. I feel a rush of sympathy for this strange unlovable woman who had so *adored* Emily Gosse.

In the evening I read Philip Henry Gosse's *Memorial*. I frequently turn back to that tragic photograph, trying, and failing, to recognise in it the attractive, intelligent woman with whom I had been acquainted. I am only able to read the text in short spells; I am too much perturbed by the intimate details of each step in his wife's illness and decline. Every word spoken between them in her last hours was recorded, every action; he had sat beside her bed, with his pencil and his notebook:

'As she lay still, she said, 'I shall see his bright face, and shall shine in his brightness, and shall sing his praise in strains never uttered below.' I have no doubt she alluded to a deficiency which she had always regretted; for want of ear and voice, she had never been able to sing.

Even up to the last her mind was set upon doing her Master's work; and on this very last day, one of the servants was seated at a table by her bedside, with heaps of Tracts and Messengers before her, folding and addressing each, under her dictation.

It was her last act of earthly service.

In the course of the evening, as I was hanging over her, she said, 'O that I loved Him more!' I replied, 'You will soon.' She said, 'Yes, I hope so!' and then, with an expression approaching to archness, she added, 'I don't love Satan!' 'Nor sin,' I suggested. 'No; and I don't want to enjoy the pleasures of sin for a season.'

As night drew on, a change became manifest. The physician had said that the whole blood in the system was poisoned by the cancer, and that the rapidity of its downward course was beyond that of any case he had ever witnessed. The breathing became shorter and more laborious, accompanied with much heaving of the chest. Soon after eight o'clock she experienced a partial paralysis of the tongue, causing her speech to be thick, and with difficulty intelligible. In allusion to this, and in the dread that she might linger some time without the power of speech, she said, 'The Lord has hitherto raised me above circumstances. He has made me to ride upon the high places of the earth, and now He has brought me down; and now He has made me fear.' 'Fear what, my darling?' I asked. 'Paralysis.'

A little before ten, she murmured, 'I'm going home - I must go home!'

'Yes,' I replied; 'What a blessing that you have a home to go to!'

She immediately added, though almost inarticulately, 'And a hearty welcome!'. There was here an allusion to one of her last three tracts, 'A Home Welcome', as its title now stands, but which in her MS had been entitled, 'A Home and a Hearty Welcome.'

The two maids, who truly loved their mistress, refused to go to bed, and they with me continued to watch for the end. After a while my precious sufferer said, 'I shall walk with Him in white; won't you take your lamb and walk with me?' This last sentence she repeated twice or thrice, as she saw that I did not readily catch her meaning. I believe, however, she alluded to our dear little boy. Her speech was now so thick, that a great deal of what she said was unintelligible; only a sentence now and then could be made out.

Presently she said, ' 'Tis a pleasant way - more pleasant than when I could not pray for what would make you unhappy.' I suppose that she referred to the circumstance that, within the last day or two, I had been able solemnly to resign her into the hand of Him, who for a season had lent her to me, and who now reclaimed His loan.

She looked on us hanging over her and said, two or three times, as if the thought of eternal union were delightful, 'One family!' and then added, 'One song! - one family, one song!'

At times she dropped into a momentary slumber, during which she still spoke, incoherently. In one of these murmurings, on putting our ears close to her mouth, we could make out the words - 'Open the gates! Open the gates and let me in!' Ah! The 'blessed of the Lord' had not much longer to 'stand without!'.

About a quarter to eleven, I spoke to her of the freeness of gospel grace, which she had proclaimed so fully in her Tracts; when she replied, 'I see it!' 'See what, love?' I asked. 'I see the freeness of gospel grace that I have set before others; but in extreme weakness'; immediately adding, lest the expression might be misunderstood, as meaning dimness of apprehension of the truth - 'in extreme weakness of body.'

Soon after this, she turned her dimming eyes on me, and said, 'Dear Papa, I'm all ready.' 'What has made you ready?' I asked. 'The blood.' Then she added, after a momentary pause, 'The blood of the Lamb.'

This precious testimony was the last sentence that issued from her lips. It had been her joy in life to proclaim the sufficiency of that blood, and now she died on it.'

I must have made some sound of disgust or grief because Duncan, who has been sitting near me, looks up.

'Do not distress yourself so, my love. Why do you continue reading it?' He comes to me and takes the book, then holds my hand. 'Listen to that thrush! He has been occupied feeding his children all day, and he still has energy in the evening to sing his heart out to his love.' He squeezes my hand and smiles. 'I wish I could sing to you.'

'Have you been labouring all day too?'

'What else?'

'What would you do if I died? Would you leave here and fly off to Africa, like the swifts?'

A crowd of the aerial acrobats is swooping and screaming with delight above the houses, rejoicing in the golden haze of the late-evening light.

Duncan releases my hand and frowning, looks away. 'You should not talk like that. Gosse's unpleasant little book has made you morbid. I shall not even acknowledge your question by giving it an answer.'

We both look out at our small garden, without speaking. Despite the lateness of the hour, white butterflies flutter between the dusty-blue spikes of lavender, pausing here and there to suck the nectar. I imagine their proboscides, tight black coils, unfurling as each probes for the flower's sweetness. I see the proboscis as clearly as if it has been mounted on a glass slide and a microscope is before me. I blink to wipe away the image and then rest my head against Duncan's waistcoat.

'I shall not be morbid. Will you fetch me Miss Shipton's book from beside the bed? I should like to remember Emily Gosse as Anna wrote about her, in the early days of their friendship. And then we shall retire to bed.'

'And will this chapter then be closed?'

'Yes. I am certain it will.'

So it is that, as the last glimmerings of the long northern day fade away softly into darkness, I hunt through the pages of *Tell Jesus!* Each time I find one of Anna's descriptions, I read it aloud to Duncan.

' "Directly I saw the face of Mrs Gosse I longed to know her better; she was fair and appeared more youthful than her years, from her small delicate features and the artless childlike smile which lighted her countenance when animated. I have seen it literally sparkling with joy, when unexpectedly brought into contact with those who loved her Lord." Listen, Duncan — "I marked her steps and they chimed sweet music." And this. "The love of God in Christ beamed through her words and life. She did not cavil at my crude opinion nor combat my errors ... neither did she appear amazed at my ignorance" ... "Her usual quiet smile and unbroken composure" ... "I never saw her ruffled with anyone, even if the wrong were directed against herself personally.'

'Was she a saint?'

'Wait, there is much more. "She was unselfish. I longed to keep her only to myself. The natural wilfulness of my character desired more of her society than the Lord saw fit to accord me ... I seem to feel the loving presence of her hand upon my shoulder now, as she looked tenderly in my face through the tears that glistened for what I had suffered." And there is more, concerning Emily's sympathy and compassion in her teaching. But this does not concern Anna directly.'

'Was Emily truly like that?'

'Anna sees her in relation to herself. She saw her also as a good mother — she did not see her as a wife.'

Duncan nods slowly. 'It sounds as though Miss Shipton was somewhat blinkered by her love.'

'I saw her as someone with a strong conviction about one thing — the saving grace of the Blood of the Lamb. She cared passionately for Henry and wanted to help him, but I wonder if she did not see Willy as a *responsibility*. Henry loved Willy.'

'I wonder if the new Mrs Gosse has caused some division within the family? Gosse's natural history books were formerly so lively. The Lord was invoked frequently, of course, but Gosse himself had done so many interesting and amusing things. His latest books have become so serious — the diatribes are quite vituperative.'

I am now lying on the sofa by the lamp and Duncan takes *Tell Jesus!* from me and places it and the *Memorial* inside the davenport.

'I would like to burn those books,' he says, and although he pretends to tease me I know he is serious. 'But think of the Gosses in this way — you should think of them as two sea-anemones, tentacles extended.' He raises his dark eyebrows at me and makes a little snort of laughter. 'One at each end of a see-saw. Above the fulcrum, in the centre of the board, there is a rock, representing the Lord. You may think of it with a capital R if you wish. Emily's tentacles are spread around her, reaching behind to other people, pulling them towards the Rock. Gosse's reach out to the Rock, pulling it towards the natural world. And of course their tentacles also reach towards each other. Do you see it?'

His eyes glint in the lamplight and I nod because I see the picture clearly.

'The Rock is firm, the forces the actiniae exert are balanced.'

'Then one is removed.'

'Quite so. And you can see what happens. The Rock slips towards the Henry

Gosse end and becomes a burden. Gosse must now try to extend himself beyond the empty Emily end to touch the distant people, to re-create the balance. The Rock becomes dominant, it is no longer a steadying influence, and Henry's hold on the natural world is reduced.'

I think about the metaphor. 'It is clever. You are clever.'

'I am not certain where Willy and the new wife fit in.'

I smile, tiredly. 'I cannot think clearly any more. I am so weary.'

Immediately he becomes anxious and helps me to my feet.

'How is our darling child? We shall take a new metaphor in order not to blaspheme — he shall be our Rock. And let us now forget about the wretched Gosses for ever more. Come now, I shall help you both up to bed.'

He stands close behind me, reaching round to cup my breast and belly with his hands; I press myself against him, feeling him, feeling our child, full of longing for them both and for our future.

'I shall carry our child for you. Walk slowly to the door ...'

He laughs softly as we try to step in unison; the absurdity of what we are trying to do makes me giggle.

'Ah! I felt him jump! Our own little rock, our pebble.'

CHAPTER 34: HAZEL

I sat on the bench outside the concourse coffee shop at Reading Station, my head swivelling like a tennis spectator as I searched for Jamie. He was grim-faced and sweating as he pushed through the crowd of kids who were hanging around and smoking, and I stood up and called to him. He hurried over to embrace me; hot Jamie, smelling of the dusty sweetness of bird-feed.

'The traffic's bloody awful, and I couldn't find a place to park except on a yellow line. Are you all right? You really worried me.'

I put my arm through his and we went out to the Land Rover and drove to Caversham. We parked by the river and walked through the park until we found a bench well away from children and strolling pensioners. Wind rattled the leaves of the poplars, and ugly pleasure boats vied with swans for space on the Thames.

'What did you tell Lynn?'

'That I had to go to Reading to see about some vitamin supplements for the feed. Which is true — I do. Later. What about Matt — is he all right on his own? You said he was pretty upset.'

'He knows I've come to see you and that we're not telling Lynn — because we're embarrassed about our mother and want to keep it to ourselves. I didn't much like leaving him but he said he'd be okay, and that he wouldn't do anything daft like going to see Elizabeth.'

'Hmm.' Jamie looked sideways at me. 'You sounded pretty upset yourself — you are, aren't you? First, tell me in detail what Matt found.'

I told him about the pictures, and how Matt had discovered them two days ago and had brought them home. I said that I thought Matt was perhaps, now, more upset at the long-term deception rather than the content. Jamie had been staring at the distant boats but now he turned to look at me.

'What about you, Haze? What upset you most about all this?'

He put his arm along the back of the bench and squeezed my shoulder. Strangely, now that I'd managed to get through the explanation, my teeth had started to chatter and my hands were freezing.

'I feel sick. But why? I'm behaving like a naïve kid. And yet you're so calm. Don't you mind at all that Mummy turned out to be a lesbian? Oh — you *knew*! You knew she was having an affair with Elizabeth Wilson, didn't you? And you kept quiet about it, too. Is that true, Jamie?'

Jamie, slow Jamie, slow to reply, looking over at the boats again.

'I had some sort of inkling.'

'How? Explain to me.'

'It was nothing much.' He puckered his lips, chewing the inside. 'Remember that horoscope-thing that she liked, right at the end, you'd read it to her just before I came down to Polkenna? And you said she'd asked you to put it under her pillow?'

'Uh-huh.'

'She made me put it in an envelope and send it to Dr E. Wilson at Nancarrow. She made a big secret of it, made me come close so she could whisper even though you were downstairs. And I wasn't to tell you, she said, because you were unkind about the horoscopes and you'd probably tear it up.'

'I wouldn't have!' I was hurt.

'No. I'm sure she knew that, too, but she didn't want you to start asking questions, did she? If you think about it now.'

'What about you?'

'She told me to mind my own business!' Jamie gave a quick grin, 'and then she just pretended to go to sleep. Or maybe she really was asleep.'

'But —' I was puzzled. 'But why did that give you an inkling that she was gay? That's nothing.'

He didn't answer, just stared into the distance again, but he took hold of my hand and stroked the back of it with his thumb. Gently, as though it was a pheasant chick's neck.

'Jamie, for God's sake! Come on! Did you see them together, or something? You have to tell me.'

He cleared his throat.

'No. But — okay, well, I'll tell you. I knew Ma was that way inclined. I've known since I was about seventeen, when we lived in that grotty little brick cottage in Gloucestershire. I don't know if it'll help you understand this Elizabeth Wilson business, I'm not a psychiatrist, Haze, I don't know the right way to do these things. But listen — it's all right, don't panic or get cross, *you* knew about it then, too.' He was looking at me really anxiously. 'Little sis, little Hazel. I'm really scared about reminding you, because you'd forgotten. You'd made yourself forget. But perhaps it's better to try to remember it now.'

His hand was trembling slightly and that frightened me, because I couldn't remember why I should be scared. A horrible cold tension was building up inside me, pressure was growing inside my head.

'I'm forty, Jamie. What's the matter? Tell me.'

'Well, do you remember how Ma used to run painting classes to earn some money?'

I nodded. When we were younger there'd been a trail of earnest people, mostly women, mostly middle-aged, filling the house with gossip and laughter. Mummy must have been thirty-ish or forty, teaching people how to paint.

'There was a woman, Judy — Jude — that used to come to that cottage, in her late twenties, I guess, short black hair and tanned skin. I used to fancy her myself.'

I tried to picture her, but couldn't.

'Were she and Mummy lovers, then — is that what you're trying to say?'

'We'd gone up the lane on our bikes, and we'd found a little dog wandering around on its own. It followed us and we spent ages playing with it. We thought it was lost and had great plans for keeping it …'

'Go on.'

'We also had this idea that we'd smuggle it up into my bedroom. We knew that Ma had a class and that some of the folks had stayed on — so you wrapped the dog in your jumper and we went tiptoeing up the stairs. The dog thought it was great joke, of course, and was wriggling around but we managed to be pretty quiet. Trouble was, Ma's bedroom door wasn't closed properly so we heard her and Jude …'

'Stop. Let me think.' I made myself think back; think back, try to see the stairs, the door. The little dog had been warm and squirming in my arms.

I'd just been able to see them through the crack in the door. No, I was making that up, I had only heard them.

'We knew they were in there.'

'You just ran away, Haze, and you went so fast downstairs — and so quietly, too. You just vanished! And I couldn't find you for ages, I looked and looked. I was really scared.'

I could see it all very clearly now. The little dog, the little dirty-white Highland terrier, and its soft wet nose and grinning mouth, and its skinny body, light as a bird, so light I was scared I'd crush it if I held it too tight. Squirming in my jumper. Yes, I had run away and hidden. After a while, I'd seen Jude come hurrying out and get into her car, that was parked in the lane. Jamie had come out later, he must have stayed hidden inside.

The shuddering started: I shook and shook, and thought I might be sick. Jamie hugged me and stroked my hair, over and over; stroke, stroke, stroke, slow and regular. A woman with a pushchair stared at us: lovers' quarrel.

Jamie rocked me gently, and whispered, 'It's all right, Haze, it's all right. I'm here.'

Rocking and rocking. Warm protective arms, comforting smell of fresh sweat. Did I fall asleep? My eyes were closed. Was it minutes or hours later when I spoke, mumbling the words against his chest?

'You came and found me in that old shed in the field. It was like this.'

'Mmm. And then you seemed to forget everything that happened that afternoon. When I found you, you were so white and still, just hiding there in that filthy old shed on your own — and you never mentioned a thing about Ma and Jude. Jude disappeared off the scene, anyway, I think Ma tried to protect us for a bit. Talk about shutting the stable door. But it was like you blanked it all out, and at least I was old enough to recognise what had happened to you, the shock of seeing Ma like that, and so on. Everyone always comments on how dreamy you seem to be, but I know there are things bottled up in there … like a fermenting pickle jar!'

He tried to laugh, and I just nodded. All these years! I'd known about Mummy but hadn't known; I'd refused to let myself recognise what was obvious. She must have hidden her feelings and her relationships (there must have been others, now I began to think about it) throughout all those years.

'Jenny Baird? Shortly after we first went to Polkenna?'

'Yes.'

'And you knew about all this, Jamie, all the time? D'you think other people knew — was it common knowledge?'

'As far as others go, no. Ma was surprisingly discreet. Hard to believe, isn't it? But people can come and go at the Shell House without being seen, if they come the top way. And anyway you know how Ma thrived on secrecy and plots.'

'It seems almost unbelievable that I've been so blind to all this. But you always knew?'

'I usually had some idea, and Ma knew that I understood and would never make a fuss or anything because of *you*. Haze, I know you always thought she didn't care about us and just did what the hell she wanted, but that wasn't always the case. She tried really hard and somehow, I don't know how, managed to keep her relationships secret from you — not because she was ashamed of them but because she was worried about how you'd react. If you wanted to hide from the truth, she didn't want to force it on you.'

'I was away at University, or on field courses in the vac, I suppose. And you weren't at Nancarrow for long, in any case. And Dave and I got married early ... But I'm still amazed she didn't let anything slip, even when she was doped up at the end. Apart from one thing — which I've only just seen as significant.'

'What was that?'

'It doesn't matter. Just a silly thing she said.'

The idea of my mother's secrecy as symptomatic of her sensitivity towards me was a new concept entirely, and I'd need some time to think about that. I shifted away from Jamie; my face felt steamy and creased and my shoulders ached.

'Do you think you're going to be all right about this now?' Jamie asked. 'I've been worried sick for weeks that you'd find out — ever since you mentioned you and Matt had been going to Nancarrow — and that it would bring on some sort of crisis. But there wasn't anything I could do, except hope that you'd come to me.'

'Where else would I go? I have always come to you.'

'You might have confronted Elizabeth Wilson directly.'

Oh yes. Elizabeth Wilson. I'd almost forgotten about her.

'I wonder why Mummy turned to women? She was happily married to our father, wasn't she — can you remember what they were like together?'

'I don't know. We were too young to notice or to question that, I suppose. I'm sure she was happy, insofar as anyone is ever completely happy. Who knows about anything? Other people's marriages are always a mystery.' He shrugged.

'Anyway, you're right — knowing this helps explain about "the Elizabeth business", and why they both kept it so quiet. After all, why should they publicise their affair anyway, it was nobody else's business and elderly lesbians always provoke snide comments, anyway. And if the daughter was known to be ultra-sensitive about the matter, well ... Silly, really, it looks as though I got my knickers in a twist about not much. Our mother was a lesbian, Jamie. So what?'

'Yeah. I can see why you're bitter. But I can see why she didn't let on, even at the end, because she knew you'd be likely to come across Dr Wilson, and anyway it would have been self-indulgence on her part at that stage.'

'At least I could have talked to Elizabeth about her on equal terms, instead of which ... oh no, what can *she* be thinking about all this?'

'Look, Matt's the one to worry about now, Haze. You're going to have to think how to talk it over with him. You said he really likes Elizabeth — they've obviously hit it off together— so he's going to feel really screwed up by this. And seeing nude pix of his gran can't be helping.'

'No. Poor old Matt.' I stood up, feeling cramped, and confused by my thoughts. 'Let's walk a bit, and think this through.'

We walked along the heat-crisped yellow grass beside the river and, for a while, we looked at the painted narrow-boats and hired cruisers that chugged and surged up and down the waterway, and talked about Suzy and John, and, of course, Jamie's birds and his preparedness for the season ahead. We bought ice-cream cornets at a van and ate them as we stood watching mallards bobbing in the wash. Coots clucked metallically as they scurried into the reeds. Jamie pointed out the laborious four-winged fluttering of blue desmoiselles. A small mass of damp grey feathers washed to and fro with the wavelets; a dead moorhen chick.

'Must've been hit by a boat — run over in the water. Hey, do you remember, last time you came to stay, you gave me a hard time about birds having souls? Trying to stir things up, as usual!'

Run over. *Aaagh.* It was like a physical blow and icy bile rose in my throat.

'Oh no. Oh God. The dog. The little dog.'

I shook my head, swallowing hard, and Jamie grasped my elbow.

'What's the matter? You look as though you're going to be sick.'

'You never asked what happened to the little dog. I was going to call it "Muffin" and you said it should be called "Pooch".'

'I assumed it must've run away again. You ran away — so did he. Ma wouldn't have let us keep him, anyway. No?'

'No. Jude killed it.'

'*What*?'

'I was carrying Muffin when I ran out into the garden, but he escaped. I went and hid behind the wall in the big field, and Muffin was running around all over the place and wouldn't come back. I kept calling him, but I didn't want to chase after him, I wanted to hide. Then eventually Jude came rushing out in a hurry, and she jumped into her car. Of course it was pointing in the wrong direction and she had to turn it round. Muffin was in the gateway opposite when she reversed. She couldn't have seen him because she just ran him over.'

'Bloody hell!'

'She saw what she'd done, after she turned round — and she got out and picked up his poor little squashed body. He was such a *mess*, Jamie, there was blood everywhere, she got covered.'

Oh God, oh God!

'And she went over to the gateway and threw him behind the hedge — and scuffed away all the blood. She threw the dog behind the hedge. Her shoes were bloody. And she was making horrible moaning sounds, she didn't seem like a *person* at all. She was moaning, making horrid noises. I thought — I was only young, I must have been muddled and terrified — I thought she'd turned into a sort of monster.'

'You saw all that. Oh Lord, my poor little Hazel.'

'That's why I ran away the second time, and hid in the shed. I never spoke about it, or even thought about it again — until now.' I was gripping Jamie tightly. 'That poor little dog! It was so *horrible*.'

Jamie was completely silent; his chin rested against my head and I could feel him breathing. Eventually he said,

'So it was nothing to do with seeing Ma ... But why did you run off when we heard her and Jude, indoors? I always thought it was because you were so shocked or disgusted.'

'I was bound to have been shocked, yes, but not as shocked as all that. I probably just wanted to get away — and I certainly wouldn't have wanted her to find us spying. Or even to know that we were in the house. It must have been like David when he fell off his bike as a teenager and got knocked out, he said he never did remember what happened during the minute or so before. The incident vanishes, its memory never gets fixed. Seeing Muffin killed like that was a bit like being knocked out, I suppose. And Jude *terrified* me. I don't know anything about the psychology of these things, either. There was so much there to be blanked out that I suppose I just forgot about Mummy and Jude, too.'

'So for thirty, thirty-five, years — all that time Ma was pussy-footing around with her lovers and swearing me to secrecy on her behalf, all because some poor bloody dog didn't have the *wit* to keep away from cars. I don't believe it. How did we get ourselves into such a mess?'

Jamie sounded completely bewildered; he squatted down at the water's edge and poked at the bedraggled little corpse with a stick. The skin on his neck was creased, and deeply tanned by the sun.

'I'm so sorry, Jamie ... But I don't think it has been such a mess, has it?'

I didn't like to see my brother hurt; I touched his shoulder, and he clasped my hand and shook his head in mock despair.

'My dear little sister. Go home and look after that great big lad of yours. Give him what he needs and the rest will sort itself out. Give him a hug from his Uncle Jamie, and that'll help you give him one from yourself.'

The previous time that I travelled home on this train, it was as cluttered and crowded as it is now. I'd been to see Jamie that time, too, but I'd been returning from the Gosse-hunting expedition. Odd to think that it was via the Gosses (but principally owing to their connection with Anne Church) that I'd become involved with Elizabeth Wilson. Matt had become involved with her too, through Jim and the boat. Or perhaps it had all started because of my hayfever. But Matt and I had followed different paths, different journeys to reach the same endpoint. My mother had been intimately involved with Elizabeth, but I couldn't decide whether her journey had been the most straightforward or the most complicated of them all. Strange how I now felt more peaceful than I had for the past year. People think that if you've got a degree from Cambridge you must be really clever, but I know that a Lower Second isn't much, and I know I'm not that bright. There are possibly some questions I might ask, of the 'what if?' variety, that might provide a few psychobabble answers about my failed relationships with men. But, really, the answers are not awfully important and, on the whole, I think I would rather leave matters as they are.

CHAPTER 35: MATTHEW

Hazel said if I was going to stay at home I might as well do something useful. She said, 'You're obviously not going to do anything constructive so you might as well be destructive,' and she set me to tidying up the garden.

So, I spent yesterday afternoon hacking at the creepers and the things that climb up the walls — a few birds' nests fell out and I felt bad about that, but they've finished nesting and have got the kids off their hands, poor buggers. One good thing that Barbara did in this garden was not to plant flowers and have stupid flower beds that would need weeding. Not that I'd know which were weeds and which weren't. But there I go again. I don't give a *fuck* what Barbara did; it's not her place any more.

We need to do something different with the place. So this morning, after I'd stuffed all the cut rubbish into bin-bags like a good boy, I dismantled the stupid bloody sundial or whatever it's supposed to be. It never worked as a sundial, anyway, or at least only in the summer when the sun was high enough, and even then only for a few hours. I picked up all the stupid bloody Hepworths (I can't *believe* I bothered to give stones names!) and piled them in an unartistic heap against the side wall. I even brought 'Babs' in from the front, though I was tempted to kick her down the hill. (Oh, childish, childish. I can behave like such a *kid*!)

I quite fancy getting rid of that honeysuckle or whatever it is, and painting a mural. Or having a graffiti wall. Matt woz 'ere. Matt 4 Caz. Perhaps something a little higher-class than the muck that's written in the college bogs.

Hazel's gone up to Reading (why Reading?) to meet Uncle Jamie, because she says she wants to talk to him about their mum. She doesn't want me to speak to Liz 'til after she gets back. I just don't fucking care any more, it's all a fucking mystery. But I'm on my own, locked away in here like — like what? I dunno. Like the *world*'s full of lepers and I'm the uncontaminated one!

Dad rang last night while we were both here, and when we rang back wanted to know why the answerphone had been on. He rang to speak to Hazel, something about their almost-divorce, not very important apparently; but he wanted to speak to me, really. He and Gail are going away for their hols in a few days' time, and they wanted to know if I was going back there because they'd need to 'make arrangements' to leave the fridge on or leave a key, or some such. The baby's due in November, Gail's getting pretty big, he said, so they thought they'd go and 'chill out' by the sea somewhere. Oh, very hip, my Dad — 'chill out'! 'Where are you going? Norway?' I quipped. So very droll. Gail sent her love, he said. I told him not to worry, I had a job here and I was probably going to stay with my girl-friend if I went away.

'Are you? Are you going to visit Caz?' Hazel asked (she'd still been in the room) and I shrugged because I'd only thought of it that minute. 'I thought you were saving money to go abroad with some of your college friends.'

'Yeah. Maybe. We've not organised anything yet.'

Hazel nearly picked up the phone when it rang again, but then she remembered and waited for the answerphone to kick in — and wonder of wonders, talk about coincidence, her ears must have been burning blah blah, it was Caz, so I snatched the phone and cancelled the machine before she had time to finish her long spiel. Anyway, we chatted a bit, and I said I was thinking of coming up for a week-end — and she was really pleased. I got her work number, and I've just phoned her again today at the time when she said she'd have her employer's kids settled in front of *Sesame Street*. We had a really good natter, a lot of banter but some serious stuff, too. Because hearing her makes me realise that I do miss her and want to see her again. What's so cool is she really likes me, too. I wanted so much to tell her about all this crap that's going on, and of course I can't, but she could tell that I was a bit down, and she was really sweet and wanted to come and cheer me up.

That's what made me think of a graffiti wall and writing 'Matt luvs Caz' and so on.

Jim'll be here any minute, unless he's had a heart attack *en route*. He phoned earlier to say he was coming over to Polkenna to go to the travel agent and the bank, and could he drop by? But I didn't hear the phone because the radio was blaring out into the garden. I decided I'd really like to see him but I was too scared to phone back. In the end, I decided that if Elizabeth answered I'd just put the phone down (heavy breathing first?) and keep trying until Jim picked it up. My luck is in again because he picked it up first time and I said I was on my own, and to go ahead, come right over. Then I got worried in case Elizabeth was going to bring him, but I needn't have — the guy's crazy, he said he was going to *run* over because he needed to get his lungs and heart pumping!

So, I hang the rake and snippers back in the outhouse and put a couple of beers in the fridge and get one for myself. There's nothing worth watching on the telly — *Sesame Street*'s finished — and I dig out one of Hazel's old Stones tapes and put it on the cassette-player loud, so that I can hear it in the garden.

I have to sit on the middle terrace because there's still some prickly stuff from the creepers lying round at the top, and so I just sit, having an occasional drink from the bottle, and looking round the garden, wondering what to do with it. The wooden pillar of the sundial's still there, like a bent dick (so why the hell did Barbara have that in her garden*?*). *Jumpin' Jack Flash* drowns out the stupid tweeting birds but not the gulls, and there's a weird smell in the air, like somebody's burning seaweed or old tyres. It's everybody's dream of a Cornish summer holiday, the time to show off your winter clothes.

A couple of white butterflies think the weather's okay, though, and come flittering and tumbling down the rock-face at the back, beating their wings enough to cause hurricanes in all of the Far East. There's a few purple flowers left on the bush in the corner that I call a butterfly bush and Hazel calls something posher, and the butterflies muck about on that for a while and disturb a really fancy one that has big blue eyes decorating its wings.

Which of course (and it's Barbara's fault for making me play the metamorphosis game) makes me think of Peter Pascoe and the *camera obscura* at Nancarrow. I didn't want to think about Nancarrow. But all the thoughts that have been rumbling round in my head come together to make me think of how you could use the *camera obscura* to spy on people in the garden.

Hazel put the rolled-up drawings of Barbara in her bedroom. I unroll them enough to check the initials and dates pencilled in the bottom corner. Allan died three or four years ago, but I don't know when — but at least two of the drawings are dated before that. I don't bother to look at the drawings — but then I remember what Elizabeth said about faces, that time when we were talking about illustration and representation and so on. There was the stuff about wearing your experience on your face, and how an artist might try to catch an expression that seems representative of the sitter's character.

So I pull out the oldest drawings and try to concentrate on Barbara's face. She hasn't got any clothes on, in one of them, but she's dressed in the other, so I can cover up most of the naked one. It's just that, well, she's my grandmother and I *never* saw her naked, even though I often looked down her front. But old women are fairly gross. She did have big boobs, though, really big and soft, so I was able to imagine being suffocated to death when she hugged me, when I was a little kid, and I'd get a bit giggly and embarrassed. Even when she had one cut off, the other was still big and sort of swing-ey — and she didn't bother much about the special padding to equal things up. That was quite embarrassing for me, I tried not to look. But I sneak a quick look at the nude drawing of her, in any case, the one where she's only got one breast ... and I try to imagine ... No, I don't, I stop myself pretty quick. Stop. I disgust myself — but then again, it's only to be expected, now that I know about her and Elizabeth ...

I go back to comparing the drawings of Barbara's face. I have to admit that Elizabeth is very good. If you know the sitter as a lover not just a friend, would that show in your interpretation of the sitter's expression? I can't decide. All I know is that Elizabeth knew Barbara well enough to draw her naked at least a year before her husband died. But Peter Pascoe said Allan hadn't used the *camera obscura* for several months before his death. Oh, what the hell! I dunno, I don't care. What does the *timing* matter. It happened, didn't it?

Christ! Someone hammering on the door, using the knocker on the front door. Nobody does that. I creep to the bedroom window and squint down, but the angle's wrong — and then Jim moves back from the door and looks up at the windows.

'Matt! Hey, Matt? Are you there, man?'

I open the window so I can stick my head out.

'Hi! Go on round to the side.'

'The gate's stuck, man. I can't get in.'

I'd bolted the door again after I fetched Babs: Hazel's instructions. I tell him to wait (what else can he do?) and hurry down to let him in, resisting the temptation to peer up and down the street in gangster style before I close the gate again.

Jim smiles his Tom Cruise smile, but he's breathing hard and his face and chest are shiny with sweat. His tee-shirt's hanging from the pocket of his shorts.

'Shit, that hill's steep!'

'You didn't try to run up *that*?'

'I'll be honest with you, Matt, I had to take a break halfway,' he says, a bit pompously I think, but then he laughs. ' 'Course not. I was half-dead by the time I reached the village — had to run all the way round by the bridge, too, because the tide's out. Give me a drink before I die!'

'Phoo!' I wrinkle my nose. 'You need a shower — you needn't think you're going to sit on our pretty chairs like that.'

'Don't you like those pheromones? Are you going to come and shower with me and show me how it works? Second thoughts, don't bother — you need a shave.'

'I know how mine works, Jim. Oh, piss off!' I grin. 'I'll get you a towel — there's a beer in the fridge. Anyway, I've been ill. I'm off work, that's why I haven't shaved.'

'You sure hurried off the other day. I thought then you looked sick.'

'Yeah. As a parrot.'

I sit on the stool in the kitchen while Jim showers and we shout at each other over the water noise. He's going on about how tough the run was (it turns out he came over the cliffs with all those ups and downs) and how he really needs to work out, he's getting kinda soft. He has the door open — he didn't look too bad when he stripped, and I sit up straight and try not to think about my beer-gut — and he keeps sticking his head out from behind the curtain and grinning. It strikes me that last time I saw him he was not this bright and frisky.

'What've you been taking?' I ask. 'You're very full of yourself today.'

'Ah-hah. I'm *high*, man — I'm just on my way to book my ticket home.'

'What? I thought you weren't going for ages.'

'Ten days' time. I just got a call from Paul. He's taking leave after this course he's on, but he's only got two weeks so we're planning on going hiking in the Grand Tetons.'

'Where's that?'

'Wyoming. Fabulous mountains.'

'Right.' I feel really deflated. 'So that's it, then — you're finishing up and going home?'

'Yeah. I have to go to London early next week to talk about some data and take in a show, see the sights — and then I leave from there. Hey,' he's finished showering and has wrapped the towel round his waist, 'I'm real sorry, Matt, I wasn't hearing what you're saying. I'm sorry. You know what, you should come and visit us. Next spring or summer.'

'That'd be cool. It's been cool having you around — you've been a good mate. There's a comb on the window sill.'

He's got his shorts on now and is rubbing his hair dry and raking his fingers through it. Seems like Jim makes a habit of showering here.

'Now that's a word you don't use around biologists. Mates we've not been! Not for want of trying on my part, you'll note. Are you sure you won't change your mind, Matt?'

He flashes me that grin again, but his eyes aren't grinning, so I get the beer from the fridge and hand it to him, quick, at arm's length.

'Here, stick that down your shorts and chill out. You're way too old for me.'

We go through to the sitting room end and I remember something about Elizabeth's study. (I don't want to think about Nancarrow, but need to think of something to say.)

'Talking of mates and biology — why's Roger Trenton such a prat?'

'Has he been propositioning you, too? Or is he still after Hazel?'

'Fuck off, Jim, this is getting boring. One-track mind, or what?'

'Sorry. Carry on.' He looks suitably contrite.

'There's this framed poem in Elizabeth's study, have you seen it? Roger was there and was showing it to me. Apparently it was made up by her husband, and it's all about the sex life of snails.' (God, I've come back to that again. What is it with sex, I can't get away from it today. Huh. I wonder why that is?)

Jim's sitting sideways in the armchair, hanging his legs over the arm.

'I can hardly wait to read it.'

'It's all about hermaphrodites, and snails without willies! Rog was trying to be witty about it, and he says,' (I try to imitate Roger, but fail) ' "The only thing left out is queer sex — for which, of course, there's absolutely no biological precedent. And which is certainly a waste of biological energy, which an animal could better conserve and use elsewhere." In chasing after Hazel, I suppose. Though she wasn't having any of it, thank Christ. Stupid lech.'

'He isn't that much of a prat, you're wrong there, you know. You're just uptight because of Hazel, and feeling threatened and protective. You mainly think he's a prat because he *looks* like one, don't you see? He approximates the archetypal British scientist that we see at conferences — American, too, if it comes to that. Or Scandinavian. Prat implies stupid, which he's not.'

'Well, he's homophobic. He thinks the reason so many people are gay is because it's just a fashionable trend.'

'Matt, people have all kinds of reasons for being homophobic. Don't forget his age — and he's strictly hetero. When you're gay — okay, let me re-phrase that! — because I'm gay, I've learned to put up with those kinds of attitudes and fool remarks. They're unpleasant, right, but there's no point in getting uptight about it. I'm not going to change anyone's mind about gays by preaching at them. Or even going on marches and protests. Personally, I'm not that kind of active gay — or activist, I should say.'

'Could've fooled me,' I say, a bit grumpily.

'Oh come on, Matt. I'm only putting on an act because I know you can take it. And I'm sorry if I play it a bit heavy sometimes.'

He bends a leg to scratch his bare foot, and it reminds me of something Uncle Jamie showed us when Suzy and I were kids.

'Can you touch your nose with your big toe?' I ask. 'You're only supposed to be able to do it when you're a kid. Like wrapping your arm around your head to touch your ear — no, that's wrong, maybe that's when you're adult.'

We put down our bottles and try, and both find we can do both these things easily, though the big toe thing is at the risk of ripping our shorts or bursting our balls. I stand up to rearrange myself and put on some music, and Jim's hair has made the chair wet so he goes to get some paper towel to wipe it dry. When he comes back, he says, by the way he's got some stuff, and I look like I need calming down. Seems like a good idea, and I put on suitable calming music while he cuts and rolls, and soon we're both lying back in our chairs, passing the spliff and letting the smoke drift from our mouths. Jim still wants to talk about sex but after a while it's in a lazy kind of way.

'Anyway,' he's saying, 'sex is *fun* for the human species. I guess animals don't find it so much fun — think of pigeons, the actual mating's just classic "wham, bam, thank you mam". Scarcely even any thanks, if you watch. The sexual imperative's there, the necessary urge, but it all looks to be transient to a human, a bit of enjoyment at the time, maybe, but mainly only the inbuilt urge to mingle your genes.'

'That would make a good advertisement for Levis. Why don't we write off, we might make our fortunes.'

He isn't listening.

'But with us it's the act itself that's so good, and the foreplay — and anticipation,' he rolls his eyes meaningfully, 'as well as the joining together. And males and females aren't just switched on once a month or once a year, they can do it any time, so in theory it's a great thing to do at any time.'

'Fills in the odd dull moment.'

'It's fun, it's *sexy,* and because it's not just about mixing your genes any more, why not do it with anyone? If someone turns you on, and you're both willing — do it!'

'Very 'sixties, free love, bell bottoms and all that. Flowers. Is this what you call "not preaching"?'

'Ahh — come on, Matt, I'm just trying to rationalise this seriously. Why there's "no biological precedent for queer sex" or whatever Roger said. What I am saying is, gay sex in humans is not only unsurprising, you might even *expect* it.'

'Actually, what you're getting around to saying is that people who object on moral grounds — or aesthetic grounds — are just making a big fuss about nothing. Then why aren't we all bi?'

I'm trying to use some big words and to concentrate on what Jim's saying, but not succeeding too well.

'Because people find it morally or aesthetically distasteful! That's to do with upbringing and social considerations. And that wasn't exactly my thesis anyway, because there is the biologically *important* question of passing on your genes — which is the serious part of the fun.'

He stops for a bit and we sit and ... think, I suppose.

'But then we have to start thinking about long-term partnerships — and why gays like to go for them, too. Less hassle?' He pauses and takes another drag, then sighs, exhaling too soon by mistake. 'Hey, guy, this is getting *heavy*. Let's leave it at that. Sex is FUN!'

He passes the spliff and I take it and mutter, 'Sex is fun. Yeah. Unusual viewpoint. Sounds like something you should write on my graffiti wall.'

'Where's that? Is that in the john, too?'

'It isn't anywhere yet. I had this idea about using one of the walls at the back — but I guess Hazel wouldn't be so keen. It wasn't a serious idea, anyway.'

'You've already got the front wall and the bathroom wall covered with stuff, all those shells and pictures. You may as well cover another one with words. Yeah, and have another dedicated to sound. Windchimes and reeds —'

'A water-curtain trickling onto — what? Different-sized metal cups. Would that make a good noise? A water version of a rain-stick.'

We fool about a bit then, thinking we're very witty and creative, and Jim tries to think of more things to write on our graffiti wall; our *hypothetical* graffiti wall, or maybe it's a virtual wall, or even hidden from us in another universe. He wants to list why sex is fun, says he can show me a thing or two; but by then we are very, very relaxed ...

Finally I make some strong coffee, and I have to make Jim a peanut butter and jelly sandwich (except we don't have peanut and the jelly's marmalade) to give him strength to get to the bank (except we're too late, the bank's closed). But the travel agent's still open, so he needs to get going; he says I should come with him because he can't remember where he's going, he thinks he needs a ticket to somewhere called Gondwanaland, and can I lend him a sweatshirt because it's cold and grey outside.

As I pass Hazel's bedroom door on my way down again, I suddenly have this crazy idea. I go into her room and get Elizabeth's drawing of the front of the house.

'Did you see this?' I say as I unroll it and Jim puts on the sweatshirt. 'Elizabeth did it for my grandmother. Good, isn't it?'

Jim's head pops out and he pulls his hair out of the neck and clenches it together into a rubber band that he's found in his pocket.

'Wow, that's really neat. What incredible detail. That's a really nice thing to have. I noticed there's a shell broken — now you can replace any that go missing. Neat.'

'Yeah.'

I roll it up again. I'm sure he'll mention it to Elizabeth and so she'll know definitely that the pictures are missing; this should get her thinking.

After I've checked that no-one from Nancarrow's coming to collect him, I say I'll come down to the village with him, and we agree to try to meet again before he finally leaves, but we both know that we've already said goodbye.

I feel pretty twitchy out in the open, it's like I'm supposed to be in hiding from some evil force, and after I leave Jim at the travel agent's, I go down to the ferry steps. The tide's coming in, but I could see from the house that it would still be far enough out. The water's still too low for the ferry to run, only the bottom of the slipway's covered, so Jim will have to go round by the bridge again.

I'll be looking with different eyes this time. The mud stinks and there's a dead fish — crab bait, probably — stranded on the pebbles. I stand back and stare at the side of the steps, just like last time. I look from all angles, again; the wall's green and weedy, but there has to be something there, even though it'll be a few years old.

I get out my trusty Swiss Army knife that Dad gave me for my thirteenth birthday and slide the big blade under the hanging weed and lift it up. I'm doing this, hacking as I go, mowing the lawn, when Billy Martin walks down a couple of steps and just stands there and stares, sort of leering.

'What're you doing down there, laddie? Hiding from lover-boy or something? I just seen 'im back there along the road. Or maybe you're carving love-'earts on the wall?'

He looks even bigger from where I'm standing, and he's got a bandage all up his forearm. His denim waistcoat flaps over his bulging gut.

'Hi, Billy! How're you doing? Haven't seen you in The Anchor much lately.'

'I was in there last night and I didn't see you either. Been missing me, 'ave you, me lover? You've only got to say the word!'

He grins at me. Why do all these guys keep making passes at me?

'I was off sick. What have you done to your arm?'

'Sliced it cutting bait. Should be out on the boat today, but the doc told me to stay off. What *are* you doing then?'

What could I tell him? Oh well.

'My grandmother painted a picture of this wall, because she said there was something special on it. But I'm damned if I can see what. Whatever, it's not going to make me rich.'

'I'll come down and 'elp you then. You need to use a proper knife, look.'

He lifts the right leg of his denims and pulls a sheath knife from his sock; its blade looks sharp and sturdy.

'There's the beauty that sliced my arm! She'll slice away this muck, too, look. Yeugh!'

The blade slips through the weed as though it is green hair.

But after a few minutes of this he gets bored. He's shown off his knife and there's nothing on the wall to see. We both peer at it, but there's nothing but small barnacles, mostly empty and dead, and a few limpets. I'm getting well embarrassed, too, and can't think how to get rid of him.

'She was 'aving you on. Nothing 'ere, me lover. I was 'oping you'd be finding us a pot of gold!'

'Ah well. But thanks for your help, Billy.'

He wipes the blade between his finger and thumb, and then on the bottom of his denims, and slides it back into the leather sheath.

'You could buy me a pint to show your thanks,' he says, slyly, and I nod.

'Sure. I'm on my way home now, but next time you're in The Anchor. See you. And take care of that arm!'

He winks at me, and goes back up the steps. He'll have a good laugh with his mates tonight! He's not as bad as he looks, but I'm glad to get rid of him. I wonder if he spoke to Jim. Funny that he mentioned a pot of gold. Didn't I say something to Hazel like that, back when she started burrowing through that case of books? She didn't find any treasure, as far as I can see.

I have another quick look at the exposed part of the wall and now, rather than concentrating on the shape of the stones, I try to focus on the barnacles. They're a bit like shells stuck on a wall. It looks pretty random, but then I notice that near the bottom step the bigger barnacles, mostly dead, are arranged in a sort of circle. It's difficult to pick out because there are quite a lot of tiny ones messing up the picture — I suppose they're new arrivals. But I think there probably is a circle, and in the centre is a rough circular mark that looks like the scar a limpet makes. They wander around when the tide comes in, and go back to the same place later and grind down the rock to make a tight fit. There might well have been a limpet there when Barbara painted the ferry steps. A circle with a limpet? Something to do with the circles and the central *Tiphobia* on the house? Not very exciting. I suppose she and Elizabeth had been waiting on the slipway for the ferry and had seen it and shared some corny joke or other. No doubt *deeply* significant. And for sure the steps don't look anything like as attractive as they do in her painting.

Nothing much there; but even so I'm quite pleased with myself for getting to the point of that painting. On my way home I buy myself a hot doughnut — a ring doughnut, naturally — and head back up to the fortress at the top of the hill.

CHAPTER 36: ELIZABETH

While driving over to Polkenna, I recall that Matthew once stated that the larvae of *Cryptocotyle* were 'malicious' — 'malicious little buggers' — because they invaded the winkle and multiplied. Perhaps 'malignant' would have been a better term. The anthroposophists treat like with like: iscador, the parasitic mistletoe, is used to treat cancer. That is of course based on a misconception, because cancerous cells are mutated self and the parasite is entirely foreign; yet both invade the self and outwit the body's defences. So too do lies and speculations — altered truth and innuendo; both are invasive and threaten the system's homeostasis.

And now, finally, it's time to attempt to unravel the lies, and re-create a level of stability.

The most recent lie occurred yesterday afternoon, when Matthew apparently showed Jim the drawing of the Shell House and told him that I had given the drawing of the Shell House to his grandmother; Jim was most impressed. I don't understand Matthew's motive although, at the simplest level, I suppose he reasoned that I would thereby be made aware of the drawing's absence.

Hazel, in contrast, was so much more straightforward when she telephoned last night.

'You're probably aware that Matthew has taken some drawings that belong to you,' she said. 'We'd like to return them, but I think we might all find it rather more comfortable and private if you would come over to Polkenna. This won't be an interrogation. You perhaps feel that the matter is none of our business, in some respects, at least. But I would so much like you to come, particularly for Matt's sake. He's respected you and has been quite unhappy.'

I agreed, we arranged a time; for Matthew's sake and mine. We were both cool and polite, for we are all civilised people. Matthew respected me. Past tense. I try to be dispassionate: this is a curious situation in which to find myself.

I park above the Shell House and walk down the stone steps, looking down into Polkenna as I do so. How often I used to do this, confident that I was unobserved. At the bottom I stand back to look at the façade, aware that Hazel and Matthew will see me, and I find that it's unchanged. Except that the *Tiphobia* has been crushed, smashed to pieces; the shattered fragments still lie on the ground.

I am so shocked that I have to struggle quite hard to regain the strength and resolve that I had earlier forced upon myself. How could he have known? How *did* he work it out? Barbara would have said that he was telepathic or had second sight.

I'm uncertain whether I should walk around to the back, so I knock on the porch door. Hazel appears at the window and indicates that I should go round. The fuchsia still overhangs the path with its superabundance of slender red flowers. The garden has been tidied, savagely, and the white stones upon which the shadow fell are piled against a wall. A Japanese stone garden, but angst not Zen.

Hazel is unsmiling but not unfriendly as she waits by the open French windows. She wears a long blue skirt with dark pink flowers, made of some light, floating material. Again I feel at a disadvantage; I have not given enough thought to my appearance and I feel old and frumpish.

The interior of the house has naturally been altered, and is lighter and tidier, more sparsely furnished than when Barbara lived here. But we are not meeting to discuss the décor. I notice at once that there is a roll of drawings on top of a strange little table near the front door.

Matt is standing by the sofa, and is pale and ungainly, slightly stooped, with puffy eyes. I suppose he may be hung over, and today he looks no more than a boy.

'Thank you for coming,' Hazel says. 'This is going to be rather uncomfortable for all of us, so perhaps we should get the discussion over. And then have some coffee, or something stronger, if we feel like it, at the end.'

I agree, and choose an armchair and then, because I wish to have the stronger position, I say, even as we are seating ourselves, that I think I should start.

'We won't talk about how Matthew obtained the portraits — I feel that I, in any case, was partly to blame in my carelessness. That you have the drawings is a 'given' factor so we should proceed from there. Incidentally, instead of referring to Barbara as "your mother" or "your grandmother", may I refer to her directly by her name? It might make our discussion easier.'

They are both sitting watching my face; when I am talking I feel safer and in control of myself. Hazel nods slightly.

'So. Since it's probably clear that Barbara and I had a very intimate relationship, I expect you want to know when that relationship started. It started about four years before her death. In fact, the first of those portraits, the one which shows her seated at the table that used to be at the other end of this room, marks the start.'

Matthew sits forward and is about to interrupt, so I say quickly, 'Yes, you'll want to know about Allan, too, and I'll come to that aspect in a few minutes. But perhaps I should first give you a chronology, if we may call it that, of the relationship between Barbara and myself. If I give you the dry facts, then that may cover some of the questions you want to raise.'

I look at each of them in turn, and this time they both nod, Matthew with a sour and cynical expression.

'Firstly, we were extremely circumspect. We rarely met at Nancarrow, and usually here — which, as you both know, is surprisingly secluded, despite being part of Polkenna — or somewhere else entirely. Allan died within about a year of the start of our relationship. Your mother, Hazel, with her great reliance on prediction and fate, then decided that our relationship was ill-fated — "was not meant to be" — and insisted we should part.'

'Perhaps she only fancied you when it was more dangerous — when your old man was around.'

'Matt!' Hazel is horrified, but Matt just stares at me coldly as she continues, 'Why was it always my mother pulling the strings? Deciding when you would be together or apart, who should know this or that. When you look back, she just seems to have been entirely selfish. I don't think she really ever thought about other people's feelings.'

She doesn't seem to be angry or bitter, merely bewildered; but it is possible that I am misjudging her mood, it is so difficult to tell.

'It may seem like that now, to you, Hazel. But I could give you so many examples to show you that you're wrong. She did care about other people, she cared very much about you and your brother. And especially about Matthew. It wasn't selfishness that drove her decisions, I think one could say it was the strength of her *irrationality* that drove her. And one can't counteract irrational beliefs with logic or special pleading.'

'I didn't know my mother at all, it seems. I'm sorry about that now, and I'm sure you could tell us a lot. But that's all private to you.'

Matt nods. 'The Barbara you knew couldn't have been my Granny B. But that's okay, I suppose. My version of her was okay for me. We don't want to hear about your version.'

'No. So, where was I? Barbara had left me. Back to the dry facts, although I suppose you may imagine how I felt, losing both Allan and then her, but that's quite irrelevant to the *facts*. Then her primary cancer was diagnosed and it was necessary for her to have a mastectomy, quickly. You came here, Hazel, to care for her. Your sister-in-law came, other local friends helped, too, taking her for radiation therapy, doing her shopping. Health visitors and doctors checked on her, and I kept out of the way, at her request. I spoke to her on the phone, I wrote — she, of course, could neither write nor paint for a long time, her arm was too weak. I knew she was feeling ill and miserable and I was desperate to be with her, but she wanted me to stay away. And indeed, I went so far as to go to America for several weeks.'

My mouth is dry so I stop, and ask Hazel for a drink of water, waiting silently with Matthew while she fetches it. I take a few sips and then continue.

'So. It took a few months before she felt sufficiently recovered to realise that she still had a life to live, and since she also knew that the prognosis might not be good, her life might be short ... well, apparently the "signs", mainly the stars, indicated that she and I should be together again. Allan was dead. I'm sorry, I don't mean to make Barbara sound calculating, she wasn't at all like that. Her reasonings were often complex and not necessarily based on logic, so I sometimes found them difficult to follow. I was just very happy that we were re-united. We were able to visit each other more freely, although still with discretion, and I think she felt as great a love for me as I did for her. But then the secondary tumours were diagnosed and she knew there was no hope — and, as you know, she didn't want to submit herself to further therapy. You, I'm afraid, were called in to help, Hazel, and I left. Again, although I have tried to keep this strictly factual, you can imagine how I felt — being kept apart, yet knowing that daily she was dying a little more.'

'Yes.' Hazel is clearly disturbed, but she too is attempting to remain dispassionate. 'But — keeping this factual, as you say — I can see why you kept your relationship quiet when your husband was alive. But why did you do so afterwards — why not tell us, and then you could have been completely open about everything? I think I may know the reason, but I'd like to hear *your* explanation. Because the continued secrecy seems to have been the most harmful part for all of us.'

'Two reasons, Hazel. Because more than two people were involved. Barbara wanted to protect you. She was very worried about what might happen to you, mentally, if you had to confront this aspect of her character, her homosexuality, lesbianism, call it what you will. I can't really go into this, Hazel, because apparently there was some incident when you were young — I don't know, I understand you were very shocked. She was adamant that you should be protected. I don't know whether that was the right approach to take or not, but she deeply cared, you should realise that.'

'I think I —'

'Wait a moment. So we had to keep it quiet, and that meant continuing the discretion and secrecy. It was quite difficult — your mother was not the most discreet of people! And I had to respect those wishes even after her death. This put me in an increasingly difficult position, as you can see — I'd no idea that you were both going to become regular visitors to Nancarrow and that we'd have so much contact. In fact, Hazel, I began to suspect that you *did* know ...'

'Did you? You were wrong. I suppose the Gosses were responsible for my visits ... and that all goes back to the suitcase —'

Matt interrupts at last, thumping his fists on his knees.

'There are so many things, so many *clues*. There's a load of things ... What's your second reason?'

'Barbara thought you'd be disgusted,' I say, baldly. 'Two old women. You *are* disgusted, aren't you, Matt? You will not have enjoyed looking at the portraits. And actually, even if we hadn't kept it quiet from you, we would not have blazoned it abroad — we weren't dying to come out of the closet, not at our age or stage of life. It would hardly have been well-received.'

I look at him, and he puffs out his lips and gives a nod.

'But I do want to say that our relationship was not merely sexual. I loved her very much, and we shared a great deal of laughter and companionship. We seemed to complement each other in so many ways. I also think that if you had been given time, over the years, to get used to the idea, it would have seemed quite acceptable. But that was impossible, for the first reason that I gave you.'

'Yes. It was so stupid, really. You see, Elizabeth, I went to see my brother Jamie yesterday, because, well, the drawings — oh, I don't know, their implications, I suppose — disturbed me in some way. I didn't understand why and I began to feel Jamie might know something more about my mother. Anyway, you don't need to worry about psychological damage or anything like that, because Jamie explained everything to me. I've remembered everything and I've explained it to Matt. So he understands your reason. And we both understand why you had to keep the secret going, don't we, Matt?'

'Yeah.' He adds, generously I think, 'And I do see that it was getting pretty sticky for you, especially with us hanging around Nancarrow all the time. Better blame it on the little winkles as well as Hazel's Gosses. Okay,' he clears his throat, 'I want to say a few things. Yeah, I suppose I do find it — the physical side — disgusting, but that's probably just ageism. You can't help growing old.' He gives Hazel a quick, tense smile, I don't know why. 'And one of my best friends is gay, as you know. In fact gays seem to be taking over the world. But what is beginning to really worry me is Allan. What about your husband in all this? I mean, if you and my grandmother were so madly in love, wasn't having him around a bit *inconvenient*?'

'Matt, what are you suggesting?' Hazel is horrified; she seems to know what he is driving at.

'Hazel told me last night that she'd found out that he died from drowning.'

I am so surprised at this line of attack that a ghastly laughter begins to bubble up inside me. I begin to laugh. Now they are both horrified. I manage to stop, and I apologise.

'That was blunt! You think I murdered him to get him out of the way. That's so grotesque — so unexpected!' I laugh again, rather grimly. 'I'm sorry. Matt, I'm not even going to go into details about my husband's death. I can only just begin to think about it, let alone talk about it, even after all these years. Suffice it to say that I was in Glasgow at the time. And that I bitterly, bitterly regret having been away.' I add, talking to Hazel, 'No doubt there's an account of the inquest in the newspaper archives. Please do *not* ask Peter Pascoe, he was dreadfully upset.'

Matthew is very awkward and apologetic but I haven't finished.

'There are two more things that you need to understand.' I have to be very careful here. 'Allan was growing increasingly incapacitated, he was very weak. I believe Peter told you that he couldn't even get up to the *camera obscura* towards the end? He was fading, and he knew he hadn't got much longer, so he was busy trying to do as much as possible. Also — and you really should know this — he and Barbara were good friends. She didn't visit often and she could be rather overpowering —' I smile at Hazel who smiles back in acknowledgement, 'but she made him laugh. She used to tease him, you know the way she could …'

Then I suddenly remember an example that will help my case.

'In your lavatory — there used to be a framed extract from Leonardo da Vinci's works. Allan made that for her. Do you still have it?'

'Of *course*, that's completely Allan's style, isn't it? Relevant quotations on the wall — and I bet he enjoyed thinking how to produce the writing back to front. I remember now, you mentioned something about da Vinci up in the *camera obscura*.'

'Yes. Allan had a translation of the notebooks. Da Vinci was interested in the paths of light rays, and devised optical instruments and so on.'

Matt leaps up and collects a couple of large sheets of paper from the table. There are sticky yellow marks on their edges where they must once have been stuck together, and he unfolds them and places them side-by-side on the floor in front of me. Hazel stands up to look.

'What's this, Matt?'

'I found them in the cupboard in my bedroom, ages ago, and I couldn't understand what the heck it was — it's such a mess and it wasn't Barbara's thing to draw patterns. But when we put the kaleidoscope attachment on the *camera obscura* these were the sort of patterns we saw. I was looking through her stuff yesterday — when I knew there was a link between the two of you —' he looks at me, 'and came across it again. And I knew then exactly what it was. It's pretty rubbishy but then drawing wasn't her strong point. Why didn't *you* do it?'

'So she kept it!'

I pick up one of the sheets, remembering so vividly the occasion when she drew it, the two of them side by side at the viewing table, Barbara leaning over the paper that had been sellotaped in place, and Allan sitting on his chair giving her instructions. I had been reading proofs of one of my research papers, working to a tight deadline, but I had occasionally come up the two flights of stairs to the attic to find out how they were getting on. I could hear their noise, the laughter and the conversation, from the landing, and I had felt excluded, even jealous. Peter Pascoe had been jealous, too, because he had been sent back into the garden.

I realise that I have been staring at the pattern for some time and that Hazel and Matt are waiting for me to say something more.

'Allan had always planned to record the various patterns, for no particular reason other than his own amusement. He thought about making photographic prints directly from the images but that would have required a proper darkroom with chemicals and running water, and was getting beyond his capabilities,' I explained. 'And he could no longer trace the patterns very well himself. Anyway, he took Barbara up there because he thought the patterns would appeal to her because of her interest in mandala. She spent ages trying to draw and paint that, she wished she hadn't started — but she was determined to find some meaning in the pattern!'

'Funny to think of Granny B being up in the attic, too,' Matt says, but Hazel is wanting more information.

'Mandala. Elizabeth, I think you'd better explain about mandalas.'

'I'm not sure I can. The original mandalas are Eastern, Asian, such as those of the Tibetan Buddhists. They're highly complex and significant and depict, I think, the steps on the road to perfection. Buddha usually lies at the centre, and there's lots of intricate painting and gold leaf in some of the more elaborate *thankas*. They're also used by astrologers — you have only to think of their zodiacal charts — and were used by Jung.'

'Ah!'

'Jung rather hijacked them, as far as I can make out, to draw diagrams of the psyche, with the Self at the centre, and the orbiting Ego —'

'That's the Queen Scallop,' Hazel interpolates. 'A pun, I suppose?'

' "Queen". The language is a little outdated, but yes. To go back to Jung — Jung used mandala in therapy, getting patients to draw their own. Apparently the shapes that patients incorporated indicated their mental state, but you had to be extremely knowledgeable to interpret the symbols. Another angle comes from the astrologers, who found shapes and colours that corresponded with their predictions. Circles are highly significant —'

Now Matt says 'Aha!'

'Concentric circles, closed circles may indicate the serpent Ourobouros, or infinity, or completeness — whatever you want to imagine, really.'

'A circle is a comforting thing, especially if you're inside it,' Hazel says. 'But didn't you find all that sort of thing rather irritating?'

'In a way, yes, although I suppose the tortuous thinking behind it fascinated me. But some of the articles and explanations appal me in their blind dogmatism — and arrogance. I'd like to say that they are harmless, but they are not. Barbara left me because of her belief in fate, not because of any rational assessment of our situation.' I shake my head. 'I'm sorry — let's move away from the specifics.'

'My mother accepted her own death more calmly, though, as a result of — oh yes! Jamie sent you the horoscope. Did you understand it?'

'He told you that? No, I didn't, I'm afraid. I kept it for a while, but it made me angry and I eventually threw it away. Matt, I think you need to explain that loaded "aha!" You've been biding your time, haven't you? Perhaps you should bring across the drawing of the façade.'

'I was hoping you'd notice it.' He unrolls the drawing and places that on the floor, too, holding one corner while he points to the concentric circles on the right. '*Tiphobia*. It was yours, wasn't it? The central point in concentric circles.'

'Yes. How on earth did you know about *Tiphobia*? I don't remember the details of the reasoning behind the pattern, apart from the most obvious things, but I put *Tiphobia* at the centre because it is — *was!*— a very special shell. It was our joke, a sort of visual pun. It portrays the Self, and it's not what it seems. That's perhaps not a joke that you will appreciate at the moment — that Barbara was not what she seemed, to you either. There's another joke "shell" in the façade, too, but it's much older.'

'The "bullet", the fossil of a shell that was inside the animal not outside.'

'The belemnite, yes. Barbara obviously explained that to you. *Tiphobia* is twice a joke in the context of the local marine shells, because it's from Africa and it's also a freshwater shell, from Lake Tanganyika.'

'But it's so thick and sturdy!' Hazel says.

'Quite. It belongs to the thalassoids, which means "marine-like" — there's a group of shells in that lake that have thick walls and all kinds of ornamentation, just like sea-shells, in fact. When the first species were discovered last century it was even proposed they had a marine ancestry, although that's no longer an acceptable idea. Whatever the reason, those thalassoids are very unusual — the area is now protected to save them from collectors.' I give a little grimace, thinking of the shattered shell. 'I was very lucky to obtain those two. They live in the deeper water but a fisherman had brought them up in his nets. Your aim was very accurate, Matthew. And I wish I knew why.'

'Jim showed me what was in those drawers in his study, that first time I went over. I wasn't snooping. I thought the shell looked familiar, but I didn't think any more about it until I saw your drawing.'

We are all rather silent for a while, but I sense that the atmosphere is less tense and that we have begun to unravel the deceptions and lies, and to have made some sense of them. The malignancy is being rooted out, but an important step remains.

'You can keep the drawing of the façade — I always intended that it should be a present for Barbara, in any case — but I would appreciate it if you would return her portraits, Matt. They are rather personal, and dear to me.' (As were the circumstances of their execution.)

Hazel and Matt look at each other, and Hazel nods and goes off into the kitchen to find a carrier bag.

'What did the barnacles and limpet mean, on the ferry steps? Is that another of the mandala things?'

The ferry steps? Then I remember the painting in the drawing room.

'Good gracious! You really *are* sharp! How on earth did you …? You are astonishingly good at adductive thinking!' I'm suddenly amazed to feel myself blush. 'Your grandmother said it … it was a symbol for herself.'

I can feel a laugh bubbling up inside again, but this time it's a happy laugh, and I can see Matt still doesn't understand.

'I can give you a clue. It's reminiscent of graffiti on a toilet wall, a boy's stylised drawing of a woman. But this was after her mastectomy.'

He thinks about it and then he begins to laugh, too, slightly shamefaced and a little awkwardly; but at least it is a beginning.

Matt and Hazel both come round to the front of the house to say goodbye. We look at the broken mandala and we discuss, not very seriously, the possibilities for restoration and renovation of the façade. Hazel mentions a shell beach in North Devon where she once found thirty species of shell, including wentletraps; when I tell her that I learnt that 'wentletrap' is Dutch for staircase, she is very amused. Philip Gosse went to the same beach, she says (and she grins at Matt, taunting him to laugh) and so did her mother's great-great-aunt.

I carry my roll of portraits up the steps, then look back. The two of them stand there, Matt with his arm around his mother's shoulder; two more generations of Lewishams, all of them so different from each other. I had never expected to revisit this house and it's probably unlikely that I shall ever do so again, but that will, I suspect, depend on Matt.

Driving home to Nancarrow in the mild damp Cornish morning, and attempting to sing along with a happy, optimistic Scarlatti sonata on the radio, I notice swallows lined up on a wire and I, too, am filled with optimism and a longing to return to Africa: there's a particular group of snails that might provide data to support the ideas that I have been developing in the past few weeks. Why not go now, while I am still able? I'm sure I can raise the money through a grant.

When I park the car outside the house I notice that the garden is already growing out of control, the plant life exercising its free-will in Peter Pascoe's absence, and I reflect that I shall have to find a new gardener, someone to keep an eye on things when I go abroad.

The tide is high and waves are splashing against the jetty and soaking the stone, but Jim and Roger have moved the boat, which now sits on wooden blocks outside the garage. The wind funnels down the valley and on the jetty a plastic *7-up* bottle, half-full of liquid, wobbles to the top of the slope and then rolls jerkily, unsteadily, into the sea. As so often, I think of Allan, and this time I feel almost lethargic with the peace that stills my mind. It would be so very easy to believe that he, with his poor thin arms, had tried to turn his wheelchair and had, by accident, without premeditation, rolled down into the sea. I stand for a while and watch the half-submerged bottle as it bobs in the water; if I were superstitious, I am certain I would hear Barbara's voice telling me it was a Sign.

CHAPTER 37: ANNE: 1908

Paignton, Devon
March 1908

E.W. Gosse, Esq.
17 Hanover Terrace
Regent's Park
London

Dear Mr Gosse,
    Last Christmas I was presented with a gift from a long-time friend who had been fortunate — as had I — to have had the privilege of being tutored by your Father on the shores of North Devon in 1855. That gift was a book, <u>Father and Son</u> — written by an anonymous author — upon which considerable praise and many congratulatory reviews had been bestowed.
    You may imagine that I turned to it with great interest, hoping to find therein some tales of those early happy times upon the shore — for it was on the sea-shore, at Ilfracombe, that I (as the former Miss Anne Church) first met you and made a drawing of a shell at your behest. You handed that <u>foreign</u> shell, that had been conveyed here by your father from the shores of Jamaica, to the lady who was my chaperone, and who was to become your own Mother's greatest admirer, Miss Anna Shipton.
    I hesitate to ask you also to recall that we met the following year under very sad and terrible circumstances, when I accompanied Miss Shipton to visit your poor Mother at those dreadful lodgings in Pimlico. I took you for a walk and bought you roasted chestnuts — but unhappily the experience did not have the desired effect of raising your spirits and offering you some respite from the sick-chamber because the nuts were too hot and burnt your mouth. Little did I imagine then that the small boy whose hand I held would become, fifty years later, a literary figure of some repute, with a Newnham-educated suffragette for a daughter and a <u>naturalist</u> son who (to my envy) had made an expedition to the South American Andes before he reached the age of twenty.
    Perhaps you question how it is that I am acquainted with such recent information about you and your family — but if you have noted my address, the answer may have already presented itself. I should also say that my late husband, Mr Duncan Robertson, and I were indebted to your Father for stimulating in us an enthusiasm for the actiniae and other marine creatures — indeed, your father was kind enough to

quote us at length in his <u>Actinologia Britannica</u>. Moreover, he did me the honour of naming a new species of sea-anemone after me — <u>Stomphia Churchiae</u> — in recognition of the happy times that he and I had spent anemonizing together on the shore.

It is now more than twenty years since I was widowed and moved from Scotland to the milder climate of the South Coast of England. It gave me the greatest happiness to meet with your Father and Mrs Eliza Gosse on several occasions before he died — your step-mother and I continued our friendship until she, too, passed on. It was through them, and their constant allusions to you and your family, that I learnt a little of your progress, and I have continued to follow it until this day.

I present all this information not as a digression but by way of explanation.

Mr Gosse, your book <u>Father and Son</u> has distressed me more than I can say; I cannot think of any other book that I have read that has so profoundly shocked me.

I am astonished that you saw fit to publish, in full, one of your late Father's letters to you — a private letter, a letter written to you in the anguish of his loving heart, intended only for the eyes of his beloved son. It was readily apparent to all of us who were privileged to know and love him that your Father loved you very dearly (even, perhaps, as you intimate in this ill-judged biography, excessively — but there can be no <u>fault</u> in that. Does not our Lord preach the doctrine of Love?) To have printed his letter thus, for the eyes of the world to see — and to <u>scoff</u> at, as seems to have been your intention — is the gravest betrayal of your father's love.

Who can doubt that your Father was a man who — beneath the undeniable dogmatism of his faith — was capable of the greatest and most tender love? All of us who knew him well and saw beneath his stern and shy exterior could not fail to love him and admire him. For your Father, to have had a son — and through him, grandchildren — was to have been granted a Gift beyond compare and he never ceased to give thanks, even as he worried about you. My late husband and I were never to be blessed with children ourselves but if we should have had a son, who wrote so publicly and critically about <u>us</u> and the intimate details of our family life, I am certain that our hearts would have been broken and our lives made empty beyond despair.

There was an occasion — not long before he passed away — on which I visited your Father and Mrs Gosse and he had, that very day, received a letter from your daughter. Great was his joy; and his tenderness for his grand-daughter — 'my darling little Teresa' — at times almost overwhelmed him. You, too, were frequently in his conversation — he was eagerly anticipating your visit at the end of the week (I have some recollection that it was to be Teresa's birthday, her tenth perhaps) when you had promised to take him collecting at Goodrington Sands.

It is in the nature of Fathers and their sons to think differently about the world — but it is not in the nature of many sons to publicly <u>deride</u> the love, however it is shown, that is borne towards them.

You have done Philip Henry Gosse a very grave injustice — in the name of 'literature'. I pray that the Lord will make you compassionate, and that you and your Father will be reunited in joy and harmony in Heaven.

Yours sincerely
Anne Robertson (Mrs)

PS. I have in my possession some crayon drawings of actiniae, and a watercolour of Oddicombe Beach, all executed by your Father — which I was able to purchase at the auction of his house at Marychurch. I shall treasure them for whatever short period remains of my life.

NOTES AND ACKNOWLEDGEMENTS

The Gosses
I have been intrigued by Philip Henry Gosse since I first read Edmund Gosse's *Father and Son* in the late 1960s; the exquisitely illustrated copy of *Actinologia Britannica* in the library of the Department of Zoology, University of Glasgow, where I held a Lectureship, was further inspiration. Information and quotations for this novel were gleaned from many of PHG's books: *The Canadian Naturalist* (1840), *A Naturalist's Sojourn in Jamaica* (1851), *Seaside Pleasures* (1853), *A Naturalist's Rambles on the Devonshire Coast* (1853), *The Aquarium* (1854), *Tenby* (1856), *Omphalos* (1857), *Memorial of the last days on earth of Emily Gosse* (1857), *Evenings at the Microscope (1859)*, *Letters from Alabama* (1859) and *Actinologia Britannica (1860)*. Also invaluable was Edmund Gosse's *Life of Philip Henry Gosse*; and to hold and examine hand-written notes, poems and letters (for example, those between PHG and Emily; Willy and PHG; PHG and his grand-daughter Teresa) at the Cambridge University Library was a moving and thrilling experience. I was also able to look through some of the Gosse material held in the Manuscript section of the old British Library (when it was at the British Museum — thanks to Sally Brown for her help); and I am very grateful to the then Librarian, Christopher Sheppard, of the Brotherton Library at Leeds University for providing me with photocopies of the Kingsley-Gosse correspondence — Emily's leatherbound diary is also in their archive.

For convenience I have moved the location of a few of the documents: for example, the photograph of Emily Gosse, taken on the day she died, is tipped into the Cambridge University Library's copy of the *Memorial* (although I ensured Hazel did not see it there).

I am very grateful to Jennifer Gosse for her hospitality, helpful conversations and enthusiasm; and to Ann Thwaite, for discussions, meetings, and an enjoyable joint expedition to the Natural History Museum's branch at Tring to look at the bird-skins that were collected by PHG in Jamaica. Ann's biography, *Edmund Gosse* (Secker & Warburg, 1984) has long been a favourite of mine (it was from this that I gleaned information about items sold at the auction of PHG's house — see Anne Church's letter in Chapter 37) and I was delighted when she asked me to read and comment on the manuscript of her biography of Philip Henry Gosse (*Glimpses of the Wonderful*, Faber and Faber, 2002).

Anna Shipton
Although Anna Shipton really existed, I have entirely fictionalised her character and background; that she knew the Gosses well is apparent from her book *Tell Jesus!* and her mention of their tracts elsewhere. In *Tell Jesus!* she describes how she chaperoned a young lady and her friend to Gosse's Ilfracombe shore class — that she chaperoned Anne Church (and the entirely fictitious Sarah Nisbet) is my invention.

Most of the incidents in this novel involving Anna Shipton have been taken from her own books — *Tell Jesus! (1863), The Lost Blessing (1870), Waiting Hours (1873), The Promise and the Promiser*. In *Rivers among the Rocks (1881)* she meets the 'Laird of B— and his lady' while sitting out a storm in Italy.

The Laird of Ballavich and his lady
The names and characters are entirely fictitious; but the 'Laird of B—' in Shipton's *Rivers among the Rocks* was apparently a great sailor, and had indeed sailed on the

Mediterranean. It is not impossible that Anna Shipton met the 'Laird of B— and his wife' again in Scotland and was taken to visit the schoolmistress (see Shipton's *Waiting Hours*)

Anne Church receives several mentions in Philip Henry Gosse's *Actinologia Britannica*; the anemone *Stomphia Churchiae* was indeed found and described by her, and was named after her by PHG.

Duncan Robertson is also mentioned in the *Actinologia*. There is no evidence whatsoever that Anne and Duncan married in real life — or even met! Their characters are entirely fictitious.

Natural History Museum, London

For information on the work of the Parasitology Unit, I am indebted to Dr Vaughan Southgate and Dr David Brown. I had very useful meetings and correspondence with Vaughan about hybridisation of schistosomes (his office at that time was in the West Tower) and other matters. Many years ago I copy-edited the second edition of David Brown's seminal work on *The Freshwater Snails of Africa* (Taylor & Francis, 1994) and it sparked off many ideas (and allowed me to choose *Tiphobia* as Elizabeth Wilson's 'joke'). Subsequently, David's detailed and fascinating descriptions of his work 'snail hunting' in Africa provided a wealth of information, and his discussions with me about what I had written were invaluable. Any factual errors, it goes without saying, are mine not his!

Ethiopia and Eritrea

In addition to Dr David Brown's descriptions of Ethiopia in the 1950s and 1960s, I was also able learn a great deal from a former PhD student of mine, Dr Stefan Gunnarsson of Uppsala University in Sweden; Stefan's family have for many decades been associated with the missionary work of the Swedish Evangelical Church in that part of Africa. Dr David Rogers and Dr Sarah Randolph of Oxford University treated me to an evening of slides of the time they had spent in Ethiopia.

Additional information

So many other people provided snippets, large or small, of information, and I am very grateful to them all: Elizabeth Boyle and Don Baran for information on housing in Glasgow in the 1850s; Diana Reynell, restorer, for information about Victorian shell pictures and grottoes; the herbalist Michael McIntyre, of Oxford, for information about Indian Blood Root and other herbal treatments for breast cancer; Norman Hammond of the Solway Shark Watch for information about basking sharks; Gill Foster, of the Cumbria Local History Federation for pointing me in the direction of information on Dickens' and Wilkie Collins' stay at Allonby.

Our family copy of Chambers' Encyclopaedia for 1884 (purchased at an Oxfam shop in Glasgow for £10 in the mid-1980s) has been a continual source of information and distraction.

George Lewes' articles, *Seaside Studies* and *New Facts and Old Fancies about Sea-anemones*, are to be found in *Blackwood's Edinburgh Magazines* for 1856 and 1857.

I am grateful to Oxford University Press for permission to reprint the extract from page 182 of *The Notebooks of Leonardo da Vinci*, edited by Irma Richter (1980).

Italicisation of species' names
Despite the fact that italicisation of generic and specific names of plants and animals was not uniformly adopted in Victorian times, and some readers may find it a distraction (as implying an unintended emphasis), I have nevertheless used it throughout because, to a biologist, the lack of italicisation looks completely wrong!

Special thanks must go to Melvyn Bragg, Matt Ridley and Ann Thwaite for giving up precious time to read advance copies of this novel; I am very greatly indebted to them for their kindness and their comments.

Daniel Mitchinson at Firpress was unfailingly helpful and good-humoured, and I'm particularly grateful to him for the cover design. The shell-lady was made by Rachel Lackie on a rainy day by the sea in the late 1980s: it gives me special pleasure to be able to use it, so many years later, on the cover! And above all, I am extremely grateful to my husband, John Lackie, for his endless support and encouragement throughout the writing and publishing of this novel.